PRAISE FOR KAMERON HURLEY

"*The Mirror Empire* is epic in every sense of the word. Hurley has built a world – no, worlds – in which cosmology and magic, history and religion, politics and prejudice all play crucial roles. Prepare yourself for sentient plants, rifts in the fabric of reality, and remarkable powers that wax and wane with the stars themselves. Forget all about tentative, conventional fantasy; there's so much great material in here that Hurley needs more than one universe in order to fit it all in."
  Brian Staveley, author of The Emperor's Blades

"Taking epic fantasy down challenging and original paths. Thoughtful and thought-provoking with every twist and turn."
  Juliet E McKenna, author of the Tales of Einarinn series

"For me [*The Mirror Empire*] did all the things a fantasy should do – holding our own societies up to the light by reflecting off worlds that are very different. Add in a magic system where the users are only powerful some of the time, and semi sentient vegetation that is possibly more of a threat than the magic users, and I happily sank into this book with a satisfied sigh."
  Francis Knight, author of Fade to Black

"Bold, merciless, and wildly inventive, Kameron Hurley's *The Mirror Empire* begins an epic tale of worlds at war that will linger long in readers' imaginations. If you're looking for original and challenging fantasy, this is definitely the series for you."
  Courti̇ ̇ ̇ ̇ ̇g

00674612

"*The Mirror Empire* is the most original fantasy I've read in a long time, set in a world full of new ideas, expanding the horizons of the genre. A complex and intricate book full of elegant ideas and finely-drawn characters."

Adrian Tchaikovsky, author of the Shadows of the Apt series

"There's a powerful yet elegant brutality in *The Mirror Empire* that serves notice to traditional epic fantasy: move over, make way, an intoxicating new blend of storytelling has arrived. These are pages that will command your attention."

Bradley Beaulieu, author of the Lays of Anuskaya trilogy

"Kameron Hurley's a brave, unflinching, truly original writer with a unique vision – her fiction burns right through your brain and your heart."

Jeff VanderMeer, author of Annihilation *and* Finch

"Kameron Hurley is ferociously imaginative – with the emphasis on the ferocious. She writes novels that are smart, dark, visceral and wonderfully, hectically entertaining."

Lauren Beukes, author of Zoo City *and* The Shining Girls

"Kameron Hurley's writing is the most exciting thing I've seen on the genre page... What Hurley's writing has (and it's something not one in a dozen genre practitioners seems able to generate) is passion. It doesn't hurt that there's also a rare freshness to the material, and a heady dash of high octane noir worked into the mix."

Richard K Morgan, author of The Steel Remains *and the Takeshi Kovacs novels*

"Hurley reuses old tropes to excellent effect, interweaving them with original elements to create a world that will fascinate and delight her established fans and appeal to newcomers. Readers will blaze through this opening instalment and eagerly await the promised sequel."
Publishers Weekly (starred review)

"Hurley intelligently tackles issues of culture and gender, while also throwing in plenty of bloodthirsty action and well-rounded characters. This is a fresh, exciting fantasy epic that's looking to the future and asking important questions. "
SFX

"*The Mirror Empire* is a fresh, vigorous, and gripping entrant into the epic fantasy genre, able to stand toe-to-toe with any of the heavyweight series out there. I cannot recommend this novel highly enough."
SF Revu

"*The Mirror Empire* is both a chance for fantasy fans to get to know Hurley's writing, and for previous fans of her work to see what she can do in a new vein. And for readers new to her work, this is in many ways the best place to start."
SF Signal

"The most important book you'll read this year."
Ristea's Reads

BY THE SAME AUTHOR

God's War
Infidel
Rapture

KAMERON HURLEY

The Mirror Empire

THE WORLDBREAKER SAGA
BOOK I

ANGRY
ROBOT

ANGRY ROBOT
An imprint of Watkins Media Ltd.

Lace Market House
54-56 High Pavement
Nottingham
NG1 1HW
UK

angryrobotbooks.com
twitter.com/angryrobotbooks
Worlds begone

An Angry Robot paperback original 2014
3

Copyright © Kameron Hurley 2014

Map by Steff Worthington.

Kameron Hurley asserts the moral right to be
identified as the author of this work.

A catalogue record for this book is available
from the British Library.

ISBN 978 0 85766 555 3
Ebook ISBN 978 0 85766 557 7

Set in Meridien by Argh! Oxford.
Printed by 4edge Ltd.

All rights reserved. No part of this publication may be reproduced,
stored in a retrieval system, or transmitted, in any form or by any
means, electronic, mechanical, photocopying, recording or
otherwise, without the prior permission of the publishers.

This book is sold subject to the condition that it shall not, by
way of trade or otherwise, be lent, re-sold, hired out or
otherwise circulated without the publisher's prior consent in
any form of binding or cover other than that in which it is
published and without a similar condition including this
condition being imposed on the subsequent purchaser.

This novel is entirely a work of fiction. The names, characters and
incidents portrayed in it are the work of the author's imagination.
Any resemblance to actual persons, living or dead, events or
localities is entirely coincidental.

For Renny, Heidi and Ryan:
the thief, the queen, the jester.

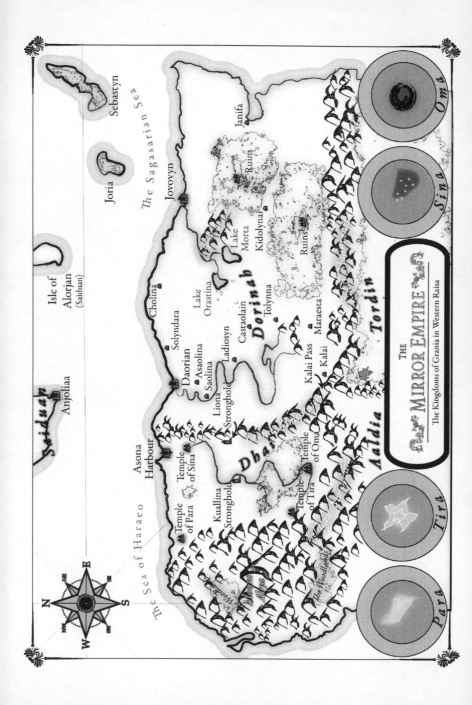

"We take our shadows with us."
Dhai saying

PROLOGUE

When Lilia was four years old, her mother filled a shallow dish with Lilia's blood and fed it to the boars that patrolled the thorn fence.

"Nothing can cross the thorn fence," Lilia's mother said as she poured the blood onto the hungry, gnarled fence. The boars on the other side licked up the blood. Lilia liked the boars' yellow eyes and wrinkled, mucus-crusted snouts. They reminded her of hungry babies. The thorn fence kept out the semi-sentient walking trees and conscription gangs who sometimes climbed up from the churning bay that clung to the base of the cliffs. The cliffs and the fence should have protected them forever. Her mother was a blood witch and never doubted her power. If you fed enough blood to a thing, her mother said, it would do all you asked.

Lilia traced the scars on her mother's arms and her own, and she believed her.

Until the day something crossed the fence.

It was high autumn, and the leaves were falling. Lilia sat on a shallow, chalky outcrop overlooking the toxic mix of lavender poppies and bulrus ivy that cloaked the heath between her village and the thorn fence. A sea of colorful leaves swirled through the air. She had dressed herself in tattered white bone-tree leaves, pretending to be the Dhai hero Faith Ahya. She played alone, rubbing her face with dandelion heads and pretending she could fly. Her mother hated it when she played that game, because it meant climbing up onto the outcrop and launching herself off it, arms outspread, hoping with each leap that some great wind would take her into the sky.

The pale green light of the satellite Tira bathed the world in a burnished emerald glow. The broader sky was a brilliant amber wash. It was the only color Lilia knew the sky to be. Tira, the life-giver, had been ascendant as long as she could remember.

Lilia scrambled to the top of the outcrop once again and spread her arms. This time, surely, the wind would carry her. As she prepared to jump, she saw the trees on the other side of the heath tremble. She froze. The thorn fence stood between her and the trees. Whatever stirred there, she resolved to face it bravely.

A wave of fuzzy gray treegliders leapt from the forest canopy. They spread their webbed limbs and glided down into the field of poppies – dozens and dozens of them. The big-eyed creatures bounded toward her, hurling themselves onto the thorn fence. First one, then two, then six, eight, twelve. Impaled on the hungry thorns.

Lilia shrieked and slid down from the outcrop. The barrier's tendrils wound about the treegliders' trembling bodies. She scrambled forward, desperate to free them.

"Take me, take me!" she cried at the fence, holding out her scarred arms. "Let them go." She tripped and fell in the field of poppies.

A great snuffling, crackling sound came from the forest. She poked her head above the poppies. Immense white bears with jagged black manes broke through the trees. Forked tongues lolled from their massive, fanged mouths. Their riders wore chitinous red-and-amber armor and carried green-glowing everpine branches as weapons, the sort imbued with Tira's power. Lilia knew those weapons well – her mother used them to kill wolverines and walking trees.

Conscription gangs sent by the Dhai in the valley to gather people for their great war carried those weapons, too. Lilia had heard dark stories of children bundled away in the night. Fear of being hauled off to join a terrible army overwhelmed her compassion, and she choked on a sob. She clawed her way back into the shadow of the stone outcrop. I am a terrible coward, she thought. Now everyone will know.

The riders barreled toward the thorn fence, trampling the dying treegliders. When they reached the fence, they raised their weapons and cut it down as easily as cutting a fresh tulip. Lilia willed herself to be still. If these people could cross the fence, they could do anything, and that scared her more than being thought a coward.

They galloped past Lilia's stone outcrop and away – toward the towering mass of webbing that cocooned the trees around her village, protecting it from the seething, semi-sentient plants that roamed the woodland.

Lilia grabbed a loose stone at her feet and ran after them. Maybe she couldn't face them directly, but they would not expect her to come up behind them.

She wasn't certain when she first noticed the smoke, but by the time she came to the creek that marked the boundary of the village, gasping for breath, the smoke choked her. Great gouts of flame ate the cocoon sheathing above her, exposing the village to the dangers of the woodland.

She stumbled into the circle of the village. Found screaming chaos. The taste of smoke was bitter. She ran toward her mother's holding, an immense banded cocoon that hung from the birch tree at the far end of the village.

From the folds of the smoke, a bear emerged.

Lilia shrieked and clutched the stone like a talisman against evil. The bear rider's weapon was extended, glowing green and bloody, the hilt protruding from a dark seed implanted in her wrist. The rider wore no helm, so Lilia saw her face. She was indeed one of the Dhai from the valley, the ones her mother told her to stay far, far away from, even if times were lean.

Lilia held her ground. Raised her stone. Her mother had taught her how to heal a hundred types of wounds and illnesses, and shake loose a bone-tree's prey, but no one ever taught her how to fight. She did not want to join the army.

The bear snarled at her. The rider laughed.

"Li!" Her mother's voice.

Lilia threw the stone and missed. The air felt heavy. She tasted copper. Glanced back. Her mother stood behind her, arms raised.

A great blinding-tree burst from the bare ground between Lilia and the rider, taking Lilia again off her feet. The blinding-tree sprouted brambled arms and sprayed a great rain of acid, a dew that ate at skin, hair, and armor alike. It coated the rider and her mount – and splashed across Lilia's right foot.

Lilia screamed and tried to wipe it away as the rider squealed and thrashed.

Her mother caught her hands. "Don't touch it!"

The flesh sloughed off Lilia's foot, revealing bloody tendons and bubbling, melting bone. The acid numbed her flesh as effectively as it disfigured it. The hem of bone-tree leaves on her makeshift dress hissed and smoked.

As Lilia wailed, her mother ripped the dress from her body, leaving her in a thin slip of linen. Lilia thrashed. Her vision swam. She was suddenly light-headed. I'm going to die, she thought. We are going to waste so much blood.

Her mother dragged her along, swift and silent as the world burned around them. Lilia was struck dumb, too horrified to speak. Within the sticky drapes of the trees, the immense cocoons where her people lived were burning. Great charred hunks of the cocoons fell, a rain of fire and flesh so mortifying that it took on the surreal aura of a dream. Women fled through the undergrowth, dressed in their twisted green regalia for the Festival of Tira's Descent. There was to be feasting tonight. Blood soup. Stuffed moths. Dancing. But it was all gone now, all in ruin.

When they came to the other side of the blazing village, her mother kicked open a discarded immature cocoon.

"Hide here," her mother said. "Like a snapping violet."

Lilia climbed inside. Her mother's skin was slick with sweat and blood, though Lilia did not know where the blood had come from. When Lilia looked back from inside the cocoon, her mother pressed something into the soft flesh of Lilia's wrist and murmured a prayer to Tira. Lilia saw a red tendril marked into her own flesh: a trefoil with a curled tail.

"It will bring you back to me," her mother said. "Come back to me."

"I'll come back," Lilia said. "I promise I'll come back. Please don't leave!"

"You'll find me," her mother said, and clapped her hands. The broken flesh of the cocoon reknit itself.

"I promise, Mam. Don't leave me."

Lilia pressed her face against the edge of the cocoon, where some insect had worried open a hole. She saw her mother standing before a dozen riders wearing chitinous crimson armor. They sat rigid on their massive bears. The bears' yellow eyes glinted. The lead rider menaced forward, a severe-looking woman with a tawny face and broad jaw.

Lilia went still, like a snake. She put her hands to her mouth, fearful she would cry out and give her mother away.

"Where is she?" the rider asked.

"Gone, Kai," Lilia's mother said.

"You're a liar." The Kai's weapon snarled out from her wrist, a lashing length of everpine that hummed with a pale green light. "You don't have enough blood to kindle a gate."

"I do now," Lilia's mother said.

Lilia felt the air condense, as if the weight of the world pressed down on her. She closed her eyes and put her hands over her ears. Heavy air meant someone was drawing on the power of Tira to reshape things. But covering her ears did not cut out the screaming.

The ground trembled. When Lilia opened her eyes, her mother stood above her, covered from head to toe in blood. She ripped open the cocoon and pulled Lilia into her arms.

"I knew you wouldn't leave me," Lilia said.

But Lilia could see something over her mother's shoulder. Four paces behind her, a dark, tattered shadow rippled across the fabric of the woodland, as if some great beast had rent a hole in the stuff that made up the sky. Between the black tatters Lilia saw hints of another woodland, a field of black poppies, and some hulking structure in the distance. The double hourglass of the suns' light was reflected from a massive glass dome there. The light hurt Lilia's eyes. Beyond it, Lilia saw the faint red blot of the third sun in a lavender-tinged blue sky, suffused with the green light of Tira in the distance.

Lilia blinked and gazed up into the sky above her, on her side of the rift. She saw the same hourglass suns, and the third red sun. But the sky on her side was amber, not lavender-blue. And as the suns sank in her sky, the horizon was a brilliant, blazing crimson, as if the suns bled. Why was the sky different on the other side?

"It's time to be brave," her mother said. "You remember what I said about being brave?" She set Lilia down and pushed her toward the tear in the world. "I've opened a gate. Hurry now. I'll bring the other children and follow after."

"But, Mam–"

"No questions. Be brave. You remember what I said about the Dhai from the valley, and what would happen if they came here among the woodland Dhai? Go now, Li, before it's too late and this was all for nothing."

"I'm not a coward," Lilia said. Her eyes filled. She wanted to throw herself at her mother's feet. Instead, she rubbed the tears from her eyes and stumbled forward.

She fell through the waving tatters between the reflected worlds, tumbling into the field of black poppies under the new sky. She looked behind her.

Her mother had turned her back on the gate. The Kai stood before her, bloody everpine weapon in hand, a tangle of poisonous vines crawling up her opposite arm. Blood wet the vine. The Kai swung her weapon.

The weapon crushed Lilia's mother's collarbone. Her body crumpled, a mangled succulent.

The Kai stepped over her mother's body, shiny crimson armor soaked in blood and shredded plant matter. The vine on her arm was shriveling now, turning to brown dust.

The Kai reached for Lilia–

But her fingers stopped short on the other side of the parting of the worlds, as if they met some invisible barrier. The Kai's face twisted in anger.

"Motherless woodland fool," the Kai said. "I have other cats to whip. Oma is rising, and we will rise with it."

The air around Lilia contracted. The world pulled her down, as if she had gained three times her weight. She put her hands over her ears. Closed her eyes.

When Lilia opened her eyes, she stood alone in the field of poppies in the middle of a deep, wooded glen. The tear in the world was gone. She saw the emerald light of Tira high in the lavender-blue sky, and the hourglass of the twin suns. Her foot ached badly; the numbness was wearing off. She saw the bloody, melted flesh of her ruined foot covered in dirt and curious flies.

Lilia retched.

"Child?"

A plump woman stood at the edge of the clearing. She had a kind face and a thick mane of silver hair; swaths of it peeked out from beneath the broad hood of her coat. She held a large walking stick.

"Where is Nava, child? Your mother? Where are the others?"

Lilia held out her wrists. "Please cut me," she said. "If you're a blood witch too, you can bring her back."

The woman recoiled. "Child, drop your hands. Don't speak that way here, no, no. Things are very different here. I'm Kalinda Lasa. You're to come with me, you understand? And no more talk of blood witches. Witches, of all things? Tira's tears."

Lilia kept her hands outstretched. "I made a promise." Her voice caught. "I have to find my mother. I promised."

"We all want a good many things, child, but it doesn't mean we get them," Kalinda said. "I'm sorry. The world – all worlds – are bigger than the both of us and your mother, too." She glanced at Lilia's foot. "If you want to keep that limb, we must go quickly."

"My mother," Lilia said, and finally dropped her hands. It was like grasping at air. Already the horrifying morning felt like a terrible story that had happened to someone else.

"Your mother is dead, likely," Kalinda said. "You'll meet her fate, too, unless you come with me."

"But I have to–"

Kalinda gently took her arm. Lilia felt numb. Her attention grew hazy. The light here was so different, dazzling, as if she'd come from a place where she only saw things through a haze of smoke. It was the sky, she realized, staring up at the blue-lavender wash. The sky was so different.

"You can keep your promise," Kalinda said softly, "but do so when you're a woman, not a little girl. Your mother will forgive you for waiting awhile longer."

Kalinda brought her to a small camp on the other side of the field and bound her foot. Then she loaded Lilia into the back of a bear-pulled cart. They traveled some time before halting at the steps of a grand temple. Lilia recognized it as the structure she had seen when she first peered through the tear in the world.

"A pity you have no magical talent yet," Kalinda said, gazing up at Tira's waning light. "But we all have our place. The Temple of Oma will look after you, child. Keep your head down. Don't cause any trouble. And don't tell any wild stories. You've been ill, and your mother is dead. That's all they need to know. No blood witches. No armies. You understand?"

Lilia nodded, even though she didn't understand at all.

"You'll be safe here," Kalinda said. "Until they come for you again. But we'll be ready then, won't we?"

It was only after Lilia woke the next morning in her simple bed in the Temple of Oma scullery and saw that the red tendril her mother had pressed into her flesh was gone, the skin red and blistered as if she'd been washed in poison ivy, that she wondered if she herself was just some shadow, another person's memory from some other life.

It was in the Temple of Oma, many months later, that Lilia met the Kai a second time.

"You're welcome here," the Kai said to Lilia and the twelve other girls and boys admitted to the temple that season as they lined up in the great foyer to meet her, safe behind the crown of webbing that kept out the worst of the toxic plant life that still crawled across the valley. This Kai had the same severe, unwelcoming face that Lilia remembered from their first meeting. But she wore no armor, and her wrist bore no seed of a retracting weapon. If she knew Lilia at all, she did not show it.

"And what brings you here?" the Kai asked.

"My mother," Lilia said. "Some people say she's dead, but I'm going to find her."

The Kai smiled, but it was a sad smile. "You're a woodland Dhai," the Kai said. "I can tell from your accent."

"And you're one of the Dhai from the valley," Lilia said. "But where is your army?"

The Kai laughed. "Army? I'm not sure what the woodland Dhai tell their children, but there is no army here. We are a peaceful people, just like you."

"But I saw you with a sword."

"I'm sorry, child, I've never picked up a weapon in my life." She hesitated, then said, "It must be very confusing to lose your family. Don't fear. We're your family now. Everything may seem very different for a time. But we'll help you get through it."

Lilia thought to ask her about the sky, too, but the Kai was already moving on to the next child.

The Dhai people in the valley were not at all what she thought they were. In truth, she wondered if these were really the same people who burned her village, or if she'd dreamed the whole thing after all.

For many years after, Lilia dreamed of treegliders. Some years, she even forgot about her promise to her mother. But when she was fifteen, well after Tira's descent, when Para, the Breathmaker, bathed the world in blue light, she made a sketch on the back of a book in the temple library. She drew the trefoil with the tail her mother had pressed into her flesh. Then she handed the book over to her best friend Roh – a novice learning to draw the breath of Para – in the hope he'd find some record of it in the temple libraries she didn't have access to. She wanted to know how much of her memory of her former life was the terrified fantasy of a young girl.

"What's this for?" Roh asked as he pondered the paper, bouncing back on his heels.

"I've been a coward too long," she said. "It's time to be brave."

He laughed. She didn't.

That night, for the first time in over a decade, Lilia did not dream of a bloody Dhai army.

1

Because ruin so often came from the sky, borne by fickle satellites
on erratic orbits, Shao Maralah Daonia did not think to look
to the sea until it was too late. She expected the next wave of
invaders to come in over land after falling from a tear in the sky,
the way they had the last six years.

Instead, the invaders came in on the morning tide. They drove
before them a boiling swarm of vegetal flesh – a massive black
surge of death that slithered up the coast like ravenous snakes
of acidic kelp, devouring all it touched. Six cities had fallen to
the same onslaught in six weeks, driving Maralah and her army
further south. Now they came for the seaside city of Aaraduan,
last stronghold in Saiduan's northernmost province.

Maralah expected they would take Aaraduan just as easily
as the other cities, but not before she evacuated her Patron,
burned the archives, and took a legion of them with her into
death. She did not mind dying here. Her brother's army was only
half a day away, slowed by spongy tundra and permafrost made
unpredictable by the summer's heat. When he did finally sweep
into the city, after it was taken, she relied on him to murder any
stragglers she could not finish herself.

Maralah summoned an air-twisting parajista at the height of his
power to secure Aaraduan's inner and outer gates with shimmering
skeins of air and soil. She gazed at the cracked face of the ascendant
star, Para, glowing milky blue in the lavender sky. She cursed the

invaders for not coming ashore fifteen years earlier, when her star, Sina, was ascendant, and she was the most deadly power in Saiduan. She felt only the most tenuous connection to her violet-burning satellite now, and could do little more to aid in the shoring up of the gates than give orders. Her days of calling lightning and fire from a clear sky were long behind her. If all here went as she foresaw, she would die before seeing Sina again.

Maralah marched into the hold to watch the burning of the archives. A half dozen sanisi – Saiduan assassins blessed to call on the stars, as she did – tossed ancient records of bamboo, human skin, carnivorous plant exoskeletons, finger bones, and the pounded carcasses of winged insects – most of them long since extinct – into the roaring hearth. On some other day, one not so mad, Maralah imagined the Patron of Saiduan himself sitting beside the hearth with a book of poetry, tracing the columns of text with his worn fingers as a sinajista conjured a flame for him to read by. But the Patron would never sit here again. The room itself would be eaten soon, and the sanisi with it.

What records they could not save, they destroyed. Maralah had heard the same reports from every city – the invaders went first to the libraries and archives, drawn there like spotted beetles to the nectar of claw-lilies. Whatever knowledge they searched for, she would rather see it burned than give them the satisfaction of having it.

Like the other sanisi, Maralah dressed in a long black coat of firegrass and fibrous bark that touched the heels of her boots. She wore a knee-length padded tunic and long trousers. The hilt of her infused sword stuck up through her coat, a twisted branch of willowthorn that glowed faintly violet. The weapon marked her as one of Sina's soul stealers. Even in Sina's decline, the weapon retained its power. She could still kiss a conjurer to death with it.

The youngest of the sanisi, Kadaan, looked up from the stacks. His dark hands were smeared darker with soot. As a boy, it was Maralah who put a Para-infused bonsa weapon in his hand, a gnarled yellow branch that burned blue when he drew it. She ensured he was apprenticed to the best parajista she knew, a man who taught him to channel Para's breath to unmake the weather and push down walls of solid stone with a strong breeze. It was she who took responsibility for his fate now.

"We're nearly done here," Kadaan said. "Let me die on the wall with the others. I won't become their slave." Maralah saw the fire reflected in his bright eyes. Oh, to be twenty-odd years old again. And foolish.

The archivist who oversaw the purging of the archives, Bael, was already well gone with what he chose to save. Maralah wished she could have sent her youngest sanisi with him.

"The ones at the wall will be dead in an hour," Maralah said. "Killing a single biting tendril achieves nothing. You must burn out the weed's nest. Keep burning."

Maralah stepped into the corridor outside the archive room, seeking relief from the oppressive heat. She heard a great yawning sigh move through the hold. Maralah let her fingers linger on one of her shorter blades and walked into the long mirrored hall that faced the coast. She gazed across the jagged black city still bundled in a husk of late summer snow, to the harbor where the invaders anchored their fantastic bone and sinew boats. She'd had to sneak the Patron, his broodguard, and the archivist out across the mosquito-filled tundra in the other direction, hoping her brother's army found them before some group of foreign scouts.

She looked for the source of the sigh but saw no evidence of it. From this vantage, the sound of the slithering plant life devouring the walls was indistinguishable from the thrashing of the sea; they drowned out all else.

She rested her hands on the warm railing. The holds this far north were ancient things, grown and manipulated by long-dead tirajistas, back when they had been called something else, something far more fearsome. Those sorcerers had since become priests, torturers, and engineers, because their work still breathed and grew; it lasted. But something that was grown could be eaten. And the invaders knew it.

Maralah heard the low, keening sigh again. She pulled at the collar of her coat. Some may have thought it was just the wind blowing through empty corridors, creeping through wounds in ancient living walls, stirring paper lanterns whose flame flies had long since died. But she knew better.

Maralah drew the short blade at her hip, pivoted left, and thrust deep into the shadows of the curtained balcony behind her. The blade met resistance. Slid through flesh.

A figure hissed and yanked its body from her blade. As it stepped into the light she saw it was most likely a man – always hard to tell, with Taigan – but yes, she could see the snarled beard that clothed his face now. He was especially particular about which pronoun others used, depending on his latest manifestation.

"Taigan," she said as he pulled out of the shadows, clutching at his bleeding side. She sheathed her blade. "You have gotten soft... and noisy."

"Release your ward on me," he said, "and you'll see just how soft I am." He took his bloody fingers away from his side. The blood around the wound began to bubble and hiss as he repaired himself. She smelled burnt meat.

Taigan dressed in oiled leather and a padded brown dog-hair coat. He carried no visible weapon. Tall and dark, he wore his hair shorn short, and he stooped awkwardly: wreckage from a wound she had inflicted on him, one he could not repair himself, not unless he persuaded another sanisi with her talents to assist him, and only when Sina was again ascendant. When the Patron stripped Taigan of his title four years before for betraying him, Maralah removed the ward that bound Taigan to the Patron. Maralah suspected the Patron would have killed him, if killing Taigan was possible, but his talents were too useful to see him waste away in exile in some fishing village.

"Was she the one?" Maralah asked.

Taigan shifted his weight as another cold wind curled in through the windows, bringing with it the smell of the sea and the acrid stink of the plants. "She died in the ruin of a ragged gate," he said, "so let's hope not. Perhaps all of those who can open gates are dead, and you can let me go in peace."

Maralah went back to the rail and watched the invaders disembark from their bloated boats. The men's chitinous armored forms rippled up the beach. All men. She had yet to see a woman among them. They rode no dogs or bears, brought with them no pack animals or siege engines, only the burbling plants and fungi and red algae tides, and those they tugged with them from coast to coast, like fish dragged along in great nets.

As she watched, a bit of the sky tore above the ships, like something from a fantastic nightmare. She had a glimpse of some... other place where the sky was a murky amber-orange, as if on fire. A rippling shadow crossed the sky there, a black mass that made her skin crawl and her breath catch. The sky shimmered again, and the seams between her world and... the other closed. She let out her breath. She pointed at the sky. "The world is ready to come apart on its own. There's an omajista more skilled than you who can control it."

They had started seeing those mad tears in the sky eight years before, in the far, far north. She had not believed the sightings at first, thought it was just some drunk tuber farmer enchanted by especially brilliant northern lights. But no. Oma, the dark star, was creeping back into orbit. The worlds were coming together again far sooner than anyone anticipated.

"There will be an omajista among the Dhai people who can open the way," she said. "There always is, when Oma rises. You don't have that many Dhai to pick through. We only need one."

"The Dhai are weak-minded cannibals. Let the invaders take that maggoty country and their omajistas with it."

Maralah had fought the invaders on every coast, in every province, at the height of every snowy peak. When she sought out her father's house in Albaaric after the fighting, she found only a weeping ruin and the slimy remnants of red algae smearing the walls at knee height, where the highest tide had reached. She and her brother had not spoken to her father or sisters in twenty years, but she went to the house in search of living kin – a near-cousin, a second-mother, even a village brother – despite the silence. She found nothing but the taste of smoke. They never left the bodies, these invaders. What they did with them... Maralah did not care to guess. But rumor had it they had a taste for blood.

"The city is done, Taigan," Maralah said. "Now you must decide if you'll perish with it."

"May your roads run long, then," Taigan said, grimacing.

"And yours," Maralah said. "Don't come back without an omajista. A real one. You understand?"

"They've reached the walls," he said.

Maralah looked. Black, slithering plant flesh swarmed the shimmering blue walls, even as the structure spat and hissed at them. The sanisi standing at the top of the walls raised their hands to call on the ascendant star Para, Lord of the Air, for protection.

When she looked back, Taigan had gone.

Maralah took the worn hilt of her weapon and pulled it from the sheath at her back. The room cooled. A soft violet light emanated from the length of the willowthorn branch. In response to her touch, the branch awakened; the hilt elongated and snapped around her wrist twice, binding her fate to the weapon's. She watched blood weep from the branch, gather at its end, and fall to the stones. The weapon sang to her, the voices of hungry ghosts, all Saiduan, all collected in the living weapon when Sina was at its height. The invaders did not have ghosts, because their souls were not of this world. A pity, that. Her weapon was always so hungry.

Maralah swept the sword over her head and slammed it into the living flesh of the hold. Violet light burst across her vision. The weapon keened. The hold wailed as a massive wound appeared on its face. Thick, viscous green fluid gushed from the hold, pouring across her forearms, her boots. Her weapon licked greedily at the soul of the hold.

She prayed to Sina it would be enough to survive the night.

2

High summer, the festival season, when the Temple of Oma played host to dozens of traders and craftspeople, all of them eating and sweating and drinking in the temple's great banquet hall. During her decade in Oma's temple, Lilia had learned how to navigate through its mass of humanity like a skilled sea captain.

She spent her time in the temple scullery cleaning sinks with morvern's drake and bottling honey from the giant spotted beehives in the back garden. In the afternoons, she hobbled up the long tongue of the grand stairway, favoring her mangled right foot – which had never healed properly – and changed the bed linens for the temple's novice Oras – the parajistas, tirajistas, and sinajistas who would claim the title of Ora on passing their initiation. The other temples – those dedicated to Para, Sina, and Tira – only trained one type of jista, but Oma's temple claimed the very best of them all, bringing them together into one very powerful – and, in Lilia's opinion, very arrogant – bunch.

As Lilia came downstairs, dragging a bag of dirty linen too massive to take through the scullery stair, she saw her friend Roh waiting for her next to the heavy carved talon of the banister.

She hesitated on the stair. He saw her and grinned. His grin could fill a room. It pierced her heart every time she saw it, because that grin made her want to trail after him like some love-struck fool, and she had seen enough novices and drudges acting just that way around him to realize how silly it was.

A plump novice named Saronia passed behind him. Seeing him grinning at Lilia, she said, "You should be pickier with your affections, Roh. You can afford to be."

Roh paid her no mind. He offered a hand to Lilia and said, "Leave the laundry. I want to show you something."

Saronia rolled her eyes. Two others had joined her, smooth-cheeked, well-fed novices from Clan Garika. They wore the blue tunic, trousers, and green apron of novices; their hair was shorn short and dark, like Roh's – like Lilia's. "All she's good at is laundry," Saronia said. "Didn't your mothers ever tell you you should flirt with Garikas, not drudges? My mothers know yours, you know, and they wouldn't approve."

Roh rounded on Saronia. "Go wrap your head in a litany," he said. "Maybe next time you'll remember it, then, instead of dropping Para in the middle of building a vortex."

"I'm more talented than–"

"You're talented at getting people to think you're talented," Roh said. "I could bury you chest-deep in laundry and you wouldn't be able to breathe your way out of it with Para."

"You're an arrogant child."

"And you're a terribly jealous woman," Roh said, "because my mother could have been yours. Too bad you were barely gifted and she gave you away."

There were five genders in Dhai – female-assertive, female-passive, male-assertive, male-passive, and ungendered. Saronia always used the female-assertive for herself, while Lilia thought of herself in the female-passive. But Roh happily used the ungendered pronoun in reference to Saronia. It was considered a rude thing, of course, to use the wrong one, but it seemed to especially annoy Saronia.

"I'm telling Ora Almeysia you said that."

"Go ahead. And I'll tell her where you light off to after dark," Roh said.

Saronia curled her lip and turned away.

Lilia waited until they were in retreat, then started down the stairs again. Her clothes were the same as the novices', only the simple gray of the temple's drudges to their brilliant novice blue.

Roh hopped up the steps to meet her. She had a desperate urge to put her hands in his silky hair and draw him closer. But she pulled away from him instead and averted her gaze.

"I found that symbol," he said. "The trefoil with the tail that you drew."

He pulled the book she'd written in out of his tunic pocket. She also noticed the edge of one of Kalinda's letters peeking out, which she was fairly certain she'd never given him. Had he stolen it?

"Where?" Lilia said.

"First, tell me how it helps you find your mother," he said. "I asked around, Li. You're supposed to be an orphan."

"It's my business, Roh."

"You asked me to help."

Lilia tried to snatch the book back, but Roh was too fast. Spry, light on his feet, it was always difficult to tell how much of that was his dance training and how much was him playing with the forces of Para. He fairly floated away from her, lighter than air.

"How will you evade me when Para is descendent?" Lilia said. "Your tricks won't work then."

"By then, I'll be a fine fighter," he said, "married to a dozen powerful sinajistas who'll protect me from you."

Roh was at least six years away from becoming a fully trained Ora – one of the jistas trained in theology and ethics across the Dhai valley – and Para would be descendent far sooner than that. Even with its erratic orbit, it wouldn't dominate the sky more than another two or three years. Sina was coming around next. She wondered how Roh would get along then, because she couldn't imagine him being happy without a satellite to call on.

"So, are you going to tell me what it means or not?" Lilia said. She had slept very well the last week after turning over the symbol; not one shrieking treeglider or bloody-eyed bear. It reinforced her convictions. She was old enough to make good on her promise. She wasn't such a weak little girl anymore.

"It's just upstairs," he said, pointing.

Lilia saw no Ora watching them from the great spiraling bloom of the stairs. Above, the hourglass of the twin suns blinked at her through the giant dome that capped the temple's foyer, twelve floors above her. She squinted. The afternoon meal had already been prepared and washed up. They wouldn't be looking for her for some time. Even though she was just a drudge, she often took part in strategy games with the novices, and even some Oras, but her next game wasn't until the early evening.

"Alright," she said, and set the laundry out of the way, just outside the entrance to the scullery stair that ran behind the banquet hall. She made to go back to the main stair, but Roh gestured for her to go up through the scullery stair instead.

She limped along behind him, dragging her mangled foot. Kalinda had ensured she didn't lose her whole leg, but she was missing two of her toes and much of the ball of her foot, and the melted flesh and scar tissue left behind wasn't pretty. Roh once asked her if it hurt. Only when she looked at it, she told him. When he laughed at that, she knew they would be friends.

They went up four sets of stairs and passed two other curious drudges. Kinless and ungifted, just like Lilia.

"How far are we going up?" Lilia asked. "I'm not allowed above the sixth floor."

"I won't tell if you don't."

Her foot was already throbbing. Her breathing was labored. She felt the tightness in her chest that often signaled a seizing of her lungs. She firmed her jaw and leaned her weight on the rail and kept going. What she lacked in physical power she had to make up for in endurance and patience.

When they passed the eleventh floor, Lilia's chest hurt. She hated that Tira had hindered her in so many ways. She tugged at Roh's tunic. "We can't go up there. That's the Kai's quarters and the Ora libraries. Drudges aren't allowed." She took a moment to catch her breath.

"Do you want to see it or not?" Roh said. "The Kai's sick, so they've moved her a couple floors down. There's nobody up there. Do you want to know what that mark means or not?"

"Why can't you just tell me?"

"Because you have to see it."

Roh came to the top of the steps. They were in the corridor outside the Assembly Chamber, where the Kai often met with the elder Oras and clan leaders. Lilia had never seen it, but she knew it by the markings on the door.

Roh pushed open the door, an ancient construction of amberwood banded in iron and marked with the Dhai characters for "come together." Lilia crept after him.

Inside the chamber, a massive round table of black walnut dominated the room. As they were at the top of the temple, the ceiling here was a tapestry of colored glass. The hourglass of the twin suns made up its center, directly above the table, illuminating it like some divine shrine to Oma. Lilia moved further into the room and saw the whole sky represented in the glass: the double suns, sometimes called Shar, the little red sun, Mora, and all three of the satellites – blue Para, green Tira, purple Sina. At the very edge of the patterned glass, closest to a second archway leading to a sitting room, was a fourth star, nearly black. The elusive Oma. Lilia did not see it represented often. Fingers of blackness followed it, like a great, spiny growth had crawled into the glass. On the other half of the ceiling were the moons – little Zini, irregular Mur, and great white Ahmur and its hazy tiara of satellites.

"Li," Roh said.

Lilia pulled her gaze from the ceiling. Roh stood next to the great wooden table, pointing at the middle of it.

She saw a mosaic of patterned stones at the center of the table. It was a map of Dhai.

Roh tapped a section of the map at the edge of the woodlands, all the way on the other side of the country, past Mount Ahya, along the Hahko Sea. A jagged dart of green stones there made up a finger-length peninsula. Set just to the left of the peninsula was a piece of jade carved into the precise shape of the figure that Lilia's mother had pressed into her flesh. It was shocking to see it, after all this time. She'd half thought she made it up, along with everything else that happened that day in the woods.

"You going to tell me what it means now?" Roh said.

"It means I'm not crazy," Lilia said.

"Well, that's debatable."

Lilia leaned across the table to get a better look. She traced the shape of the jade: a perfect trefoil with a long, curled tail. Pain radiated up her bad leg, but she hardly noticed it. She saw other symbols, too, which she didn't recognize. A triangle with two circles where the Temple of Para should be; a circle with two lines through it in the woodland around Tira's temple; a coiled curl with a circle at the center near Sina's temple; and a square with a double circle inside over the Temple of Oma. There was one more near the Liona Stronghold that marked the mountain pass that separated them from Dorinah – a trefoil with four tails, one at each compass point.

"What do these all mean?" Lilia asked. "There's no temple or stronghold here. I know. I've been there. But it's marked like the others."

"You should find out," Roh said.

She pulled her hand away. "That's the other side of the country. Through the woodlands." She wasn't gifted. How was she going to get all the way out there by herself?

"So what are you going to do, clean up after novice Oras your whole life?" Roh crossed his arms. He was almost as tall as her, and more than a year younger, but leaner and stronger. For a moment, she wished she could have his perfect legs and powerful confidence.

"I'm glad you found this," she said. She got down from the chair and made her way back to the scullery stair.

"Listen," Roh said. "I can't leave the temple without permission, but you can. You're just a drudge."

"Thanks for reminding me."

"You know what I mean."

"Do I?"

He sighed. "My mother once asked another seer about my fate," Roh said, "because as much as she tried, she couldn't see it. The seer told my mother I'd die an old man in an orchard. I'd be a farmer, with six spouses and dozens of children."

"A parajista farmer? I can't imagine that."

"Me either," Roh said, "but Para's going to be descendent in another few years. What if it never comes back?"

"It always comes back."

"Well, the seer saw something different," he said.

Lilia gazed at the dark shape on the ceiling that followed Oma. "They always come back," she repeated.

"Maybe," Roh said, "maybe not."

"You were passed some good pieces in life," she said.

"Is everything some strategy game to you?"

"Well, yes," she said, as she'd been thinking of kindar, a cooperative board game played with wooden pieces meant to represent family members. Roh had a large family, multiple mothers and fathers and siblings and other relations. "Be happy with how things turned out. You have a family that loves you."

"*You* don't love me," Roh said.

That startled her. "What are you talking about?"

His color darkened, which surprised her even more. Parajistas from powerful Clan Garika did not make eyes at kinless drudges.

"We're good friends," she said. "Is that not enough?"

Lovely, arrogant boys like him only loved a person until they loved them back.

She turned and stumbled down the steps, gripping the rail hand over hand to keep from falling headlong back down all twelve flights. Her breathing was better, but she would need to see the temple physician. Spending time with Roh had gotten more and more confusing of late. He left her more frustrated than anything. Her focus was the promise she made her mother. That's all.

She made it down almost a floor before she heard voices coming from below.

Lilia tried to step back, and fell. Roh grabbed her arm to steady her. He released her almost immediately and apologized for touching her without asking.

"It's all right," she said. "Someone's coming." Lilia tried to get past him up the stairs, but there wasn't any room.

"You can kiss me," he said, staring over her shoulder as the voices grew closer.

"What?" she said.

"What other reason do we have for being up here?"

"Para, Roh, stop ironing my head."

"I'm not trying to annoy you," he said.

"Since when?"

"Can I kiss you?" he whispered. "Should we tell them we're doing laundry, maybe?"

It was a rude and sometimes dangerous thing, to touch without consent. No one had dared do more than grab at her sleeve since she was twelve. People in the temple might play strategy games with her, but no one cared to court her. She wasn't entirely sure she was ready.

"No," she said.

"What are you doing up here?"

Lilia jumped. Roh let out a squeak. Lilia covered her mouth to keep from laughing.

Ora Almeysia, Mistress of Novices, rounded the stair ahead of them. Almeysia was tall and wiry, like a bird, with a nest of tangled white hair knotted in pale ribbons.

"I'm sorry," Lilia said. Her cheeks felt hot. She glanced at Roh. His color, too, had deepened, and that made her want to laugh even more. All this sneaking around for a mark on a map that she had no idea how to reach.

"We're going," Roh said.

"Rohinmey Tadisa Garika," Almeysia said. "This is not the first time I've caught you where you shouldn't be. I want you in my study at dusk. We'll mete out your atonement for this indiscretion. And you... who are you?"

"Just a drudge," Lilia said.

"Drudges have names. What are you called?"

"Lilia Sona."

"No clan."

"I'm a woodland Dhai," Lilia said.

Almeysia snorted. "Woodland. Not surprising, then, to see this sort of behavior from *you*. I've told the Kai time and again not to permit you feral dissidents here. The scullery master will be informed of this trespass. Go, before I toss you to the pitcher plants."

Lilia squeezed past skinny Almeysia and limped down the steps as quickly as she could.

They made it down four more flights before Roh said, "Why was Almeysia taking the scullery stair? She's allowed to be up there. She could have taken the main stair."

"She was talking to someone," Lilia said. "I heard voices."

"But she was alone."

"Should we start spying on her, since we've already broken a temple law?"

"It wasn't a very *big* temple law," Roh said cheerfully.

"I bet when you're that old, you'll talk to yourself, too."

"It's a lot like talking to you," he said, "only I get a lot more compliments."

They walked down the rest of the stairs in silence. Little lightning jabs of pain spread up Lilia's leg from ankle to knee. Every few breaths, she coughed. She focused on her breathing and pushed out of the scullery stair and back into the banquet hall. A few Oras generally worked there between meals, sipping cinnamon tea or smoking Tordinian cigarettes, but she saw no one there now. She limped to where she had hidden the laundry, hoping Roh wouldn't follow.

That's when she saw the stir of figures standing under the entrance to the foyer. At least a dozen novices and drudges fixed their attention on the giant amberwood door.

Lilia came up behind them, dragging the laundry. A very tall, dark man stood in the foyer, speaking with four of the senior Oras. He wore a long black coat. She saw the hilt of a blade sticking up through the back of it. In Dhai, only trained members of the militia were allowed to carry weapons.

"Who is he?" Roh asked as he came up behind her.

One of the novices, a boy named Kihin, glanced back at them and said, "He's a sanisi, all the way from Saiduan."

"I've seen sanisi in books," Roh said. "He doesn't look like a sanisi. Not a real one."

"Ora Ohanni found him trying to get through the webbing around the garden," Kihin said. "I guess they don't have web fences there. My father says–"

But at that moment, the sanisi raised his voice and turned toward them. "Bring me to your Kai or I will cut my way to her. I'm here to save your maggoty, cannibalistic little country. Against my better judgment."

The sanisi's gaze met Lilia's. He frowned. She stepped behind Kihin, trying to avoid the stranger's look. Roh glanced back at her.

"My name is Taigan. I need to speak with the Kai," the sanisi repeated. As Lilia peered around Kihin, she saw the sanisi still looking at her. "If things are progressing here as they did in my country, it's time you all stopped dancing around the olive trees and prepared for war."

3

Ahkio started awake in the arms of three strong women whose names he was pleased to remember. His cousin Liaro lay sprawled naked beside him: a long, lean man with a face that would inspire no poetry. The number of infused everpine weapons and baldrics scattered across the floor reminded him that their bedmates were members of the Dhai militia posted at the Kuallina Stronghold.

It was not an unpleasant way to start his morning.

After untangling himself from bed, Ahkio snuck out the back of the house to avoid bumping into his housemate Meyna and her child. Her husbands were likely off working in the sheep fields, which made his exit that much easier. He walked down the ramp leading to the knotty exterior of their living house. Most homes in central Dhai were hollowed out of gonsa trees, their crowns so great they blotted out the sky. It took a good half hour of walking to clear the shadow of the gonsa trees and reach the Osono Clan square.

The dozen students he taught religion and ethics were already assembled under the immature gonsa tree next to the square, the one that would be big enough to house a proper school in another twelve years, when Tira became ascendant, and the tirajistas would use that power to sculpt it. In the distance, he saw the silky threads of the webbing that dissuaded the worst of the walking trees from inundating the square. Most homesteads beyond the webbing had only thorn fences and homegrown defenses like fox-snaps to protect their families and livestock from creeping vegetation with a taste for blood and bone.

"Ahkio!" the students called when they saw him, and he waved, for a moment forgetting to be self-conscious of his hands. The children had stopped asking about his scars when he told them he once fought a fire-breathing bear. It was a prettier story than the one their parents might have told them.

"Today, we talk about Dhai government," he said.

"Does this mean you'll tell us about your mother," one of the girls asked, "and how she died so your sister could become Kai?"

Ahkio winced. "Terrible things sometimes happen to Kais," he said, "like what happened to my parents. We'll discuss that when we speak of the line of the Kai, and I'll also tell you about Faith Ahya, who birthed the first of us."

Ahkio tried to smile, but it took a great effort. His sister Kirana was Kai now at thirty – almost eleven years older than him – and talking about her supposed divinity always made him uncomfortable. His sister hadn't blazed down from a satellite the way it sounded like Faith Ahya did in *The Book of Oma*, though there were days he wished she had. Mostly, she was just his sister – a warm, sometimes aggravating, and often wise woman who believed in him even when the rest of the country wanted to see him exiled for madness after the death of their parents.

"Government is not determined by Oma," Ahkio said. "If you learn nothing else in this class, remember that. It's created by people like you. When we were slaves to those Dorinah witches across the mountains five hundred years ago, a woman named Faith Ahya fell in love with a man named Hahko, and the Dhai people followed them and their kin out of bondage in Dorinah, not because of their brute strength or cunning but because of their faith in the vision Faith and Hahko spun for them. This was the refuge they created. Now each of you is a part of building its future."

Only one student rolled her eyes. Ahkio made a note to tell her some terrible story later about how people from Saiduan spirited away arrogant young students who didn't listen to their teachers.

"Oma," he muttered aloud, because he realized he'd heard precisely that type of story from the Oras in the temple when he was younger. He was going to end up an old man teaching the children of shepherds to fear monsters in the woods.

At midday, most of his students went home to help move their family's thorn fences so they could rotate their sheep from one plot of community land to another. Ahkio napped and spent some time at the local tea house playing kindar with Saurika, the clan leader of Osono, a pleasantly plump, beady-eyed old man who kept claiming his leader piece long before he'd swept Ahkio's family pieces off the board.

"You're a cheater," Ahkio told him.

"You're one to talk," Saurika said. "I taught your sister to play kindar, and now I see you using my own defenses against me."

Later in the afternoon, a few students returned for a lesson in arithmetic, something Ahkio was not nearly as qualified to teach as religion and ethics. When he tired of it, he invited everyone home to dinner with Meyna and her husbands.

They arrived at Meyna's house and sat at the big communal table out back – Ahkio, three of his students, his cousin Liaro, and Meyna's husbands, who were also brothers – big Hadaoh and skinny little Rhin. The brothers shared a father, and one could see their kinship in their faces, their postures. Hadaoh stood at the outdoor stove, poking at the embers and drinking from a mug of wine. Rhin rubbed Meyna's swollen feet and told her some bit of gossip from the square about a merchant's new husband. Meyna was hugely pregnant with her second child. Her first, Mey-Mey, was two and danced around the table with a large day lily stalk, singing nonsense songs about angry sparrows that lived in the bellies of bears.

The night was hot, and moths circled the lanterns along the path to the house. His students were deep in a discussion with Liaro about the virtues of the country's second Kai, and whether or not Faith Ahya actually glowed when she appeared to prophets and seers.

Ahkio kept his hands tucked beneath his long sleeves. He gazed out past the students to the lights and laughter coming from the families nearby who were doing just as they were – congregating for good food and good company on one of high summer's last vital nights. He heard someone swear and stab out into the darkness at some flailing thing. The woman came back from the shadow beyond her table carrying a limp flower, its sticky tentacles still seething. She tossed it into her outdoor fireplace. Even from a hundred paces away, Ahkio heard the plant hissing.

"Ahkio?" Meyna said.

He started. "Yes?"

"Go get me wine, love. It's your turn to fetch drinks."

Ahkio touched thumb to forehead in a mocking way – an overly formal gesture between kin – and rose from the table. He paused a moment to admire her. She tilted her head, smiled; she was beautiful by any measure and a formidable businesswoman.

"Are we drinking to our engagement?" he said.

"And what would you add to our house?"

"A pretty face isn't enough?"

"You're not that pretty," she said.

Liaro laughed. "Now you're just playing," he said. "If I didn't bring Ahkio along to the tea house, I'd never lure over an accomplished woman."

"Liaro has the truth of it," Meyna said. "Those militia women in the house this morning surely kept you quite busy."

"I'd give it all up for you," Ahkio said, and though his tone was playful, his heart fluttered when he said it, because it was true. He would give up a great deal to marry Meyna and her husbands. More than he'd admit.

"Fetch us a drink," Meyna said warmly. "We'll discuss it."

He grinned and pushed away from the table. Liaro called after him, "Don't fall for it, Ahkio! She says that to everyone!"

Meyna said something less than complimentary in turn.

Ahkio walked around the side of the house and opened the entrance to the cellar. As he started down, something caught his attention. In the dim light of the flame fly lanterns at the front of the house, he saw someone on the porch.

Ahkio hid his hands in his sleeves. He called to the figure. "Welcome, kin. Food, rest, or company?"

The figure raised its head, and Ahkio's chest tightened.

It was Nasaka, one of the Oras from the Temple of Oma.

The last time an Ora had come for Ahkio, his parents were murdered, and he was saved from a fiery death by his screaming sister and Nasaka's glowing willowthorn sword.

Nasaka was a lean whip of a woman, well over fifty, hawk-nosed and gaunt, with a firm mouth and broad jaw. She was his aunt – his dead father's sister – and people often remarked that she and Ahkio bore a resemblance to one another. The resemblance annoyed him. He'd rather look like some useful farmer.

She wore dark colors. Not temple colors. That meant she had traveled without wanting the locals to recognize her as an Ora. The scholarly magician-priests of the temples weren't well favored in most clans. They dirtied up Dhai politics. As if Dhai politics weren't dirty enough.

"Just a smoke, I'm afraid," Nasaka said. "Come sit with me, Ahkio."

Ahkio hesitated. Dread knotted his stomach. He heard Meyna's laughter behind him. He wanted to turn around and pretend he had not seen Nasaka at all.

"Has my sister sent for me?" Ahkio asked. He leaned against the porch rail. He, Rhin, Hadaoh, and Meyna had built the railing the year before, when Mey-Mey had started to walk.

Nasaka pinched her fingers to the end of her pipe. A soft glow lit the end of the pipe. She began to puff. She drew her fingers away, shaking off ash. It was a trick Ahkio was surprised the old woman could manage. She was a sinajista, and Sina had been descendent many years. What little power Sina's gifted still retained wouldn't amount to much more than calling up a tiny flame or perhaps removing an uncomplicated ward.

"You certain?" Nasaka said, gesturing with the pipe.

"I don't smoke," Ahkio said. "You're thinking of Kirana. How *is* my sister?"

Nasaka exhaled a long plume of smoke. "Your sister is dying," she said.

Ahkio was glad for the rail then. "You're wrong," Ahkio said. "Kirana is Kai, and Kais don't die without heirs. I've spent all morning teaching that to children."

"Just because a thing has not yet happened does not mean it can never happen," Nasaka said. "She is dying. And she has summoned you. There is no one else, Ahkio. You knew this day might come."

"Kirana isn't going to die," Ahkio said. Of the two surviving children of the former Kai, Kirana was the one who could channel the power of the satellites. When Tira was ascendant, she could heal the blind and coax a morning star vine to become a sturdy ship's rigging. The rest of the time, she excelled at talking down disputes among bitter clan-rivals and managing trade negotiations with the Aaldians and Tordinians to the south.

Ahkio taught ethics to the children of shepherds.

Nasaka exhaled more sweet-smelling smoke. It was a foreign blend of cloves, purple hasaen flowers, and Tordinian tobacco, a spicy, not unpleasant scent that clung to the woman night and day: a smell uniquely Nasaka. It put Ahkio in mind of the temples, and another burning, a long time ago.

"I hoped you would marry," Nasaka said, "a good strong Osono girl or two. It was why I permitted you to leave the temple."

"Kirana married, and see how happily that turned out. You never got your heirs from her and what's-his-name."

"And look where we are because of that. I have a dying Kai and only her weak, irresponsible brother to tap for the seat."

"My life is *here*," Ahkio said. He looked into the dim yard. The moons were rising. "I've kept house with Meyna and her husbands–"

"Oh, Meyna this, Meyna that," Nasaka said, and her tone let Ahkio know the low regard she held for her.

"Don't speak ill of Meyna in her own house."

"I need you at the temple tonight," Nasaka said. "Clan Leader Saurika has someone prepared to take over your classes."

Ahkio thought about telling her no. He thought about running off into the sheep fields. But telling Nasaka no never ended well. He knew that as well as anyone.

"Is she really dying?"

"I wouldn't be here otherwise."

"Who did it, Nasaka?"

"It's some illness."

"Then call some sensitive tirajista who can still channel Tira in decline, and she'll fix it. Don't take me for a fool."

Nasaka sucked at the end of her pipe. The silence stretched. Then, "Whatever her illness, it can't be cured. It's gotten worse, Ahkio. I'm sorry. I don't know how much time she has, and I want you to sit with her before the end."

Ahkio pressed his hands to his eyes. Took a deep breath. "Was it Tir's family?" he asked. "Rhin and Hadaoh's father?"

"I suggest you pack your things and come with me," Nasaka said. "If it was, then this house is no longer safe for you."

Ahkio turned away from her. He went back around the house to where his kin had gathered. He could not still his hands. Politics had caught up with him, years after he thought all those terrible days were dead and burned.

The remains of dinner smeared the bowls and plates. Eating sticks and hunks of half-eaten bread littered the table.

Meyna held Mey-Mey, asleep, in her lap. Hadaoh was relating a story about birthing a lamb. Rhin conferred with one of Ahkio's students, scribbling something in charcoal on the wooden table.

Liaro grabbed at Ahkio's hand with his rough, calloused fingers. Ahkio had given him blanket consent some time ago, and the unexpected touch calmed him now. Liaro set his black stare on Ahkio.

"Something tells me that Ora isn't here to propose marriage," Liaro said, and from the look on Liaro's face, on everyone's faces, Ahkio had done nothing to conceal what he felt.

"How did you–"

"I sent him for wine," Meyna said. "You were dallying. He saw Ora Nasaka. Is it true?"

"Kirana's summoned me to the temple."

Meyna cut a look at the house. He wanted to take her smooth, unblemished hands in his. He wanted her to tell him everything would be all right, and she would propose in the morning, and they would be his family now. Kirana was not dying. He wouldn't be left all alone.

But all Meyna said was "Be careful."

Rhin and Hadaoh exchanged a look. "We should speak to Yisaoh," Rhin said.

Their sister, Yisaoh, had contested Ahkio's mother for the title of Kai just ten years before. Ahkio had thought Meyna inviting him into their house meant the end of all those bad feelings. He was not his mother. But Meyna's expression had darkened. As Ahkio stood there rubbing his hands, the mood of the table sobered. Whoever had come for his sister would come for him next, he knew. He knew it and still rebelled against it, because to step back into the temple with Nasaka meant she would try to turn him into everything he hated.

"I want to stop the world right here," Ahkio said aloud. "Just like this."

"Too late," Liaro said, and pushed away from the table.

4

Roh drew himself up outside the painted door of the sanisi's quarters and raised his hand. Fear flooded him, but he held his ground. He had convinced one of the drudges in the kitchens to send him up with the sanisi's meal of rice and curried yams. Roh found himself salivating over it during the entire climb to the sixth floor. It was well past dinner, but he'd been too excited to eat.

Now he waited with the cooling yams and rice on a tray, both terrified and hopeful that the sanisi would answer. Finding the sanisi in the foyer had been like discovering some mythical being from a ritual retelling come to life. He didn't know how long the sanisi would stay, but he wasn't going to give up the opportunity to learn something from him. Or figure out a way to run off to Saiduan with him.

Roh pushed open the door – there were no locks on doors in Dhai – and called, "I've brought-"

He looked at his feet as he entered, careful not to trip over the tapestried carpet. He heard something hiss. For a moment, it sounded like a spitting lily, and he wondered how such a dangerous plant had gotten into the temple.

Then he saw the flash of metal, the flurry of movement.

It was a blade.

Roh threw the tray ahead of him and stepped back. The blade met the tray and sliced it in two. Rice and bits of yam spattered the walls, the rug.

Roh rotated his body and crouched low, making himself a smaller, thinner target. He held out his forearms to take the worst of the onslaught and called on Para for aid. It was like drawing air through his skin, air only he could sense, only he could breathe – and power only another parajista could see. His fists tightened. He held the breath of Para there, just beneath his skin. He concentrated on the Litany of the Palisade to construct a shield of air. The air began to condense around him, grow heavy. A brilliant blue mist swirled around him: a blessing. Para was fickle and didn't always respond when he called. Even now, the shield he wove came together slowly. Far too slowly.

He heard harsh words in Saiduan and peered through his raised arms. The sanisi stared at him, blade pointed at the floor. Roh let go of his breath, but not Para. His knuckles grazed the solid wall of misty blue air in front of him, formed a moment too late.

"Is there no privacy in this country?" the sanisi said in heavily accented Dhai.

Roh straightened. He let go of the litany. The air around him returned to its regular pressure. His ears popped. The blue breath of Para dissipated.

Roh stared at the mess of rice and broken yam pieces scattered across the room. One half of the tray rested near his foot. The other had settled behind the sanisi. Roh imagined that could have been his head. It was a stupid mistake. He should have known better.

"Sorry," Roh said. "I'm Rohinmey Tadisa Garika, a student of Ora Dasai's. Forgot about Saiduan privacy. I meant no offense. We're very open here."

The sanisi sheathed his blade.

Roh had not gotten a good look at the sanisi back in the foyer. Now that he was up close, he realized he had made a false assumption. The sanisi was tall, far taller than any Dhai, and dark, with twisted rings of black hair knotted close to his head, though it looked like it had been shorn short not many months back. The ends were ragged. It was the sanisi's face, though, that made Roh pause. The hair that graced the sanisi's upper lip and the sides of the cheeks was soft and downy. Roh had seen pictures of Saiduan men, and they all had short but noticeable beards.

"Are you a woman?" Roh asked. He used the Saiduan word for "woman", worried he might be using the wrong pronoun.

The sanisi narrowed her eyes. "I am a good many things, depending on the day."

"I didn't think women could become sanisi. I've never seen a picture of one."

"And I've never seen a picture of a fool Dhai boy. Yet here you are."

Roh squared his shoulders. "I know things."

"What does a petty pacifist know of the empire?"

"I know enough," Roh said. "I know that's not an infused weapon. It's just metal. Sanisi carry infused willowthorn and bonsa and everpine branches, like ours. If I can see that, Ora Dasai will, too."

"Perhaps I was not always thus," the sanisi said. "And your elders see less than you suppose."

Roh pulled at Para. His skin prickled. But Para rebelled. The power of its breath surged through his body, then sputtered out.

The sanisi laughed, a bitter bark. "You try to bowl me over with your little training exercises and you will know the power of the dark star. I have no qualm with incinerating you, mouth-breather."

"The dark star? No one can draw on Oma. It hasn't been in the sky in two thousand years."

"About due then, isn't it?"

"Why are you here?"

"You're not the only one who can see things, boy. If your masters learn of your indiscretion, it could be bad for you."

"I'd like to be a sanisi," Roh said. "They don't teach us how to fight here the way you fight. Para will be descendent soon. I won't have an advantage unless I can fight. Really fight."

"Advantage against what? Wandering trees and pitcher plants?"

"I need to change my fate," Roh said.

The sanisi murmured something in Saiduan about foolish boys and bait for wolves. "Your fate?" she said. "That is easy to see. But I'm not here for you."

"Who are you here for?"

"The Kai."

"But *I* could go with you! Are you taking novices or–"

"Your speech is exhausting."

"I just–"

The sanisi half turned away, then reconsidered. "You're the boy who was with that scullery girl," she said.

"Who?"

"That crippled girl."

"Lilia?"

"I wonder," the sanisi said, "what does a pretty parajista with a fiery interest in death have to say to a plain-faced crippled girl?"

"You have a weird way of seeing people," Roh said. "I don't know why being plain matters. She's very smart."

"I suppose when you don't seek to own a thing," the sanisi said, "its beauty matters less."

"Will you teach me to fight?" Roh asked.

Someone knocked at the door. "Permission to enter?" Dasai's voice, speaking perfect Saiduan.

Roh sighed. It was the sewer dregs for a year, for sure.

"Do enter," the sanisi said.

Roh stepped away from the door, and Dasai came in. They regarded each other for a long moment, then Roh looked at his feet.

"I apologize deeply for the impolite behavior of our young people," Dasai said, in Dhai this time. "We are quite isolated. Unfortunately, that means our young don't often engage foreign visitors. If this child caused offense–"

"Offense was given," the sanisi said, "but can be mitigated. Thus far, I have been instructed to bathe in a great underground chamber, given flowery clothes smelling of rotten plant matter, and had rice thrown at me. Yet my purpose for this visit has yet to be fulfilled. I understand you heard word of my coming from my Patron. I should not have been unexpected."

"The acting Kai is now prepared to meet you," Dasai said. "I do apologize for the delay. Ora Chali is waiting outside to escort you."

Dasai motioned for the sanisi to move into the hall. Roh saw his own older brother, Chali Finahin Badu, standing there with hands clasped, his too-long hair hanging into his eyes. Most people didn't guess that Chali and Roh were brothers – they shared a family of two mothers and three fathers but were not blooded relations.

Chali's eyes widened when he saw Roh, but he said nothing. Roh knew he'd hear about it later. Chali was always telling Roh how something or other Roh did hurt Chali's chances of being Elder Ora of Tira's Temple someday.

"Ora Chali, escort our guest upstairs, please," Dasai said. "I will be but a moment."

Roh half hoped Dasai would be so busy with the sanisi that he'd just send Roh downstairs.

Chali and the sanisi moved down the hall. Roh waited.

And waited.

"You're angry," Roh said.

"I am furious," Dasai said. "There is a game here you don't understand. You could be exiled."

"Exiled? We were talking. Just *talking*!"

Dasai lowered his voice. "That is a Saiduan assassin. He has killed more people with his own hands than inhabit this temple."

Roh wanted to correct Dasai on the sanisi's gender but thought better of it. Dasai was still using the male-assertive pronoun, while Roh now thought female-assertive was more appropriate. The sanisi had carefully used none in reference to herself.

"One ill word from that man," Dasai said, "and the Saiduan Patron sends one thousand men like him into Dhai. They murder every last one of us. *Every one*. They wanted us dead two millennia ago. They nearly succeeded. Don't think they won't look for a reason to come here and end it." Dasai struck the floor between Roh's feet with his walking stick. "And all because one vain boy could not stomach his fate."

"I'm meant for greater things," Roh said. "Anyone can see that."

Dasai grimaced. Roh hated what he saw – disappointment, anger, disgust. Roh knew he was supposed to be like every other Dhai, like Lilia, just doing what he was told, having babies for Dhai, growing crops in the same spaces, fighting back the same toxic plants from the fields, using Para only to build, to defend, to grow. But to grow them into what?

"It's not enough for me," Roh said.

"Then maybe this temple is not the place for you."

"No, no!" Roh said, because exile was worse. Exile meant Dorinah, to become a slave, or the woodland, to get eaten by some blinding-tree. And then he laughed, because maybe that's how it would all play out – they would exile him, and he'd join some woodland exiles, and teach them farming. And he'd die a farmer.

"Sleep, Rohinmey," Dasai said. "Tell Ora Almeysia I excuse your tardiness. Just... sleep. We'll discuss atonement in the morning."

Roh wiped at his face and hurried to the scullery stair. The risks he took were real, he knew. But the risk of being exiled still paled next to the risk of squandering his life. He pushed and pushed, and nothing ever changed. His parents had tired of his constant questions and boundless energy. It was almost a relief to them when the Oras who came to Clan Garika tested him for sensitivity to the satellites and discovered he could draw on Para.

But when Para was descendent? He'd be an unlovable burden again.

Roh sat on the scullery stair steps. He needed to think his way out, even though it wasn't his strength. Lilia was the one good with strategy and problem solving.

The flame flies in the lanterns cast flickering light in the dark stairwell. He heard a voice from below, murmuring words he could not quite make out.

Roh leaned around the curl of the corridor to get a look at who was coming up.

It was Almeysia. Again. Talking aloud in the scullery stair. Again. But she was not alone this time.

Almeysia walked up the stairs with a hooded woman. Roh knew the figure. It was Yisaoh Alais Garika, daughter to the clan leader of Clan Garika. Roh had seen her often enough there to recognize her generous shape and strong jaw, even with her face cowled in the dim light.

Roh stood. He expected Almeysia to admonish him. But when she saw him, she came up short. The expression that crossed her face was one he had never seen on an Ora – guilt mixed with a terrible fear. Yisaoh tipped her head downward, drowning her face in shadows.

Almeysia wet her lips and said, "Rohinmey. You should not be here." They were three steps below him.

"Yisaoh," Roh said, "I didn't know you were in the temple."

Yisaoh raised her head. She was a tall, handsome woman with knotted curls of dark hair tied back from her face, and a broad, slightly crooked nose, the result of a break many years before, the last time Para was ascendant. Roh remembered that because if it had been any other time, some tirajista or sinajista could have mended the bone before it healed wrong. But her face looked more hollowed, thinner than he remembered, and this close now, he saw the bulk of her figure was made up of her thick coat.

"Oh, child," Almeysia said. "You always could see too much."

Yisaoh moved up one step into the cramped space. Roh turned, to give her room to pass. She grabbed his arm.

He was so startled he froze. The Saiduan were dangerous people, but not Dhai. Not his own clan mate. Why would she touch him without consent?

Pain burned through his belly. It came so quickly and unexpectedly that he gasped. His legs gave out. Yisaoh cradled him. He saw her pull a blade from his stomach. Saw wet blood.

His blood.

Roh grabbed at her hand, smearing blood on his fingers. The blade came down again. He saw the stain of blood bloom across his tunic and apron. He made a half-hearted attempt to clutch at his wound, to stop the bleeding. Yisaoh's hand came down again. Pain blotted out sense.

Almeysia knelt over him. She closed his eyes with her leathery hand.

"You didn't tell me there were novices here who could see through hazing wards," Yisaoh muttered.

"I didn't realize," Almeysia said. "Oma's breath, I didn't know."

Roh saw himself standing in an apple orchard, holding the hand of a small child.

"They've arrived," the child said.

5

The Temple of Oma grew from a knotted rocky spur at the tip of a mountainous peninsula called the Fire Thorn. They glided over the spur; Ahkio peered out from within a bubbled chrysalis that followed the giant living Line system connecting the temples and clans. The vegetation of the peninsula was burned out twice a year, so all Ahkio saw were the stubbly amber tips of newly seeded foraging grasses. It reminded him of the fields of Osono. They came in parallel to the peninsula. He had a view of the carved stone bridge that connected the spur of the temple to the greater land mass. As he and Nasaka passed inside their shimmering blue chrysalis, he heard the thundering roar of the river below them, continuing its quest to carve away the spur from its parent.

The translucent webbing that circled the gardens of the temple stretched from the bridge all the way around the spur. The webbing had caught many small insects. Captured flame flies and gleaming night dragons struggled in its grasp, lighting the web with a thousand twinkling lights. The temple itself was well lit, considering the time of night. Ahkio saw the telltale flicker of flame fly lanterns hung inside crystal chandeliers. The great dome of the temple glowed with a soft, ambient light, a beacon for weary travelers. Everything about the Temple of Oma was like a dream. He had not grown up in Dhai, and when he returned to it as a boy and saw the living temples and massive gonsa trees and delicate crimson spiders that patrolled the webs, he believed anything was possible. It made him want to cast off his parentage and board a ship at random in the harbor and head off to places unknown. What was the rest of the world like, if this was home? What wonders lay outside the great gates of the harbor?

"Bump here," Nasaka said. Ahkio braced himself as the bubbled chrysalis of the Line met the open lip of the Line chamber in the Temple of Oma.

Four Oras already waited for them in the chamber. They had long, pained looks on their faces as if Kirana were already dead.

Elder Ora Gaiso, the plump woman who oversaw the management of the Temple of Oma, made a sweeping gesture as they arrived. Their chrysalis immediately burst.

Ahkio covered his head.

"Was that necessary?" Nasaka asked as the shattered bits of the chrysalis melted and flowed into the depression at the center of the floor.

"There's more news," Gaiso said. She was a broad, imposing woman with a dart of white in her black hair.

Ahkio also recognized Elaiko, Nasaka's young assistant, and Dasai, the ancient Ora who had taught Ahkio history and governance before he left the temple. He was the same Ora who told Ahkio the story of the Saiduan who'd come to take away bad students. Dasai held out a hand in greeting. He had a mean face, long and narrow, and he kept his mouth pursed when not speaking. He had already lived well over a century, and though Dhai were known to live a hundred and fifty years or more, few retained their wits and stamina as well as Dasai had.

"The Kai asks for you," Dasai said. Dasai had a slight Saiduan accent. He had spent many years studying in that country, though he spoke little of it.

Ahkio folded his arms.

"Like that, is it?" Dasai said.

"There's another issue," Gaiso said, moving her bulky body between them. "I tried to send you word before you got on the

Line. We have a Saiduan sanisi here. He's asking for the Kai. We can't permit that. Not in her condition."

"Where's Ora Almeysia?" Nasaka asked. "I'm convening the Elder Ora council immediately."

"She's with Ora Masura," Gaiso said, "trying to get her fit for company."

"Is Ora Masura drinking again?" Nasaka asked.

"Like a drowning Tordinian priest," Gaiso said.

"Will you ascend with me, Li Kai?" Dasai asked. "Your sister asked for you, and I'm not sure we can wait much longer."

Dasai led him into the hall. Nasaka hung back to speak with the others.

"Nasaka won't tell me what's wrong with Kirana," Ahkio said.

"It's not known," Dasai said.

"How's it possible not to know what's wrong with the Kai? Did someone poison her?"

"Eight physicians and four tirajistas have visited her. None can name the illness."

"Someone close to her did it, then."

"Let's not start painting stories."

"Nasaka thinks I'm in danger if I stay in Osono. She thinks whoever did this to Kirana is after the seat."

"You should really use Ora Nasaka's title. It's respectful."

"I'm aware," Ahkio said. He hadn't called Nasaka "Ora" in almost a decade.

Paper lanterns lined the corridor. The Temple of Oma, like the Temples of Para, Tira, and Sina in many of the holds in Saiduan, was a living thing, a slumbering beast created in some distant time. The walls were smooth and bore a greenish tint. If one tried to dig deep enough into the skin of the hold, it would weep and ooze a sticky amber sap. Whether plant or animal or some combination, no one knew. But the sinajistas said the holds had souls, vital energy that could mend wounds or melt flesh.

The Line chamber was on the eleventh floor of the temple. Ahkio expected they would travel up to the Assembly Chamber and Kirana's rooms on the twelfth floor, but instead, Dasai took him down two floors to the novice practice rooms and Ora studies. They passed open archways where novice parajistas practiced moving objects: building small towers of stones and blocks with skeins of air, or creating little vortices and waterspouts in pails. Ahkio couldn't channel their star, so he did not see the blue breath they manipulated, only its result. The novices barely glanced up from their work as Ahkio and Dasai passed.

Dasai brought him to the end of the hall, down a short stair, and through another corridor. Ahkio had never been to this area of the temple before.

"Why did you move her?" Ahkio asked.

Dasai raised his hand to a broad door of amberwood. Ahkio saw that the door was banded in thorn vines, the same kind that made up the thorn fences that protected livestock in the clans.

"We feared for her," Dasai said.

"If you think she's in danger from someone *inside* the temple, why bring me here?"

"Li Kai, if I had the chance to go back and bid my family farewell before their deaths, I would have leapt at the chance. This is yours. Don't spoil it."

"I'm afraid, Ora Dasai."

"We're all afraid, child," Dasai said. "It's what we do with that fear that sets us apart. Bid farewell to your sister."

Dasai murmured a prayer to Sina and opened the door.

Inside, the windows were covered. The darkness was complete.

Dasai picked up a lantern in an alcove and shook the flame flies awake. The flickering light cast wide shadows, illuminating a raised bed draped with sticky webbing. Ahkio heard someone else breathing in the darkness – wet and ragged.

Ahkio approached the unfamiliar bed and sat on a stool beside it. Dasai brought the light closer. Ahkio took it.

Kirana's face was a gaunt mask with deep circles under the hollows of the eyes. She had the look of their mother: the long, plain face, high forehead, sloping nose, strong, square jaw. Her black hair was thin and tangled, tied at the nape of her damp neck. Displaced curls clung to her forehead. Her skinny hands clasped at the bed sheets like claws.

It was high summer in Dhai, and Ahkio felt cold.

"Ahkio," she said. The clawed hands reached for him. He took her fingers. Her eyelids flickered. "Asked for you... weeks ago. There's something coming."

"You'll meet it," Ahkio said. Weeks ago? He glanced at Dasai.

"I was never Kai," she said. "Everything's burning."

Ahkio rubbed her warm fingers. "That was a long time ago," he said.

"Get the others out," Kirana said. "Out!"

"Ora Dasai," Ahkio said.

Dasai stood at the end of the bed, his face mired in shadow. "Call if there's a need," Dasai said.

After Dasai closed the door, Kirana urged Ahkio to lean in close. She smelled of rot from within. He saw his father in her, his mother, and the dead sisters his mother had buried before they had names.

"Don't go," he said. He pushed the damp hair from her face. Her skin was hot. She looked so much like their mother... "You promised," he said. "You promised me you wouldn't die like they did."

For over a year after that day in the Dorinah slave camps, when he watched his father's head lopped off and saw his mother burn, he had expected Kirana to die, too. The dreams got so bad, they stalked him during the day. The Oras, especially Nasaka, thought him mad. It was Kirana who brought him back from madness, Kirana and her promise.

"You said–"

"I can't make the future, Ahkio," she said. "It's yours now. I shouldn't have pulled you from the fire, I know. Another woman would have chosen Mother instead, wouldn't she? But I chose you, brother. You were supposed..." She started coughing, great hacking sobs that shook her body. Blood appeared at her mouth, flecked the sheets. "It was all..." she gasped. "All wrong, this turn. I've made it right."

"Hush, Kira," he said softly.

"But you should know... about Yisaoh." She gazed up at the long lines of poetry running along the ceiling. Ahkio tried to read them, but the light was too dim. He said a prayer to Sina instead.

Ahkio tried to pull his hand from her grip. "I'll get you tea. Do you–"

She squeezed his fingers. "I'm too late." She coughed blood onto their joined hands, and said through bloody lips, "Dhai's peace..." Her fingers clenched his once.

She made a strange strangling cough, almost a sigh.

"Don't," he said.

Her eyes lost their focus. Her fingers relaxed in his.

Ahkio bent over her body. The flies in the lantern began to dim as they settled. Kirana's fingers cooled in his hands. He prayed to Sina to take her soul, and Oma to bless him with wisdom in her absence.

He sat next to his dead sister in silence. The world did not move. The air did not tremble. Nothing was different at all, except he was alone now, because someone had killed his sister.

He did not weep. He had wept over their parents for a year. It changed nothing. He knew what he needed to do.

When the door opened, Ahkio lifted his head. His neck and shoulders were stiff.

Nasaka stepped through the archway, her expression stern. "We must meet the sanisi now. The Ora council is ready."

"Kirana," Ahkio said.

"Has she passed?"

Ahkio stared into Kirana's slack face, the still-open but blank eyes. He thought of Meyna. Oma, how he wanted to go home to Meyna and Rhin and Hadaoh and Mey-Mey. But they weren't going to be his kin anymore, were they? It's why they had never married him. They knew this day would come.

Someone would kill the Kai, and Ahkio would take her seat. Did they hope he would grant them favors on that day?

"We have a duty to Dhai," Nasaka said, following his stare. "We must get you dressed in something befitting your... title."

"That's like you," Ahkio said. His voice broke. "You'll watch another Kai perish, just like you watched my mother die. You pull all the strings."

"No," Nasaka said. "I don't watch Kais die. I call tirajistas to save them. I use my sword to defend them. They may die regardless. But I always act. You're the one who bides his time, waiting for someone else to make his fate. So get up, Ahkio. I don't pull strings. I pull the people attached to them."

"I'll find out who killed her, Nasaka, if I have to burn this whole temple down around me."

"One fire at a time," Nasaka said. "That sanisi upstairs is asking for you."

Ahkio stood.

6

Lilia sat on the edge of the bed in the infirmary, waiting to hear the worst. The temple physician, Ora Matias, pressed two cool fingers to her chest. He watched her face as she took a deep breath. Halfway through her exhale, she began to cough. She kept coughing for several minutes, even after he gave her a sip of water.

Above, the dome over the infirmary let in the light of the triad of moons. The flame flies in the lanterns filled the darker spaces. The soft organic walls here had been smoothed over in lavender plaster. Lilia found the temple infirmary very soothing. Though most were kind to her in the temple – when they noticed her – it was the Oras in the infirmary who brought her relief from pain and discomfort, whether from her twisted leg or labored breath.

Matias was new to the temple, though, and she had not been in since his appointment. He was an agreeable-enough person with plump, ink-stained fingers and a habit of smoothing over his eyebrows.

"It's a very mild case of asthma," Matias said, "as I'm sure you know. A girl with lungs like yours should be a seamstress or a typesetter, not a laborer. I always wanted to be a typesetter, you know."

"Then why are you a physician?"

"Well. Talent cannot be wasted. Tirajistas must serve Dhai. It's not a terrible profession, and it still impresses my mothers."

"I know I don't look very strong," Lilia said. "But I like the exercise. My leg's worse when I don't use it."

"I can't argue with that," he said. "But be careful. Let's give you something to ease the constriction. Have you been given wax wraith before?"

"Ora Shotai always gave me mahuan."

"Let's go with what you know works, then." He went to the vast wall of medicinal jars at the far end of the room. "You've been like this all day?"

"The scullery master sent me here after bed check. I was coughing so much, it bothered the other drudges."

"Ora Matias!"

Lilia heard fear in the cry. She was on her feet even before the woman entered. It was Ohanni, the temple's dancing teacher. She carried a limp form in her slender arms. The body was lax, like a doll. But it was the blood that made Lilia's stomach seethe.

The body was covered in blood. Soaked in it. One arm hung free. Drops of blood collected at the ends of the fingers, spattered the floor.

Matias stood frozen at the wall of medicinal jars, mouth agape.

Ohanni carried the body into the room. Behind her were two novices. Their aprons were rusty with blood.

It was only then that Lilia realized the body was Roh's.

Ahkio leaned over the table in the Assembly Chamber at the top of Oma's temple. He watched the gathered council and wondered which of them had murdered his sister, and to what purpose. He was a little unsteady, so he sat in the chair to the right of the Kai's seat, the chair reserved for her heir, which he'd sat in only once, the day they returned from the Dorinah camps and Nasaka called the circle of Elder Oras and the temple's Ora council – the same faces he saw now.

Gaiso frowned at him from the other side of the room but did not break in conversation with her assistant. Elder Ora Masura of the Temple of Tira waved to him from the hall. Masura was a splendid, regal old woman, and one of his mother's many lovers. She came around the table and asked to take his hands.

He consented, only because he did not want to draw her suspicion; he was exhausted and angry, and he feared what he would say. She took his scarred hands in her smooth, cold palms and blessed him.

"It's been a decade since I saw you last, hasn't it?" she said. "I wish it were under better circumstances."

In truth, it had been twelve years since he sat with these people. He could have gone a lifetime without sitting here again.

Gaiso dismissed her assistant and rounded on Ahkio. "Has the Kai passed, then? Is that why you're here?"

"Are you questioning my right to be here?" Ahkio said softly.

Gaiso looked taken aback. "What did you say?"

"I'm so sorry, Ahkio. No one wanted this," Masura said.

"I wanted twenty babies," Gaiso said. "I was made Elder Ora of Oma's temple instead. We don't all get what we want."

Masura made a sound of distress. "Don't speak as if your life decisions were not made just as politically as your cousin Tir's."

"For a clucking, drunken little bird," Gaiso said, "you spend far too much time aggravating cats."

"I see you're all getting along as expected," Nasaka said from the doorway.

"Who else is coming?" Ahkio asked. He wanted to see the reactions of the other Elder Oras to Kirana's death.

"Just Ora Almeysia," Nasaka said. "Elder Ora Koralia of Sina's Temple and Elder Ora Saraba of Para still haven't sent a response. Ora Dasai will be here, of course. He's bringing up the sanisi now."

"It's curfew for the novices," Gaiso said. "Ora Almeysia will be doing a bed check. Let's start without her. I don't want to keep that sanisi waiting any longer."

Nasaka nodded to Ahkio. "I see you found your seat."

"I expected you wanted me in another."

"That will do," Nasaka said.

Ahkio glanced next to him at the seat of the Kai, his sister's seat. He wanted to sit there just to spite Nasaka, but though he made to press himself out of his chair, the rest of his body would not obey him.

He heard footsteps in the hall.

A young Ora entered – one Ahkio did not know – and made a sweeping gesture as the sanisi pushed up ahead of him. The emissary's rudeness was shocking.

"May I present Shao Taigan Masaao, a sanisi messenger from Saiduan," the Ora said.

The sanisi was tall, taller than Ahkio expected. He easily towered head and shoulders above Ahkio, like some giant. For all that, he moved like water, with a slightly hunched posture that made Ahkio wonder if he'd been injured.

"Which of you is the Kai?" Taigan asked.

Ahkio put his hands on the table and made to stand.

Nasaka waved him back, said, "I'm afraid you've reached us at a difficult time." She had not yet made it to her chair, the one at the right side of the Kai seat, reserved for the Kai's religious and political advisor. "Let us sit–"

"What I have to say is for the Kai," Taigan said. "We have very little time to chatter on about complications and niceties and backward Dhai customs."

"Excuse my tardiness," Dasai called from the hall. He limped in, leaning heavily on his cane. "Thank you, Ora Chali," he said, dismissing the sanisi's escort.

Chali looked more than happy to leave them, and ducked past Dasai into the hall.

Taigan peered at each of them in turn. His gaze settled on Ahkio. "You're no Ora," the sanisi said. "What is your function?"

"I am the Kai's brother," Ahkio said.

"Ah," Taigan said. "A boy. Yes, this explains much. You're not gifted, though, are you? You're not who I was looking for. Is this all there is? No other relation to the Kai? I have no time to be politic."

"Let us be seated," Dasai said. He clutched the top of his walking stick tightly. Ahkio wondered how many polite rituals and welcomes they had already trampled past.

What he wanted more than anything was to go sit by his sister's side. He should have been here when she got sick. If she'd called him weeks ago, why had no one told him? They could have uncovered together who cursed her with the illness that took her.

"That won't be necessary," Taigan said. "Oma is rising."

Ahkio raised his head. "What?"

"Not according to our stargazers," Nasaka said.

"Then they are ill informed," Taigan said. "Oma, just like any other star, has been known to appear suddenly. One cannot always track its path. Now I tell you its effect is being felt across my country. With Oma come invaders. Such is as it's always been. This time, they've found a way to come through before Oma's full appearance."

"Who are these invaders?" Ahkio asked. "What do they have to do with us?"

"The last time Oma rose," Nasaka said, "two thousand years ago, the Saiduan invaded what was then Dhai, when we ruled the continent. There is always a great power that unseats another during Oma's ascent. Always. I do not contest that. But I see no proof of Oma's rise here besides your word."

"If you had seen what I have seen, you would not question it," Taigan said.

"Shao Taigan," Dasai said, "we respect you greatly. Yet you do not use the speech we have come to expect of the Patron's emissaries. What is it we can do for you, sanisi, during your time of trouble?"

Ahkio saw four figures dressed in red come into the Assembly Chamber. They were members of the militia posted to the Kuallina Stronghold; he knew them by the pins at their collars. The temple itself had no standing militia. They must have traveled in on the Line behind him and Nasaka. A bit of fast thinking on someone's part. But not mine, Ahkio thought. They told me as little as they could. He glanced at Nasaka and wondered how much she'd kept Kirana in the dark, too.

The sanisi laughed at the militia. "You think yourselves safe?" Taigan said. "You may be able to hold for a time, it's true, with your defensible pass, and the mountains to the west, and that harbor wall to the north, but they will devour you eventually. Oma is rising. These people will rout you."

"What can we possibly offer in assistance?" Dasai said.

Taigan gritted his teeth. "Scholars," he said.

"Eh?" Gaiso said. "Book people?"

"Your best translators of ancient Dhai," Taigan said. "That is what my Patron requests of you. It may help turn the tide."

Nasaka folded her arms. "You have Dhai records that predate the last Rising, then," she said. "Records that could help you find out how to turn these people back. But of course, they're all in ancient Dhai, aren't they, and you've killed all the Dhai in your empire who can read them."

Taigan said, "The invaders destroy our archives. Strange, no? They could target supply lines, terrorize civilians. They do that, yes. But the archives are first."

"So send the records here," Ahkio said. "We could find—"

"Impossible," Taigan said. "We have two thousand years of records. Do you know how many holds we pillaged to collect it? We can't risk putting it on a cart to some indefensible country."

"So we must travel to Saiduan," Dasai said.

"It was a very long time ago," Taigan said. "All this death and killing of the Dhai people. You speak as if it was I who did this thing. We have let you alone here. Imported your infused weapons. Are we not friends now?"

"What do we get in return?" Nasaka asked.

Ahkio thought that a bit bold. He wondered if she'd been bold enough to kill Kirana... but to what end? He rubbed his face. And now Oma. He couldn't imagine Nasaka was as ignorant of that as she pretended. Kirana talked often of Nasaka's obsession with Oma's rise in prior ages. Oras' powers were ruled by the fickle stars. Many were consumed by the study of their erratic appearances.

"In return?" Taigan said. "In return, you will live. Is that not enough? In return, we may be able to push back these invaders on Saiduan's shores, instead of seeing them spill all across the world the way they have in the past. When Oma rises, the world breaks. This is written in every holy book."

"We should have a treaty," Ahkio said. "Kirana would request it."

"Papers?" Taigan spat. "You would ask for papers when the very world is being ripped apart–"

"The Li Kai is right," Nasaka said.

"Paper," Taigan said. "It means nothing."

Nasaka leaned toward him. She was as tall as Ahkio, wiry, but though the sanisi dwarfed her, she stood before him like a woman twice his size. Ahkio saw her again in the Dorinah camp, slaying legionnaires with a weapon he had only before seen her use to chop wood.

"It means something to us," Nasaka said.

"It will take weeks," Taigan said.

"So it will."

Ahkio glanced up at the representation of the heavens above him, and the dark stain of Oma. Oma was an embodiment of the gods, the Book said. It was not supposed to be a true star. A philosopher-astronomer once said that Oma's rise was actually just an eclipse of the satellites, a brief moment when all three stars crossed paths in the sky. Two thousand years. Who knew what it really was?

"These invaders," Ahkio said, "where are they coming from? Which direction?"

"Boats," Taigan said, but Ahkio saw something in his expression that troubled him.

"From the east, then?" Ahkio said. "Or the south?"

"They come from..." Taigan muttered something in Saiduan. "They come from the sky, sometimes."

Masura spoke for the first time, her tone incredulous. "The *sky*? Have you been drinking, sanisi?"

Ahkio heard someone running in the hall outside. The militia turned toward a blue-clad Ora who burst through the door. One of the militia members held up a hand. The Ora stopped, gasping for breath.

Gaiso stood. "What is it?" she asked.

"Murder," the Ora said. Ahkio recognized her as Nasaka's assistant, Elaiko. She wasn't much older than Ahkio.

Ahkio saw Nasaka tense. He was keenly aware of the weapon at her hip. She had yet to bare it, but he was waiting. It felt like an inevitability now. He regretted running from this temple just when his sister had needed him most. Now he was left alone amid a sea of scheming Oras, murder, and rising stars. He was not ready. But he stood anyway. His sister once affectionately called him a coward, and it was true. He wanted a quiet, honest little life.

Oma, it seemed, had other plans.

"There's blood all over the scullery stair," Elaiko said, "like bad tea. He's in a storage room."

"Who?" Dasai asked. "Let's not make a bear out of a fly."

"Rohinmey," Elaiko said. "I'm not making up some fish story, Ora Dasai. Roh is dead."

Lilia choked on a cry. Adrenaline flooded her. She watched the infirmary as if from a great height.

Ohanni set Roh's body onto Lilia's bed. A blooming tear ran across his gut; she saw the wet glistening of his intestines beneath bloody clothing and torn skin. More rents in his clothing indicated numerous wounds. Blood pumped profusely from one of them.

"Ora Matias?" Ohanni called, but Matias was still standing, shocked, by the shelves.

Lilia tugged off Roh's apron. "Help me get his tunic," she told Ohanni. She was surprised at how calm she felt. His blood smeared across her own scarred wrists, and a terrible thought bubbled up from a long time ago – *we are wasting so much blood.*

Ohanni helped with the tunic, her breath rapid, fine beads of sweat bathing her face. Lilia wondered how long Ohanni had carried him. She was not a large woman.

"Press here," Lilia said. She put Ohanni's hands onto Roh's thigh. "Press hard. To the bone."

Ohanni did. The flow of blood eased from the worst of the wounds. Lilia wadded up Roh's novice apron and pressed it against the major wound itself. Blood and death. A hungry thorn fence. She remembered bleeding out into a shallow dish to protect her village from harm.

Matias joined them at Roh's side. He wiped at his eyebrows. "Oma," he said. "This injury is too much. Tira is descendent. I can't fix this."

Lilia thought him a fool. She had seen worse, with her mother's patients. She knew the major arteries in the body. She had learned basic anatomy with everyone else in the temple. But closing a wound as bad as Roh's was beyond her.

"Please, Matias," Ohanni said. "You must try. This violence... someone did this to him. It's not as if he tumbled off the stage during some grand jeté."

"I'm sorry, Ora Ohanni. He's dying."

Ohanni made as if to draw her hand away from Roh's thigh.

"Don't!" Lilia said. "He will bleed out."

"There are no tirajistas with the skill to fix this," Ohanni said. "Ora Almeysia is the most sensitive, but she doesn't specialize in matters of the body. Can you ease his pain?" she asked Matias.

"He is nearly gone," Matias said. He pressed his hands to Roh's wrist. "There is nothing to ease."

"Try!" Lilia said. "Won't you try?"

"Child, I'm sorry," Matias said.

Ohanni drew her hands away.

"No," Lilia said. She pressed her hands there instead, hard. "Close the artery. Stop the bleeding."

"He has lost more blood than I can replace," Matias said. "Even if I could find every source of damage–"

"Is this him?"

Nasaka's voice. She strode in ahead of a young man, handsome, with scars on his hands. Lilia had not seen him before.

"I'm sorry, Ora Nasaka," Matias said. "He's lost too much blood."

"Sina's breath," Nasaka muttered. She came up next to Matias. She wore a willowthorn sword. Lilia had never seen an Ora with a sword. "This boy can't die, Matias."

"The blood–"

"I don't care about the blood. He *cannot die*. Wash your hands. Are you a physician or a soap maker?"

Matias hurried to the stone sink at the center of the room.

Roh's breathing was almost imperceptible. Matias was right. Lilia knew that, but she pressed hard anyway, though her hands ached and her chest still burned. She coughed and coughed.

Matias pulled the apron away from the wound. He carried sinew, a needle, and a delicate knife.

"I cannot see for all the blood. Mop this up," he told Lilia.

She grabbed a cotton towel as he widened the wound to find the nicked artery. Blood dripped from the towel down her fingers, to her elbow, to the floor. Lilia didn't notice the arrival of others in the room until some time later, when their voices became loud and angry.

"This is not his fate," Dasai said, arguing with Nasaka. "Call another surgeon. He's the one child in a hundred for whom the seers saw a peaceful fate. We cannot lose this boy."

"There is not a tirajista in the world powerful enough to turn this," Nasaka said.

"Not a tirajista," said the tall, dark man in the doorway. It was the sanisi Lilia had seen in the foyer, Taigan.

"He's gone, I'm sorry," Matias said. His face was covered in sweat. He was spattered with blood.

Roh's face was slack.

Lilia's fear and terror finally bubbled up from the dark place she had hidden it. Her throat closed. She coughed harder; her head swam, and her vision was going dim. Blood covered her arms to the elbows. With enough blood, all things were possible.

She pointed to the sanisi. "Are you a blood witch?" she said. "A blood witch can save him. My mother could save him."

The others, the Oras, looked confused. She suspected they thought her mad. But she knew the look on the sanisi's face. Wonder. Recognition.

"Save him," Lilia said.

"There's a price," Taigan said.

"He's dead," Matias said.

"No," Lilia said.

"A beat or two of his heart remains," Taigan said. "I can save him. But I have a price."

"I will pay it," Dasai said.

"Let's not be irrational–" Nasaka said.

"We will pay your price," Dasai said. "This boy has an important fate. Remake him."

"I expect he does," Taigan said. "You have seers. You know what's coming, don't you? Your little dance upstairs was less than convincing."

Nasaka and Dasai exchanged a look. Nasaka said, "We know that our seers do not see peaceful futures for this generation of children. But this boy has a peaceful fate. He should not die this way."

The sanisi pointed at Lilia. "You are the price. Give her to me and you can keep the boy."

All gazes turned to Lilia. She pushed herself away from Roh's body, gasping for air. She could hardly breathe, hardly think. He knew what a blood witch was. Now he knew what she was, too.

"Our people are not for sale," Nasaka snapped. "We are not chattel. Save the boy because it is right. There need not be a price."

"That is my price," the sanisi said. "The boy for the girl."

Lilia stared at her bloody hands. Then Roh. She remembered watching her mother's body crumple. Too small to stop it. Too powerless to do anything at all.

"We won't," Nasaka said. "Find another way."

Lilia said, "Do it. I'll go."

The sanisi made a sweeping gesture with his hand. The pressure in the room increased, like being underwater. Roh's body shuddered. His back arched. For one blazing moment, Roh's body was suspended above the bed, screaming. The blood that smeared the room peeled away from the floor, their clothing, their skin, and burst into the air. It clung to Roh for one terrible moment like a second skin.

Lilia put her hands over her ears.

Taigan dropped his hand.

Roh fell back to the bed. Lilia smelled burnt meat. She broke into another fit of coughing.

Matias ran to the medicinal shelf and brought back a cup of foul-smelling water.

Lilia choked it down as the Oras gathered around the bed.

"Oma," Dasai said.

"Yes," the sanisi said. "One does not need to believe a thing is true for it to be fact. Oma is rising. I've channeled Oma since I was a child, and my power gets stronger each season. You are looking for an omajista? There is your proof, and your little ward-unmaker back to you. Fully formed."

Roh's skin was no longer broken; there was no sign of injury but his torn clothing. Lilia grabbed at his tunic. The blood that coated him was gone, eaten up as hungrily by the power in the room.

"How did you know he can see through wards?" Nasaka asked. "Not one Ora in twenty here knows that."

Lilia lay still next to Roh as her breathing eased. They paid her no attention, as if she were only some dying fish.

"He saw through mine," the sanisi said. Now he looked at Lilia. "And he saw through yours, too, didn't he?"

Lilia felt cold. She remembered Kalinda's words: *"We'll be ready for them next time, won't we?"* But she was not ready. Not at all.

"You asked what I'm really here for," the sanisi said. "I'm here for the girl. But you already knew that, didn't you, Lilia?"

7

Zezili Hasaria, Captain General of the Empress of Dorinah's western legion, paced the damp hall outside the Empress's audience chamber in wet boots and a set of clothing she could not remember ever being washed. She wore her chain mail and her metal skirt knotted in dajians' hair. Her battered sword and dagger hung at her hip, both solid metal. She didn't trust infused weapons. She cradled her helm under one arm.

Being summoned from the coast while her force lolled about getting drunk waiting to mount an offensive on the isle of Alorjan filled her with trepidation. The Empress did not pull her captain generals from the field so lightly. Zezili swore as she waited, muttering old Dhai curses, in case anyone of importance happened by. More people feared her when she spoke Dhai. It reminded them of her mixed face and manners, and her deviant propensity for slaughtering her own kind.

The big double doors to the audience chamber opened, and the Empress's white-haired dajian secretary, Saofi, said, "The Empress regrets she cannot see you at this time, Syre Zezili Hasaria."

"She's left orders, then?" Zezili said, trying to conceal her annoyance. Saofi was a plump, matronly woman, easily fifty or sixty, and had survived a long service to the Empress. That made her nearly as valuable as Zezili. Zezili did not often measure her own worth compared to that of dajians – Dhai slaves – but

Saofi was obviously of mixed parentage – Dhai and Dorinah, just like Zezili. And sometimes the similarities chilled her. The secretary's mother had sold her. Zezili's mother had claimed her. One woman's choice made all the difference.

"She has something prepared, yes," Saofi said. "She told me earlier she may be unable to make this audience. This way, please. I'll give you her missive."

Saofi led Zezili through the drafty hall. The Empresses of Dorinah had torched their organic holds and rebuilt them from stone and iron over eighteen hundred years before. It meant their holds were cooler, less permanent, and required much more maintenance than the tirajista-built holds that littered the lands of their neighbors. Zezili found the idea of maintaining this massive heap of stone exhausting.

They passed a pair of dajians refilling the lamps along the hall. A girl no more than ten hung from the ladder, leaning far over to the next sconce. When the girl saw Zezili, her eyes got big. She dropped the oil decanter.

Zezili snapped up the decanter before it could clatter to the stones. Oil sloshed onto her hand. She shoved the decanter back at the little dajian. "You'll set the whole cursed place on fire," she said.

The dajian babbled apologies. Zezili saw Saofi watching them. She should have just let it fall. She half thought to dump the oil on Saofi and set her aflame, just for effect, but knew she wouldn't get her orders then.

So, Zezili settled for shoving the decanter at the older dajian holding the ladder, who hadn't lost her senses in the face of a captain general. Then Zezili forged on ahead of Saofi.

"I don't have all day, secretary," Zezili said.

Saofi hurried to catch up. She had a shorter stride. As they came to Saofi's office, Saofi selected the key from among the various useful secretarial items she had dangling from the chains of her chatelaine. She opened the door and retrieved a small purple letter from her desk.

Zezili took it and broke the royal seal: the Eye of Rhea stamped into a generous gob of gonsa sap.

My dearest Zezili,

Pull your legion back from the coast. You're to partner with my new foreign friends for a domestic campaign. They will meet you at your estate in a few days' time with your orders.

Do all they ask, and question them only as you would question me.

I remain,

Empress Casanlyn –

Zezili skimmed over the honorifics after the Empress's name. Zezili did not question the Empress's orders, ever. It was one reason she kept her place at the head of the legion. But she didn't much like the idea of packing up back home and blindly following some foreigner, even at the Empress's order. She hoped they weren't Saiduan or Tordinian. Saiduans were arrogant, and Tordinians foul and uncouth, even by her standards.

"Is this a serious letter?" Zezili asked.

Saofi shrugged. "You would know better than I."

"Why didn't she see me personally? Why call me out here and then send me home again?"

"I don't pretend to know the mind of the Empress," Saofi said. "I take her orders, just as you do."

"We're nothing alike," Zezili said.

"As you say."

Zezili pushed her helm back on. Her ears were cold. She bunched up the letter. It had been a waste of time to come all the way to Daorian for this. She could be at home fucking her husband.

"Luck to you," Saofi called as she stepped into the hall.

Zezili bit back a retort. Every word would get back to the Empress. She walked down to the kennels and had the kennel girls bring out her dog, a big black brute named Dakar whose shoulder was as high as Zezili's chest. He had dark eyes and a scarred muzzle, reminder of a skirmish she had taken him into along the coast of the Saiduan island called Shorasau. She had always preferred dogs to bears. They were easier to train and stank less.

She rode through the great gates of the stronghold of Daorian and into the city that took its name from the hold. Daorian had been built on the ruins of the Saiduan city of Diamia before it. The city was a patchwork of government houses to the east, merchants' quarters organized by profession, and poorer shacks and tents along the water, where the fishers and sea-trade people lived.

Big, somber-colored awnings stretched over the sidewalks where city-owned dajians tended to the lanterns set up on long poles lining the road; the dajians bore the look of their Dhai relatives but could hardly be called Dhai when they'd spent the entirety of their lives owned by the Empress. Women and girls filled the streets, dressed in bright tunics and long trousers and skirts, embroidered coats and wide hats. Little dajians followed after their owners, carrying shopping baskets; many had babies tied to their backs with lengths of colorful fabric. Most dajians were easily recognizable by their drab gray clothing, their smaller stature, their tawny complexions. Many were also branded with the mark of the family who owned them.

Zezili watched as the dajians streamed past, hurrying after tall women whose hair was curled or beribboned, pinned or sewn in place, and adorned in combs and jeweled pins. Zezili had learned how to tie hair up like that, a lifetime ago, before her mother had put a sword in her hand.

She rode past the booksellers and merchants' stalls and into the religious quarter, where all of the lanterns were wound with red paper. The open awnings of the men's mardanas lining the streets of the quarter were red, the sidewalks lined in brick.

The Temple of Rhea stood at the end of the red-lantern road, its spires outlined by the gray sky. The Dorinah flag flew from the three topmost peaks of the stone towers: the Eye of Rhea on a background of purple.

"Syre Zezili!" someone called. "My favorite unwashed snapdragon. How are you?"

Zezili turned. A bear-drawn carriage pulled up next to her. The lacy curtains were swept back from the window, revealing a bright, rouged face with eyes heavily lined in kohl.

"Tulana Nikoel," Zezili said. "Looking for a treat in the mardanas?"

"Nothing so amusing," Tulana said. Her dark hair was arranged atop her head in a pile of forward-facing curls that had been sewn into place and knotted with yellow ribbons. It was not the most intricate style Zezili had ever seen, but nearly. The Empress's gifted jistas, the Seekers, had little to do but sit around and braid each other's hair between enemy-killing, road-building, and ditch-digging. Tulana's little sloe-eyed shadow, Sokai, sat with her, gazing off in the opposite direction. Zezili had made a pass at him once during a campaign, and he hadn't taken it well. Men had no sense of humor.

"I didn't think the Empress let you out of the Seeker Sanctuary without a leash," Zezili said.

"Being gifted is often a curse," Tulana said, "but leading the gifted can be advantageous. Tell me, has the Empress called you here to speak of a campaign? I have six new parajistas hungry for experience in the field."

"You know I can't say," Zezili said. "But when I can, you'll be the first to know. Say hello to Amelia and Voralyn." They were the only gifted women Zezili could tolerate, in large part because they often lost extraordinary amounts of money to her at cards.

"I will say hello to their purses for you," Tulana said.

Zezili grunted and turned Dakar away. From the corner of her eye, she saw Tulana's bright expression darken. Zezili suspected

Tulana's tolerance for Zezili was only slightly higher than Zezili's for Tulana. But Zezili's legion, without gifted Seekers, was just a mob of women with pointy sticks when facing the gifted forces of an enemy. She had to work with Tulana and her little jistas more often than not.

Dakar carried her to the limits of the city, where a charred black ring marked the outer edges of habitable land. She gazed across the rolling hillsides covered in tangled summervine and creeping deathwart. Most of the trees had been cut, but there were still many dangerous semi-sentient things crawling along the roads. Workers burned off the plant life for twenty feet on either side, ensuring that nothing took root.

Zezili passed time that afternoon to eat and pray at a way house run by the owners of an adjacent silk farm. She was not fool enough to give up her daily prayers to Rhea and her daughters, though she did not consider herself particularly religious.

Her husband, Anavha, had often begged her to move the household back into the city, where he would find more of his own kind and could worship in a proper temple. But she preferred to keep him out here, safe from the dangers of the city. As was custom, Zezili had allowed her sisters the use of Anavha until they had done with their own broods. Then she moved her household to the country, away from the lascivious stares of older women and the poisonous influence of mardana men.

She arrived at her house just after dusk. Her estate was not grand, but adequate for her station. Lights burned in the windows. The latticed shutters were open. An apple orchard stretched out behind the house, and beyond that, Zezili kept a small vineyard that produced the estate's wine. She saw a gaggle of dajians with flame fly lanterns patrolling the orchard. Burning out encroaching strangle vines and sap thorns took constant maintenance.

Zezili dismounted. Her housekeeper, Daolyn, emerged from the round gate, followed by two of the house dajians. The dajians took Dakar's reins.

"How goes my house?" Zezili asked Daolyn.

Daolyn was mostly dajian, short and dark-haired, though her hair was going to white. She had the high cheekbones and tawny cast of a dajian, but her eyes were Dorinah gray, and she had put on a healthy amount of fat over her broad frame. Zezili trusted no one else with the affairs of her house.

Daolyn inclined her head. The night was cool. She wore green divided skirts and a short coat with an embroidered green collar. She had sewn the Eye of Rhea onto the two big outer pockets.

"Your house is well, Syre Zezili," Daolyn said. "We did not expect you for several weeks."

"The Empress had other plans," Zezili said as they walked into the inner courtyard. "How is my husband?" A fountain bubbled in the eye of the yard. A circular door from each of the house's three main rooms led into the yard.

"He has been melancholy," Daolyn said.

Zezili walked into the common room. "I suppose I should bathe before I settle," she said, glancing at the padded benches and chaises and the tapestry lining the floor, so recently uncurled that its edges had been strategically held down by items of furniture. Daolyn only put the tapestry rug out when Zezili was home; she would have hurriedly unrolled it the moment the dajians in the yard alerted her that Zezili was coming down the road. That touch inspired in Zezili a feeling of contentment she could almost call happiness.

"You must strive to keep him busy," Zezili said. "Idle hands ruin good boys. We'll have visitors soon. Prepare the house for company."

After bathing and having her hair washed, combed, and tied with red ribbons by a new house dajian Daolyn had purchased in her absence, Zezili dressed in long red trousers and a red undershirt embroidered at the cuffs and hem. Daolyn brought her a new handsome short coat of red silk stitched in silver at the wide sleeves, with three silver-threaded frogged ties at the front and blooms the color of blood embroidered at the collar.

"Will you allow your husband to attend supper with you?" Daolyn asked.

"Yes," Zezili said, "and bring the account books. I need to review them. This new campaign will keep me occupied many months, I'm sure."

Daolyn inclined her head.

Zezili walked back to the common room, where the dajians had pulled out the low dining table from the wall, set it at the center of the room, and put cushions down on the floor. As Zezili waited for her husband, the dajians brought out mushroom and leek soup, served cold, garnished with basil.

She heard a rustling at the door. Anavha stood in the broad archway. Had it only been a month since she last saw him? He wore a white girdle that pulled in his waist just above the hips. He was, of necessity, slender. She believed men should take up as little space as possible. He wore his black hair long over his shoulders, tied once with a white ribbon. Those men allowed to live were, of course, beautiful, far more beautiful than many of the women Zezili knew. Anavha was clean-shaven, as she wanted him, lightly powdered in gold, his eyes lined in kohl, eyes a stormy gray, set a bit too wide in a broad face whose jaw she had initially found almost vulgar in its squareness. He stood a hand shorter than she; she easily outweighed him by fifty pounds. She liked him just this way.

She warmed at the mere sight of him. She wanted to push Anavha onto the table, and pull his body into hers.

"Wife," Anavha said softly. He knelt with head bowed.

"Rise," Zezili said.

Anavha stood. Zezili took him by his slender forearms and looked into his eyes. He averted his gaze.

"Come, husband, eat with me." She released him.

He sat at the other end of the table.

"Do you yet know how long your leave is?" Anavha asked.

"A week. Nine days. We will have visitors for some of that, though. I have a long assignment we must prepare for."

"A campaign?"

"Nothing so glorious. A personal favor for the Empress. I'm not sure how long it will be. Hasn't Daolyn kept you busy in the greenhouse?"

"She has kept me at that well enough, and no doubt the greenhouse is enough for Daolyn in her evenings, but I hoped perhaps you would be willing, should you be gone for such a long campaign, to perhaps furnish me with some reading, perhaps?"

Zezili must have shown her disapproval in her face, because he interrupted before she could dissent, hurried on. "Just the daily papers from Daorian. I know your feeling about books, and Daolyn feels that way as well, but surely, what harm is there in papers? Just some news from outside? There was a silk merchant through here last week, she—"

"I regret that we have had no children," Zezili said. A sore subject indeed, in any company. "I have heard that a man assisting in the raising of children often finds some fulfillment from it, but I'm here to take life in Rhea's name, not give it."

"You should just dedicate your body to her as well, then," Anavha said. A bit too cutting for Zezili's taste.

Zezili's anger stirred. "You *would* like that, wouldn't you?" she said. "Having a sexless woman for a wife? Yes, you'd like taking solace in none but your own body. Because that's all I would allow you. My sisters have no use for you. Who will touch you then? Or will you content yourself to be a mad little thing, running after dajian effeminates?"

She saw Anavha clenching his fists, saw the anger in him, and saw it dissipate into tears. Rhea only allowed him tears.

"You don't let me go anywhere," he cried. "I can't see anyone. These dajians, they don't even speak proper Dorinah."

Sometimes, Zezili wished she could allow him to shove a sword into a dajian. It was the best way she had found to silence sorrow.

She stood and squatted next to his little quaking form, brushed the hair back from his cheek. "Shush now, shush," she said, and wondered what sort of mother she would have been if she'd had to deal with children. She would have done what other women did, of course – farm them out to the dajians and get on with her work.

"Shush now. Am I so terrible a wife?" She took one of his soft, slender hands, pulled it to her chest, inside her coat, and pressed it over her breast. "Tell me you have no desire for me at all," Zezili said. "Say you would rather fuck nothing than fuck me, and I will have it done."

"You're horrible," Anavha said. "You're horrible."

"I'm not horrible," Zezili said, rising. "I'm your wife."

As she watched him weep at her feet, she thought of the faces that watched her in the city; the disgust, the outrage, that some mongrel slave could hold such a station, and own such a husband.

She took her husband, then – right there next to the table.

He was the one thing in her life she controlled completely. And she loved him for it.

Despite the Empress's instructions, Zezili found herself unprepared for the visitors that showed up on her stoop the next day. Two women – one little and slightly dark, with the features of a Dhai, and one taller, plumper, with the broad gray eyes and complexion of a Dorinah – entered the courtyard under Daolyn's escort.

"I'm Sai Hofsha," the smaller woman said. Her accent was strange. Not quite Dhai. "Empress Casanlyn sent you word of my arrival?"

"Is that a title or a name?" Zezili asked.

"Call me Hofsha," the woman said. "Sai is a... title, yes." Her hair looked like it had been cut with a razor, then crimped and curled into some unrecognizable country style.

"And you are Syre Zezili," Hofsha continued. Her smile was large and glorious, yet unmistakably disingenuous. "This one is Monshara." She waved dismissively at the other woman.

Zezili glanced at stone-faced Daolyn; what she thought of their visitors, Zezili could only guess.

"Do you have papers?" Zezili asked Hofsha.

Hofsha laughed. "Papers? Oh, no, I'm not some slave, some dajian. I'm here from the Empress. Surely she told you to expect me?"

Zezili frowned. "You are not... what I expected."

"I'm never quite what anyone expects," Hofsha said. "But no worries on your part, my friend. I won't actually be the one managing this campaign with you. You'll be partnering with Monshara here." She jabbed a finger at her plumper companion again. "She's one of our top generals. You should get along well. She speaks very good Dorinah." Hofsha seemed to find this funny and smothered a laugh behind her hand.

Zezili sized up Hofsha's companion. Her expression reminded Zezili of Daolyn's, as if they both sought to shutter up emotions better left unexpressed. Monshara held herself like one of the Empress's noble councilors. Her pale, round face and eyes, the black hair, the broad nose and narrow jaw – it was all very Dorinah.

"Where are you from?" Zezili asked her. "Not here, surely? I'd have heard of you."

The general's mouth twisted. Not a smile, but a grimace. "Gold head to you," she said. "Perceptive." She spoke Dorinah with no accent, which was even more perplexing than the odd accent of the Dhai-looking woman.

"Are we dining?" Hofsha asked. Big grin. The grin would not leave her abhorrent face.

"Yes, of course," Zezili said. "Daolyn, bring tea and – what would you like? Are you some kind of vegetarian cannibal Dhai?"

"Nothing so exciting as that," Hofsha said. "Bread and cheese will do."

"Cheese?"

"Ah, there are some differences, I remember," Hofsha said. "Jam, then. Bread and jam."

Zezili motioned Daolyn toward the kitchen and ushered the visitors into her sunken sitting room. She couldn't help but wince when she saw them walk across her unrolled rug. They sat on opposite ends of the divan. Monshara leaned slightly away from Hofsha, as if the foot of space between them already was not quite enough. Hofsha, for her part, leaned forward, as if ready to leap into Zezili's lap.

"I understand that this is a difficult time for you," Hofsha said.

Zezili raised her brows but said nothing.

Hofsha said, "I'd like you to work with Monshara to purge the dajian camps."

"The slave camps?" Zezili said. "That's over eight thousand dajians."

"Indeed," Hofsha said. "It's a large task but necessary."

"Necessary for what?" Zezili asked. She had expected some grand invasion – command of a dual force to overtake Tordin or Aaldia to the south.

"It's necessary," Hofsha repeated. "That's all you need know." The smile was ever-present. "Monshara has... much experience with this type of assignment. I hope you can come to an agreement and work well together. I know our government and your own Empress have great hopes for the success of this campaign."

"And who is your government, exactly?" Zezili asked.

"All in good time," Hofsha said. "Can you complete this task?"

"I know how to kill dajians," Zezili said. "If your friend here can help, it's another pair of hands. That's something."

Monshara was not looking at either of them but at something above and behind Zezili. Zezili glanced back; the woman was staring at the gilded mirror above the hearth. It was a tarnished silver mirror with a bit of greenish color in the frame, as wide as Zezili was tall.

"You make mirrors?" Monshara asked.

"What? No," Zezili said. "I buy them."

"Not that one, I think."

"It was a hobby of my mother's. Not mine."

"But you have her blood."

"I have a lot of things my mother doesn't approve of."

"But she taught you this skill? How to build mirrors and infuse them with the power of the stars?" Monshara asked.

"What has that got to do with anything?"

Hofsha's smile had vanished. She, too, was staring at Zezili with genuine interest now. "You know how to work mirrors?" Hofsha asked.

Zezili shrugged. "It was a long time ago. Before I took up fighting. I made a few in my youth. Not well. They are worthless like this, though. I can't channel any of Rhea's daughters, the satellites, so you can't see some foreign place through them or see yourself better than you are. They're just dead things. Not of much use for military operations."

Hofsha and Monshara exchanged a look. It was brief. Not friendly. But knowing.

"If you were gifted, you could," Hofsha said.

"What a stupid thing to say," Zezili said. "I don't like senseless chatter. I thought we had a much larger campaign planned, so my second, Syre Jasoi, is on her way to assist in discussion of strategy."

"We've already settled on strategy," Monshara said.

Hofsha said, "You're to act as Monshara's second in this matter. She has created a plan for dissolving the camps. I trust you will obey her in all things."

"You trust I... what? You're foreigners. You know nothing of this place or its people."

Hofsha stood and clapped her hands loudly. "Good! That's settled."

Daolyn arrived with the tea. She hesitated in the doorway.

"Thank you," Hofsha said, "I have other matters to attend. I expect you'll both get on well."

"I need to discuss this with the Empress–" Zezili said.

"You're welcome to it," Hofsha said. "Until then, Monshara, I expect you'll handle this all admirably, as our sovereign would expect."

Monshara just looked at her. Zezili found she could not read the expression at all. Annoyance? Anger?

Daolyn set the tea on the low table and escorted Hofsha out.

Zezili let the silence stretch between her and Monshara. Monshara gazed at the mirror again.

"Your force is five thousand?" Monshara asked.

"Give or take. We have a few out with blue fever this time of year."

"Well, we won't need that many." Monshara pushed the tea tray aside. She pulled a leather case from her shoulder. Removed a map. She pinned the map to the table with the empty cups. It was a map of Dorinah, with each of the dajian camps marked in red.

"My people have refrained from alerting the camp officials of our intent, of course," Monshara said. "With a campaign like this, rumor will travel quickly. That's why I chose the camp here, in Saolyndara, first. It's the largest."

"Has the Empress addressed what will happen to our labor here, with the dajians dead?" Zezili asked. "This seems like a very dramatic move, without precedent."

"It's of no consequence," Monshara said.

"Without dajians to—"

"It was my understanding that you had a head for killing, not governing," Monshara said. "If your people can't handle this—"

"My people know how to put down a dajian," Zezili said. "I just want it known that I'm not wasting time on some slippery dog chase."

"You have such strange speech," Monshara said. "Like an educated slave."

Zezili rankled. "You're one to talk of slavery, riding about at the call of some Dhai."

Monshara's expression hardened.

"Syre Zezili?" Daolyn called. "There is an issue with your husband, Syre."

"Tell him to wait."

"I apologize deeply, Syre. But it is quite urgent."

Zezili sighed. "If you'll excuse me."

Monshara stood as she exited.

Zezili took Daolyn by the arm as soon as they entered the courtyard. "What's this? You know how important this is?"

"I'm sorry, Syre," Daolyn said. "But your husband has… done something."

"Done something?"

Daolyn gestured across the yard, to the door leading into Anavha's chambers. Zezili went there. The door yawned open at her touch. She came up short.

At the center of the room, Anavha's double bed had been neatly sliced in two. The front half remained, canted forward now on just two legs. The rest was... gone. Zezili saw a scorched mark in the floor at the front of it, roughly circular. Beside it, Anavha sat back on his heels, clutching himself. He was barely clothed. Zezili saw blood on his hands, and a knife next to him.

Anger and terror seized her. She went to him. Took him by the arms. Shook him. "Are you hurt?" she asked.

His face was slack, smeared in tears and clumps of gold makeup. She saw three neat cuts on the inside of his bare thigh. The new wounds stood out in stark contrast to the older scars running parallel to them, some just a week old.

Her grip loosened. His self-harm was an unfortunate habit but not life-threatening. She suspected he did it to get attention.

"What happened?" she asked.

He shook his head.

She slapped him lightly. He began to cry.

"What happened?" she asked. Softer, now.

The ruin of his tear-smeared face, lacking the artifice of the perfect makeup, made him look much younger. In that moment, she was reminded that he was little more than a child.

He said, "I opened a door."

8

Lilia stood among the scattered lanterns in the temple garden, clutching a pack to her chest. Her personal belongings were almost nothing: an extra pair of clothes, a dog-hair coat, sandals, the mahuan powder for her asthma, and Kalinda's letters. The books and strategy games that had sustained her days were all property of the temple. She had arrived at the temple with the clothes she wore, and it appeared now that she would leave it with little else.

"Have you ridden a bear before?" Taigan asked.

Dawn was a hazy gray promise kissing the edges of the darkness. Though it was warm, she found herself shivering.

"A long time ago," Lilia said. "They were not so tame, though. My mother spoke to them."

Taigan snorted. "I expect she did. When did you come to the temple?"

"After my mother died. Kalinda brought me."

"Who's Kalinda?"

"A friend of my mother's," Lilia said.

Taigan pointed to her wrist. "And did Kalinda give you that?"

Lilia looked at her hand. "What?"

"The ward? You can see it, can't you?"

Lilia realized the wrist Taigan pointed at was the same one where her mother had burned the trefoil into her skin. "There's nothing here," Lilia said. "I don't see anything."

Taigan laughed. "You will," he said. His certainty made Lilia fearful. She had given herself away, and he'd come for her, just as Kalinda warned her.

The sanisi turned as two novices approached, leading a hulking white-and-brown bear that must have weighed a ton. It wasn't until that moment, when the sanisi took the bear's reins in his slender fingers, that she realized what she had done. Everything had happened very quickly.

"Up," the sanisi said. He brought the bear beside her. The stink of it was nearly overpowering.

Lilia took a step back. The bear snuffled at her; its yellow eye seemed enormous, the size of her fist. Its great bifurcated paws dug impatiently into the soft ground. Fangs protruded from the upturned snout. It flicked its forked purple tongue at her; the yellow eye narrowed, slitted like a cat's. The bears were native to the woodland and used their tongues to sample potentially deadly plants before ingesting them. That was why her mother kept one in the village. It helped them avoid contaminated vegetation or new mutations of familiar plants that may have become poisonous. The broad, split paws also made it effective at getting through marshy woodland. They were faster in the marsh than most people.

"I can't go," Lilia said.

"Too late," Taigan said, and took her by the waist.

She was astonished by his strength. But even more at his rudeness. He had touched her without asking. Once she was in the saddle, he took the bear's rein and walked beside it.

"You should ask first," Lilia said, indignant.

"Ask about what?"

"You can't just grab a person."

"Those with strength rule over those without."

"Strength doesn't make you better. It makes you a bully."

"You agreed to come with me, girl."

"You could be less rude," she said, and looked back at the temple. But there was no one to see her go. Just the novices stepping back into the shadows, as if fearful they too would catch the sanisi's eye and be taken away. She feared that she was some sacrifice, a token sent to appease their northern neighbors, to ensure another five hundred years of peace. They would not miss her. Tomorrow, they would not remember her name.

She choked on a sob. She'd given herself away to save Roh, and now she had no idea how she was going to get to the woodland coast to find her mother.

"Hush now," Taigan said. "The first thing you must learn is that there is a time to mourn, and a time to act. Now we act."

Ahead of them, the great webbed netting that encircled the temple garden from the wild heath and untamed lands between clan territories loomed large. A parajista waited at the webbed gate. She pressed her hands forward and sliced through the gate with a cone of air.

The sanisi led the bear through. They traveled across the stone bridge connecting the rocky spur that housed the temple and the broad plateau it had been separated from. The plateau was barren of all but the most harmless of vegetation, most of it burned out. The sanisi took them to the head of the precipitous path that cut into the edge of the plateau. Down and down they went into the valley as the suns rose and Para's light entered the sky with it, bathing the world in a blue wash. As they walked, the sanisi kept his short blade out. Squelching tripvines and bramblewash sensed their heat and motion, and slithered their way across the path. The bear ate most of what assailed them, but for the bigger plant life, the sanisi used his blade to hack and cut and beat back. Lilia clung tightly to either side of the high seat of the saddle. No one traveled the spaces between the temples and clans without a trained Ora by their side, preferably one skilled in drawing on the dominant body in the sky.

After hacking off the clawing fingers of the fifth yellow pox plant of the morning, the sanisi said, "Why your tirajistas haven't irradiated this filth continues to baffle me."

"Where do you think it all came from?" Lilia asked. "The Oras say we were the ones to blight the world, during the war with your people, two thousand years ago."

Taigan frowned. "I cannot contest that. The world was a heaving wasteland after that. It took two thousand years just to become half-habitable again."

"It wasn't just us," Lilia said. "You're no better."

Taigan gazed at the wriggling tendril of a creeper spitting green, acidic bile into the dirt. "No," he said, "We are not."

Lilia leaned forward in the saddle. "Why did you save him?" she asked.

"What?"

"Roh. Why did you save him? Why trade him for me? I'm nothing. I'm nobody."

The sanisi shook his head and tugged the bear forward. It caught up the wriggling tendril with its tongue and ate it.

"I think you know," Taigan said.

Lilia looked away.

They traveled until midday and stopped for a rest on a scorched patch of ground that had been prepared for the purpose. The sanisi tried to feed her some kind of meat, which she refused. She foraged for fleshy tubers and the fat rose cones her mother had taught her to find. The sanisi turned up his nose at her fare and ripped into his meal of dead animal flesh. After letting the bear graze, they moved on. North. To the sea.

In the early afternoon, they came to a crossroads. Lilia only knew Dhai by maps. She hadn't left the temple since Kalinda dropped her there. But maps told her that northwest lay Clan Sorila, populated mostly by timber farmers and plant sculptors, and northeast was Clan Garika. She knew from the letters she received from Kalinda that she kept a way house on the road to Garika.

Taigan began to pull them northwest, to Sorila. She bit her tongue, wondering if he would uncover the ruse. She waited a few minutes before she said, "I'm glad we're going to Sorila. I have family there."

"You said you have no family."

"My mother is dead. But I have an aunt and cousins in Sorila."
Lilia had told many lies in her life, but telling that one, to a sanisi,
felt the boldest by far.

He drew the bear to a halt.

"Never lie to me," Taigan said. "It is a useless endeavor."

"You could be nicer," she said.

"No," he said.

"*Everyone* could be nicer," she said.

"And what a world that would be."

"You build the world through your actions," Lilia said. "Yours
are very poor."

"You argue like a mewling toddler," he said. "The last girl was
less talkative."

"What girl?"

"Let me sit a moment in peace."

This was the second longest conversation they'd had. She
wondered what a rollicking noisy night in Saiduan sounded like.

"How did you know about the symbol on my wrist?" Lilia
asked as Taigan started forward again.

"I can see it."

"How?"

"Because I draw the breath of the same star as the person who
made it," Taigan said, "the blood witch you call mother, yes?
Blood witches, ha. Only one people calls them that. Wards are
complicated things, stitched together with litanies created just for
the purpose. But yours is one I recognize. It's a simple hazing
ward. It makes it difficult for people to see and remember you.
Useful, I imagine, in your state."

"What's my state?" Lilia asked.

"Don't you know by now, little bird? Why would anyone try
and protect you, a little nameless drudge?"

"Because she loved me," Lilia said. "My mother put this ward
on me, and she loved me very much."

"Your mother wanted to save you for someone else," Taigan

said. "She was an omajista, based on the color and composition
of that ward, and she likely suspected you would be the same."

"There aren't any omajistas," Lilia said.

"Not many," Taigan said. "Not yet. We'll take off that ward
tonight. I suspect it plays a role in reducing your sensitivity to Oma."

Lilia gripped her wrist. "I'm not an omajista, or a blood witch,
or anything like that."

"Nor are you a woman grown," he said, "but you will be."

"I'm nearly five years past the age of consent!"

"In Saiduan, you'd still be a veiled child. Please, your chatter
hurts my head."

Lilia considered him the way she might a kindar piece on a
board. What was his strategy? Surely the Saiduan didn't want to
kill her. But she couldn't imagine they would keep her in their
care when they found out she wasn't gifted.

Dusk came much sooner under the massive canopy of the
trees. Lilia only saw the dim lights of the way house when they
were nearly on top of it. The way house was a large, sinuous
thing hollowed out of a vine that wrapped its way up the trunk
of a bonsa tree that must have been a thousand years old. For
the last hour, Taigan's pace had quickened. He glanced back more
often. Now that the way house was in sight, she worried he might
go past it.

"Are we stopping?" Lilia asked.

"Someone is following," he said.

"So we aren't stopping."

"We must. They're worse at night, and harder to sense."

"Who?"

He led the bear into the light of the way house. "Come now,
get down." He called up at the way house. "Hello there; send
someone out!"

Lilia thought it was very rude.

Taigan reached up to grab her.

She batted his hands away. "Ask first!"

"Do you want help off the bear or not?"

"Yes," she said, and held out her arms.

When he pulled her off, she dropped to the ground and said, "See? Was that so difficult?" It took her a moment to find her balance. Her legs were sore. She clung to the side of the bear.

The sanisi muttered something in Saiduan, and she wished she'd paid more attention in Dasai's classes.

Lilia walked toward the light of the house. She heard the hiss of the sanisi's blade.

She expected to see something terrible as she turned – a rogue walking tree or some slithering nightwalker. Or, worse, the sanisi's sword impaling her. But the attackers were human. Three men stepped out of the shadows, moving so quickly, she did not have time to scrutinize their faces. They bore the blue-glowing bonsa blades of parajistas in their fists. As they raised their arms, though, she saw the hilts were not wrapped around their wrists the way the militia's did.

No, these blades protruded from the men's wrists – hungry, snarling brambles that grew from some dark seed implanted in their flesh.

She panicked.

She'd seen those weapons before.

Lilia dropped beneath the bear and scrambled toward the way house, dragging her bad foot behind her. She heard the hissing kiss of the blades and the roar of the bear. But instead of going inside, she ran around to the other side of the way house. The ground immediately outside the house was scorched and safe. She crouched there and waited, listening to the fighting.

The sanisi could not save her from those men. Only one person had kept her safe all this time, and only one woman would believe her about those strange weapons. Could Kalinda help her again?

Taigan cursed. Lilia saw a burst of blue light.

She darted further into the woods, away from the purls of blue light. Her breath came fast. She tried to slow her breathing as she slogged, fearful of her poor lungs. She limped through snaking creepers and sticky pox tendrils and emerged again on the road, behind the sanisi and his attackers. She saw the bear snuffling off back the way they had come, spooked by the fight.

She hobbled forward, making soothing sounds, and – with great effort – climbed onto its back again. She glanced behind her only once. She saw the blue arc of the weapons, still whirling, the battle still undecided between Taigan and... who? The same people who'd come for her before, so many years ago. She had made a promise, and she intended to keep it. But things were spiraling out of hand, and she didn't think she could do it alone.

"We'll make our own fate," she murmured to the bear, and urged him forward, back to the crossroads, back to Kalinda Lasa.

9

Ahkio stood at the eastern wall of the Assembly Chamber, staring out the wall of windows overlooking the Pana Woodlands. Para's bluish light kissed the horizon, herald of the double dawn, which was just a few hours off. The light washed over deep green adenoaks and clumps of pale lime-colored bamboo and less savory things that rolled out across the plateau and into the distance. Clouds boiled over Mount Ahya, obscuring the summit. It was a rare day when one saw the peak.

He had come up here to be alone after the disturbance with the sanisi downstairs, but as ever, Nasaka found him. He knew the footsteps behind him were hers, even before she drew a breath and said, "They're getting ready to prepare your sister. I suggest you spend your grieving hours with her."

"If Oma isn't rising, that sanisi made a good show of it," Ahkio said.

Nasaka held a green sheaf of papers in one hand; the other rested on the butt of her willowthorn sword. "We hoped it was a century distant," Nasaka said. "But as with all things as they pertain to the gods of the satellites, our calculations can only be approximate. They bend us to their own will."

"He came here looking for omajistas," Ahkio said.

"That's a grand leap in logic."

"Is it? He asked for Kirana first. She's a powerful channeler, Nasaka. I'm not. And that girl..."

"We test every child in Dhai," Nasaka said. "Could we have missed one, especially one not able to draw on a star we haven't seen in two thousand years? Certainly."

"And Kirana?"

Nasaka sighed. "We... speculated she may have some power besides that of a tirajista. The last few months, things were... strange with her."

"She said she asked for me weeks ago."

"She was not in her right mind, Ahkio."

"Do you think she was killed for it?"

"Perhaps." Nasaka set the pages on the table and came to his side, gazed with him toward Mount Ahya and the creeping dawn. "Do you want a part in saving all of this, Ahkio? Or will you run home to Meyna?"

"You're giving me a choice?"

"With or without you in this seat, we are headed for civil war," Nasaka said.

"War? In Dhai? That's not possible."

"The Garikas will contest your right to the seat. The Raonas will ask that I find your mad Aunt Etena and put her in it. And then there's the matter of Oma..." Nasaka shook her head. "I suggest you sit with your sister now, before her body is prepared. The rest can wait until morning. But think clearly on this, Ahkio."

"What changed?" Ahkio asked. He peered at her, but she did not meet his gaze. "You called me here to make me Kai. Now a sanisi tells us Oma is rising, and you say I can go home and pretend none of this happened?"

"I hoped having you here might spare you," Nasaka said, "from whatever fate befell Kirana. But now... Now I worry that harm will come to you no matter what way I move you."

"Like a piece on a board?"

"No. Like an ungifted man trying to fill a seat that's only been held by gifted women."

Ahkio referred to himself with the male-passive pronoun, and it was the same identifier Nasaka used when he said "man." Ahkio always thought the pronoun very accurate, even complimentary – he was a teacher, a lover, a man who wanted four spouses and dozens of children, but somehow, the way Nasaka said it, it felt like an insult.

"Why does being a man matter?"

"To some, it matters," Nasaka said. "More importantly, with Oma rising, having an ungifted man on the seat is even worse. They will tear you from this temple with their teeth and insist on a politically savvy and gifted woman."

"Who killed her, Nasaka? Who wanted civil war now, of all times? The Saiduan?"

"That's a question I can't answer yet," she said, "let alone prove."

"But you suspect the Garikas?"

"I always suspect the Garikas. Yisaoh will come for your seat soon, I guarantee that. I've already set things into motion in preparation for that."

"They'll come for me whether or not I'm here."

"Not if you renounce the seat."

Ahkio had nothing to say to that. He watched Para bubble up over the horizon like a great bristling urchin. He thought of Kirana downstairs, her final words a mad cacophony of nonsense. He did feel very young, very small; Kirana had happily seen him off to Osono, away from Nasaka's poisonous influence, and the ongoing headache of Dhai politics.

"I'm going to go and sit with Kirana," Ahkio said. He turned away, crossed the room.

When he looked back, Nasaka still stood at the window, her lined face made brilliantly ominous by the blazing blue light of Para.

Ahkio walked downstairs. He grabbed a flame fly lantern from its niche in the hall, shook it, and brought it with him to Kirana's room, where the curtains were still closed.

He moved to the stool by the bed. He saw Kirana's slack face staring back at him. She seemed smaller. The smell of her voided body wafted up from the bedding, mixed with the smell of her sickness, but he still paused there, and gazed at the body of the woman who was once his sister.

He looked behind him, so he wouldn't miss the stool as he sat to pay his last respects. He remembered when he and Kirana did the same over their parents' bodies. Huddled together, trying to understand the loss. This wake was for kin only, a few hours of stillness before the funerary attendants arrived to perform her final rites, the washing and liturgy, ensuring her soul was well gone before preparing her for the funerary feast.

As he turned, he heard a noise behind him, a rustling sound.

He thought perhaps one of the windows was open, letting in a soft breeze to stir the curtains.

The curtains remained motionless.

But his sister was sitting up in bed.

Ahkio's gut went icy.

Bodies sometimes moved. Even after death, they could move. They...

Kirana turned to look at him. Her eyes were glazed over, unfocused. Her hair fell into her gaunt face. She threw her legs over the side of the bed. Stood. She wore a thin white dressing gown that clung to her skinny legs.

Ahkio couldn't move. "Kira," came out in a strangled whisper.

"Listen," she said.

She took hold of the front of his tunic in her clawed hands, and pulled him forward. She was nearly a head shorter than he, her face awash in the light cast by the lantern he still clutched.

"The heart is for you," she said. "She'll let you through, but you must find her. You will see me again, but not as I am. They're coming, Ahkio. You must meet them."

He gasped; he was suddenly short of breath. The air felt heavy, like soup. He feared some sinajista had called her back from death. If that was so, or if she'd pulled herself back from Sina's maw, he didn't have much time.

"Who was it?" he said. "Was it Nasaka? Kirana, who killed you?"

"I did," she said, and released him.

The lantern fell from Ahkio's hand.

10

When Lilia came to the crossroads, she did not halt the bear, though foam lathered its snout. She pulled out a short blade sheathed behind her with the sanisi's other supplies, and used it to cut back the worst of the plant life that barred their path. Her wrists and ankles were covered in red welts and broken thorns. A giant swinging vine nearly knocked her from her seat. She untied the sanisi's supplies and used the cord to tie herself to the saddle.

She sent Kalinda letters six times a year, on the major festivals and religious holidays. Kalinda had her address them Way House Hyacinth, Mark 21, Oma to Garika. It meant Way House Hyacinth was at the twenty-one-mile mark on the road that ran from the Temple of Oma to Garika. Dhai had no regular mail service; it was all taken up by traveling merchants and delivered along with other shipments.

When Lilia came to the door of the way house, she was bleeding and exhausted from her tangle with the hungry plant life along the road. She slid from the bear, filthy and aching, and climbed the steps of the porch with great effort. The door – as all doors were in Dhai – was not locked.

She stepped inside.

Kalinda Lasa sat at one of several round wooden tables at the center of the room, speaking to two older women and a boy. Another young woman stood to the rear of the room, leaning easily in the doorway to the kitchen. She moved immediately forward when Lilia entered. The others stayed seated.

Kalinda cocked her head at Lilia. She was much older than Lilia remembered. Her white hair was wound about her head in one easy spiral, as if some tornadic wind had shaped it. She wore a bright red skirt and purple blouse beneath a leather vest buckled at the front with three large, eye-shaped silver buttons.

"Are you all right, child?" Kalinda asked as she rose.

Lilia had a terrible fear that Kalinda did not remember her. Oma, she had come all this way and given up the only friend she had for nothing.

"I'm Lilia Sona, and there is a sanisi coming here for me. Maybe something worse."

Lilia saw recognition pass across Kalinda's face. Lilia's relief was so sharp that her eyes filled with tears. There is a time to mourn, and a time to act, the sanisi had said. She wiped her eyes.

"It's all right, Gian," Kalinda said.

The tall woman who had been standing far across the room was now within just a few paces of Lilia. The woman, Gian, took a step back and crossed her ropy arms. Her long, dark hair fell nearly to her waist in a thick braid. Lilia found herself a little jealous of it. No one in the temple had long hair.

"Get inside," Kalinda said. "Gian, bolt that door. You remember how? Lilia, come with me." She gestured to the others at the table. "Go home. Quickly and quietly. Wake our guests and send them on their way. We need the house clear."

Kalinda came forward. Her plump, round face was heavily lined, very serious, the thin lips pressed tightly into something that was not quite a frown.

"When did they come?" Kalinda asked.

"A day... two days ago. He wanted me to go with him."

"You specifically? Did he forcibly take you?"

"No. He saved my friend. I agreed to come with him."

"Come downstairs. Gian, you too."

Gian reentered from the kitchen, carrying a large beam with her. It was a knotted thing, silvery with some still-living plant compound that Lilia did not recognize.

"Why does he want me?" Lilia said. "Why are there people chasing me?"

"Come," Kalinda repeated.

Lilia followed her into the cellar. It was built among the roots of the massive tree that made up one wall of the way house. The large roots bore carved compartments for storing foodstuffs and supplies. Lilia passed row upon row of pickling jars and fibrous, knee-high seed pods that held water and wine.

Kalinda walked to one of the tree roots at the back of the cellar and released a catch that let a chunk of the root pull away. Inside was a dark space. She held a flame fly lantern ahead of her. As they entered, Lilia saw that the room was a perfect sphere lined in the decayed skin of an old bladder trap plant. Lilia recognized the shape from her classes in ecology and vegetal manipulation. She had heard they grew beneath the soil of trees like these, feeding on bears, giant shrews, and careless people, but it was the first one she'd seen up close.

Kalinda set the lantern on the carapace of some giant dead thing, its form lost as it was digested by the bladder trap. Whatever the bladder trap secreted, it kept this creature more or less mummified.

"Tell me precisely what happened," Kalinda said.

Lilia told her. Not just about the sanisi, but about the mark on her wrist the sanisi said he could see, the map on the Assembly Chamber table, and the familiar weapons of the sanisi's attackers.

"Why did you go looking for that mark?" Kalinda said.

Lilia straightened. "I made a promise to my mother."

"You were a child."

"I'm not a child anymore."

"No," Kalinda said, eyeing her. "You are not."

"What happened all those years ago matters," Lilia said. "I

thought I was mad, or misremembering, but whatever happened that day is the reason these people are after me, isn't it?"

"You should tell her," Gian said.

"Yes, I must," Kalinda said. "Your mother led a resistance against the Kai, and powerful people wanted to destroy her and take you. They thought you might be powerful too, someday."

"The sanisi thinks that," Lilia said. "But I'm not gifted."

"Someday you might be," Kalinda said. "Your mother was supposed to send you and six other children here that day, so we could protect them. But only you showed up. I came back to look for the others after I brought you home, but there were none. I suspect the other side has them now. You're all we have."

"We?" Lilia said.

"The resistance," Gian said. "Against the Kai."

"But what's the Kai done?" Lilia said.

"It's complicated," Kalinda said.

"It's not the Kai you know," Gian said. Kalinda shushed her.

"We need to hide you again," Kalinda said. "The sanisi will easily find you here."

"No more hiding," Lilia said. "Take me to the place on the map."

"We can't do that," Kalinda said. "There's nothing there."

Lilia got angry. She was exhausted and bleeding from her trek through the seething forest, and it felt like a betrayal. "I came here for your help. If you can't help me, I'll go back to the sanisi."

"You're as stubborn as–" Kalinda broke off, started again. "This isn't some duck chase, child."

"I'm not a child. I'm far past the age of consent. I won't consent to go anywhere or do anything until you take me to that place on the map. That was my home, Kalinda."

"It's not what you think it is," Gian said.

"That sanisi may be just behind you," Kalinda said, "or, worse, his attackers. Let's leave this place together. We can discuss our destination on the way."

Lilia hesitated. It was her best option. She nodded curtly.

"Good girl," Kalinda said.

But as Kalinda withdrew, Lilia felt the same way she did when the sanisi asked her to trade her freedom for Roh's life. It was as if she had been offered a choice that was not a choice at all.

Kalinda and Gian moved around Lilia as if she wasn't there, busying themselves with packing and preparing. They left her alone with the flame flies. Standing in the dark while the world moved around her, while others made decisions about her fate, had been a constant her whole life. She felt pulled in every direction, with no control over any of them.

She picked up the lantern and moved toward the back of the bladder trap. At the far end, the spiky protrusions that kept those trapped from exiting had been cut away, so the long tube of the trap that led to the surface could be reached freely from either direction.

If she left alone now, she would eventually be eaten by something unsavory. And where would she go? The Woodlands? The coast? Where could a hunted Dhai go when it was not only foreigners who hunted her, but her own people?

Trapped. No matter which way she turned.

Lilia set the lantern onto the table. She heard a commotion above her. Pounding at the door. Loud voices.

She looked again to the bladder trap's tiny exit. She had no map but the one from her memory, and no gift but the knowledge of woodland plants her mother had passed on to her.

But she'd made a promise to her mother and to herself. She was done with doing other people's laundry and being pushed around in service to other people's causes.

Lilia hooked her good foot into the side of the bladder trap and pulled herself up through the kill hole. She hauled herself forward on the nubs of the old spiky protrusions. They dug into her chest. She had to let out her breath to squeeze through. For one horrible, black moment, she thought she was stuck. She huffed out more air and pushed into the open air.

Outside, dawn was still only a promise on the horizon. This time, she did not look back, not even once. She located the blue blush of Para as it rose through the trees in the pre-dawn sky. She stumbled out onto the road heading east, to the woodland, to the sea.

11

Yisaoh Alais Garika came to meet with Ahkio the next day, just as Nasaka predicted. Ahkio stood in the kitchens, watching his sister's body being prepared, as Nasaka told him of Yisaoh's arrival. The funerary attendants washed Kirana's body in rose water and cardamom. They laid it on a stone slab in the temple kitchen on a blanket of fragrant bonsa leaves. Funerary chefs from the temples of Sina, Para, and Tira joined the scullery master of the Temple of Oma to carefully split open the Kai's torso and remove all vital organs. The heart, liver, and intestines were set aside and given to novice attendants. The intestines were cleaned and soaked in salt water. The liver and heart were washed with saffron; the liver was prepared with garlic, onions, and hasaen tubers. They divided the heart into sections and fried it with leeks and butter. They drained the blood into a broad silver bowl, for use in making blood soup and sausage later. The head was reverently removed and reserved for interment in the bowels of the temple catacombs.

Ahkio had never seen his parents honored in this way and had always regretted it. Seeing someone die and accepting that death were far different things. Watching her prepared, smelling the savory aroma of her flesh and organs cooking, helped wash the memory of her post-death awakening. Had it been a vision? Or had she truly been strong enough to reclaim her soul from Sina for a few stolen moments... only to tell him she'd manufactured her own death?

"Did you hear me?" Nasaka asked. She stood at his elbow, grim and surly as ever.

"I heard you," Ahkio said.

"Have you met Yisaoh before?"

"Not since before I went to Dorinah." In fact, he had a very difficult time remembering her face. She would have been twenty or so back then. He remembered pining after her for at least a year; a cool, aloof figure, witty and capable. He had always liked her strong hands.

"I'll need an answer, then."

"About?"

"Will you eat your sister's heart tonight and take her seat in two weeks, or shall I set another plan in motion?"

"Your only other option is to find my mother's sister Etena," Ahkio said. "But my mother didn't want her on the seat, and Kirana didn't either. She's probably dead in the woodlands by now."

"I have several options," Nasaka said. "Etena is not one of them. She disappeared a long time ago."

"They'll all lead to civil war."

"You could save us all the trouble and simply agree to marry Yisaoh."

"She wants to be Kai," Ahkio said. "Not the Kai's Catori. I don't think she'll settle for second."

"You have a better idea?"

"I'll marry Meyna."

Nasaka's laugh was bitter. "Over my rotting corpse."

"Noted," Ahkio said. He turned away. "Is Yisaoh upstairs in the Kai's study?"

"Ahkio, you can't be serious about Meyna."

"It's the best solution," Ahkio said. He'd been thinking about it all morning, remembering that warm night around the table before Nasaka came for him. "Her husbands are Yisaoh's brothers."

"If you won't marry her, you had best be prepared with a very smart way to pacify her."

"I intend to ask her about Kirana."

"Oma's breath, Ahkio, don't go accusing the Garikas of murder. I'll come up with you."

"No. They hate Oras far more than they hate me. Stay here."

"I don't advise it."

"I'll take that under advisement," Ahkio said, and walked back through the massive banquet hall, past drudges and novices and the occasional Ora sitting down to the midday meal. He considered Yisaoh kin. Her brother Lohin had married Kirana. But the link that decided him was her kinship to Rhin and Hadaoh. She could not contest her own family marrying him; with Meyna came Rhin and Hadaoh. He thought of the spill of Meyna's hair and her broad smile. He wanted her here beside him more than anything. Even she could not argue the logic of it.

Ahkio went up to the Assembly Chamber. Two militia flanked the archway leading into the waiting room outside the Kai study. But the waiting room was empty.

The door to the Kai's study stood open. Ahkio saw Yisaoh sitting on one of the padded chairs in front of his sister's desk. Well, he thought, at least she had the decency not to sit in Kirana's chair.

Yisaoh rose at his appearance. She was solidly built, wide in the hips. Her long blue-green skirt and tunic were plainly made, unfrivolous. She had a long face and heavy brow. He found her crooked nose endearing. She took him in with a steely gaze.

"Yisaoh Alais Garika," he said.

"Li Kai Ahkio Javia Garika, kin," she said.

It was, indeed, a mouthful.

His sister's portrait gazed at him from the far wall, one of eight to stare back at him from the portraits of five hundred years of Kais. His mother's most contentious action as Kai had been to break the line of succession. For five hundred years, the line of the Kais had followed that of the most gifted male or female. But his mother's older sister had been gifted to the point of madness, and his mother had taken it upon herself to change the rules. His mother, not his Aunt Etena, took the title of Kai. And now he was left with it. Though Kais throughout history had been a variety of genders, he would be the first unable to bear an heir to term from his own womb, as he didn't have one. And that difference wasn't going to sit well with some people.

Ahkio sat in the guest chair opposite Yisaoh. Moving behind the big desk reminded him too much of Nasaka. Yisaoh was already formal and defensive. More hierarchy among Dhai rarely resulted in anything but increased defensiveness.

She resumed her seat.

He had forgotten to order tea. Had Nasaka thought to send someone for it? She would take it as an affront. He had lived in a proper house with Meyna and her family for so long that he had no idea how anything got done inside a temple.

"Pardon, Li Kai, I know I come at a troubling time," Yisaoh said. She rubbed the stained ends of her fingers together. He forgot she smoked. Tordinian cigarettes, likely. His sister had loved them.

"I expect you aren't here to talk about taxes," Ahkio said.

He fished around in his sister's desk, looking for her smoking box. It would have been comforting indeed if Yisaoh came to him about taxes. He knew all about tax law.

"No," Yisaoh said. "With your sister being prepared downstairs, I–"

He found the cigarette box, a black lacquered box as big as a ledger. "Can I offer you a cigarette?"

She hesitated. "No, thank you."

"I don't smoke, and my sister is dead." He pushed the box toward her. "Is this enough, or is there something else of my sister's you'd like?"

Yisaoh steepled her fingers. "A mouthy ethics teacher. That's what Kirana called you."

"And where is my sister's husband?" Ahkio asked. "Your brother Lohin? I expected him." Ahkio sat across from her. He adopted an open posture, arms on either side of the seat, legs uncrossed. It took a great deal of effort not to snap up like a morning glory at midday, but she was here to find weakness.

"He sends his regards," Yisaoh said coolly.

"Thoughtful."

"I see there's no sense in dancing around," Yisaoh said. "I never was a good dancer."

"I doubt that very much."

"I am here to ask you to renounce your claim to the seat."

"I'm afraid I've chosen not to do that. It's not what Kirana would have wanted."

"So you're doing this for Kirana?"

"Yes."

"Not Ora Nasaka, of course?"

"It's no secret Nasaka and I don't get along."

"There have been questions about your right to the seat," Yisaoh said, "based on your true parentage."

"My... what?" He folded his hands, realized what he was doing, and released them again. He tried to look at ease while pondering what she meant. He could think of no legitimate issue with his parentage except for lost, mad Etena. Had the Garikas found her after all? When his mother exiled Etena, Tir's family all but declared an open campaign against his mother's family. Kirana had fought them off with a great deal of diplomacy and, it was rumored, an inordinate amount of affection for Yisaoh.

"People talk, Ahkio. Kirana and the three dead babies before you were all obviously your mother's children. But you look nothing like your mother."

He laughed. "Is this all you have? Yisaoh, there are far more important things at issue here. First, who poisoned my sister with some gifted charm that no tirajista could cure? Who wanted this seat badly enough to commit murder for it?"

Yisaoh shrugged. She looked at his sister's portrait on the wall. "An interesting question," she said. "Perhaps this was done by someone who knew that times in Dhai are about to become very dire, and we needed someone of strength on the seat."

"Someone like you?"

"I would offer you a seat as my Catori, my consort, but really, a boy not of the Kai's womb has no right even as consort."

"You're less charming than I supposed, based on the amount of courtesy Kirana showed you."

"Should I be charming? No. I hold the might of clans Garika and Badu in my fist. What do you have but the backing of some nattering old Oras?"

"Oras who can call on the power of the stars? I'd say I have a great deal."

"You'd threaten me with the power of the gods? You'd use Oras against your own people? Are you truly so monstrous?"

"If this is about power for Garika, I'll marry Rhin and Hadaoh and Meyna. But if this is about you, I cannot help."

Yisaoh was rubbing her fingers again. "They are the weakest of my brothers. You think I'd stand for some honey-headed sheepherder in this seat?"

Ahkio heard a clatter from the waiting room. Elaiko entered carrying a tea tray. "I've brought cinnamon-orange tea," she said. "My family's most popular blend."

"Ah, yes," Yisaoh said. "Elaiko. My father buys your family's tea. That's my favorite blend."

"Oh, is it?" Elaiko said.

"But of course you knew that."

"Thank you," Ahkio said. Elaiko placed the tray on the table.

Elaiko pressed thumb to forehead. "I'll be just outside if you need anything," she said, and left them.

"That is a coy little bird," Yisaoh said.

"A gentle description," Ahkio said.

"You misunderstand my intent with this meeting," Yisaoh said.

"Do I?"

"My father seeks to give power back to *all* clans, not just Garika. Assuming–"

"Your father, if you'll pardon, is a liar," Ahkio said. "I know precisely what your father wants, and I'll burn down the temple before I see your father pronounce you Kai of Garika and rename our country after one of his children. You've been trying to get this seat into your family's hands for decades. I'm offering you a fair compromise."

"My father said you would speak of tradition and history and say only, 'It's always been done this way.' He said–"

Ahkio quoted from *The Book of Oma*, "*Our country could see a thousand years of peace before the rising of Oma. That peace does not forfeit our strength but disciplines it. We must rely on that peace and our lines of kin to survive. When Oma calls us to defend–*"

"And he said you would quote the Book at me," Yisaoh said.

"I think that's enough," Ahkio said. He had been fair. He talked sense. Why wouldn't she see it? "Tell your father I can't grant his request. Tell him that any militia or sons or daughters or spouses or cousins of his he sends here will be treated with the utmost courtesy, but if another one threatens me, and in so doing threatens this country, I'll exile his entire family. Spouses. Sons. Daughters and all. I'm not pleased to be in this seat, but I respect the words of the Book. And what you and your father are proposing is heresy."

"Those are brave words from a shepherd."

"I teach shepherds. I'm not one." Ahkio stood. "It has been an occasion, Yisaoh Alais Garika."

She moved reluctantly to her feet. "I am disappointed. I hoped you would show sense. Your sister understood what was coming, even if the Oras covered their eyes. She kept a house in Garika and listened to my father and our stargazers when no one else would. You could have learned much from her."

"You're talking of Oma?"

"Ah, so they've purported to figure that out themselves now, have they? My father told Kirana and Ora Nasaka about Oma's rise years ago. We knew it was twenty years from rising, at best. Not a century."

"That's impossible."

"Is it?" Yisaoh gestured at the desk. "I suspect you know very little about your sister and her alliance with us. Perhaps you should learn more for yourself and stop relying on lies from scheming Oras."

"I'm not going to take that apple, Yisaoh. I know how divide-and-conquer politics work. The Oras are mine."

"The Oras belong to themselves. Don't you ever forget that. You're just a means to an end."

Ahkio called out to the militia posted at the doors. "Will you please escort Yisaoh Alais Garika from the Temple of Oma?"

Yisaoh's eyes were black. He saw her father's strength in her, a hardening of the jaw, blind purpose.

"We did not kill your sister, Li Kai," she said, "however convenient that would be for you. But you are ill prepared for what's coming. My family is ready. We'll take this seat any way we must."

"I invite you to try."

"Go eat your sister," she said.

The militia took her away.

12

Kalinda Lasa had fought many battles with many people, but this was the first she fought against her own people.

As she came up from the cellar, she saw the front door smashed in and three men standing in the remains of it. The men were indeed hers, not the local version. She knew them immediately, though many Dhai would not be able to spot the difference on sight. Those with lazy minds got themselves caught up in the cut of a coat, or the cast of a stranger's skin, or the cant of one's nose, but that told her very little. What she looked for was the way they held themselves and interacted with others, how they approached a problem. All Dhai here were proud, but passive. They exuded a calm politeness that tested Kalinda's patience. But it was their open, friendly approach to each person they met – as if they were all intimate family members – that was the biggest tell. These men stood in her house with shoulders straight and chests puffed out. They watched her with the alert, wary gazes she saw on war veterans, not the open faces of a rural militia.

"I suspect you aren't here for a room," she said.

The dark wounds at the men's wrists bloomed. Two of them sprouted glowing blue bonsa blades. The third, an everpine branch. They gripped the more pliable ends of the living weapons with their fists and marched forward.

Kalinda already held Para's breath beneath her skin; the Litany of Breath played at the back of her mind. She shifted to the Litany of the Spectral Snake and wrapped the men in skeins of air, trying to force their blades back into their bodies. But they had anticipated her. Blue mist bloomed around them.

Para suddenly fled from her grasp. Fickle Para. She yanked it back and opened herself again to its breath. She rebuilt her spectral sword and lashed out.

Her twisted skeins of Para's breath met a misty wall that engulfed the figures. The waves of blue emanated from the men on the left and the right – the parajistas. The middle one was likely a tirajista, based on the everpine weapon. Kalinda stepped away from the doorway and grabbed a sturdy club from the bin of canes and walking sticks she kept near the door. When Para's breath was unstable, it was good to have a solid backup weapon in case of failure.

The men advanced, weapons out.

Kalinda held her ground. Giving more of it showed weakness.

The men surrounded her. She pulled on Para and condensed the air around her into a solid blue bubble, reciting the Litany of the Chrysalis. The men were young but well-trained. Yet they had not knifed through her defenses immediately, which meant she had a slim chance of outwitting them.

Kalinda wrapped spiky protrusions of hazy blue air around her club. She thrust it forward, testing the bounds of their barriers. Their blades sliced through her defenses. She batted them back. Sealed the tears. The Litany of Sounding was a burning brand in her mind, and her defenses were a manifestation of that – concentrated thought made real. The patterns they used to create their wall were intricate. It was difficult to find a way to untangle it.

But as with any task that required perfect concentration to maintain control of a notoriously inconsistent power, there would be errors. Kalinda switched to another litany. Focused slivers of air zipped outward from the contours of her body, hammering their barriers.

One got through. She saw the man rocket back, drop his weapon. It snarled back into his wrist.

Her reaction was instant.

Shaping the power of Para took concentration, and breaking it, even for a moment, left a certain softness, an incompleteness of form, a corrupt pattern of Para's breath that was easy to cut if penetrated at the right moment. She focused her next blast at the weak point her sliver had penetrated. Their barriers burst. Para's twisted breath broke into a thousand unbound particles.

Weapons buckled. Snapped.

She squeezed the air around their limbs. Bones cracked. Screams. The air pressure in the room eased. Their concentration, like their bones, was broken.

She cut into them again, thrusting forward with the spikes of air that lengthened the reach of her club, bashing open their heads. Blood spattered the room, clinging to the surface of the condensed air she wielded, giving further form to the instruments of death and protection they had battled with. A portion of one of their barriers still stood, protecting the torso of the man nearest her feet. She saw the blood and brain matter of the man's companion stuck to it. She hammered the man's knee twice, and the barrier crumbled. The blood and matter dropped to the floor with it.

She pummeled the man's head until it was unrecognizable. Stepped back. She walked to the third man, the one injured by the initial spike of air. He clutched at his side. She heard him murmuring a litany, saw snaking tendrils of some poisonous creeper plant tunneling up through the boards of the floor. She sliced off the tails of the plant with a buzz of air. Then she crushed the man's head.

Kalinda dropped her barrier. Para's misty essence evaporated. She was wheezing hard. Cold sweat soaked her body. She slid to the floor. Sat against the door. The bodies bled out across the living boards. The floor had been shaped by some long-dead tirajista, created to soak up organic matter and allow heat from the thrumming heart of the tree beneath them to flow freely. She watched the boards darken.

And she remembered a time, very long ago, when killing people was as routine to her as birthing them.

Kalinda pushed herself up.

Gian pushed in from the kitchen, her blue bonsa weapon out. "Kalinda!"

"Hush," Kalinda said. "They're through. Hurry downstairs and wait for me. I have a few things to gather upstairs."

"Who are they... *were* they?"

"The Kai's," Kalinda said. "My hope is they were trailing Lilia and didn't come specifically for us. If the Kai knows we're here... well. We have far greater concerns. I want Lilia taken to the other side as quickly as possible."

"She doesn't want to go."

"I didn't want to kill these men," Kalinda said, "but my only other option was our deaths. She will come around when she realizes what her choices are. Go."

Gian pounded down the stairs. A good girl, Gian. Kalinda had chosen that one well. It was difficult to keep a gifted girl out of the temple system, but Kalinda had done it and never regretted it. Gian's loyalty was hers now, not the temples'.

Kalinda walked up the curl of the stair and into her room. Pulled a trunk from beneath her bed. The lock had no key. It had to be removed by force. She used a simple burst of air to break the lock. Inside was her blued weapon: a yellow bonsa branch as long as her arm, infused with the power of Para. An implanted weapon here, in this world, would have given her away. All that remained of the retractable weapon she once wielded was an old, twisted scar on her wrist. She pulled her knotted baldric over her vest and sheathed the weapon. She scratched at the little glass bead embedded on the inside of her arm, reassuring herself it remained intact. The night was cool but not cold, so she left her dog-hair coat. She shed her skirt and pulled on more robust traveling pants, dark as the leather of her baldric.

She had a number of people to speak to and plans that had to be set in motion. It was too early for this kind of fighting, far too early. Nava's child, Lilia, should have had another decade to prepare. By then, her studies at the temple would have been finished. One more year, and Kalinda would have taken her aside and begun her formal training. She could have revealed everything more slowly – the coming-together of the worlds, and the bitter war on the horizon – but now... all was in ruin.

Kalinda tugged on the pack stored in the trunk and knotted the long ends of it around her torso. She started downstairs quickly. If they went now, they might be able to make it to the Line station at the Kuallina Stronghold and arrive at the coast by dusk the next day.

She came into the main room.

A blast of air took her off her feet, threw her onto the stairs. She cried out. The pain and shock muddied her reflexes. She reached for the Litany of Breath too late.

Long whips of air pulled her back up. Threw her against the wall again. She saw a splash of blackness across her vision. For a moment, she thought she had lost all sense, because though she knew it was air that held her, she could not see the blue particles of Para's breath. Whatever power this was, she was blind to it.

A tall, dark man approached her, dressed all in tattered black. He wore a long coat and an expression to match. It had been many years since she last saw a sanisi, but the look he gave her was familiar.

"Neat work you did here," the sanisi said, walking across the bloodied floor.

Her head ached. She tried to focus. Still, she saw no breath of Para. Poor time for the star to elude her.

"Stop that," he said. "I'm stronger and better trained, and Oma gives me access to the power of every satellite. You'll exhaust yourself to no purpose. Where is the girl?"

Saiduan had omajistas, then. Things were progressing very fast indeed. She caught a hint of Para. Drew deep, battered at his barriers. Her concentration faltered. She dropped the litany once, twice, a third time.

"I told you to stop," the sanisi said.

"This game is bigger than you," Kalinda said, "played between many different worlds far more powerful than this one. You will lose."

"She's just one," he said. "There are others."

"Among how many millions?" she said. "How long did it take you to find her? And how much longer do you have until it's all over, until they've destroyed you so utterly that you become as we are here?"

"Ah, but you aren't from here, are you?" the sanisi said. "You're one of *them*."

"It's a long contest."

The sanisi walked toward her. Leaned in. They were separated only by a sheet of tangled, translucent air. "A contest I am better suited to in this moment. Let's discuss." He drew his weapon, a plain steel blade.

"Crude," Kalinda said. But she did not doubt his ploy would be effective.

She gritted her teeth and hissed out one final litany. The air she had trapped within the glass bead embedded in her arm burst, spilling the poison it carried into her blood.

Her body began to tighten and seize. They had told her there would be no pain.

The sanisi did not drop his barrier. She remained caught against the wall while her muscles tightened. Her jaw locked.

She wished then that her final words had been better. She wanted to sing of her own life. Her battles and her babies. She wanted to tell the last person she was to ever see the journey that brought her to this world, and how terribly hers was broken. She wanted to spin long about the horrors this sanisi would encounter in the coming months. Words of anger and warning. Portent.

Her vision blurred. The sanisi's face was unreadable.

"A peculiar game," the sanisi said. "I wonder. Are you saving her life to ensure your world survives or ours?"

Kalinda felt the darkness coming. Her stomach began to clench. Pain radiated through her torso. But she had been told there would be no pain.

13

When Anavha Hasaria – then Anavha Lasinyna – was five years old, he hit his sister on the mouth. She had called him something – a name, an insult – he couldn't remember. She bawled and punched him back, in the throat, and told him he was unnatural. Then she told his mother.

His mother took him by the ear and brought him out to the chopping block outside the kitchen, scattering the dajians. She took one of the big, bloody knives left there from the gutting of chickens, and pushed up his skirt. Her big hand covered most of his thigh. She cut him, there on the inside of his thigh, a cut that surprised him more than it hurt. He screamed as the blood welled.

"This is the way Rhea rewards violence in boys," she told him. "Commit enough of it, and she will bleed you dry. You touch any of your sisters again, and I will cut you piece by piece and feed you to the dogs."

The wound had healed slowly but completely and did not even leave a scar. It taught him how deeply he could cut.

Anavha did not understand, at first, his difference. He looked like his sisters, longhaired and thin. One could not tell them apart unless they were dressed up to go somewhere and his mother made him wear a girdle and coat, and belled trousers, usually white. He hated the color, because he always got it dirty. It did not matter when his sisters got their own clothes dirty.

That was natural, his mother told him. Girls did such things. They spoke with loud voices.

When Anavha turned ten, his mother brought him to the religious quarter, and the priests said Rhea had spared him for her service. He was to be owned by a woman and her kin, to bring them pleasure, and children, for the good of Dorinah, the will of Rhea. The men in the mardanas told him he was blessed. Boys who survived to puberty were restricted from brute physical labor. They did not cook, did not clean, and were not to be engaged in any strenuous education beyond the sexual. Men led a life of leisure, never to worry about money, subsistence. The fact that he still breathed proclaimed Anavha's importance to the world. Yes, young boys coveted what Anavha and the other men were. They envied the endless preparation: the dressing, the washing, the oiling, the styling, because it meant they were alive.

Anavha learned his purpose in the mardanas. He began at fourteen, awkward and unsure, encouraged to learn from poor women seeking children or pleasure who paid the temple eight dhorins for the privilege. He couldn't become erect. He was introduced early to a philter drunk with wine that kept him hard for hours; he would lie in bed at night, still in pain from three hours of copulation and an induced erection that could not be fulfilled, merely worn off. His body was not his, they reminded him. It belonged to Rhea.

It was in the mardanas, his first year, that he began to cut himself. Small cuts on the insides of his arms. Just enough to release a thread of blood, leave no scar. He would sit in his room in the mardana listening to the sounds of pants and cries coming through the walls. He sat naked in front of the mirror, studying his every pore, the angles of his body. The blood would come, and he'd dab at it with a little kerchief he kept in a drawer. When the kerchiefs got too stained, he burned them.

At fifteen, he was wed to a woman whose name he knew by reputation: Syre Zezili Hasaria, the most passionate and devastating of the Empress's commanders.

He did not meet Zezili Hasaria until the day of the wedding in Rhea's temple in Daorian. He felt very small in the immense temple, cloaked in white, coat and hood, tunic, belled trousers. Zezili's four sisters were also there, eyeing him over; though there was some resemblance among them, he did not mistake any of them for her.

Zezili dressed in Rhea's purple – purple trousers, tunic, lavender short coat. She wore a black leather belt and ornamental sword, a jeweled dagger. She was, indeed, handsome: tall and broad-shouldered, boldly feminine, with a spill of straight dark hair knotted with purple ribbons. She was a little dark, being half dajian, and her brows nearly met over large, dark eyes. Zezili held herself defensively, as if she expected a fight to break out at any moment. When Anavha stood next to her, he found he was a hand shorter than she. He liked the solid bulk of her, the steadiness.

She will take care of me, he thought. She will protect me.

His first night with Zczili, she made him strip in her bedroom in her country house. She cuffed him across the mouth, drawing blood. She told him to kneel. He was so startled, he did not even cry out.

She took his chin in her hand and said, "You're mine. All of you. Every bit of you. You'll service my sisters, because it's required. But never forget you're mine."

She took out a blade and cut her initials into the flesh between his shoulder blades. When she finished, he was trembling. He heard her set the knife down at her feet deliberately, with a solid thud. He saw the sheen of his blood on the blade. She licked at the blood of his wounds. He gasped. She reached for him and found him, absurdly, embarrassingly erect.

"Well," Zezili said with a laugh, "they paired me well."

Zezili was a brutal mistress, demanding, violent. She entertained herself with him until his vision was hazy, pain and desire twisting his insides, turning his voice to a high-pitched wail, begging for release. Yet when she finished with him, he felt somehow obscene, disassembled. She knew him for what he was.

And he loved her for it.

He sat awake nights and cut himself while she was away; the insides of his arms, his thighs. He spent time examining the big blue veins in his wrists, wondering if Zezili would mourn him if he died, or simply have him replaced, as she would her dog or one of her dajians.

But he always put the knife back down and stored it at the back of the drawer of his dressing table behind a box of white powder, among the kerchiefs. He hoped Daolyn would find it someday, or Zezili, and ask, "What's wrong?"

When Zezili came home for leave this time, she dragged him to bed immediately. Then again twice the next day.

After, he bathed. She attended her foreign guests.

He sat at the end of his bed and began the old ritual, the simple cuts. The knife was comforting in his hand. The knife was something he could control.

He concentrated on the lines, the perfect symmetry. It calmed him.

As he cut, the air around him stirred. His vision blurred. Blood welled down his thigh. A strong wind knocked him back. Bloody haze crept across his vision. The knife slipped, plunged deeply. He cried out.

The world opened.

He fell against the bed, knocking his head. But then the bed was gone. He continued to fall back into... nothing. Darkness. He screamed and scrambled back toward the light. Cold bit at his skin. The air around him swarmed with a fiery mist.

As he groped back into the room, the door opened. Daolyn stood there. Her face contorted. She put her fist to her mouth.

Anavha sat on his knees. Began to shake. His ears popped. The black portal winked out. Half of his bed went missing with it, and the red gauze across his vision lifted. The floor was scorched. Something tickled his lip. He wiped his face and saw his nose was bleeding. The terror was so deep, he could not move. Could not think.

Zezili shook him.

His wife was shaking him.

He told her about the door.

She slapped him.

Anavha began to cry in earnest.

"But he's not a sorcerer," Zezili said. "He was tested as a child, just like anyone else."

Anavha had washed and dressed. He stood now outside the sitting room where Zezili met with their local priest and barely gifted tirajista, Karosia Soafin. The foreign guest had been sent to bed in the quarters across the courtyard. Anavha should have been asleep as well, but the fear and terror of what had happened still coursed through him. He spit out the draught Daolyn had given him to soothe his nerves.

"It's possible to miss one here and there," Karosia said. "My concern is not that he is gifted. My concern is the manifestation of his gift."

"I requested a commonplace husband," Zezili said. "If he's gifted, I won't have him in my house. Those boys go to the Seekers, not the mardanas."

Anavha wanted to claw open the door and beg her to reconsider. Surely it was some kind of fluke. An accident.

"Is it possible it was someone else?" Zezili asked. "Some untrained itinerant passing through who attacked my house?"

"It is... doubtful," Karosia said.

"It must have been an outsider."

"Syre Zezili, my deep concern here is that the ability your husband has manifested has all the hallmarks of a skill we haven't seen in thousands of years. This is a matter for the Seekers. We should call Ryyi Tulana."

"Rhea's bloody bit," Zezili said, "I have no time for this. He was tested. He isn't gifted. And what kind of gift is that? Opening spaces to nowhere? Disintegrating furniture? Who ever heard of that? All I need to know is if he'll harm himself or others again."

"Without assessing his abilities, I cannot say. If you'll allow me to bring him to the local Seeker escort for an assessment–"

"He's not gifted."

"Syre Zezili, I must humbly disagree. He may even have a very special talent. He may be able to draw on the power of all satellites, perhaps even, well, the dark star... It's uncommon, but the astronomers say-"

"An omajista? No. That's all myth and nonsense."

Anavha pressed his palm to his fluttering heart, trying to calm it. Some part of him hoped to be taken away, to ease the monotony. But hearing Zezili insist that he stay comforted him. Somewhere, beneath all the anger and rage, she loved him very much.

"I'll have my dajians keep a close eye on him," Zezili said.

"If you are to keep him here, I suggest that one of my order come to check on him, especially if, as you say, you are to be deployed on a long campaign."

Anavha heard a rustling. Someone standing. He moved away from the door.

"Thank you for your counsel," Zezili said. "I will take it under advisement."

Anavha hurried through the morning light streaming into the courtyard and hid in his room. Daolyn and the house dajians had removed his old bed and set a temporary mattress in its place. He toed the scorched floor. They had not been able to scrub the marks out. The stones themselves had melted.

He sat in front of his vanity mirror and scrutinized his face. Zezili was right, of course. He wasn't gifted. It had to be some accident. Some trick. Zezili had many enemies. He opened the drawer at his side. Stared at the bloody knife and kerchief there. Perhaps he just needed to be more careful for a while. There was no telling who would want to hurt him to strike at Zezili.

When the door opened, his heart leapt. He expected Zezili. But it was just Daolyn. She closed the door and came up behind him. She began to unplait his hair.

"Where's the usual girl?" Anavha said. It had been many years since Daolyn took the time to do his hair.

Her strong fingers loosened the tiny plaits. He watched his dark, twisted hair come free, one lock at a time.

"You'll need to be careful now," Daolyn said.

"Why?" Anavha said. "Zezili will take care of me."

"Only so long as you are useful to her," Daolyn said. "Only so long as she believes she controls you." She began to knot the front of his hair up, to create a crown that ran from his left ear to his right.

"I am hers," Anavha said. "She knows that."

"Perhaps," Daolyn said. "But perhaps things will change."

"They won't change," Anavha said.

"The only constant is change," Daolyn said. "Be ready, child."

"You don't understand what it's like," Anavha said. "I'm all alone here. All I have is Zezili."

Daolyn tied off his braid and began forming a new one, her face neutral. She smoothed the back of his head, like his mother had done when he was a child. "It must indeed be difficult," she said, "to be so alone."

"It is," Anavha said.

She completed the rest of the hairstyling in silence, the perfectly obedient dajian Zezili always said she was.

But her words unsettled him. He wanted to take the knife from the drawer and throw it away. What would happen if he cut himself again? What would happen if Zezili was wrong?

14

Zezili's week of leave was complicated again by the arrival of her near-cousin, Tanasai Laosina, as Zezili and Monshara completed their plans for their assault on the largest of the dajian camps, circling around each other in Zezili's increasingly cramped estate.

Tanasai's arrival was heralded by pounding on the door and the screaming of Zezili's name. Her usual greeting. She enjoyed getting drunk and blaming the hardships and shortcomings of her life on Zezili.

Zezili had given Daolyn permission to admit near-kin, but even Zezili was surprised when Tanasai burst through the estate and pounded directly into Zezili's chamber where Zezili sat astride Anavha.

Tanasai shouted, "Why did she give you this campaign? I was up next for a grand campaign and you gutted it!"

Zezili pushed herself off Anavha and stood, naked. "What's this about?"

Tanasai's dark eyes were wild, red-rimmed. She sounded as if she'd been drinking. She pulled off her helm, letting loose her matted mane of stringy curls.

"I come home and the whole city's talking about it, her giving you some secret campaign. Is she having you take over my legion, too? Is she trying to take off my title?"

Anavha was reaching for his clothes, making little ducking motions, as if hoping Tanasai would not see him.

"She said nothing of the sort," Zezili said. "Go sit down. I'll dress. Daolyn will bring you some... tea."

"I want answers, near-cousin," Tanasai spat.

Tanasai trudged into the courtyard.

Zezili dressed and met Tanasai in the sitting room. Tanasai had already broken the lock on the liquor cabinet and acquired a flagon of wine.

"So, what's this business?" Tanasai asked.

"I'm fucking my husband," Zezili said. "What's *your* business?"

"You know what I'm asking."

"It's just an errand for the Empress. Not a campaign. We won't invade Aaldia or Tordin without you," Zezili said.

"You better not."

"I'm on leave."

"And making the most of it," Tanasai sneered.

"I don't have to pay for sex," Zezili said. Zezili had shared Anavha with her four blood-sisters, but not Tanasai. She couldn't abide the idea of *Tanasai* touching anything that belonged to her.

"She always liked you best," Tanasai said, and Zezili wondered if Tanasai meant her mother or the Empress. Likely both. Zezili's mother had hated Zezili, but when Zezili's mother's sister died, she had hated the burden of caring for wild-haired Tanasai more.

"You know what you came to know," Zezili said. "Go tend your pasture of drunks."

Tanasai's face flushed a deep red. She shoved her helm back on. She sputtered something – maybe something in Tordinian – that sounded like a curse and stepped abruptly out of the sitting room, carrying several bottles of Zezili's liquor. She marched through the courtyard, screaming at dajians as she went. Tanasai had good reason to want to lead a legion against Tordin. It was the only way she would make a name for herself that wasn't synonymous with that of a drunkard.

Zezili followed her to the door. Daolyn locked the gate behind her.

"Do I have to let her in anymore?" Daolyn asked.

"No. If I'm not here, don't let her enter. She won't be happy until this campaign is over and the Empress sends us to fight the people we should actually be fighting."

The rest of her leave passed uneventfully. Anavha cried a bit over some perceived hurt or other, and Zezili ignored him until he became docile again. He had no more… episodes. She chalked up the business in his room to some outside anomaly. On the day of her departure, he threw himself at her feet and cried and begged her not to go. Zezili curled a lip in disgust. She made Daolyn pull him off.

She dressed in a clean tunic and newly polished armor, and cinched on her skirt of metal and dajians' hair. Daolyn checked all of her straps and knots, and Zezili took her leave. Daolyn closed the door behind her. Zezili patted her massive dog, Dakar, in greeting, fed him a treat, and mounted.

Monshara already waited there, sitting atop a massive black-and-white bear. Dakar did not take well to the bear. Zezili could both hear and feel him growling low. She thumped his rump. Training bears and dogs to tolerate one another started early; she had made sure to select him from a kennel that raised him alongside bear cubs. But there was no accounting for individual dislike. She wasn't fond of Monshara or the bear either.

"There's been enough fucking in your house for eight women," Monshara said.

"I fight better than I fuck, if that's any consolation," Zezili said.

"I look forward to finally seeing it."

They traveled northeast, to the city of Cholina, and met Zezili's second, Syre Jasoi, and three hundred of the five thousand members of Zezili's legion. Jasoi had cleaned up for the occasion and smelled heavily of pomade. She had knobby knees and a pinched, fox-like face, but she was good with a blade and smart on the field for a Tordinian.

Monshara inspected the lines of women for nearly an hour before finally reining up beside Zezili. "They'll do," she said. "Some are very drunk, however."

"We're only killing a few dajians," Zezili said, "not invading Saiduan."

Monshara barked a hollow laugh. The laugh went on and on, far more laughter than Zezili thought the joke warranted.

"Will you introduce me?" Monshara asked when she recovered.

Zezili grimaced but spurred her dog forward and called to the line, "This is Monshara, my co-general. You will obey her as you would me. Disobeying her is disobeying me. I will personally mete out punishment to any woman displaying insubordination. You'll be stripped and lashed to start, and hung if necessary. Our duty in the coming months is a simple but critical task. I received it from the lips of the Empress herself." Zezili paused for effect. Tried to think how she'd have responded if her own superior told her what she was about to propose.

"For centuries, the dajians have been a plague on our country. Cannibalistic parasites whose cheap labor keeps you all from cozy jobs in your old age. You spent your youth on patrols, putting down petty dajian insurgencies instead of conquering land for the Empress. You've wasted the better part of your lives policing a people that are little better to us than pack animals. Now the day has come to put our country in order. Our Empress has tasked us with their removal. We free our country from their tyranny. We free ourselves. We march to the Saolyndara camp to the north, and we offer their blood to Rhea. Today, we take back our country."

The cheer then was more exuberant than Zezili expected. She plastered a grin onto her face. I'm Dorinah, she thought. If there was any doubt, today will prove that.

The killing started not long after. They purged three small camps of half-starved dajians near Saolyndara, rounding them up from the local farms that rented them for day labor. Zezili killed at least forty herself, with her own hands. It was a strange, senseless sort of killing that drove Zezili to drink after. She had no trouble killing people for a cause, but this was a waste of her talent and the talent of her women. There was no honor in it, no satisfaction. It was like murdering litters of puppies.

What was the Empress trying to accomplish? She had to know how much this would disrupt the harvest next year. Half of Dorinah would starve if the dajians were dead. Zezili wanted to ask Monshara but feared the answer. *Do as you're told,* the Empress would say. *Don't you trust my love for you?*

Then they cleared the big camp inside Saolyndara proper. They murdered eight hundred and forty-seven dajians there.

As Zezili sat in her tent that afternoon, penning a long, laborious letter to the Empress, the muddy blood of the dead caked her boots. The day was clear and warm, but the blood had turned the field to mud.

Monshara met her in the tent after the count was made. She removed her shiny armored helm and regarded Zezili with gray eyes.

"What?" Zezili asked.

"You were right," Monshara said.

Zezili grunted.

"You are better at killing than fucking," Monshara said.

"You best consult with my husband before making that judgment."

"I could consult or know for myself."

Zezili snorted. "I don't rent him out."

"Not him."

"I'm still not interested."

"A shame." Monshara put her helm back on, so when Zezili finally looked at her, she could not see her expression clearly. She half thought the woman was joking.

"It's a week's travel to the next camp," Zezili said. "If you're itching, Cholina has a good mardana."

"It's not that kind of itch," Monshara said, and left the tent.

Zezili frowned. She heard something drip onto the page, and saw a spot of blood. She looked up. Someone had tossed a bloody severed arm onto the top of the tent. Blood had soaked through the thin hide.

She grimaced and moved to the other side of the table.

Saolyndara's done, she wrote. *Eight hundred and forty-seven dajians dispatched at the main camp, at your order. We begin our march to our next camp tomorrow. I will update you at its end. I do hope you will give me a more challenging campaign. My women make better fighters than butchers.*

She sealed the letter.

Outside, she heard someone keening.

The cry was cut short.

She scratched out "forty-seven" and wrote "forty-eight."

Monshara ducked back into the tent. "Are you coming?"

"For what?" Zezili asked.

"We're opening a gate," Monshara said. "My sovereign wants to meet you, and I don't want all this fine Dhai blood to go to waste."

15

Two weeks after his sister's death, Ahkio took the title of Kai. He stood at the center of the great Sanctuary in the heart of Oma's temple, bathed in the crimson light of the double suns streaming through the red face of Oma represented in the domed glass above him. The elder Oras were all in attendance, as well as the temple's novices, full Oras, and their assistants, but as Elder Ora Gaiso bathed his hair in his sister's blood, he saw that just half the country's clan leaders sat in attendance. Nasaka had told him that before the ceremony, but hearing a thing and seeing it were different experiences. Fear and horror gripped him suddenly, powerfully, and he could not shake it. Nasaka had offered him a way out of taking up this burden, and he'd refused it. Now he was alone amid a sea of faces who saw an ungifted boy given a sacred title that few, if any, believed him capable of holding for any length of time.

He glanced over at Nasaka. Her face was, as ever, unreadable. She sat at a table with Elaiko and the clan leader of Sorai – Hona Fasa Sorai, her assistant, and another young woman, very fair, in her mid-twenties, who Ahkio took to be Hona's daughter.

Eight letters to Meyna had gone unanswered. Still, Ahkio searched for her face among those sitting behind Nasaka at the great yellow adenoak tables. The only kin of his he saw were distant cousins, twice or three times removed. Only Liaro had written him, a letter of sympathy for Kirana's death. Ahkio kept it

under his pillow where he slept now, in Kirana's large bed behind
the Kai study, at the very top of the temple.

Nasaka rose from her place at the table and picked up the silver
plate that bore what remained of his sister's preserved heart. She
brought it to the dais and offered it to Ahkio.

Ahkio took a sliver of Kirana's heart. He had eaten most of her
heart the day after she died; the act of eating her heart amid this
stoic crowd was largely symbolic. He sent up a prayer to Oma
then, because in all likelihood, Oma was close enough to hear
him, now: *if I'm not the right person for this seat, you need to show me
another path.*

He swallowed the flesh of his sister's heart and became Kai.

The funerary chefs and kitchen drudges brought in the dishes
prepared from his sister's well-salted body – blood sausage and
blood pudding, fried liver, sweetly seasoned ribs and delicate
finger bones dipped in lemon juice and butter. The meal was
complemented by honey wine and blackberry liquor, as well as
other delicacies such as roasted fiddleheads, bracken tops, and
nasturtiums.

When the ceremony was finished, he made polite talk with
the clan leaders and Oras. Nasaka stayed at his side, too close for
his comfort, and after an hour of too much wine in the too-warm
Sanctuary, he evaded her by escaping to the privy at the end of
the hall.

He sat there listening to the rush of water running underneath
the bank of stone seats and purling down the washing sinks,
until three novices burst in, eyes bright, voices loud – already a
little drunk.

Ahkio pushed out of the privy and nearly fell into Elaiko.

"Kai," she said, and he winced. He wished he were as drunk
as the novices.

"There's a man here for you," Elaiko said. "Your cousin?"

"There he is!"

Ahkio knew the voice. He hurried past Elaiko, toward the
great foyer.

Liaro waved to him from the bottom of the stairs, a lumpy pack slung over one shoulder.

Ahkio held out his arms, and Liaro stepped into his embrace.

"Oma, cousin," Ahkio said. "You don't know how good it is to see you."

"I came as quickly as I could," Liaro said. "Sina, look at your hair! Is the ascension over?"

"I would have liked you here sooner. Where's Meyna?"

Liaro cleared his throat. "Ah. Meyna. Well, about that-"

"What are you doing out here?" Nasaka asked, pushing her way out of the Sanctuary.

Ahkio sighed. "Can I have two minutes of peace with my cousin?" he said.

"Are you expecting Lohin to come in this late?" Liaro asked, gesturing back toward the foyer. "I passed him and some Garika militia on the way in. Seemed odd they didn't show up sooner."

"Kirana's husband?" Ahkio asked. "With... militia? We invited Tir's whole family – Lohin, Yisaoh – just as I invited Meyna and her husbands. No one responded. Are you sure it was him?"

"Could have been some dancing minstrels dressed like militia, I suppose," Liaro said, "but I expect that's even less likely."

"How close?" Nasaka asked. She gripped the end of her willowthorn sword, and the branch snarled itself around her wrist. Ahkio's stomach dropped. He knew what was coming, knew it and still tried to deny it.

"They're just a few minutes behind me," Liaro said. "On the plateau. What? Is that bad?"

"Blood and ashes," Nasaka swore.

Roh woke in the infirmary, rattled awake by a seething tide of nightmares. The black spill of light trailing Oma clawed at him, engulfed him. The world was a sea of red rain that strangled the fields and washed away the Temple of Oma, cracking the great dome, showering jagged glass onto novices and Oras, severing limbs and making ribbons of their organs.

It was the smell he noticed first, like burnt black tea. Para's light spilled through the glass ceiling – which he was surprised to see whole after the dream – blinding him in blue light.

"Roh?"

His brother Chali stood over him, round face scrunched with concern.

"Where's the sanisi?" Roh asked.

"He left some time ago. Are you all right? The whole family came to see you. Ora Nasaka sent them away yesterday."

"I need to talk to Ora Dasai."

Chali held out a hand. Roh took it. Chali was almost thirty and acted like he knew everything, but Roh had never seen him look so scared. "Stay in bed," Chali said.

"I feel fine," Roh said. Hunger pinched his stomach. He wasn't sure how long he'd been in bed. "What day is it?"

"The new Kai's day of ascension. You've been out almost two weeks."

"Two weeks? The Kai... is Kai Kirana dead?"

"I'm sorry," Chali said. "You've missed a lot. Yes, she passed. Her brother, Kai Ahkio, has taken her title."

"Where's Li?" Roh said. "Was Lilia here? My friend." She was always in the infirmary. He had a memory of her next to him.

"You mean the girl who went with the sanisi?" Chali asked.

"He took *her* and not me?"

"You should rest."

"I need to see Ora Dasai. The sanisi should have taken me."

"You were nearly dead. Rest. Ora Dasai is taking a group of scholars north. He wanted to make sure you were all right before then. I think he feels responsible."

Roh clutched at his stomach, searching for a wound that was no longer there. He pulled at the front of his tunic and realized it wasn't his. He wore a white tunic and trousers, like an invalid, instead of his novice clothes. When he raised up the tunic, he saw no wound, no scar.

"I was hurt, wasn't I?"

"Someone attacked you," Chali said. "We hoped you could say who it was."

Roh searched his memory. He remembered pain and surprise; a deep betrayal. "I don't know," he said. "Chali, Ora Chali, I need to go north with you."

"That's not my decision, Roh."

"But you're going," Roh said. "Ora Dasai asked you, didn't he?"

"If I want to be an Elder Ora, travel abroad would help my case," he said. "In eighty years—"

"Eighty years!" Roh said. "I don't care about what happens in eighty years. I care about *today*."

"I'm going to get Elder Ora Gaiso," Chali said, and stood. He left Roh's side before he could say any more.

Roh sat at the edge of the bed, staring at his hands. Something terrible had happened after Dasai sent him downstairs. Why couldn't he remember?

He found a clean set of clothes on the other bed. They were drudge clothes – gray tunic and trousers, and no green apron. He expected to feel weaker, but his legs held his weight, and he did not tremble. It must have been a very skilled tirajista who saved him. He dressed carefully and waited. And waited.

Loud voices came from the hall. He crept to the door, barefoot, and opened it. The corridor outside the infirmary curved before reaching the foyer, so he couldn't see anything from there. But he heard the strange sound of hissing weapons; the same sound two infused swords made on meeting. It was a sound he had never heard outside a practice yard.

Roh recited the Litany of Breath. He held the breath of Para close, just beneath his skin, and ran into the corridor, toward the sound of the fighting. He ran headlong into a massive clutch of whirling bodies – red-wrapped militia, green-aproned novices, and full Oras, all coming together in a violent melee. He saw the blue mist of Para's breath suffusing the parajistas he knew, but saw no structures being built, no woven weapons. Using gifted arts against the non-gifted was the gravest of crimes. But as Roh watched blood spattering the temple floor, it seemed like a terrible prohibition.

He ran into the sprawl to see if he could figure out who they were fighting. As he did, he saw the Kai's brother, Ahkio, run past him, back toward the Sanctuary. Roh knew him from his early days at the temple, when the Kai's brother visited her more often. Ahkio's hair was matted with blood; the ascension ceremony, Chali had said. Was someone trying to take the country now, before the Kai came into power? Three militia members sprinted after Ahkio.

Roh did not hesitate. He grabbed the nearest militia woman by the collar of her tunic and yanked her back. He jabbed her twice in the kidneys, just as he'd learned in his defense classes. He took her everpine sword. The hilt curled around his wrist. He ran after the others. Ahkio entered the Sanctuary just as the two militia turned to see what had become of their companion.

Roh jumped up and jammed the fist of his weapon into the face of the one closest to him. He felt bone crunch. Blood spattered. He swung his blade just as the second man thrust forward. Their weapons met. Roh rolled smoothly away, ducked behind him, and hacked at the back of his legs. The second man fell.

Out of breath, his blood already pounding with adrenaline, Roh pushed into the Sanctuary – and stopped short. He still held Para beneath his skin. He itched to send an attacker spinning off into the void.

Almeysia stood at the center of the Sanctuary, facing Ahkio.

She raised her gaze to Roh's, and he knew.

It was not a full memory. It was not some arcane knowledge. Just instinct. Something terrible passed between them in that moment. It was her fault. She had attacked him in the hall. Closed his eyes, so he could not see.

Almeysia was a tirajista, but a very sensitive one. It meant she could draw more deeply on Tira than many of her contemporaries, even in decline. Roh knew that, but he shook off his sword and channeled Para anyway.

The floor of the Sanctuary shook. Roh spun up a vortex of air as a slithering fanged vine burst from the floor of the temple, cracking through stones and overturning tables.

Roh pressed forward, unfazed, as the vine lashed at him, battering itself against the whirling winds. He ignored Ahkio's defensive stance and focused more intently on his creation, intensifying the howling winds. He had never felt so powerful.

The fingers of the vine burst apart. The trunk split in two.

Another vine surfaced. Then another.

The third one nearly broke his concentration. Roh stumbled back. The vine caught him around one leg.

Ahkio stepped forward, grabbed Roh's discarded sword–

–and sliced Roh free.

Ahkio was yelling something at him, but Roh knew the minute he lost his focus, Almeysia would conjure something to eat him. He pressed forward across the cracked stones and shattered bits of the tables, the burst vegetal matter and broken thorns.

He hadn't mastered the ability to hold a shield and deploy an offense at the same time. Almeysia hounded him with more and more attacks. He broke a stout rattler tree, and severed woody varga vines, all the time advancing on her position.

Almeysia had to work harder for her manifestations, though. As he came forward, he saw she was drawn and trembling. Sweat soaked her tunic.

He was younger, fitter, and his star was ascendant.

The Sanctuary doors burst open behind him.

A blast of air took him off his feet. He created a fast bubble of air to cushion his fall and landed lightly on the other side of the Sanctuary.

Almeysia took the full force of the attack. The great stone lanterns of the gods ringing the altar smashed against the far side of the Sanctuary. Almeysia went with them, tossed to the floor like a tangle of seaweed.

Roh let go of Para. The tension that had held him upright left his body. Exhaustion rolled over him. He sank to his knees.

On the other side of the Sanctuary, Nasaka and Ohanni stood with Ahkio. Ohanni was a parajista and still had a whirling cone of air circling her, churning up dust and debris. Roh could see the misty blue shape of it, sapphire streamers whirling from her fingers.

The Sanctuary was a ragged mess of twisted, seeping plant flesh and broken tables. Tattered paper lanterns tumbled across the floor. The tiles of the floor were broken, jagged in places where Almeysia's plants had torn through.

"Oma's breath," Ohanni said. "Did you do this, Roh?"

Nasaka strode across the Sanctuary to Almeysia. "She's alive," Nasaka said. "Bring a draught, Ora Ohanni. I want her drugged. And you–" Nasaka turned to Roh. "You stay where you are. You have much to explain."

Roh stared into his hands. He had never been in a fight before. Not a real one.

He fell to his knees, trembling. He should be retching, he knew. He should be horrified at causing harm.

But he had never felt so alive.

16

The boar spiders swarmed Lilia at the edge of the Woodland. Each spider stood as high as her knee and whispered forth from deep burrows hidden by floxflass nests. Lilia froze, the way her mother had taught her. The spiders clambered up her trousers. One perched on her head. She closed her mouth and breathed through her nose, trying to stay calm. Boar spiders were like hornets – they only bit when provoked – but she was hungry and exhausted, and the fear that roiled over her was paralyzing.

The swarm continued to gain strength. She must have stepped on a nest. Nests were often connected, and her misstep had triggered others in the area. She closed her eyes so she did not have to look at their fangs.

A poor way to die, she thought, before even stepping foot in the woodlands.

She began to count her breaths. Something heavy, much larger than a spider, crunched in the undergrowth.

A vortex of air blasted her from above. She flailed, barely kept her feet. The tendrils of air bundled up dozens of spiders and propelled them into the dark woods around her. Lilia heard them land in the trees and crunch in the undergrowth. Several smashed wetly into massive tree trunks.

She opened her eyes.

Gian stood before her, just a dozen steps down the path, blue-glowing bonsa sword in hand. She looked much taller out here, formidable, like some historic hero from a tapestry come to life. A bear snuffled behind her, licking its snout.

Lilia patted herself down, skin still crawling with the memory of the spiders. "I was all right," she said.

Gian smirked and came forward. "Of course you were."

Lilia scrambled away from her, back into the hanging ivy that flanked the path. "I'm not going with you."

"Aren't you?"

"I'm sorry. Tell Kalinda–"

"Kalinda's dead."

"Oh, no."

"A sanisi," Gian said. She sheathed her weapon, putting out the blue glow of it, surrendering them again to the dim light that filtered through the forest canopy. Lilia wasn't sure of the time of day. She'd been walking for hours, and her bad leg throbbed. Her breath came so heavy, she'd had to stop twice and take her mahuan powder.

"Taigan killed her?"

"Is that his name?" Gian surveyed the woodland around them, as if looking for more spiders.

"Shouldn't you be an Ora? You can channel Para. All the jistas become Oras."

"Not all," Gian said. "Some become healers and seers, those with poorer gifts." She leaned in to Lilia, peering at her as if she were a mystery that needed unraveling. She had broad cheekbones and black, black eyes. Lilia thought she might stumble into them. "And some of us believe in freedom of the individual over the tyranny of the common good."

Lilia wasn't sure what that meant but let it lie. "What are you going to do, now that you've found me?"

"Lot of things I could do, couldn't I? Wrap you up in a vortex and cart you back to my safe house. Maybe just cut you in two and leave you here."

"You sound like the sanisi," Lilia said.

"Don't try and shame me," Gian said. "It was my aunt killed back there. The woman who saved you, and me, and at least a hundred other children from that hungry war and the Kai's army back home."

"What war?" Lilia said. The Dhai had no armies. She shook her head. "You're trying to confuse me."

"Maybe," Gian said. Lilia wasn't sure she liked the way Gian looked at her. "How far away is this place you think you lived?"

"It's on the coast. The other side of the woodland. In the northeast. There's a peninsula that juts into the sea."

"Fasia's Point. Yes, I know it."

"It has a name?"

"Most things do."

"We can lose the sanisi in the woodland," Lilia said, trying quickly to come up with a rational reason to plunge ahead. "He'll know every road. Take me to Fasia's Point. By the time we come back, he'll have lost us."

"What happens after Fasia's Point?"

"Then, I'll... I'll go wherever you want." She held out her scarred wrists, an old habit. "I swear it."

Gian stared at her outstretched arms. "Your mother was a blood witch, wasn't she?"

Lilia dropped her arms. "Where did you hear that? No one says that."

"In the valley, they don't," Gian said. "In the woodlands, they do. And... other places." For the first time, Gian pulled her hand away from her bonsa sword. The branch loosened its hold on her wrist, retracted. "I'll take you to Fasia's Point so you can see what's there. But you won't find your mother."

"I promised I'd go back."

"So after I take you there, and we lose the sanisi, and you see what you can see, you go where I want. No fuss. No arguing. No running off into the night alone."

"Why does it matter?"

"Because I made a promise, too, to Kalinda. I promised no

harm would come to you, and I'd deliver you to her people. I make good on my promises. In that, we're alike."

"I'll go," Lilia said. Roh's life for hers, fulfilling her promise for Gian's... she was trading a good many things these days, all of which involved her freedom. She was done bargaining, but Gian didn't need to know that yet.

They spent the rest of the day climbing up into the hills. Lilia knew they entered the Woodland proper at dusk, because that's where the formal road ended. They traveled instead on a mossy path lined in red roses and fireweed. The trees, too, changed, from elegant and well-groomed bonsa trees to tangled rattlers and stinging foreshore. The trees grew twisted and massive, like a maze constructed by a mad giant with a very perverse idea of how to channel Tira. But it was the bone trees that evoked the Woodland the most for Lilia. She saw her first in many years as they climbed through a crush of rattler trees that grew across the path, Gian's bear chomping through what they could not clear themselves. The bone tree stood alone in a little clearing, no taller than Lilia. Its dirty yellowish trunk and spiny branches were made of literal bone, the remnants of the small mammals and birds it caught in its clawed branches. The creatures were drawn by the sweet smell of the poisonous sap it secreted. The sap killed all nearby plant life, too, hence the patch of dead ground ringing the tree. A dozen long-toothed, grinning skulls made up one branch of the tree, twisted together with amber sap and a shimmering silver webbing of organic matter. The skulls were no bigger than her palm. They were treeglider skulls.

That night, they camped in an area Gian carved out for them just off the path. The cyclone she called cleared a perfect circle of poisonous vines and biting saplings. Lilia poked around in the underbrush, looking for bladder traps or root hooks.

"How's your leg?" Gian asked. She crushed a handful of scorch pods together and lay flat on her belly in front of their flickering light to kindle a fire.

"Fine," Lilia said. In truth, the pain had become constant. She rested when she could but considered it a point of pride to keep up with Gian.

"Really?"

"No. But when people ask, they don't really want an answer. They want reassurance that it's all right not to care."

Gian pushed herself up, wiped her hands on her tunic. "Is that so?"

"I know how people are."

Gian unpacked sticky balls of rice and dried mangos. "You must not know a lot of people," she said, and offered the food to Lilia.

Hunger got the better of her. Lilia ate quickly and fell asleep not long after. She woke briefly when Gian bent over her with a thick bedroll. "I brought two," Gian said. "Get inside before the bugs eat you up."

Lilia crawled into the bedroll and slept like death.

Gian woke her at dawn the next day, and they started out again. Gian led the way with her sword, hacking at vegetation that clogged the path.

"Tell me a story," Gian asked as she hacked away.

"What about?"

"Temple life. Baking. Did you do a lot of baking? What do ungifted people get up to there? It'll be more than a week to Fasia's Point, maybe two, at this pace."

So, Lilia told her stories of strategy games and dancing class. She talked about Roh and Saronia and the temple's great library. At night, when Lilia's legs cramped up, Gian came to her side, asked to take Lilia's feet into her palms, and pressed the balls of her feet forward to help lengthen her seizing muscles.

"Did you have any lovers in the temple?" Gian asked.

They lay next to one another in a clearing deep in the hills, staring up through a rare break in the canopy at the great patterned map of the stars above them. Lilia had never seen so many stars – the blackest time of the night, between Para's rise and fall – lasted only a few hours. She had never sat up that long.

"No," Lilia said. "I'm not like other Dhai."

"You're just fine for a Dhai."

"What about you? Did the sanisi... did he hurt anyone else at Kalinda's?"

"There's just me here," Gian said. "I came alone."

"What do you mean?"

She sighed. "We'll be at Fasia's Point soon. You'll know why you need to come with me then."

"What did you want to be?" Lilia asked.

"What?"

"When you were younger."

"I'm only twenty."

"Did you always just hit people with a sword for Kalinda?"

Gian laughed. Lilia loved to hear her laugh; it was a rich, deep laugh. She wished she was better at telling jokes, just so she could hear it more.

"I want to save the world," Gian said.

"Is that all?"

Gian turned onto her side, propped herself up on one arm. She caught Lilia with her black stare, and Lilia's heart raced. Gian leaned forward, as if she might kiss her. Which would be an absurd thing to do without consent. But Lilia did not move. Gian paused, her face a breath from Lilia's.

"It's full of many things worth saving," Gian said.

It took nearly two weeks to reach the coast. They had to abandon the bear outside a tangled woodland it could not squeeze through. By then, the sticky rice was nearly gone, supplemented with fiddleheads, acorn meal, and whatever half-digested fruit remains that had fallen into the massive pitcher plants littering the boggy areas around springs and streambeds.

Lilia smelled the sea long before she saw it. When they pushed into a ragged clearing and beheld the edge of the plateau and pounding violet waters below, she caught her breath. The sky was pale lavender along the horizon and brilliant azure blue above, on fire with the light of Para.

"Familiar?" Gian asked.

"Yes," Lilia said. "The smell is, at least."

"Just a little farther north," Gian said. "That's when the plateau breaks off into the sea."

They followed a game trail the rest of the day, keeping the sea to their left. Lilia spotted a treeglider staring at them from the lowest branches of a rattler tree, its eyes bright. Somewhere distant, Lilia heard the familiar hulking crash of a walking tree.

They drove deeper into the plateau. Gian kept asking her if anything looked familiar. But Lilia saw no signs of her old village – no decaying cocoons or the charred remains of seedpods.

Then Lilia saw it.

A gray spur of rock jutting up from the weeds on the other side of a broad clearing. She knew that ledge. She had played there. It didn't look nearly as tall, of course. What a foolish child she'd been, to think that she could fly if she just had enough faith.

Lilia hurried across the clearing, looking for the remains of the thorn fence. But there were no bunches of sticks or charred root balls. All she saw were the shriveled poppies, their leaves browning with the coming of low autumn.

Gian called after her. Lilia kept going.

She scrambled around the rock ledge and up the low hill, following the creek. As she came over the rise of the hill, she half expected to see the massive webbing that protected her village. She was out of breath and wheezing hard, harder than she had the whole trip.

Lilia gasped and stumbled. Caught herself on a nearby tree. Ahead was a grove of birch trees. Massive butterfly cocoons as long as Lilia's arm hung from their branches. A few of the cocoons were as large as Lilia herself. She saw scattered seedpods on the ground, just big enough for a small child to hide in. In the distance, on the other side of the hill, she heard the thrashing of walking trees and shuddered. There was no webbing here to keep them out.

She saw no broken old trees or char in what should have been her village; nothing had been touched by fire here for hundreds of years, at least. The grove itself was not inhabited. She saw no paths. No stone structures.

This place had never been her home.

Gian came up behind her. "Is this it?"

Lilia nodded. Her chest hurt.

"I need my mahuan powder," Lilia said, wheezing.

Gian retrieved the powder. She bent next to Lilia, mixed the powder with water, and made her drink it.

Lilia coughed and coughed. She pointed to the chalky outcrop below them, obscured now by the woods they had traveled through. "That's where I saw... the riders. The Kai and her militia. It was... It was right *here*."

"Strangled heart," Gian said. "Don't you see, yet?"

"Hey there!"

A man rounded the top of the rise in what had been Lilia's village. He raised a large walking stick, then began climbing down toward them.

Gian rose. "He's a woodland Dhai," she said.

Lilia finished her mahuan powder as the man came toward them. The day was hot, and he was bare-chested. He wore what looked like fibrous trousers. A linen tunic hung from his belt. He carried no pack, only the walking stick.

"Are you traveling alone?" he said. "You valley Dhai?"

Lilia noticed his accent now; she had met a few other woodland Dhai at the temple. She didn't have much of an accent anymore, but his felt warm and familiar.

"Is there a village here?" Lilia asked. She coughed. "Maybe... they moved?"

"Village?" he said. "No. I'm sorry to bother you, but if you're traveling on your own, you should know there's a man in the woods, a hunter. Foreign. Saiduan. I've been through three family camps now, all dead. I bedded down with another group just last night. Two girls there said he's been looking for one of ours." He glanced at Lilia. "Young temple girl, they said."

"Thank you," Gian said. "We'll keep an eye out."

He gestured behind him. "There are family camps just up the peninsula, if you're looking for rest or company. You look thin. Are you hungry?"

"We're fine," Gian said.

Lilia noticed then that he'd come from the direction of the crashing trees. No one – especially not a woodland Dhai, who should know better – would have trekked up the other side of that hill through a herd of walking trees.

She glanced behind them, back at the game trail they'd followed along the coast. "Ahead of us?" she said. "You mean the camps are behind us, where *you* came from."

He grinned. Too hard. "Not sure I follow." He pointed back up the hill with his stick. "I came down from there."

"You doubled around," Lilia said. "You circled behind us and came up the hill to pretend you were ahead of us. Why were you following us?"

Gian put her hand on the butt of her willowthorn sword. The hilt of it elongated and curled around her wrist.

"Hold on now," the man said, raising his free hand. "He said you were a temple Dhai, but you do have the eye of a woodlander, don't you?"

"I don't want to kill anyone," Gian said. "I suggest you move on and tell the sanisi you couldn't find us."

"Afraid I can't do that," he said, and Lilia noticed a trembling in his voice. "He sent me to track you. I turn back now and he kills me and my family."

"Then we are at an impasse," Gian said.

The man grinned again.

He lashed out with his heavy stick.

Gian yanked her sword out, too late. His stick thumped her in the chest, sent her stumbling back.

He grabbed Lilia's arm.

Lilia shrieked and kicked at the dirt. She remembered chitinous red armor. Heavy air. And the trefoil with the long tail. She closed her eyes until she saw the bright, burning image of the trefoil in her mind.

It will bring you back to me, her mother had said, but it had brought her back to the wrong place.

Lilia kicked the man in the knee. He cursed, stumbled back. Swung his stick. Lilia covered her face.

Pain seared her skin. Brilliant light surged across her vision. The image of the trefoil burst in her mind. A whump of air knocked her back. She landed hard on her tailbone. The man screeched.

Gian ran forward. Lilia's head ached; she began to tremble violently, uncontrollable spasms that shook her whole body. Her jaw clenched. Gian killed me, she thought.

The man was screaming. Screaming. The way they had screamed in the village.

"It's all right," Gian said. She made little shushing sounds. "It's all right."

Lilia thought Gian was talking to the man, but as her vision cleared, she saw Gian crouching next to her, one hand on her forehead, the other on her sternum, holding her down as she jerked and flailed on the forest floor.

The fit lasted several minutes. When it was over, Lilia was exhausted, spent.

Gian asked to take Lilia into her arms and carried her back down the hill to the clearing near the rocky outcrop. Lilia had not realized how strong she was. Lilia buried her face in Gian's hair and wept.

Gian held her while she cried.

"It's all right," Gian said. Her voice sounded distant. She was staring off into the woods. "I drew too much. I hurt you, too. I'm sorry. I won't let that happen again."

"You can't do that," Lilia said. "You can't hurt the ungifted like that."

"I used up a great deal of power," Gian said. "It was my fault. Sometimes, I panic and pull too much. Kalinda says it'll burn me out someday."

"What did you do to him?"

"I flayed him," Gian said. "Don't go back there. I'll get his heart and his liver. We'll eat well tonight."

"The sanisi will find us."

"He's close, no doubt," Gian said. "But we'll keep moving. My people aren't far from here. It's why I agreed to take you. Just another day to the northeast, and you'll have your answers."

Lilia saw the bloody body of the man crumpled on the hill. Gian could do anything she wanted with her. She wasn't bound by temple rules. Why had she taken Lilia's bargain, then?

"Kalinda wanted you kept safe from the Kai," Gian said. "My friends can protect you better than I can."

"Kalinda brought me *to* the Kai. I live at the Temple of Oma where the Kai *lives*. Kalinda never saved me from anything. She delivered me to her door!"

Gian stood. "I need to prepare his heart and liver," she said. "Do you like dandelion greens?"

Lilia pressed her fists against her eyes. "Why won't you tell me anything?"

"You'll understand when you meet the others," Gian said. "I did what you asked and brought you here. Now you fulfill your end. You join me."

Lilia watched the hourglass of the suns begin to set in the blue-lavender sky above her. Lavender, not amber. The leaves here were just beginning to turn, far up in the forest canopy.

Lilia struggled to her feet. The sky. The leaves. The village.

"What is it?" Gian asked.

Lilia walked back down to the stone outcrop. She gazed toward the clearing where the thorn fence had been, and stared at the sky. The blue-lavender sky. She covered her mouth.

"Lilia?" Gian asked.

"Oma," Lilia said. "The sky. It's the wrong color."

Gian's expression was unreadable.

Lilia persisted. "I thought it was because Tira's descendent now. But the sky here, right here, wasn't this color when I lived here. When the village was here. It was amber, and it caught fire at sunset, like a crimson cloak. Oh, no; oh, no..."

"Lilia, I'm sorry," Gian said. "I can explain–"

Lilia's legs gave out. She leaned against the rock outcrop. Terror squeezed her insides. "That's why everything is different here," Lilia said. "Dhai has no conscripted army here. The Kai wears no armor. This isn't where my village was at all, is it?"

Gian shook her head.

Lilia burst into tears at the sad expression on Gian's face. It was pity. Pity for a foolish child piece on a kindar board who suddenly understood the whole world was make-believe.

"I'm not from this world, am I?" Lilia said. "And neither are you and Kalinda. That's why you put me with the Kai in Oma's Temple. It's not this Kai you're fighting."

"No," Gian said.

"You're fighting a Kai somewhere else," Lilia said. "You're fighting a woman who looks just like her, from a world with an amber sky."

17

The churning mud sucked at Zezili's boots as she slogged across the remains of the camp. Her legionnaires milled about the field, gutting corpses from navel to neck to check if the dajians had swallowed any valuables before the raid. Zezili couldn't imagine dajians having anything worth stealing in a camp like this, but some had been known to flee their owners after stealing from them. She heard the grumbling of her women as she went; easy slaughter was appreciated, but not cheap slaughter. Fighting that paid in nothing but blood would sour them quickly. She made a note to have a hundred kegs of cheap wine hauled in after the next raid. Mounts – a skinny dog or pox-ridden bear – were good prizes, too, for the most exuberant killers.

Monshara waited at the center of the field. She sat astride her great black-and-white bear. Zezili had left Dakar behind; she had no interest in tacking him up just to watch some petty bit of magic.

Four riders came through the camp, riding great bears like Monshara's. They didn't look like Monshara, though. They looked the same way Hofsha had – like Dhai. Zezili's skin crawled. Were they opening a door of some kind to Dhai? Why would the Dhai want to kill dajians? They were petty pacifists. They'd vomit at the sight of blood.

"So what exactly are you going to do now?" Zezili called.

"My sovereign wishes to meet you," Monshara said. "These agents of mine will open the way. I'll keep them with the legion from here on out. We may need them."

"Opening the way... to where you're from?"

"Yes."

"Are they some kind of mutant jista?"

"Nothing so grand. These are friends of mine. Omajistas."

"Omajistas?" Zezili laughed. "There aren't..." She caught herself. What had Anavha said? *"I opened a door."*

"We put these omajistas in place many years ago," Monshara said.

"Years ago? Oma's a myth."

"Like Rhea?" Monshara said. Zezili rankled. "Oma appears from between spaces. One cannot track it like a comet. Even Para, Tira, Sina are irregular bodies. We can make estimates, but their appearances can sometimes be erratic like their powers. Oma was not close enough to open a gate in those days, when my omajistas came here. We had to force it. As we will do today. Many died."

"How many?"

"A small country," Monshara said, "called Saloria."

"The whole country?"

"Yes."

"What's worth killing a country over?"

"We knew what was coming," Monshara said. "The sky has darkened on our world for decades. Bloody sunsets, first, as whatever poisons the satellites emitted as they decayed rained down on us. Then amber skies, and now... Well. We knew we didn't have much time. When Para rose, it brought the full brunt of the decay it gathered from the spaces between things. It's diseased. Now we are, too."

"Wait," Zezili said. "Your *world*? You mean your *country*. Your country's dying?"

Monshara raised her hand in greeting to the riders. The riders made a similar salute. Best Zezili could tell, the riders were three women and one man. The man trailed after the women, as was proper in Dorinah.

The riders arrived and exchanged a few words with Monshara in a language that sounded a lot like Dhai. Was it some dialect?

"Should I step back or something?" Zezili asked.

"That won't be necessary," Monshara said.

The four riders formed a broad circle. They raised their arms. The air thickened. A massive boom rocked the field. Zezili's legionnaires cried out. Raised their hands to their ears. Zezili wondered, then, if this was all some fun ruse – have the legionnaires slaughter the camp, then slaughter the legionnaires in turn with some great trick. But that thought was short-lived, because it was at that moment that the ground around Zezili's feet began to harden.

Bloody mist roiled up from the soil and filled the sky. Zezili took a breath and gagged on coppery, blood-soaked air. Beneath her, the ground cracked and heaved. Zezili stumbled forward and caught herself on a fresh body. Blood burst from the corpse. She rolled to the side. Gazed across the field. One by one, the corpses burst and split apart, sending great gouts of blood into the already-saturated air.

She gagged on another breath.

The air began to clear as the blood coalesced into a single shimmering sphere at the center of the riders.

Zezili dry-heaved at the churned-up ground.

Above her, the flat sphere expanded into a thin-skinned bubble. Violet light burst from its center. Zezili turned away, blinded.

Her ears popped. The pressure eased.

She wiped at her eyes. Black spots juddered across her vision. Where the bloody bubble had been, a perfect disk of amber sky bled through from... some other place.

Zezili's stomach heaved again. She vomited. She heard someone laughing and looked up. It was Monshara. She was looking through the hole in the sky.

Zezili didn't know what she expected. The sky on the other side was a burnished amber, not blue-lavender. The hourglass suns were brilliant crimson, not yellow. The whole horizon glowed red, as if the ground itself emitted some wavering heat. She could not see Para, only a black mass in the sky where Para should have been, and long tails of misty black particles trailing it: the tail of an ebony comet.

The landscape it rained upon was a sea of charred hills. Zezili thought at first it was barren, but then she saw a squat, round tower in the distance, pulsing with a faint blue light.

"Are you coming?" Monshara asked.

Zezili started. "What?"

"Your second can clean things up here," Monshara said. "My sovereign wishes to meet you, as I've said."

"I can go through?"

"Yes. We've ensured that."

"Ensured it? How?"

"That's not important. Come through. You'll need a mount." She called to one of the omajistas – well, there had to be such a thing, didn't there, if they could do this? – who slid off her bear and handed the reins to Zezili.

Zezili grimaced. She hated the smell of bears. She mounted anyhow. She didn't want to make a habit of arguing with women who used blood magic to open doors between spaces. She remembered Anavha crouched on the floor of his room again, and her heart clenched. She broke out in a cold sweat. It was someone else, she reminded herself. He didn't do anything at all. Maybe it was one of these people, opening spaces to nowhere on accident. Maybe... Zezili sat straight and tall atop the bear. She needed to ask Tulana about omajistas. If the Empress had known people all along who could do something like this, she would have hidden them away with Tulana. Zezili understood now why her local priest had wanted to take Anavha away immediately.

Monshara began to move through the gate.

"Will it stay open behind us?" Zezili asked.

"Eight hundred dead should keep it open at least two hours," Monshara said. "We have time."

"And if it closes?"

"We'll be done by then," Monshara said. "We're going to the tower."

Zezili firmed her jaw. She thought of her fine estate, and Dakar, her dajians, and Anavha. If these people wanted her dead, there were far easier ways to do it.

She hissed at the bear beneath her and followed Monshara into the other side.

Dirty bones littered the field around the glowing blue tower. The air here was dry and smelled strangely of sulfur. Zezili put a kerchief over her nose, but it did nothing to keep the strange air from her lungs. She gave up and tucked the kerchief back inside her cuff.

"Who were these people?" Zezili asked.

"We had to remove a good many people," Monshara said, "to gather enough blood to open the way between the worlds. Blood witches have known how to intensify the power of the satellites through the power of blood for centuries. It was only natural we apply those same strategies to intensify the tenuous power of Oma."

"Blood witches? Worlds? Are we on the moons or something? Because you're talking nonsense to me."

"Not the moons, no," Monshara said. "It's… like looking at a series of reflections, you understand?"

"No."

Monshara sighed. She looked around the charred, shattered ground and pointed to a fetid pool of standing water in a ditch along the beaten track they followed. "When you see the sky reflected in that pool, is it the sky you know, truly? Or some blacker version, some mirror version? Pretend that beneath every reflecting pool is some other version of that sky, layer upon layer of them, with slight differences in each. The deeper you go, the more different things are."

Zezili wasn't too keen on that analogy but understood something of what she was getting at. "So, let's say you peel up enough layers, and in some reflection, the Dhai aren't slaves anymore?"

"To put it mildly, no. The Dhai are not slaves here."

"There's something I've been trying to figure out," Zezili said. "Why kill a bunch of slaves on another world, especially if they look like you? I mean, you're working for Dhai who are killing their... what, reflections? Isn't that like killing *yourself*?"

"You'll have to ask the Kai," Monshara said.

"The *Kai*?" Zezili said. "You have got to be joking."

Monshara did not answer. She slid off her mount and tied off the reins at a broad silver hitching post outside the tower. The tower itself was not as grand as it appeared from the other side. Just four stories tall, ringed in silver-rimmed windows that shimmered with little rainbows of light, as if inlaid with the wings of dragonflies.

Zezili followed Monshara up three broad flights of stairs. The tower was empty of possessions. Zezili saw a spot of blood near the door. The rest of the interior was scoured clean. Not even any dust.

As they came to the top of the tower, Zezili heard voices. Four figures dressed in chitinous red armor stood around an amberwood table. A large map lay at the center. Four red vases sat next to each leg of the table.

It took Zezili a moment to realize she actually understood what they were saying. They spoke Dhai.

The woman farthest from Zezili glanced up at their arrival. She was a dour, hard-faced woman a handful of years younger than Zezili, with a strong jaw and sloped nose. She looked vaguely familiar. Her companions turned. Two men, two women.

"Welcome back," the hard-faced woman said to Zezili, in Dhai.

"Do I know you?" Zezili asked.

"I'm sure of it," the woman said.

"You have me confused with someone else, then."

"I think not," the woman said.

Zezili tried to remember where she had seen this woman – the title, Kai, decided her. Zezili had killed any number of dajians over the years and interacted with hundreds more. But something about this one reminded her of burning flesh. And she remembered a man she murdered one day calling for his wife, calling for the *Kai*, the honorific for the Dhai leader.

"You're the girl from that camp uprising I put down," Zezili said. "That was... twelve, thirteen years ago? You pulled your brother out of that fire. He was lit like a torch. I remember."

"Is that what happened?" the woman said. She looked amused. "Perhaps that's what happened where you're from. It was different here. We met very differently."

Zezili glanced back at Monshara. "Is this a joke?"

Monshara shook her head.

"I'm the Kai," the woman said, "of the Tai Mora. You'll know me as Kirana Javia Garika, if you remember my name at all. You were a rebellious little troublemaker here, rousing your people against mine about that time."

Zezili had been a snot-nosed young recruit in the Empress's legion back then. She had killed a good many Dhai during that year; there was an uprising in the camps caused by their itinerant Kai, a religious zealot who had decided to play prophet in the camps. Those never ended well.

"No, I was murdering your parents in the camps," Zezili said, "as a member of the Dorinah legion."

"Interesting," Kirana said.

Zezili glanced over at Monshara. "What's going on? Why's the Kai in some other world?"

"There are two of us, of course," Kirana said. "Two worlds. Mirrors of each other."

Zezili started. "What?" She remembered Monshara's talk about reflections. It hadn't occurred to her she didn't just mean countries and places that were the same, but actual individuals. Two of everything? Two of Zezili? That hurt her head.

Kirana grinned. "You were never one for philosophy or astronomical theory," she said, "so I'll use small words. You're fighting Dhai here. The same Dhai you fight in your world, with some key differences." She waved her hand at the window. "Such as the scenery. And, of course, the fact that we're winning."

"Is this some kind of joke?"

"I wish it were," Monshara said.

Zezili stared at the Dhai woman in armor. She had never seen a Dhai in armor, she realized. The dajians in the camps were soft things, even during the uprisings. At most, they wore heavy leather and maybe carried a staff or battered sword. She struggled with her slim knowledge of Oma – long referred to in scripture as Rhea's Eye – and the people she saw before her. Rhea walked the world the last time Oma rose, bringing with her the Empress's people and the Saiduan. Those invasions eventually led to the end of the Dhai empire. But fighting *themselves*? Fighting... reflections?

"There's no logic to what you're saying," Zezili said. "My mother is a titled Dorinah. My father is a dajian – a Dhai slave. You've just said you're the leader of the Tai Mora, whatever that is, not the Dhai, and I've seen no Dorinah here. So I couldn't exist. I'd have no double."

"The people are the same," Kirana said. "But small things make the difference. Our people go by many names, and Tai Mora is just one of them. We still had a handful of Dorinah left for some time until just recently, working as clerks and translators for landed families. So your father was still the same Dhai. Just not a slave. Your mother was, perhaps, less free to do as she wished here. But the result, you, is... mostly the same."

"Scripture says–"

Kirana sighed. "We could sit here all day philosophizing about the nature of the link between our worlds and between our other selves. I know philosophers, hundreds of them, who do just that. I do not expect we will solve the riddle any sooner or more satisfactorily than they will. I am not looking to solve philosophical problems but immediate concerns of survival."

Zezili clenched her fists. She wasn't feeling terribly well. It was the armor, she realized. Dhai people in armor. It made her sick. "But I should know–"

"What you need to know is that my people will take your world," Kirana said. "We can do it with or without your aid, but without will take longer. That black star will continue to decay, raining death and poison until not one of us is left living. I assure you, I am very motivated."

"So what?" Zezili said. "You've outsourced your killing over there to me and my legion?"

"We're busy people," Kirana said. "You've seen how many resources it takes to send our people through. It's easier to rely on native faces to eliminate the Dhai on the other side."

"What?" Zezili said. "*All* of them?"

"Your mission is the dajians in the camps," Kirana said. "Let's focus on that."

"But you'll want to kill the Dhai, eventually," Zezili said. "Your double. Her family. The ones I didn't kill, anyway."

"Focus on your mission. I'll focus on mine."

Zezili gazed out the rainbow gloss of the broad windows behind them and saw a great construct along the horizon, in the valley behind the tower.

"What's that?" Zezili asked.

Kirana glanced back. "Ah. You noticed it. That's the mirror."

"Hard to miss."

"Your predecessor worked on it."

"My predecessor? What, so I *do* have a double?"

"You *did*," Kirana said.

"Where is she?" Zezili asked.

"She was no longer of interest to me," Kirana said. "We needed you to come through, and you can't come through if your other face still breathes."

Zezili sucked her teeth. "Ah," she said, and understanding blossomed like some dark flower in her mind. "So those slaves I'm killing *are* the twins of your people already, maybe even you. You can't go through that gate unless the Dhai are dead."

Kirana smiled. "Retain your focus, Zezili. Focus has never been your strong suit."

"And the mirror? Why do you need one that big out there?"

"Impress me with your boundless intuition, and perhaps

your fate will be brighter than your predecessor's."

Zezili thought it was meant to rankle, so she barked out a laugh instead. She half expected to wake up back in her tent, still smeared in dajian blood and ranting to Monshara about hallucinations. "You had my other self build it after she killed your family?"

"She had a few talents," Kirana said, "but ultimately, she would not cooperate."

"So you wanted to know if you should kill me, too?"

"You have her mouth," Kirana said. "Let's say this secret isn't one that will be hidden long. Best to see how you took it. Some go mad."

Zezili could understand that.

Kirana rolled up the map on the table, which Zezili recognized now as a map of Grania. Zezili saw neat lines of Dhai characters scrawled across areas of Dhai, Tordin, Dorinah, and Aaldia. Zezili spoke Dhai but had never studied the written language, so it was just scribbling to her.

Kirana held the map out and Monshara took it. "That's your battle plan," Kirana said. "Eight hundred dead to deliver that. Best not lose it."

Monshara slipped the map into a leather sleeve attached to her belt.

"Who are you battling with next?" Zezili asked. "Wars on multiple fronts never go well."

"You'll know soon enough," Kirana said. "You're dismissed, Monshara."

Zezili spared one last look at the Kai, then followed after Monshara down the long stairwell.

When they reached the bottom, Zezili walked out behind the tower, ignoring Monshara's shout, and gazed down the hill toward the great construction she had spied from the window.

A vast silvery arch split the sky. Distant figures worked in the tattered shreds of some temporary camp near it. She saw long lines of workers carrying baskets of shimmering matter toward the structure. More workers dangled from the scaffolding that skirted its base.

"Why build a mirror?" Zezili asked as Monshara came up alongside her.

"To keep the gate between our worlds open," Monshara said. "We don't have enough blood or omajistas to keep a steady gate open without it. The rebels took two hundred of our most promising omajistas a decade ago and hid them across many worlds, but mostly yours, as it's the closest to ours."

"How do you lose that many children?"

"It's a very long story. A few women made a nuisance of themselves, led by an upstart named Nava Isoail. But they're nearly all dead now. We're just mopping up."

Above the arch of the mirror, the blasted black sphere of what should have been Para glowed ominously in the sky.

"Why would she pick me for this campaign," Zezili said, "when she already killed me here?"

"I long ago gave up trying to understand her motivations. She is equal parts manic brutality and strategic fuckery."

"There's no chance she could fail?"

Monshara's face was a grim mask.

"With a face like that, you'd be good at cards," Zezili said.

"I am," Monshara said. She sighed. "We won't fail, Zezili. Our armies are vast. Saiduan was the largest enemy we had to face, and they're nearly spent. When the mirror is finished, we can easily send through as many of our soldiers as we like. No need to slaughter more here or there to fuel it, or wait for random tears in the sky. The mirror will keep the rift open until we destroy it."

Zezili remembered the mirror hanging over her own hearth, and the day she watched her mother sculpting the soft, warm metal. She wished she wasn't blind to the power of the stars then. She wished she could do something to stop whatever mad thing was about to happen.

"The metal is most vulnerable now," her mother had told her, "before it's infused with the power of Tira that gives it this glow. After that, it will never shatter. It will outlive us, just like those everpine weapons the legionnaires wield." The mirror in the distance did not glow. If it wasn't yet infused with the power of a satellite, it could be broken.

"Come," Monshara said, squeezing Zezili's arm gently. "We need to go back before the gate closes."

"How many omajistas will it take to infuse this?" Zezili asked. "I assume that's who has to give it power."

"I don't know," Monshara said, "and I don't ask. We have a different task in all of this. Best concentrate on that."

As they walked back across the scorched landscape to their mounts, Zezili understood the scope of her mission far more than she had before she passed through the gate. It wasn't about offing a few dajians. It was about extinguishing the Dhai race in her world entirely. They would not stop with the dajians. They would come for the free mixed-race Dorinahs too, the ones like Zezili, and for the free Dhai people in their toxic slice of a country. They would replace the passive little Dhai Zezili knew with a conquering horde of overlords, Dhai who had never been defeated.

Zezili gazed out at the blazing, beleaguered world. Focus on the mission, Kirana had said. Keep your head down and don't ask questions, the Empress would have said. One mission. One goal. They never wanted her to see past the next body, but from here, all Zezili could see were bodies – the bodies of the Dhai on her world, all laid out across these bone-chilling fields of char, opening the way for the conquering hordes of Tai Mora; she saw them crunching across the broken forms of their other selves and destroying Dorinah in a single day.

She had seen Dhai in armor now, and she could not unsee it.

As they crossed back into Zezili's world, into the comforting blue sky and brilliant light of Para, Zezili said, "You know, there's one thing I've always been good at."

"Killing?" Monshara said.

"Killing Dhai," Zezili said, and urged her bear onward before she could see the look on Monshara's face.

18

Ahkio clung to the banister looping about the tongue of the grand stairway where Kirana's husband, Lohin, had fallen. Gaiso huffed blood on the landing just above them, her attempt at joining Lohin and his band of Garika militia cut short by a snarling attack from Nasaka that happened so fast, Ahkio had barely had time to process it.

He felt the heartbeat of the temple beneath his fingers. His mother had told him the temples were living, breathing embodiments of the gods. Oma was already here, pulsing through this temple, bathed in the blood of militia from Clan Garika.

And to what purpose?

Lohin's breath was ragged. He was a stringy young man with a twisted mouth and kind eyes. The weapon he carried was plain metal; only the militia were issued weapons infused with the power of the satellites.

Below, in the foyer, half a dozen dead Oras and more than twenty of the Garika militia lay dead or dying. Ahkio knew because he'd counted them as he came limping out of the Sanctuary after the novice, Rohinmey, incapacitated Almeysia. But one body he had expected was missing.

"Where's Yisaoh?" Ahkio asked Lohin.

Lohin huffed at him, something like a guffaw. "I led this coup myself."

"You're the sort who doesn't act without a stronger person's backing, Lohin. It's why you married my sister."

"Kai?"

A young novice named Caisa stood below. She was a lean young woman, freckled and high of forehead, with an affinity for Para. She was the one who had pushed him toward the Sanctuary when the militia burst into the foyer. She may have saved his life from the Garikas. And the boy, Rohinmey, had surely spared him from Almeysia's wrath – whatever that may have been. Almeysia was bound and drugged now, spirited off into the bowels of the temple at Nasaka's order.

It should not have surprised Ahkio that novices would be more trustworthy than Oras. They'd had less time to choose sides, so they fell on the side of the divine Kai. It gave him an opportunity, and though he abhorred politics and twisted ethics, sitting here in this pool of death made him realize that however much he hated it, if he wanted to live, he had to embrace it.

"Do you have the physician for Lohin?" Ahkio asked. "He's fading."

"Ora Matias has been killed," she said. "The physician."

"I see." Ahkio finally saw fear in Lohin's pained face. "And my cousin?"

"Liaro's in the infirmary. We've called physicians from Clan Sorila. But Liaro isn't that bad, Kai. He's just a complainer." Her color deepened. "I'm sorry. I meant–"

"I know what you meant," Ahkio said. "Thank you."

Caisa shifted from foot to foot another moment, looking contrite, then stepped away to help with the bodies.

Ahkio noted the blood pooling on the steps. Lohin would not survive long enough for a physician to walk the three or four hours from Sorila. He wondered if Lohin knew that yet.

"Did Yisaoh tell you I'd marry into Rhin and Hadaoh's family?" Ahkio asked. "It could have spared you this."

"They won't have you."

"Why?"

His grimace was ugly. "They won't."

"You're likely going to die here, Lohin."

He whimpered. "Let me alone."

"You killed Oras, Lohin. You nearly killed my cousin."

"You aren't Kai."

"I'm Kirana's brother."

"Half-brother."

"Is that so?"

Lohin hacked up a smattering of blood. He whispered, "Your mother's babies all died, Ahkio. All but Kirana, and she was sick from the start. You aren't Javia's."

"You're saying my mother stole someone else's child? You Garikas are all mad."

"Not stole. Freely given." Lohin's breath was shallow.

"Who?"

"Who do you think?"

"My Aunt Etena?"

Lohin hacked out a laugh. "Stupid. So much stupider than your sister. Should have been you."

"Nasaka," Ahkio said.

Lohin snarled. "Her, with a stillborn baby?" he said. "Same week... Javia pushed you out... first to live since Kirana. No one believed it. No one."

The hacking stopped. Lohin's face softened. Ahkio saw the light go from his eyes; the tension left his body.

Ahkio slid down onto the steps, favoring his injured side, and sat quietly next to Lohin's body. He remembered that story. Nasaka's single pregnancy. Was there anything Nasaka wouldn't do for the Dhai? Below, the militia Nasaka had called from the Kuallina Stronghold worked to clean and bundle the dead. He saw Elaiko and Caisa working among them, directed in the task by Ghrasia Madah, head of the militia at both the Liona and Kuallina strongholds. She was a fierce little woman, wading through blood and bodies like a person well used to death. He recalled her face from many a portrait – she had led the defense

of the Liona Stronghold during the Pass War, when the Dorinahs
tried to take the country twenty years before.

Ghrasia could have sided with the Garikas, but she'd chosen
Nasaka and the temples instead. That loyalty, he knew, had
been the only thing to save them today. Without her two dozen
militia, they would have had to turn the gifted arts of jistas on the
Garikas. That would have ended any hope Ahkio had of uniting
the country. The ungifted would have turned on the temples. The
day could have been much worse.

He stood, called down to Elaiko, "Where's Nasaka?"

"Meditating in the garden, I think. Is Lohin-"

"He's dead," Ahkio said.

"I'm sorry, Kai."

"He was no kin of mine," Ahkio said.

Ahkio forged his way through the bloodied foyer, passing
Ghrasia as he did. She gave him a brief nod, and he hesitated,
asked, "When did Nasaka send for you?"

"This morning," she said. "She suspected there may be...
conflict. We arrived just in time."

"Wish she would have expressed that... concern to me," he
said.

"Ora Nasaka's methods of protecting the Kai tend toward less
information, not more."

"I'd like to change that."

Ghrasia smiled, almost a smirk. He might have found it
insufferable in a novice, but coming from this hard-faced leader
of the militia, it was endearing. "I wish you luck with that."

"Thank you for coming, regardless of why."

"I would have done the same for your mother."

"Noted," Ahkio said. His mother. Yes. Either of them.

"Noted?" she said. "Is that all you have to say, when eight of my
best lie dying here, and a good many of your kin by marriage?"

It was an unexpected punch. He rounded on her. "I have half
the country out to kill me and anyone who stands next to me. I
know *exactly* what happened here today."

He strode away before she could reply; he wanted to remember the smirk, not what came after.

Ahkio found Nasaka in the gardens behind the temple, sitting within the stone circle dedicated to Sina, her star. A great violet orb hung suspended over a massive stone base. Tremendous red-and-purple flowers wound up the boughs of the weeping trees. She sat back on her heels, eyes closed.

He waited for her to acknowledge him. She did not.

"I'm going to bring the bodies to Garika," Ahkio said. "I'd like Ghrasia to escort me."

"I don't recommend that," Nasaka said.

"Blood's been spilled," Ahkio said. "I understand why it's been done, and I need to fix it."

"You have no idea," Nasaka said.

The anger and betrayal bubbled up. Like being on fire. "I do have an idea," Ahkio said. "It has something to do with dead babies."

Nasaka raised her head. "What are you nattering about?"

"The Garikas seem to think I'm not Javia's," Ahkio said. He felt heat in his face and choked on his next words. It made him angry, because he knew. He knew without it being said. "You had a stillborn child, they said. The same week my mother had me. My father said it's why you cared so much about our safety. It's why he told you we were going to that camp in Dorinah, even though my mother wanted to go alone. You knew where we were, and that's the only thing that saved Kirana and me that day. You're my childless aunt. It made sense to me. Now I wonder if that was just the easier assumption."

Nasaka placed her hands on her knees and regarded the violet orb. "I had reports last week of a dead way housekeeper."

"Don't avoid my—"

"Dead right there in her house, untouched... surrounded by the mangled bodies of three men. Men we still haven't been able to identify. Dhai men without families. Impossible, wouldn't you say?"

"There are dead Garikas in there accusing me of not being my mother's child, saying I'm a man with no right to this seat, and you're going on about a way house keeper?"

"You know what's important, Ahkio? That this country has a legitimate Kai. Especially now."

"Ah, yes. *Now*," Ahkio said. "Yisaoh tells me you and Kirana knew about the coming of Oma for years. Is that true, too?" He hadn't wanted to bring it up; Yisaoh played a good game of dividing allies against one another, but if Nasaka conspired to lie to him about his own birth, he couldn't imagine how many other lies she'd told him.

Nasaka stood. She gestured to the wooded gardens all around them, and lowered her voice. "Can you imagine a time when none of this exists? All turned to dust. Eaten by fire. Did Kirana and I entertain ideas of Oma's rise? Certainly. But Oma has been spoken of for centuries. It so happens the Garikas were within a decade of being right. Sometimes prophets of the cataclysm get lucky. I have more important things to concern myself with now than the mad rumors of a power-hungry clan trying to get us to eat each other."

"If I married Meyna–"

"Meyna! Have you learned nothing yet?"

"I've learned plenty," Ahkio snapped. "I know that path is closed."

"And which have you picked? Or will you mire yourself in this rumor? Curl up and weep on that bloody floor in there and piss about how your life turned out?"

"No," he said. "I'll go to Garika and return their kin. And I'll exile them. Every last one of them."

Nasaka stiffened. It was a rare day he could shock her, and he found himself grimly pleased.

"If you exile the Garikas, you'll exile–"

"I know who I'll be exiling," he said.

"This is–"

"And I need an assistant, someone I can trust, to start helping me here. Not you or someone bound to you."

"I'll find–"

"I want Caisa, that novice parajista who fought with us today."

"That... would not be my first choice."

"An even better reason to have her next to me," Ahkio said. "You'll be sending scholars north with Ora Dasai soon, is that right? That hasn't changed?"

"He's selecting his scholars, yes."

"Have him send Rohinmey."

"The novice who attacked Ora Almeysia? Absolutely not."

"He was defending me from harm. I have my reasons."

"What does that boy have to do with anything? You realize we just bartered away a kitchen drudge for that boy's life, and you want to send him to Saiduan?"

"I'm Kai," Ahkio said. "It's my business. Do you understand now, Nasaka, or should I repeat myself?"

"I can hear."

"Good. You'll be interrogating Ora Almeysia?"

"Naturally."

"Bring her to Osono when you can get her to speak."

"Why Osono?"

"Because that's where I'm going after Garika. I want the person who killed my sister, Nasaka. I have no trouble angering you, or Ghrasia, or any of the rest, to find that out."

"You realize, boy, that you will only sit that seat so long as you have people, like myself, loyal enough to keep you on it."

"Dead babies," Ahkio said. Nasaka's expression was icy. Bile rose in his throat, but if she dared threaten him, he'd call her bluff. "I think you'll be loyal to the bitter end. As any kin of mine would."

Ahkio turned on his heel. He felt sick, but he pushed on without looking back. He managed to make it halfway back to the temple before he stepped discreetly behind a stand of willowthorn trees and vomited. He crumpled to the ground and stayed very still in the shadow of the trees.

Nasaka could crush him, he knew. But she would not crush her own son. Not after she'd worked so hard to give him this bloody title.

• • •

The massive Ora libraries took up the entire eleventh floor of the temple. Roh bounced in one of the grand chaises in the central reading room while Dasai stood nearby, scowling. After the fighting downstairs, most of the novices were confined to quarters, and the Oras were helping with cleanup. Roh tried to still himself under Dasai's gaze, but it took a great bout of effort. They waited for the Kai, who'd insisted on seeing them in the libraries instead of his study. It was an odd request, and Roh suspected it made Dasai even more nervous than it did him.

Roh stared at the glass-encased shelves that stretched twenty feet up the walls. He remembered spending hours in here just a few weeks before, searching through old historical texts and geography books for the symbol Lilia had drawn in the back of a book of Saiduan poetry. If caught doing research for a drudge, he expected he could lie his way out of it. Attacking an Ora, though... there was no way to talk himself out of that.

"You think he'll exile me?" Roh asked Dasai.

"Let's hope so," Dasai said. "Using the gifted arts against another Dhai... you knew better."

"I was defending myself," Roh said, "and the Kai – the Kai! – against an Ora. We can use our gifts against other Oras."

"How is it you go from your death bed to attempted murder?"

"It was self-defense!"

"Causing the death of another is always murder," Dasai said. "All that changes is the punishment."

"I think she was the one who attacked me," Roh said. "She stabbed me, Ora Dasai, because she saw me with Yisaoh."

"Yisaoh Alais?"

Roh started at the voice. It was the Kai, stepping through the broad double doors. He closed the doors behind him. His hair was still caked in the blood of the former Kai, twisted back from his face with a fireweed cord. "Ora Dasai," the Kai said. "I didn't expect you."

"The boy is my student," Dasai said. "In Ora Almeysia's absence, I wished to speak for him."

"There's nothing to speak of," the Kai said. "Rohinmey... Roh, correct?" Roh nodded. "Roh and I have some things to speak about. More than I thought, it seems. Ora Dasai, I expect you'll have preparations to make for your journey to Saiduan."

"We were waiting on Ora Chali, Rohinmey's brother. He is among my finest Saiduan speakers, and he had some business to complete here before we went north."

"Roh's brother? That's excellent. Excuse us now, Ora Dasai."

Roh looked to Dasai for direction, but Dasai merely pressed thumb to forehead and retreated. He paused at the big double doors and fixed Roh with a final stern stare before closing them.

Roh started bouncing on his seat again.

"Are you all right?" the Kai asked.

"Yes, Kai. Just... nerves."

"Ahkio, please."

Ahkio sat on a chaise at Roh's right, settling back against the pillows.

"Are you going to exile me?" Roh asked.

"Exile?" Ahkio laughed. He had a good laugh, though there was a bitter bite to it. "No, I'm not going to exile you."

The threat of exile unraveled, Roh had an irrational hope that this was going to be a romantic encounter. Would the Kai praise him for helping him, and be in Roh's debt?

"So, you believe it was Yisaoh Alais who attacked you?"

"I know it," Roh said. He told Ahkio what he remembered of the encounter, and felt suddenly light-headed. He rubbed at his belly, where the knife had pierced him. "Is it odd she used a blade," he said, "and not an infused weapon?"

"Infused weapons are registered to their owners," Ahkio said. "A skilled jista could have tied it back to the Ora or militia member it was gifted to. It makes sense she would use a blade."

"What did I see that I had to die for?" Roh said.

"Yisaoh doesn't want me on this seat," Ahkio said. "That's no secret. But it does interest me that... well, I have others to speak to about that. This isn't why I brought you here."

Roh leaned forward.

"You want to go to Saiduan," Ahkio said. "I've heard Ora Dasai and Ora Nasaka debating it, these weeks they thought you dead."

"I want it more than anything," Roh said.

"Even now?"

"Especially now."

"Where do your loyalties lie?" Ahkio asked.

"My… Oh." Yisaoh and the dead people downstairs were from Clan Garika, just like him. "I know I'm a Garika, but that's just my clan. I'm not related to Tir's kin."

"You showed me that in the temple this morning," Ahkio said. "What I want to know is if you're an Ora first, or a Dhai."

"If you asked me to swear an oath to you, I would," Roh said.

"Ora Dasai will permit you to go north," Ahkio said.

"But… he really doesn't–"

"He'll take you with him. I've asked Ora Nasaka to speak to him. But there's a condition."

"I'll do it," Roh said. He pushed his hands under his thighs, because he wanted to jump out of his seat and hug the Kai. A profound sense of relief washed over him. He had pulled on Para, and faced down an Ora in defense of the Kai, and changed his fate. He'd known all along he could do it. He caught himself grinning.

"You're happy to obey Ora Dasai?" Ahkio asked. His tone was somber. Roh's grin faded.

"I… well, shouldn't I?"

"I need you to obey me first," Ahkio said. "It's no secret things are very bad and people are divided. I need someone I can trust in Saiduan. You're a talented boy and a Garika who'll still defend the Kai. I need you to work for me now, for Dhai. You understand?"

"I think so." He really didn't care to understand. All he cared about was seeing the tundra for the first time, and fighting with sanisi, and building some big life outside a farmhouse.

Ahkio said, "My sister, Kai Kirana, is dead. It wasn't a natural death. There are many who would want her dead, the Saiduan among them."

"How... how could *I* help?"

Ahkio pulled something from his tunic pocket – a sheet of green paper with neat rows of Dhai characters set beside jagged lines of script.

"I'm not asking you to uncover any great plot. I'm just asking you to tell me the truth as you see it. I need someone there with fresh eyes who isn't Ora Dasai. Will you go to Saiduan and tell me all you see?"

"I will," Roh said. His grin was back, and this time, he could not suppress it. "Thank you, Kai."

But the Kai's face was somber. Roh tried to match his expression.

"This is the cipher of the Kai," Ahkio said. "We've used it for thousands of years to pass messages among kin. Today, I'm going to count you as kin and turn it over to you. It's how you'll send word of what you see in Saiduan and how the battle is progressing there."

Roh nodded.

"I know you're a smart boy," he said. "Ora Dasai does not speak highly of the dim-witted, nor does he try to keep them from being exiled. Hopefully, you can learn this in a few afternoons."

"I will. I promise."

"Roh, this part is important," Ahkio said. Roh sat up a little straighter. "You're not to tell anyone else what you're doing. Not Ora Dasai. Not Nasaka. No one but me. Put your trust in me, and if anything happens to you, know that I'll do everything in my power to help."

"I believe you," Roh said.

Ahkio gestured to the massive wall of shelves. "Then select a few books, and let's begin."

19

"If there are two Kais," Lilia said, "it means there could be two of everyone, doesn't it?"

Gian picked at the remains of the man's liver. The suns had set, and cool darkness blanketed the clearing.

"I know it's hard to wrap your head around," Gian said. "It was hard for me, too, when I first came here. I had a sister over there, a twin. She had to stay. She couldn't come through because she already existed here. We're twins there, but here... just one of us. Just her. So I could cross. She couldn't, unless we found the woman here with my face and... killed her. That's the rules." She shrugged. "I keep expecting to find my sister here someday. Keep expecting to look up and see my own face."

"Two of everyone," Lilia said. "Two of my mother?"

Gian's expression was difficult to read in the low light of the fire. "Yes," she said. "Two of your mother. But not of you. That's why Kalinda could bring you here. You can't bring someone over if they're still alive here. That's why my sister had to stay but I didn't."

"Where's my mother?" Lilia said. "If there's two of everyone, then, my mother–"

"Listen, Lilia, this may be difficult–"

"Where?"

"Your mother here isn't the person you knew," Gian said. "Kalinda already tried to get your mother here to join with us. But she's... she's Dorinah. And very loyal to Dorinah."

"You're a liar."

"Believe me or don't, but the version of your mother as she exists here, the one you're so keen to find, serves the Empress. Your real mother, Nava... I'm sorry, Lilia, but she's dead and gone and you must forget her. Come with us the way she wanted. Our worlds are coming together, and only one is going to live. You can help decide which one."

"Why should I believe anything you say?"

"Has anyone else had answers for you but Kalinda? Trust me, Lilia. Your mother delivered you to Kalinda, and Kalinda turned you over to me. You have to trust that you're on the right side."

"I'll find my mother in Dorinah, then."

"Have you heard anything I've said?" Gian tapped the butt of her weapon. "I'm a parajista with a sword, Lilia, and I'm telling you now – we're not going to Dorinah so you can track down some shadow working for the Empress."

Outside the temple, it was people with weapons and strength who pushed others around. If Gian was a stone defender on a screes board, Lilia would employ a flanking defense to sweep her off it. But Lilia had no pieces. And no sword.

Lilia pressed her hands to her face. Her mother had been a little pale like her, she knew. But she had never seen a Dorinah outside a history book. No one told her she had the face of those people, so maybe she did. Maybe they were all too polite to say anything. She didn't know who she was anymore – a ghost from some other world.

"I made a promise," Lilia said. Her voice cracked.

"You made a promise to a dead woman."

As Gian hacked through the undergrowth the next day, Lilia hung back, watching her swing her sword. The heat was intense. Gian had stripped to the waist. Lilia watched her, fascinated by the banded cords of muscle in Gian's shoulders as she worked beneath the sky. Lilia was strangely mesmerized by her in the warm air and felt foolish because of it. Gian was no more to be trusted than the sanisi, and she was just as ready to use force to get her way. Cicadas buzzed all around them, their song broken only by the screech of some small mammal.

Lilia trudged forward, kicking up the first of the browning leaves. She had not slept.

Gian's course wavered. She chose to go right instead of left, down a path with less vegetation.

Lilia saw a spidery red tendril curling up from the ground ahead of Gian. She knew it immediately – it was the lure of a bladder trap.

Lilia slowed her pace. Stopped. Gian continued on, oblivious. She was still eight paces from the bladder trap. Plenty of time for Lilia to call out and turn her back.

Gian glanced over her shoulder. "You coming? Our rations won't last at this pace."

"Of course, master," Lilia said. Too haughty, she knew, and immediately regretted it.

Gian stopped. Lowered her sword. "Don't be like that." Sweat poured down her face. For a long instant, Lilia wondered, again, who Gian would be, what fate she would have chosen for herself, if she was not bound to Kalinda.

"This was your choice," Lilia said.

"I like you, Lilia. You're stubborn and spiteful, just like Kalinda. Don't make this harder." She turned back to the brush and started hacking away again.

Lilia shuffled forward to catch up with her. Was she any better than Gian or the sanisi, if she didn't warn her?

"Gian–"

Gian cursed.

And plunged out of sight.

Lilia dropped to the ground immediately. She clawed her way forward the rest of the way on her belly. There were many kinds of pit traps and bladder traps in the woodland, most of them brimming with poisonous reservoirs and thorny protrusions. Many killed their prey neatly the moment they fell. Others took weeks to digest them.

"Gian!"

The ground softened under her reaching fingers. Lilia slid up to the lip of the torn turf. She peered over the edge.

Gian lay six feet below, coughing up green bile into the fleshy pit of a bladder trap.

"Are you hurt?" Lilia asked.

Gian spit more green liquid. "Dropped my sword. Nicked my leg."

"Did you drink any of that?" Lilia asked.

The green digestive juices of the plant sloshed around her. "I think so," she said.

Gian fished around for her sword. Took hold of it. As she stood, Lilia saw a gout of blood jet out from her leg.

Lilia held out her hands. "Quickly. You're losing blood."

Gian gripped her wrist with one hand and shoved her weapon into the soft flesh of the trap with the other. Lilia pushed the spines at the top of the trap down while Gian pulled them in. Squeezing through the bent spines without impaling Gian took time. Finally, both of them out of breath, Gian crawled out.

Lilia lay next to Gian, covered in blood and the plant's digestive juices, panting.

Her mother would have called her a coward, letting this woman die. The Oras would call her a horror.

"I'm sorry," Lilia said.

"I don't feel… My head's buzzing."

"It's poisonous. It's all right. Everything will be all right."

Lilia helped drag Gian away from the trap. It took all her strength to push Gian onto her side. She ripped open her trousers. The weapon had jabbed deeply into her thigh, cutting a great wound as big as Lilia's fist. A killing wound. Gian would bleed out here.

Lilia dug into the wound, pinching off the affected artery. Gian cried out.

"What kind of trap?" Gian growled.

"Fellwort," Lilia said. "We need to clean this wound." She wanted to tell Gian the poison would eat her from the inside out, but didn't think that would be helpful.

Lilia pulled a length of cord from Gian's pack and used it as a tourniquet. "You have any honey?" Lilia asked.

"No," Gian said. "No alcohol, either."

"We can use honey," Lilia said. "It'll take me awhile to find. Keep that sword close. There are bears and wolverines. Can you still call on Para?"

Gian nodded, but her face was very drawn. Lilia worried she would go into shock.

"I'll be back," Lilia said. "I promise."

She rinsed the wound with the water they had and collected a handful of scorch pods from Gian's pack. Her mother once taught her how to track and take a beehive, and she desperately needed one now. I should be running before the sanisi catches up to us, she thought. But her heart would not let her.

She found a small spring an hour up the trail. She refilled their water, then followed the heady, fragrant smell of fungus flowers. Two more hours of stalking bees the size of her thumb paid off. She knocked down a massive papery beehive and used the heat of the broken scorch pods to confuse the remaining bees.

Six stings later, she had four bricks of honeycomb. Dusk was falling. She moved quickly, following the broken branches and little stone markers she had left along her way.

When she arrived, Gian was slumped to one side. Her hand rested limply on her bloody thigh. Too late.

"I'm a murderer," Lilia breathed. "Gian?"

She came up beside Gian and rested a hand on her bare arm. It was cool, but not cold.

Lilia worked quickly in the dim light. She mashed the honeycomb inside a woody seed pod, mixing it with water and a few leaves of night dagger she'd collected.

She pulled back the tunic she'd left over Gian's wound as a makeshift bandage and recoiled at the smell. It had mortified quickly.

Lilia washed the wound out a second time, then began to pack it with the honeycomb mixture. Gian came to as she did.

"Get away!" Gian said, slapping weakly at her hands.

Lilia ignored her. She had seen her mother with feverish patients.

"I won't tell you anything," Gian said.

Lilia unknotted the tourniquet. She used it to secure the tunic around the wound again. All the while, Gian babbled.

"It wasn't me," Gian said. "I won't do it." She grabbed at Lilia's arm. "I love you," she said. "I won't do it."

Lilia tugged Gian's pack from her shoulders and pulled out their food. Most was packed in waxed linen, so hadn't been poisoned too badly. She sat over the pack for a few minutes, staring at its contents. There was enough food to get only one of them back to the valley.

She glanced up at Gian. Gian's head lolled back against the great trunk of the rattler tree.

Lilia thought of Roh, and the Temple of Oma, the Oras there who sheltered her, the drudges who worked with her, and the farmers and herders and craftspeople who cared for her after her mother pushed her through to the other side.

"I'm sorry, Gian," she said. "My place is here."

Lilia left the food in Gian's pack. Lilia could forage on her own, but Gian wouldn't be fit for it. She set a full water bladder at Gian's elbow.

Then Lilia slung the second bladder over her shoulder and skirted around the bladder trap. She looked back once because she felt a stab of longing. She wanted to take Gian's hand in hers and never let go. Her journey with Gian had been the first time in a long time she didn't feel alone.

Lilia pushed back out into the woods, into the slithering darkness. She was tired of being hunted, tired of running in circles.

It was time to hunt down the sanisi in turn. Her mother, even if it was just a shadow of her, was in Dorinah. And if anyone could get Lilia there in one piece, it was the man who could not kill her.

• • •

Taigan collected the little sparrows into his palm and breathed on them. Maralah's message was a brilliant blue fragrance excreted from the sparrows; blueberry and sugar, like something created by an exceptionally gifted confectioner.

He – for he still felt comfortable using that pronoun in Saiduan, at least for another turn of the moon – stood at the center of a little Woodland village, its inhabitants neatly and bloodlessly broken, like discarded farm implements.

Coding messages with the power of the satellites had its drawbacks. Only the very skilled could tailor a living thing to change its nature as it traveled from icy tundra to spitting sea to dripping jungle. These sparrows had likely begun their journey as flies or beetles, then birds. They reacted intelligently to their surroundings, cycling through forms according to what their tirajista shaper had encoded in them.

He tugged at little red threads of Oma's power to unravel the fragrances and turn them into Saiduan characters. It was a deft, complicated thing, taught to him by some long-dead old woman with a face like a stone slab. His peculiar birth had marked him from the very beginning as a herald of change. She was the only one who would touch him.

After he'd caught the little omajista girl, he'd sent a message to Maralah. Her response indicated she'd received it:

We broke the one Saarda found in Masaira, but the east coast was just invaded. The Patron's running out of patience, and I'm running out of sanisi. Break her before you get here. We don't have time to do it after.

Taigan sent out a little puff of air, tearing apart the misty characters. They dissipated like smoke. The sparrows, too, scattered. He watched them flit to the edges of the village, then shimmer and tremble and become small white parrots. They took flight, heading for the top of the broad canopy.

The man he'd sent out from here had not returned, but as

Maralah's message lit off, he saw the constructed butterfly he'd sent with the man fluttering toward him. Taigan pulled it apart now, catching a whiff of the sea. The smell caused a bright memory to waft up from his consciousness; he saw a game trail, a rocky outcrop, a birch orchard ringed in massive cocoons.

Not far now. He poked one last time at one of the dead Dhai, then struck back out into the woods, silent as a cat, toward the butterfly's memory of the path.

Woodland Dhai were much less cooperative than their valley brethren. They also turned out to be more skilled at channeling the satellites than he anticipated. He suspected his reputation as a sanisi preceded him here, or perhaps the invaders had already sent a scouting party, and it had put them on edge. Few bothered to exchange words before attacking.

So much for petty pacifism.

He crossed the village and stepped over the low thorn fence that kept out the baby walking trees and various creatures that made this Woodland less than welcoming. He had tracked these people hoping the little servant girl and her companion had fallen in with them. The death of the innkeeper frustrated him. Death without answers or leads served no purpose. He should have known better than to shield her instead of immobilize her.

For several days, he had been able to smell the sea. It reminded him of better days. His family had been fishing people, illiterate and ungifted. Children only went out veiled twice a week, during prayer days, and then only until age nine. Learning he was still considered a child at thirteen in the capital had been frustrating.

Some days, he thought the only place in Saiduan the invaders hadn't touched was that village he grew up in. He still looked for it on the lists of scoured cities and towns that Maralah kept in her study, compiled by sanisi posted across the empire. She inquired often which city he looked for, but he dared not say it aloud. Some part of him hoped that if he never heard of it, it would remain untouched. He hated the heat here and the cloying jungle. He wished he could bury the girl and her friends in the heat and forget them.

Taigan followed the smell of the sea, trying to pick up signs of the girl and her companions again. He marked several great insects with little tendrils of twisted air and fragrance, hoping they would offer something useful back to him.

Three hours later, one of the insects returned. He followed it to a mossy trail. When he looked up, he saw the scullery girl clinging to the tangled branches of a tree just across a clearing on the other side of the trail. Taigan did not look directly at her at first, wondering if she thought she was spying on him. If so, she was doing a terrible job of it.

But the girl did not move.

He met her look.

She scrambled down the tree, much more quickly than he expected.

Taigan moved across the clearing after her.

A cold dagger of pain plunged into his chest. He threw out his right arm, too late. The bone-strung branches of the tree that dominated the clearing closed around him like a vise. Throwing out his arm had been a mistake; the bone tree snapped his arm clean through, torquing it backward and shoving it against his body.

He grunted. Tried to find leverage by kicking away with the heels of his boots. But the tree lifted him cleanly from the ground. Its bony fingers drove into his flesh like knobby needles.

His skin burned. Punctured flesh and organs tried to knit themselves back together. It was like boiling from the inside out.

As he struggled to center his mind, he saw the girl creeping toward him, skirting the edge of the clearing.

Taigan showed his teeth. "You're less stupid," he said. He tried to rip his arm free. The bones of the tree dug deeper. His flesh bubbled. The air was filled with the smell of burnt meat.

"I have a proposal for you," Lilia said.

He wanted to mash her face in, Maralah be cast to Sina's maw.

His songs for concentrating Oma were elusive, broken to pieces like the bones of his arm. He found his focus briefly and sliced his good arm free. He reached for the girl.

She darted back.

Another bony branch curled up from the ground, pulling his arm back. He hissed.

"We both need things," Lilia said.

"You'll need a fine surgeon," Taigan said, "when I have done with you."

"I know the Woodland," Lilia said. "I don't think you do, though."

"If you think this tree can kill me, you know very little."

"You won't be conscious much longer, no matter how strong you are. That's a bone tree. It's poisonous. Like most things here."

"Where's your little friend?" Taigan asked. "You think a parajista can hold me when I burst free of this?"

"I think we can help each other," Lilia said. She spoke loudly but stayed at the edge of the clearing. He had seen enough young people bluster to recognize it. She was alone, then. He wondered how such a slip of a girl had freed herself of a parajista, and then considered his own predicament. Well.

Taigan felt the poison. It was a subtle thing, twisting through his body like a cold, snaking elixir. He had been poisoned before by any number of things, and though it would not likely kill him, it would dull his access to Oma, a connection that was tenuous at the best of times.

"Talk fast," Taigan said.

She puffed out her chest. Cheeky little child. "You need people who can channel Oma," she said. "That's why you're after me. I want to help you. I do. I know what's happening now."

"Do you?" Taigan grunted. "Then you are well ahead of me."

"Help me find my mother in Dorinah, and I'll go with you willingly."

"Haven't we already made this bargain, girl? I gave you that boy's life, and you betrayed your oath to me."

"Only because I made another oath first. My mother is a blood... she's... well, you know already. She can channel Oma."

"You have a very strange way of asking favors," Taigan said. His voice was slurred. He tried to move his fingers.

"You wouldn't help me otherwise," Lilia said. "Not even if I asked nicely."

He could not argue that. "You said your mother was dead."

"Do you always say things that are true?"

"They'll gut you open if you try and go to Dorinah alone. You'll end up a slave."

"That's why I'm asking for *your* help."

"Why not your Dhai friends?"

"You're the only person I know who isn't Dhai... and I know for sure you won't kill me."

"Do you?"

"I'm important to you."

"Cut me loose, then, or whatever it is you're going to do," Taigan said.

"You'll take me?"

Taigan saw Maralah's swirling note before him, and something older, darker – a searing brand, a ward Maralah burned into his spine, sealed with the power of Sina to ensure he did Maralah's bidding. He was almost impossible to kill, but like any other thing of flesh, he could be coerced with the right ward. It compelled him now; he could not destroy the girl, no matter how much he wished it. He fought the ward the same way he fought the tree's poison, and with the same results.

"If I escort you," he said, "you both come to Saiduan."

"All right," Lilia said.

He wondered at her lack of hesitation. She must believe her mother powerful indeed or believe him a great idiot. She had run from him once, of course. In her arrogance, she might believe she could escape again. But he knew what she did not – there were children of Oma scattered all over the country, and the more he had of them, the better his chances for success. She herself was weak. If not in spirit, then body. She would flame out gloriously, if she ever learned to call on Oma at all. He needed more than just one girl before he trekked home.

She stepped forward. He waited for something fantastic. Perhaps the parajista had already taught her how to draw Oma's breath. Instead, she stepped around to the back of the tree and kicked something at the base of it.

The tree spasmed.

Taigan dropped to the mossy ground. His body contorted; muscles tensed, flesh knit, organs regenerated. It was like some great rumbling storm churning through his torso. He hacked up a gob of blood. He wiped his mouth. From the corner of his vision, he saw the girl backing away, toward the edge of the circle.

He snapped hold of the song in his mind, the one that called the great gout of fire that the stone-faced old woman had taught him three days before he killed her with it.

But as he turned to focus it on the girl, the long length of the ward seared to his spine sent a wave of ragged fire deep into his bones. He hissed at her instead. He could not kill her. He had to deliver her.

She moved back another step. Stupid girl. He knew what she was the moment he saw her. It was a simple test. Call on Oma to murder every child or farmer or soldier from Saiduan to the southern ice flow, and discover which his body would allow him to burn and which it would not.

The ones Maralah had compelled him not to destroy with her ward, he was compelled to collect. Even the troublesome ones.

"Lead on, little scullery maid," Taigan said. "I do hope you know what you're doing."

20

Ghrasia Madah said prayers to Sina over the now-deceased kin she had brought with her to Oma's temple, and the smooth-cheeked young people she had thought of as kin. So many dead in that bloody hall two days ago, and for what? Petty politics. Power. Their names would fade from history or be erased from it because of their crimes. No one worshipped a kin-killer.

She had trained and cared for these youth at the Liona Stronghold for over a decade, only to see their blood spilled by their own people. Anger coursed through her, so high and hot that she took a long plunge in the cold pools beneath the temple. She swam through the marbled tiers of the pools, thinking of the future she was promised so long ago as a girl. Her mother was so angry when she joined the militia that they didn't speak for three years. Her mother called her a warmonger and worse. Ghrasia had spent her life trying to prove her wrong, but when she closed her eyes, all she saw were all the people who died at her hand.

Some days, she wept to think her mother may have been right.

When Ghrasia emerged from the baths, the blood-red spite of her anger was gone. She was spent. Empty. The same way she had felt when she killed her first Dorinah during the Pass War. It was always the same. The blood tore her apart. Killing was like cutting off one of her own limbs. Every time she killed, she felt like she was bleeding out with them. Losing some part of herself.

After bathing and dressing in the red tunic and skirt the drudges had cleaned for her, she walked up into the sky of the temple to meet with the Kai. The Liona Stronghold was not a living hold the way the temples were. She did not like touching the walls or the railings here. Even sleeping within them gave her nightmares.

She ran into Nasaka's little mincing assistant, Elaiko, two floors up.

"Ghrasia Madah!" Elaiko said. "I apologize, but you must have an escort in the upper tiers of the temple."

"The Kai asked to see me," Ghrasia said. "Is that not allowed?"

Elaiko made some polite noises and small talk about tea as she accompanied Ghrasia up, never really answering her. Ghrasia already knew who was in charge of this temple, but it was good to get confirmation.

The Kai stood in one of the open Ora libraries at the top of the temple, his wiry young body illuminated in the spill of the suns gleaming through the glass ceiling. She was always disappointed he did not look more like his mother, though she had to admit his beauty was still captivating. Javia had been a good friend and companion. Javia had confessed to never really understanding her young son. Reading and mathematics were a struggle for him, and he had never been gifted by the satellites. Seeing him now, Ghrasia had to push away a strong surge of desire; his was a hard beauty, the sort cut with sorrow. She had a softness for sorrow, because sorrow so often showed up on the map of her days. Sadly, a pretty face did not a politically savvy ruler make.

He was arguing with Nasaka about something. Ghrasia expected they argued a good deal.

"Kai?" she said.

He turned but did not smile. His expression was terribly serious. A small tragedy, she thought, to have that face and never smile. She tried – and again failed – to tuck that thought away. She suspected Nasaka was vetting this boy's lovers with an eye toward some political end, and warding off all the others with a large stick.

"Ghrasia," he said.

"Ghrasia Madah," she said.

"Of course," he said. He clasped his hands behind his back as if it mattered. The whole country had seen his scars, as had she, when she fought beside his cowering cousin Liaro in the temple foyer. She felt his mother's loss again. Burned up in a foreign country, driven out by fear and some terrible argument with Nasaka that not even Ghrasia understood. "Your mother was formidable in her own right."

He had not cared much for small talk when she met him in the foyer. Understandable, of course, with their feet mired in the puddle of their kins' blood. "It's an old name in our family, Madah," she said. "I named my daughter Madah."

"You have many children?"

"Just the one," Ghrasia said, and she still cringed when she said it. She had often thought to adopt more children, but there never seemed to be a good time. Liona and the militia there were more family to her than her husbands and daughter, some days. "Oma does not bestow the same gifts on everyone."

"Indeed it does not."

"You wanted to speak with me?" she said, and her tone sounded harsher than she wanted it to. It wasn't the boy's fault for dredging up so many conflicting emotions. That was her burden. "I apologize for my abruptness, but I need to prepare and send home my own dead this evening."

"Of course," he said. "I'm sorry. Nasaka was... wise to send for you."

Ghrasia glanced at Nasaka. Nasaka, too, bore a face that suffered no amusement. Ghrasia imagined Ahkio would look much like her in his old age – serious as death, his face scoured in deep lines, posture always rigid, formal. Ghrasia had not seen Nasaka smile in years; she suspected that after all of Nasaka's crimes, she had very little to smile about.

"Ora Nasaka's instincts are often correct," Ghrasia said. Even when Ghrasia never wanted them to be. She had kept far too many secrets for this woman, but then, Nasaka had kept hers as well, hadn't she?

"We're a people with very little experience in violence," Ahkio said.

"Based on what I saw downstairs, we're getting a taste for it," Ghrasia said. She felt the anger again and tamped it down. Anger solved nothing. She had chosen a sword. No one forced it on her.

"I know," he said, "and it's the beginning of something worse."

Ghrasia knew where the power was behind the boy. The same place the power had always been. "What's he talking about?" she asked Nasaka.

"We'll require your services," Nasaka said. "He wishes to return the bodies of Tir's kin to Garika personally."

"Is that so?" Ghrasia regarded the boy again. Was he coldly calculating or a simpleton? Always hard to tell with young men. Even in Dhai, their passions often got the best of them. And this one had a reputation for losing his head.

"My mother thought very highly of you," Ahkio said.

"Many others do as well," Nasaka said.

Ghrasia wearied of Nasaka's endless politics some days, but Nasaka was easily the smartest and most calculating woman in Dhai now that Javia was dead. It made Ghrasia's heart ache, even now, many years later. Because for all Nasaka's cunning, Javia had still died under Nasaka's watch. On purpose? Ghrasia often wondered. It was no accident this boy had the title now. Ghrasia suspected Nasaka had maneuvered him into it from birth, though by all counts, he never wanted it.

"If the Kai wishes it," Ghrasia said, "I will, of course, accompany him to Clan Garika. I expect you will require the Liona militia I brought with me as well?"

"It would be appreciated," Nasaka said.

Ghrasia put thumb to forehead. "Tonight, or tomorrow morning?"

"The morning," Nasaka said. "We have much still to sort here."

"Thank you, Ghrasia Madah," Ahkio said.

"Of course," she said.

"Did you want to speak with Ora Dasai?" Nasaka asked Ahkio. "The scholars leave for Saiduan in the morning."

"Yes, of course," Ahkio said. "I'll leave you to your business." He nodded to Ghrasia and walked into the corridor.

Ghrasia sighed and waited. She felt the familiar dread that came with being alone in Nasaka's presence. Nasaka's darker nature only manifested itself in private. Ghrasia stood a little taller. She could still beat Nasaka in a duel, and that was something.

"So you bumbled in here three hours late," Nasaka said, "and we nearly lost everything."

"I'm not some gifted Ora," she said. "I can't control the Line connecting the temple to Kuallina. There was some problem with the vine that links up to the chrysalis. They had four tirajistas out on that strand to repair it. I could have marched, I suppose, and shown up three days too late."

"You could have sent word."

"I'm a woman of action, not words. You're the woman of words."

"Let's not do this. I'm overtired."

"You know I would never stand for a Garika on that seat. What's really happening here, Ora Nasaka?" In truth, she never thought Nasaka would dare to make Ahkio Kai. There were too many rumors about his parentage, mostly spread by Garikas, but the way Nasaka hovered over the boy only gave them greater strength.

"Oma's rising. We've been born under the wrong star."

Ghrasia stared at the floor a long time, trying to untangle her thoughts. Javia had spoken often of Oma and the collision of worlds written of in *The Book of Oma*. Legends and mysticism, Javia had said. But Ghrasia knew better. Far greater minds than her own had written *The Book of Oma* many thousands of years ago. It was the only guide they had now. She murmured a prayer to Tira, the star she had been born under. She wished, not for the first time, that she had been born in another time, under some other star.

"You understand I won't be an aggressor," Ghrasia said. "I defend the Dhai. I don't go out and murder people for no cause or for political gain, no matter what star's in the sky."

"You insult me," Nasaka said, but her tone was flat. "I have others for that."

"Your casual attitude toward the living makes me question your own humanity."

Nasaka frowned. "You are as troublesome as–"

"Who, Javia?"

"Let's pretend to be friends, Ghrasia. Do I need to bring up your daughter's offenses again? Let's not argue about the sanctity of life."

"No," Ghrasia said. It never took long for Nasaka to bring up her daughter. Murder was murder, no matter the circumstances; Ghrasia knew that better than anyone. But Madah was her only daughter and had hardly known better when she was twelve. Mistakes happened. Ghrasia should never have gone to Nasaka for help when she found Madah standing over her cousin's body.

"You have my loyalty," Ghrasia said. "You know that. But loyalty doesn't mean I won't argue with you. I'm not foolish enough to think I won the Pass War on my own, but I know how to lead people, the sort of people who don't like you very much. So, though you may not like me at all, I would ask for your respect."

"You know you have it."

Ghrasia smiled. It improved her mood just by forcing it; an old trick she learned from her mother. "Is there anything else, Ora Nasaka?"

"Keep an eye on him for me," Nasaka said. "He knows you were a confidant of his mother's. He will trust you. I need to know what he confides."

"As you like," Ghrasia said, but the words tasted bad. "I'm going to go prepare for our departure."

Nasaka turned away. Her usual dismissal.

Ghrasia made her way back downstairs. Elaiko shadowed her until she reached the second floor, asking if she needed food or tea.

"I've been assisted enough," Ghrasia said, and she failed to hide the exhaustion in her voice. It was not going to get any easier in Garika.

Once she was free of Elaiko, Ghrasia did not go back to her room but instead walked into the long foyer that looped around the Sanctuary. Inside the Sanctuary, the dead and wounded had been removed, and little seemed amiss. She walked until she reached the large, intricate tapestry of the Liona Stronghold. The scene was meant to depict the Dorinahs at the pass during the Pass War. The massive walls of the stronghold were shown from the viewpoint of an invading horde of maned, red-eyed women. And there, at the top of the battlements, stood the Dhai, calling their fistfuls of air and fire and snarling green plant life. It was difficult to ignore that one woman stood out among them, a tall, massive figure with a long tail of black hair. Her red tunic and skirt glowed, the way Faith Ahya's vestments were said to glow when she appeared to her people.

It was a terribly inaccurate depiction of Ghrasia, but it was her favorite. Many of the other portraits included her with Javia and her family, or standing among a number of great historical Dhai and Oras and clan leaders and heroes. And in those depictions, she looked more as she saw herself – a diminutive woman whose only real strength appeared to be the squint of her gaze and the profound loyalty she inspired in those who collected around her like flies to honeyed pitcher plants. It was not a fame she cultivated. It was something she was good at. Her face, her people often told her, was open and kind. And when she spoke, she did so with authority. One did not learn how to speak with authority in Dhai, not unless they had been raised as Ghrasia had, vying for very limited resources in a very poor clan. She was not truly of Clan Taosina. Her birth mother relocated there from Clan Mutao when she was very small, after her spouses were killed in a mining accident. She gave them both the moniker of Clan Taosina and pretended the past had not existed.

"We build the story of ourselves," her mother often said.

Ghrasia stared at the glowing woman on the battlements. This was how they all saw her – a shining god who could push back a tide of evil.

But in truth, she was just like everyone else. Bowing and scraping to Nasaka and her endless political push. What was Nasaka's true intent? She had gotten the boy the title, something Ghrasia had not thought possible. What else did she have in store for them?

Ghrasia had picked her side many years ago when she shared Javia's bed, but it didn't make the idea of spying on Javia's son any easier. Oma was rising, as Faith Ahya had promised in *The Book of Oma*. And Nasaka was rising with it.

21

"The Dhai are coming," Rainaa said, "and the Patron wishes to speak to you about it."

Shao Maralah Daonia lowered her blade, resisting the urge to slice out at Rainaa with it. Maralah practiced bare-chested in the chilly air of the courtyard reserved for the women of the Patron's hold in Caisau. As a general rule, she did not prefer segregated spaces, but since arriving in Caisau, she had enjoyed the relative solitude of the women's quarter. Only half the Patron's wives lived here, and they kept their personal slaves close. She sent her usual sparring partner, Shao Driaa Saarik, south to Alorjan on reconnaissance to shore up the city for their expected retreat south. That left Maralah with many hours of solitary training here.

She took up her tunic from the slush-filled fountain and wiped the sweat from her face. The pain in her torso was less today than the day before. A broad scar rippled up her body from navel to armpit, the gutting blow dealt to her by the invaders who'd taken Aaraduan. They'd left her to die, which was a blessing of the Lord of Unmaking, for a certainty. They didn't realize she had the hold's soul at her call, to repair her to some semblance of living.

Rainaa waited patiently, clasping her little hands in front of her. She was a big-eyed northerner; Maralah could always tell by the cant of the nose, with northerners. Like the rest of the Patron's slaves, her head was shaved bald, and she wore a purple wrap around her flattened forehead. Those born into servitude had the same sloped foreheads, an easy deformation to manufacture and impossible to hide. Slaves often bore the deformity as a badge of pride; newly conquered people or those plunged into servitude by debt or misfortune weren't so marked and were treated with more distrust. But flatheads like Rainaa surrounded the Patron and his family like loyal, well-prized dogs. The Patron thought them perfectly tame.

It was a foolish complacency, Maralah knew. She had been a slave, a long time ago, and trusted not one word or expression people like Rainaa tried to sell her.

In truth, Maralah had known the Dhai were coming three weeks before, when Taigan sent word of their acceptance of his terms and told her he had a possible omajista. But she had been in the middle of burning the fields behind her during the hasty retreat of their last remaining army in the west. When she shared the news with her Patron that they had lost all but three hundred soldiers, the Dhai scholars were the last thing on her mind. Not for the first time, she wished the Dhai were some fearsome people they could hire as mercenaries, not bookmaking philosophers.

Official word of the Dhais' agreement had come to the Patron some time later, with the Dhais' terms. They must have finished hashing out some kind of paper treaty by now. As if words on paper meant anything. Maralah remembered burning shelves and shelves of old treaties back in Aaraduan. Just so much ink on paper, or hide, or bone, or whatever other fool thing they thought to make marks on.

Above her, the sky was a gray wash. At night, the cloak of the stars sometimes rippled. Staring at the night sky too long now made her seasick. She had seen the invaders coming through the tears in the sky, driving omajistas far more skilled than Taigan before them. But countering their forces without an equal number of those who could channel the dark star was impossible. If Taigan did not find more people like him, they were lost.

"I come presently," Maralah said. Her chest tightened, but she banished her anxiety in the next moment. Foolish thing, to lose even that bit of calm in front of a servant. Rainaa was one of the Patron's little partridges; her every word and wince would find its way back to him.

Rainaa bowed stiffly at the waist.

Maralah watched her go. Every time a new Patron's family ascended the throne, they killed all the prior family's men and women, and raised their children as slaves. She wondered how much it delighted former Patrons to have the descendants of their enemies preparing their meals and washing their cocks. Maralah found the whole thing unsettling.

She walked back to her rooms and changed into a clean black tunic. She changed her padded shoes for a sanisi's proper boots and donned her coat, though it was early in the season for it. Most days were still above freezing.

Caisau's hold had been patched and rebuilt hundreds of times, so it was a hodgepodge of organic and inorganic matter. She walked from the tumorous growth that was the women's court and across the sky bridge to the central keep. Air moved through the hold from its skin, but light was another matter. Skilled tirajistas had lined the ceiling with bioluminescent flora around the entire outer perimeter of the hold. Windows only made an appearance as one neared the core of the keep or one of the centralized courtyards. Wandering Caisau's hold was like scurrying up and down four or five cities, each of them trundled up on top of each other, then suddenly bursting into the open spaces of the yards with their mosaic of fountains and shimmering green gardens. Even during the worst of the winter, yards in the central keep stayed warm, heated from below by great geothermal vents that carried heated air from the nearby hot springs beneath the floor and into the walls.

That meant that as Maralah ascended, the air got warmer, and she soon regretted bringing her coat. Before the routing of the western army, she had thought they might hold Caisau another three months, maybe even all winter, but every report she received from her scouts said the invaders were marching straight for Caisau, stopping only to pick over any field or farmhouse Maralah's razing party had overlooked. It would only be a few weeks before they had to abandon Caisau and move further south. Only her brother's army remained intact, and they were still holding the east. Eighteen armies massacred in just five years, cities swallowed, villages leveled. Some days, she felt like Saiduan had turned to sand, now slowly trickling through her clenched fingers.

Maralah asked after the Patron at his diplomatic secretary's desk and was directed to his private garden. One of his personal sanisi, Ganaa, held her up at the entrance and insisted one of his body servants announce her.

Maralah remained relaxed, despite her annoyance. She had saved the Patron's life numerous times. To be treated like one of his servants, like Rainaa, sometimes grated. She thought their sense of ceremony would have broken down here at the end, but it was the opposite: the closer they were to annihilation, the tighter they all clung to ritual and ceremony.

"You may enter," the Patron's chief attendant said, and Maralah moved past him into the garden.

The garden was a riotous mass of color. Massive bamboo bird cages hung from weeping willow and birch trees entangled with ivy and holly and some hardy purple flowered thing that looked like wisteria. A great copper-colored stone at the center of the garden pushed gouts of water over its surface, where it tumbled into elaborate channels carved into the floor. Maralah walked over them; the mosaic of the grate above the streams of water was solid and very old.

At first glance, it appeared the Patron was alone. He was a tall, straight-backed man with soft hands and bright eyes. He was about her age, though she would not have believed it if she hadn't read his birth date in some scandalous rag put out by the merchants in Albaaric on the occasion of his forty-fourth year.

His face was a puckered morass of scarred tissue just below his jawline; he had grown a fine beard in an attempt to mask the scars, but it only drew attention to them. The Patron's beard had become all the rage among Saiduan men and a few hirsute women, though, and now they all grew them out and trimmed them to the same squared-off wedge at the end.

The Patron wore a single piece of jewelry – a gold ring on his little finger with a pale blue stone the size of a robin's egg. For a man so often shielded by the flesh of others, he dressed remarkably practically, a fact she had always respected. Unlike more established Saiduan families, he had fought for his seat, murdering eight of his brothers for it. Or, rather, Maralah had killed them for him. She had joined the Patron because he had an eye for economics and infrastructure, something she felt the country sorely needed. She and her brother provided the teeth. It was a cruel irony that the man she chose for peace now led them in the bloodiest assault the country had seen in two thousand years.

As he turned, she saw another sanisi on the other side of the garden, one of the younger men she had trained four years before. The Patron went nowhere without one of her people, preferably at least two of them. She had seen to that.

"Do you have any new reports for me?" the Patron asked. "Perhaps some good news, like the northern half of the country sinking into the sea and taking these blighted people with it?" He had a warm, soothing voice, the sort of voice that could lull a man to sleep, making it easier to slit his throat. But this Patron was more likely to use his voice to sway a man to his side of an argument.

"I do not, Patron," Maralah said.

"Nothing from Taigan?"

"No, Patron."

"We've finalized our treaty with the Dhai," he said. "They should arrive in a few weeks if all goes well. I'd like your counsel on who to send with them, if we're all still alive by then."

"Wraisau and Driaa," she said. "Wraisau is already in Alorjan, and Driaa is on the way there for a reconnaissance mission. I need Kadaan here to oversee the patrols."

"We're spread very thin."

"Yes."

"How many dead on the coast?"

"The last skirmish? A dozen, as well as General Araalia."

"Araalia, too? Who's taking his place?"

"I'm promoting his son."

"His son isn't even eighteen."

"There were only two hundred men left under Araalia's command. I thought to combine them with what's left of Aaraduan's forces, but two hundred men with a boy to lead them will move more quickly, and I needed someone to begin shoring up our defenses in the south. Should it come to that."

"I am sorry about your brother," the Patron said.

"I had reason to send him there instead of Araalia," Maralah said. "He would have been the smarter strategist on that field. We grew up there. But I understand your decision."

"With your children dead, it benefits—"

"I understand your reasons," she said, because if he used his warm voice to talk any longer about how the fate of her line now rested on her thirty-six year-old brother's ability to seed heirs, she might betray her annoyance. Her brother's interest in women was generally only incited by strong drink, and then only if there were no strapping men about bearing traders' tattoos. No doubt he would settle in with a family eventually, but with events taking shape around them, odds were their line died with them. She had given up seeing anyone of her blood survive the season. Her hope now was far less – that when it was all over, a single Saiduan person still lived. Maybe even a whole village. Somewhere remote. It was possible.

"I apologize," the Patron said. "I still treat you as a colleague, not a subject."

"We won the contest for the seat," Maralah said. "No doubt your sons would have treated mine differently if I had them."

"You know I rely on your loyalty now," the Patron said. "More than ever."

"I promise you, Patron, whatever I do, I do with your interests at heart."

"And what you keep from me?"

"If I were to ever keep information from you, it would be for your protection," she said.

"But you would keep it?"

"To save you? And Saiduan? Yes."

He walked to the fountain. He washed his hands, then his face. Murmured a prayer to Para, Lord of the Air. Para was not his satellite; he was a tirajista, but Maralah had caught herself praying to every god in recent days. She had never spent so much time calling Oma's name.

"Are the Dhai meant to kill me?" the Patron asked. He still had his back to her.

"No," Maralah said. "I'm sorry I set that in motion so quickly. It was a desperate effort. I knew Aaraduan was lost."

He straightened. "The Maralah I know would have died on the wall at Aaraduan."

She rolled that over. He had been distant and dismissive since she crawled back from Aaraduan alone, bleeding out from a wound that should have killed her. She might have died, even with the soul of the hold to keep her upright, if Kadaan had not come back through the upper tiers of the hold before their final retreat, doing one last sweep as she'd taught him, and hauled her out the rest of the way.

"I'm yours, Patron."

"I wonder," he said. "It wouldn't be the first time one of these invaders replaced a woman I trusted with her shadow."

"I'm the Maralah you know. No other. We've been over this."

"Is Taigan yours or mine, Maralah?"

"We're all yours," Maralah said. "I burned that ward into Taigan to make sure Taigan was yours. If they replace one of us again, you'll know."

The Patron turned and pressed himself into her space. She held her ground, so their faces were inches apart. In her boots, she was nearly as tall as he. His beard tickled her chin. She felt the heat of him and smelled cloves and brandy on his breath, his afternoon repast.

She expected a knife in the gut. It would be a fitting way to end things. Unexpected, from his hand, but fitting.

"You killed a good many men to get me this seat," he said. "I ordered more put to death to keep it."

"Yes," Maralah said. She dropped to her knees. It hurt. She wasn't twenty, and her body let her know it. She gazed up at him. He towered over her now, and in his soft eyes she saw anger and something that unsettled her more – fear. "I was yours then, and I am yours now," she said. "They can read ancient Dhai. We can't."

"Get up," he said.

She did.

"You infuriate me," he said.

"I told you I was not a soldier, nor a wife," she said. "I am a sanisi. You've trusted me to get you into this seat. Trust me to keep you in it."

He leaned into her again, so his lips brushed her ear. "I am afraid this is a fight we will lose."

"I'm not," Maralah said. She placed her hand over his left breast. She felt the spongy mass of his tirajista-manufactured heart there, warm and taut, but so terribly fragile.

He caught her wrist but did not pull her hand away.

She said nothing. Just rested her hand there, a reminder. Seven years ago, she and an especially skilled tirajista had built that bloodthirsty, plant-based organ when a bolt passed through his original heart, striking him down on the field. She still counted it among her greatest accomplishments.

"We'll win," she said. "All looked lost that day, too, when you dropped on the field. But we came back. We will always rally, Patron."

He had become more short-tempered after Aaraduan. Four of his cousins had died when their retreating caravan was ambushed by a small force of invaders. She worried he was losing his faith in her and the sanisi who had risked everything to keep his heart beating.

He drew away. "Set things up with Driaa and Wraisau," he said. "I'll want to meet with these Dhai before we let them into the archive room, though. I want to be absolutely certain there are no enemies among them. We can't have Caisau compromised."

"I understand," Maralah said.

"You can go," he said.

Maralah relaxed and moved toward the archway.

"Maralah?"

"Yes?" She did not turn. There were times when she could not bear to look into his face, because she saw the young man he had been, the sparkling, handsome youth with the black eyes that everyone – man or woman – fell headlong into, until all they could see was his vision for Saiduan, for the restoration of a bloated empire stretched far too thin. Twenty years he worked to make them stronger. But it hadn't been enough. Now, to her eyes, he looked tired and broken, and she feared that if she looked too long at him, too often, she'd see her own broken face reflected back at her.

"If you betray me," the Patron said, "by twisting Taigan or anyone else, or if you are not the Maralah I know, I will have your hair, and then your life, however little that means to you now, and however much I cannot spare you."

"I understand," Maralah said, and left him.

She made her hand into a fist. He could take her life, but she would always have his heart.

22

Ahkio wore red, the color of mourning, and rode at the head of a procession of corpse-filled carts. Ghrasia Madah and Liaro kept pace with him. Two dozen militia took up the flank and the rear. Any journey by foot outside the temple required an Ora. Ahkio had brought a dozen of them, including Nasaka's assistant, Elaiko, and Ohanni and Shanigan, two of the only senior Oras in the temple that Ahkio could stand. He also chose four novices, younger, less predictable choices like Caisa, and a boy named Jakobi, and a powerful parajista called Naori who was about the same age as Ahkio and also his third cousin once removed. She reminded him just enough of Kirana that he was willing to see where her loyalties lay after six years inside the Temple of Oma. He had specifically chosen a greater number of novices than senior Oras for this trip. They would begin in Garika but end in Osono, because Yisaoh was not the only woman he meant to meet with.

Meyna had still not answered his letters.

As they neared the clan square, Ahkio sent Caisa off with six militia to clear out Kirana's quarters. She had kept a temporary house in Garika for long political visits; he only hoped Yisaoh had not cleared them out first.

"What if they fight us?" Caisa asked. She had been humming bars of a terrible Dorinah opera for the last eight miles that she'd picked up from a way house minstrel. Now she firmed her jaw and sat up a little straighter on her bear, and Ahkio was reminded of her age. He wasn't much older than her, and he was sending her off to wrangle with an angry family who'd just tried to kill him. "That's why the militia's with you," he said. "I expect Yisaoh is going to be waiting for us in the square. They know we're coming."

"Why would she want to talk to you?"

"So she can tell me she's right and I'm wrong," Ahkio said. "If you go to my sister's rooms or Yisaoh's and you meet resistance, turn back."

He watched Caisa and the six militia members break off from the group. Caisa started humming the opera again.

Ghrasia leaned over on her bear, said, "She'll be all right."

"She has a better chance than we do, certainly," Ahkio said, and waved the procession forward.

The Garikas waited for them in the amber-tiled square of Clan Garika, tucked five miles inside the textured webbing that kept out the worst of the plant life. The massive, gnarled bonsa trees surrounding the square were draped in red. Garikas came out onto their doorsteps or stood under the awnings of their shops and trading places. The weather had turned, and a warm, drizzling rain fell. The sky was a gray wash, heavy and oppressive. Outside the square, fog moved among the trees. Ahkio was not ready for low autumn; he wanted summer to last forever.

Clan Leader Tir Salarihi Garika stood in front of the council house. He wore one red armband, all he had given over to mourning. His broad frame was clothed in a black tunic and dark trousers, and a gray overcoat stitched in silver. He had a thick beard and the same heavy brow Ahkio remembered.

Yisaoh stood just to the right of her father, smoking and smirking. Ahkio recognized Yisaoh's mothers as well – Alais, Gaila, and Moarsa. All as formidable as their daughter. He felt like an animal being sized up for slaughter.

The militia Ahkio had brought fanned out ahead of him. Ahkio slid off his bear. Liaro said, low, "You sure you don't want me next to you?"

"Just me," Ahkio said, and patted Liaro's bear. Liaro's injuries from the week before had been minor. He had strutted about the temple with three stitches on his brow and some bruised ribs, but had otherwise escaped the fray unscathed. If anything, Ahkio suspected it had hurt his pride more than his flesh. Liaro was not a man made for conflict.

Ahkio saw none of Tir's other sons, though they may have been among the crowds lining the square. His blood quickened. He wondered if he would be the first Kai torn apart by his own people.

Ahkio pressed thumb to forehead. "Clan Leader Tir," he said. Because though he suspected Yisaoh and her mothers were the true instigators of this particular plot, it was Tir who bore the title of clan leader.

Tir did not return the gesture. "Ahkio," he said.

"I've brought you your sons," Ahkio said, "and your militia." His voice sounded steadier than he felt. Summoning the courage to speak was like pitching himself from some great height.

Ahkio gestured to the militia. They unloaded the bodies. Lined them up neatly in the square. Four rows of five, including Lohin. As Ahkio watched the bodies laid out, he wondered how it had come to this. He had spent a decade hiding from Dhai politics while old wounds and rivalries festered until his sister was dead and half of the most powerful families in Garika lost kin.

"Those that survived have been exiled from Dhai," Ahkio said evenly, "as set down in *The Book of Oma.*" He waited, but Tir said nothing. Ahkio did not look away, though his left hand started to tremble. He pressed the offensive hand into his tunic pocket.

Ahkio nodded to Yisaoh. "I'm certain your daughter told you when we spoke that if your house threatened mine, I would exile you and your kin. I am here to make good on that promise."

"The Oras have given you much power," Tir said.

"No," Ahkio said. "The people did, and you sought to usurp them. This could have ended differently. I could have married into your family, Tir. We could have been friends and kin."

"You will break ties of kin to keep to a code made for former slaves," Tir said. "We are no longer those people who fled Dorinah five centuries ago. You must know by now that change is coming to Dhai. We will need strength. A new way of doing things."

"According to–"

"Don't quote the Book at me, boy."

"I will quote the Book all I like," Ahkio said. Every old person in the country wanted him to keep quiet, to take a seat and die for it, but do it quietly. "*You* broke our kinship with your betrayal. Tell me what other fate Faith Ahya and Hahko would have for you."

"You are no Kai."

"You think we need a new government," Ahkio said. "You think I'm unfit for what's coming. You aren't the only clan leader to express such concerns. That's why I've called for a circle of the clan leaders, in Osono. We'll discuss changes peaceably, as Dhai do. Not like bloody Dorinahs."

A flicker of something – surprise? – crossed Tir's face. "I would sit in that circle."

"Perhaps you don't understand," Ahkio said. "You will not be sitting in this circle. You and your family have forfeited that right. I'm exiling you to Saiduan, to the third degree."

The crowd gasped. Even some of the militia looked unsettled. The third degree meant Tir and his wives, their children and children's spouses, and their children's children would be banished. Ahkio held up a hand for quiet.

"You have an apprentice," Ahkio said. "Where is she?"

"Here," said a woman from the crowd around the council house. She was broad and tall as Tir. Hazel eyes, a bit of a squint. Ahkio had looked up her name before they arrived. She looked nothing like her grandmother.

"You're Shisa's granddaughter," Ahkio said.

"Yes. My mother was clan leader before Tir."

"Will you sit with me in Osono as clan leader of Garika?"

"Don't you–" Tir began. He stepped forward.

Three dozen militia drew three dozen glowing blades. Ohanni and Shanigan and the other Oras raised their hands, and the air in the square grew heavy. Ahkio knew the Oras' stance was a ruse; they would not unleash Para on their own people. But the heft of the air made a strong statement.

Tir grunted. "You leave me with no choices."

"You already chose," Ahkio said. "When you murdered my sister."

Yisaoh sneered at him and pointed with her cigarette. "You listen, you arrogant fool. Kirana's messes were her own. You were off fucking sheep in Osono for years. What do you know what happened with Kirana, what promises were made? We did not touch your sister."

"Only innocent novices and Ghrasia Madah's fresh-faced militia, then?" Ahkio said. "You only murdered youths drawn from your neighboring clans?"

"There is a great assumption here," Tir said. "You assume my sons acted–"

"Don't lie to me in your own square while the bodies of your sons lie next to us."

"You're a fool boy."

"A lot of old people tell me that," Ahkio said, "usually when they fear me most." His other hand had begun to tremble. He stuffed that one, too, into his tunic pocket.

"Why isn't my youngest here, Kihin? Let him at least look his mothers in the face before you cast us off to Saiduan."

"Kihin's fate won't take him to Dorinah," Ahkio said. "Ora Dasai has agreed to take him to Saiduan on a mission of importance to Dhai."

"You mean he'll be your hostage," Tir said.

"If you step away peaceably, you can make a life with him in Saiduan, when he's finished his task for me," Ahkio said.

"You've overstepped. They'll make us slaves in Saiduan!"

"Would you rather he was lying here?" Ahkio asked.

Tir's wife Alais put her hand on Tir's elbow. A moment, no

more. She was a solid woman, not yet fifty. Tir did not look at her.

"The militia waits on your decision," Ahkio said. "Half a dozen will escort you and your family from Dhai. Whether they must do so forcibly is up to you."

"You ask me to casually choose the course of my life. My children's lives. It is a decision I cannot make in a moment, a day, a month. I need time."

"You don't have it," Ahkio said.

Alais said, "We will step away peacefully."

"Alais—" Tir said.

"We will step away," she said. "He brings us our dead sons and keeps our youngest with his Oras. Do you see another path? I did not birth my sons, nor raise that of my sisters, to see them slaughtered now."

"It has always been their decision—"

"Shush," Alais said.

Ahkio felt Yisaoh's burning black gaze on him but did not look at her. A single man or woman did not make a decision his family did not support, not in Dhai. There were too many family ties to consider. Kin were too close. Tir had not acted on his own. At the very least, his spouses supported and encouraged the actions their sons and daughter took. That's why it had to be an exile to the third degree... even if it included people Ahkio wished it did not.

Ahkio nodded to Tir's apprentice. "I will see you in Osono," he said.

Ahkio held out his hand to Tir. He could not stop the trembling, and he cursed himself for it, but he held the hand there, a last gesture of goodwill.

"Don't look at me, boy," Tir said. "Your mother twisted this country, and your sister was blinded to what's coming. My family's known for years what we faced, while you relied on some foreigner to come here and set you right. You march Oras and our own militia into Garika, two forces that have never been given leave to work together. You defile your own Book. I will not speak your name again."

Tir turned into the council house.

His wives followed. Yisaoh made to do the same, but Ahkio stopped her. "Not yet, Yisaoh."

"Go soak your head."

"Would you rather I say this in front of your family?"

She walked down the steps to him. Her mother, Alais, paused in the doorway and watched her.

Ahkio moved away from the house to a barren patch of ground near the rain barrel at the side of the council house. "You know I could have done worse for you."

"Why? Because I had the heart to stand up to you?"

"Let's not play. The boy you tried to kill in the temple lived."

"I don't know what you're talking about."

"The novice you stabbed on the steps of the scullery stair, sneaking around with Ora Almeysia."

Her look was incredulous. "Don't insult me."

"You were in the temple the night my sister died. I have a witness."

"The night she died?" Yisaoh shook her head. "I wasn't there. Check the Line records in Garika. I left the next morning, the day I heard word of Kirana's death. Not before. You think I walked there, attacked some boy, and then walked all the way back – a two-day journey! – only to take the Line the next morning? What, do you think I flew home on the back of a parajista? It's quite obvious you never taught logic to your little sheep students."

She made to walk back up the steps.

He grabbed at her sleeve. She jerked her arm away. "Don't even think about touching me, any part of me. Don't come within leagues of me."

"You say you wouldn't kill a boy, but you were happy to kill me."

"That wasn't my preference. Now, if you'll give me back some measure of my own autonomy, I have things to pack."

"I'm afraid you can't go back to your rooms."

"What?"

"I've sent my assistant and a contingent of militia to empty your rooms, and Kirana's quarters here in Garika as well."

"You have no right."

"I have every right. You've been exiled."

She took a pull from her cigarette and regarded him a long moment. "You think you're clever enough to save this country on your own? You aren't half so clever as you think. I wish whoever killed Kirana had killed you instead. The country would be better off for it."

She crushed her cigarette under her heel and walked back into the council house.

Ahkio twisted away stiffly. He paused a moment in front of his bear, then mounted. He looked at the mob in the square. He needed to say something to them. Anything. Instead, he was leaving militia the color of mourning in their square. And he could think of nothing to say to that, nothing that would make it any better.

As he turned his bear about, Liaro rode up beside him. "Could have gone worse," Liaro said.

"They may kill us yet," Ahkio said.

"They'll think about it a lot harder this time."

"Let's hope."

"Did you really mean what you said, about exile to the third degree?" Liaro said.

"Yes."

"You know who else that means, right?"

"Yes."

"That includes some of my cousins. It nearly included me," Liaro said. "And it definitely includes Meyna and Mey-Mey. Rhin and Hadaoh."

"I know their names, Liaro."

"Just wanted to make sure you weren't forgetting."

"I'm not going to forget."

They were a sodden, downtrodden group filing into Osono four days later, short a dozen militia members who had stayed behind to escort Tir and his family to the harbor. Caisa had returned with her escort, though, driving a cart full of Yisaoh and Kirana's belongings, unhurt and fairly crowing at the success of her theft.

Clan Leader Saurika met Ahkio in the Osono square. It was not a market day, so there were few people out to greet them.

Saurika reached for Ahkio's hands. "Are we kissing now?" Saurika said. "I'd like to welcome you as clan family."

"I accept," Ahkio said. He kissed both of the old man's cheeks.

"Welcome home, Kai," Saurika said. "Fancy a game before we talk business?"

"I've had enough games in Garika," Ahkio said, and he was surprised when Saurika laughed.

"Welcome to the seat, Kai." His face grew serious. "You're here to see Meyna and her husbands."

"I wanted to tell her myself."

"Too late for that," he said. "We had a messenger arrive hours before you."

"Is Meyna still here?"

"I don't know if they'll see you."

"Let me go with you," Caisa said, sliding off her bear. Ghrasia had issued her a sword along the way, a plain metal blade, not infused. Ahkio worried she didn't know how to use it, but she insisted she had taken classes at the temple and was very capable.

"I'm going by myself," Ahkio said.

"I know Meyna," Liaro said. "That's not terribly smart."

"No wiser than anything else I've done," Ahkio said. "Honestly, both of you. Stay here. This is something I need to do on my own."

"We've had enough funeral feasts!" Liaro called after him.

Ahkio started the long walk to Meyna's house. He had not slept well since he left, and his pace was sluggish. He did not expect to sleep well for some time. He walked up the spongy ramp to the house. Everything looked the same. He cracked open the door and called, "Meyna? Rhin? Are you home, Hadaoh?"

No answer.

Ahkio pushed open the door.

All was in order. He saw row upon row of carved eating sticks laid out on the table where Meyna had left them. Rhin's boots, caked with mud from the sheep fields, sat by the back door. Ahkio called into the house again.

He walked onto the back porch. Stared down into the community green behind the house. A dozen children played there, shrieking as they pelted one another with sticky thorn flowers. He saw Mey-Mey sitting away from the group, surrounded by a pool of the purple flowers. She smashed their faces into one another and threw them halfheartedly at the other children.

He recognized big, broad-shouldered Hadaoh speaking to a neighbor across the green. But Rhin and Meyna were nowhere to be seen.

Ahkio walked back into the house, calling for Meyna. He heard movement upstairs. A heavy thumping. He went up the stairs that curved around the inner core of the tree, to the second level of the house.

Meyna stood at a long table in the open room at the center of the second floor. Her hands were covered in black soil. On the table, little semi-sentient orb-blood plants squiggled in the piles of dirt. Meyna brought up a hatchet and severed the red cylindrical head from the stem of one of the plants, then tossed both pieces into a foaming bucket of salt water at her feet. Ahkio had seen her cull the plants before but recognized this as something different. She was murdering all of them.

Meyna glanced up at him, hatchet raised, fingers clasping another wriggling plant. "I wondered how long you'd be," she said, and brought down the hatchet.

"I hoped you'd still be here. I sent you letters. Did you get them?"

"The Soarina sisters are coming for the plates and Rhin's unsold ceramics," Meyna said. "You'd be surprised how much Afara Soarina wants them now that they come so cheaply. But the plants... well, no one wants the plants."

"The letters, Meyna?"

She laughed. The laugh grew louder and deeper, until she doubled over, clutching her belly. She had to set down the hatchet. "Marry *you*?" she gasped. "After what you just did?"

Despite the hatchet in her hand, he wanted to hold her. He wondered if he was mad for feeling it. But this woman had held him and comforted him. She'd welcomed him into her home, made love to him, done everything but marry him.

"If you'd just answered-"

"You don't love me or my husbands. You love power," she said. She held up one of the wriggling plants. "Do you want one? I have thirty, and thirty more after that. Not much use for them where we're going. They breed like flies in the woodlands. Beautiful but troublesome little things, liable to bite off a hand at maturity. But so sweet before they become deadly."

"They killed my sister, Meyna."

"You know that isn't true. Is that what Ora Nasaka told you?"

"Yisaoh was seen in the temple-"

She lay down the hatchet. Leaned toward him. Her face softened. "It doesn't have to be this way," she said. "Come with us, Ahkio. Ora Nasaka is turning you into something horrible. I do want to marry you, Ahkio, but I don't want some Ora's puppet. Give your title to some other scheming madwoman."

Ahkio's heart raced. How long had he waited to hear her propose? Years. The dying plants wriggled on the table. He saw her hand covered in their sap. She knew what he wanted. She had always known. She offered it now because she'd run out of options. The more Dhai talked of love, the more all he could see was politics.

"It's too late for that, Meyna."

"Let me give you a piece of advice, Ahkio," Meyna said. "Your sister had a good many irons in the fire. She was obsessed with that temple and kept you out of it for a reason. She asked me to take you into my home. And I did come to care for you, Ahkio. I did. But I can tell you that whatever she was doing there had nothing to do with the Garikas and everything to do with her own obsessions. Be careful you don't become just like her."

"Kai?" someone called from downstairs. Ahkio recognized Caisa's voice.

"Here," Ahkio said.

Caisa mounted the steps. She had one hand on the hilt of her sword. She eyed Meyna's hatchet.

"Is everything all right?" Caisa asked.

"It's fine," Ahkio said. "This is a personal matter."

"You shouldn't wander around alone," Caisa said, "especially not now."

Meyna set down the hatchet. She wiped her hands on her apron. "Oh, I see," she said, sparing a long look at Caisa. "I understand now."

"Meyna—"

"No," she said. "You've done a fine job of ingratiating yourself in the temple and with its... inhabitants. I wish you the best."

"Caisa, could you please let me—" Ahkio began.

"No, let her hear it," Meyna said. "Let her know how you treat kin. Family."

The anger he'd kept so well in check in the temple struck him then. He stopped fighting it. "Family?" he said. "You took me into your home and your bed to tie me to you. And to Kirana, from what you're saying now. Did you pity me? Did she? If you'd loved me, you'd have married me. You wanted the ear of the Kai's brother. You're as bad as the Oras. At least they don't pretend their interest is affection."

"You're monstrous," Meyna said.

"Only because it's the truth," Ahkio said. "You pack up your family and you go. I don't care where. But you and Tir and all his kin have no place here. I won't have civil war. Not now. Not ever. And I'll have justice for Kirana."

Meyna placed her hands on the table. Her look was icy. "Ora Nasaka has won this bout, Ahkio, but there is a war coming. And I don't intend to lose that."

He started down the stairs. He half expected to feel a hatchet in his back. But Caisa came down behind him, blocking him from Meyna's reach.

Ahkio got halfway out the front door before he realized this was the last he would see of Meyna and Mey-Mey. He wanted to turn back, ask to see Mey-Mey, so he could tell her that whatever Meyna would say about him, it wasn't true. But that wasn't something a Kai would do.

He rubbed his eyes with his fists and walked back toward the square.

Caisa trailed behind him. She kept the silence until they were just a few steps from the square.

"That was a very formidable woman," Caisa said.

"I seem to know a good many of those."

"And you have a terrible habit of angering them," she said.

23

What impressed Roh most about the Saiduan port city of Anjoliaa was the color; bright streamers of purple, crimson, green, and gold flew from soaring windows and feathered awnings. Saiduans dressed in the same bright colors – billowing robes with wide sleeves, long scarves, and vests with broad collars embroidered in silver. Most men wore long tunics and short coats, and many had their dark ears pierced. Their hair was long and black, knotted with colored ribbons like Dorinahs. There were smaller, paler people dressed in drab colors whose hair was cut short or shaved bald, their faces tattooed in black. They were slaves, ancestors of Dorinahs imported from Dorinah before the Saiduans retreated eight hundred years before. Roh also saw some men decked out in the clothing and markings of slaves who looked completely Saiduan. He knew the Saiduan enslaved others, but for some reason, it had never occurred to him that they might enslave themselves.

Anjoliaa was tucked into a wide bowl cut into a craggy plateau jutting out from the spur of the continent. The land looked immensely old, buffeted by strong wind, scoured clean.

Roh felt as if he had come to the end of the world.

Kihin stood with him one long moment at the end of the pier when they arrived. Great blubbery harbor seals, with toothy snouts and broad, delicate fins that looked more like plumage, pushed themselves off the iron mooring rings where they lay in the sun, entering the sea with a great splash. The smell of dead fish and offal, and something altogether spicier, stranger, filled the air.

Kihin gazed across the busy pier. He shifted his weight forward, as if he wanted to stand on his toes so he could see over the crowd. "My parents are here," he said.

"What, do you see them?" Roh asked. Passage across the Sea of Haraeo to Saiduan had taken several days. They had left the Temple of Oma in advance of the Kai's mission to Garika, but Dasai had already told Kihin what was coming.

"No," Kihin said, "but they're here. Somewhere. Now the Kai has the power to do whatever he wants."

"He's Kai," Roh said.

"Titles don't confer power," Kihin said. "People do."

Roh was not in the mood to argue. The other scholars disembarked behind them. Big Aramey and soft-eyed Nioni walked together, their heads almost touching as they spoke. Chali had spent much of the trip brushing up on his Saiduan, and carried a book even now down the gangplank. Dasai set the pace with his shuffling walk, moving past Roh and Kihin and calling for them to follow. Roh was never sure if he should admire Dasai or fear him, but he did pick up his pace.

At the end of the pier, two black-clad sanisi waited for them. The taller one was a woman with long frizzy hair knotted into a braid that touched the middle of her back. A smattering of freckles bruised her face. She had a dark complexion but not as dark as the man next to her. The other sanisi was a lean man with a massive beak of a nose and hair even longer than the woman's. His was wound with a fine string of bells that seemed terribly impractical for an assassin.

It wasn't until the man moved toward them, soundlessly, that Roh realized the bells had no clapper.

Dasai bowed at the waist. It was a strange thing to see. Dasai was a grizzled, petite man with a face like the gnarled confluence of some ancient tree. Roh found it difficult to watch him show deference – even respectful deference – to anyone. The sanisi made no gesture of deference in kind, not even a nod.

The sanisi exchanged pleasantries with Dasai, which Roh decided were boring. So he pushed his way ahead and stood next to Chali.

Chali gave him a stern look. Chali had spent the whole boat ride telling Roh how much he disapproved of Roh's presence among the group.

"I'm Rohinmey Tadisa Garika," he told the sanisi. "You can call me Roh."

The man exchanged a look with the woman. "They're Dhai," he said, in Saiduan, as if it were an apology. "I'm Ren Wraisau Kilia," he said, in very bad Dhai. "This is Shao Driaa Saarik."

"You're a woman," Roh said, "like that other sanisi."

"Not a woman," she said, as if disgusted. "I'm ataisa."

"Oh," Roh said. "I'm sorry." The Saiduan had three sexes – male, female, and ataisa. Ataisa were in-between people, those who lived in the seams of things, not quite male and not quite female. There was no equivalent term in Dhai, but it was just as rude to call someone by the wrong pronoun.

"You must be talking about Taigan," Driaa said. "There are dozens of ataisa among the sanisi, but Taigan is not ataisa and not male, not female. Taigan changes often." She shrugged. "Taigan is just Taigan. And Taigan will be the first to tell you that."

Wraisau said something that sounded like a curse. Then, in Saiduan, "Taigan is not a sanisi. And he shouldn't be a woman again for a season yet."

"You know he can speak Saiduan?" Driaa said, in Saiduan. "They didn't send these ones along for their looks. Though they are terribly pretty. For cannibals."

"We'd be pretty, too, if we danced around in circles all day singing to plants and fucking each other," Wraisau said.

"Your most fervent desire, I know," Driaa said.

"One can dream."

Roh found their wry tongues and loose manner confusing. It wasn't at all like he imagined they'd be from books. "Aren't you deadly assassins?" he said.

"I apologize," Dasai said. He leaned forward. Despite his small stature, his mean face and the deep tenor of his voice got their attention. "No doubt we all have much to say to one another. But perhaps not on this pier? We have traveled many days."

Wraisau bowed, finally. Roh stood a little straighter. Maybe the Saiduan would be less rude. "Of course," Wraisau said. "I apologize. Things are difficult. I suggest you all stay close. Foreigners are often kidnapped in Anjoliaa. They do like pretty boys, especially." He looked at Roh.

"Thanks," Roh said.

The sanisi procured them bears and supplies and led the party overland around the base of the big plateau and out onto a dusty flatland. Roh marveled at every moment of it. The sky looked bigger here, vast, like the world went on and on forever. They trekked for two days across the flatland and entered a wide valley cutting through a low rise of smooth-topped mountains. Rice paddies and red grass fields draped the valley and the gentle base of the mountains.

It took another week to cross the valley, and as they turned north, the weather became cooler. The trees were different: tall and many-limbed with leaves the size of Roh's head, their bark rough and knotted, the color of burnt cream. He had no Dhai name for the trees, because they didn't exist in Dhai. Most of the vegetation was that way the farther north they went: familiar, but other. The grass was tall and leathery, brown-gold, or topped in bunches of dark seeds.

Roh had expected to see more evidence of fighting as they traveled. Wasn't Saiduan under siege? But the landscape was pristine, virtually untouched. They passed a few small villages and towns lined in red stones, but no one came out to greet them or challenge them. Stranger still, the plant life here was somewhat tame. Roh spotted what must have been a herd of walking trees in the far distance, but the roads and undergrowth were clear of snapping, deadly things. Driaa still burned the area where they slept every night, but the sanisi seemed remarkably unconcerned about being eaten by plants in the middle of the night.

"Where's the fighting happening?" Roh asked Wraisau.

"What?" Wraisau said, "Disappointed not to see us gutted and laid out?"

"Why would I want that?" Roh said.

Wraisau frowned. Driaa said something to him sharply in Saiduan, too fast for Roh to make out.

"The fighting is farther north," Wraisau said. "They haven't reached us here yet. We just abandoned Caisau to them and retreated to Kuonrada."

"With luck, you can stop this before we must move again," Driaa said to Roh, but her tone was bitter.

"Why don't you want us here?" Roh said. "We're fighting the same enemy. We should be friends."

Wraisau grinned and glanced over at Driaa. "You must admit," he said, "he grows on you."

"It's dumb talk," Driaa said.

"It's the way we all sounded before the war," Wraisau said.

"I never sounded like an illiterate Dhai," Driaa said.

"I can read," Roh said.

"Ze means you lack wisdom," Wraisau said, using the Saiduan pronoun for ataisa to refer to Driaa. "But to be honest, I could do with some company who has a little more hope than sense these days."

When they arrived in sight of Kuonrada, it was high autumn in Dhai, but here, the trees had already shed their leaves, frost covered the ground in the morning, and a cold wind came in off a tangle of craggy mountains framing the city. From a great distance, Roh saw a massive glacier wedged into the maw of the mountains above the city from which sprang the cold, clear river their caravan followed.

Kuonrada was a mountain city, a city built for cold weather and defense. It was the first big city Roh had seen since Anjoliaa. The defensive wall reared a good fifty feet above the grassy plain, an impassive face to the dark city.

As they crossed over the threshold of the stone gate and into Kuonrada, Roh rode up near the front between Nioni and Dasai, just behind the sanisi. The ground beneath them was bare stone, worn smooth. The city buildings, too, were of stone fit with the same precision as those of the defensive wall. Where were the famous living holds of Saiduan?

The city felt as old as the mountain. Its residents wore much darker colors than those in Anjoliaa. Instead of sandals, they wore boots and heavy coats lined in fur. Their hair was braided back in three long braids, one on either side of the head, another along the top, knotted with dark ribbons. They seemed taller than their southern counterparts, darker-skinned.

Passers-by stopped to stare at them. When Roh looked up, he saw the open wooden shutters of the apartments above. Veiled children peered out at them.

As they approached, the great gates of Kuonrada opened.

Roh kept pace with Chali and Dasai through the gates and into the main yard of the keep. At the bottom of a double stairwell that led up to the main door, a tall, thin man stood. He was dressed in a black ankle-length tunic stitched in silver, the sleeves wide, the collar high. He wore over it a short coat lined in white fur. His white hair was wound around his head and pinned close. Behind him stood three young men with shaved heads, dressed in drab gray tunics and short coats. They kept their gazes averted.

"Ora Dasai," the white-haired man said as the riders entered the yard.

Roh handed off his bear, and he and Nioni helped Dasai dismount.

"It has been some time," the white-haired man said. He held out his hands and clasped Dasai's forearms without permission. Roh winced at it, though Dasai didn't protest. The sanisi had largely kept their distance from them while traveling. But now that they were going to be among so many people who tried to touch him without asking, Roh was suddenly uncomfortable.

"Keeper Takanaa," Dasai said in Saiduan, inclining his head. "I trust all is well in the house of your Patron?"

"As well as can be expected. Come, my assistants will bring your men inside. The Patron asks that you dine with him tonight."

"Of course," Dasai said.

Takanaa showed them into the hold and through many broad corridors, finally stopping at a great hall that ended in a hub, with six rooms facing a central foyer that boasted plush chairs and low tables at its center.

"These are your scholars' quarters," Takanaa said, "and your shared lounge. Does it please you?"

"Very much," Dasai said.

Takanaa unlocked each of the doors. Roh and Kihin chose a room together. Roh was disappointed to see two narrow beds inside and a simple stone fireplace with banked coals. Two scuffed trunks.

"A little bare, isn't it?" Kihin whispered.

"Maybe the others are better?" Roh said. Not even a temple drudge would be expected to sleep in such spare quarters. There wasn't even a window. Roh searched for something to put onto the fire and found more coal and a few logs. He discovered candles in the trunks and lit a few to give them light to unpack by.

After Takanaa left, Roh went to look at Dasai's room. Chali stood outside the door, and moved aside as he approached. Dasai's room was much the same as Roh's.

Aramey came up behind Roh. He was a beefy man in his forties, with a generous grin and broad hands. Unlike the others, he wasn't gifted, but he had been a student of Dasai's for two decades.

"It seems we'll have to do something worthy to receive better quarters," Aramey said.

"No one of our number," Dasai said, "is naïve enough to think that anything we are given will come without consequence. I urge you all to accept no gifts, and make no oaths or promises. Breaking such things is a grave crime here. If there is a situation you find confusing, please refer whoever is speaking to you to me."

"We heard this four times on the boat," Roh said.

"And you will hear it forty more times if need be," Dasai said. "Accept no gifts, Rohinmey."

Roh opened his mouth but closed it again at a look from Chali. Roh had argued with everyone but Aramey the entire trip.

A few hours after dark, a man dressed in a long purple robe and short black coat appeared at the door of the sitting room. He knocked politely, even though they had left the outer door open. Behind him was a small bald man, dark but with the features of a Dorinah, whose forehead looked unnaturally flat.

He introduced himself as Ko and invited Dasai to supper with the Patron.

"This novice will act as my assistant during supper," Dasai said to the Saiduan, waving a gnarled hand in Roh's direction. "Is this acceptable to your Patron?"

Ko bowed. "Of course. I will escort your scholars to the shared dining hall for their supper with our local scholars."

Roh and Dasai followed after Ko through wide-ribbed corridors, some of them lined in mirrors. The halls of Kuonrada bore none of the sinuous lines and circles of Oma's Temple. Dasai shuffled slowly beside him.

There were no frescos, no tapestries. The stones making up the halls were nearly as tall as Roh, set with the close seams of the outer walls, and when not covered in mirrors, the stones were carved into scenes of violent, frenzied battles. Roh walked past a carving of a vicious wolf a head taller than him goring the life from an armored body.

"Beautiful, aren't they?" Dasai said.

"Who are all these battles with?" Roh asked.

"The Dhai," Dasai said, "and the Talamynii, before us."

Roh gazed at the carvings again. The brown, green-eyed Talamynii, the "children of the white wolf," had tamed the wolves of the continent, wolves half again as big as dogs, their more docile counterparts. But even they had not been able to stand up to the Dhai armies, four thousand years before.

Ko took them through a number of passageways, down a hall lined in black-clad sanisi – more than Roh had ever seen – and halted outside a cavernous room without windows. A tall, lean man stood speaking to two other men a pace between the table and the far wall. Two sanisi stood at either end of the table. A massive table of polished dark wood stood at the center of the room. There were four place settings of crystal. The dozen chairs ringing the table were carved in fearsome faces and padded in deep green velvet.

"It has been some time," the man said.

He could not have been much past forty. Roh thought maybe he was one of the Patron's sons, sent with apologies for his father's absence.

"Patron Alaar Masoth Taar," Dasai said.

"Ora Dasai," the Patron said.

The Patron stood a head and shoulders taller than Dasai, slender of waist and shoulder, not thin but knotted, wiry. If the Patron were two decades younger, Roh would have called him beautiful. Time had worn the beauty, made it hard and handsome, not pretty. His heavy beard covered terrible scars on the lower half of his face.

"I trust you met with no ill luck," the Patron said.

"None," Dasai said, "though I heard it said we were in good fortune to arrive whole."

"You were." The Patron's gaze moved to Roh. "And you have brought another."

"My assistant," Ora Dasai said, gesturing for Roh to come closer. "Rohinmey Tadisa Garika, a novice parajista. Excellent dancer. Competent fighter."

"You have trained with Ora Kimey?" the Patron asked.

Roh barely remembered the correct tense for addressing a Patron in Saiduan and was certain he botched it. Why did there have to be so many titles and honorifics and polite ways of speaking?

"I am the student of one of her students, Ora Ranana. Ora Kimey has retired to Clan Osono," Roh said.

The Patron's gaze lingered, as if he were evaluating a dancing partner or a sparring opponent, sizing up their skill.

"Please be seated," the Patron said. "I'm afraid all is not as well prepared as it should be."

Roh was startled to see one of the sanisi move forward and lay out six loaves of various types of bread in all different shapes and hues. He never imagined sanisi serving a Patron or his guests. They were assassins, not servants.

The sanisi brought out small bowls of other things – some kind of green slurry that looked like spinach or seaweed, diced fruit coated in cayenne pepper, and twelve kinds of fish dishes: fish heads, fish tails, cubed fish, dried fish, pickled fish. Roh couldn't figure out what types of fish they were, but the smell made his stomach turn.

Roh waited until the Patron ate. He took a slice of bread and slathered it with the various condiments. Roh filled up mainly on bread and the seaweed-spinach mixture and the spicy fruit. To his horror, Dasai partook of each fish dish in turn. Roh tried not to gag.

He knew from his classes on Saiduan culture that drinks were served after the meal, not during it, but he hadn't thought about that before eating the spicy fruit. His lips burned and his eyes watered.

The Patron glanced over at him and laughed.

"You're an adventurous boy," the Patron said. "I see why Ora Dasai brought you."

"How much information have your scholars found?" Dasai asked. Roh noticed he had stopped eating or drinking anything.

"Little," the Patron said. "We have a piece from the *Book of Miracles* that's very similar to your *Book of Oma*. We found some older historical pieces, but they all dated back just eight hundred years. What we need is far older."

"You realize," Dasai said, "that finding a two thousand year-old text telling us how the invaders come through, and how to stop them, is highly unlikely."

"Of course," the Patron said. "But if there was ever a time for miracles, this is that time."

The servants took away the still nearly-full trays. Then they brought out the watered wine and liquor. They placed four different types of glasses in front of Roh. One short and round, one tall and slender, one tall and fat, and one goblet with a long stem. Roh waited to see what the Patron did, but thankfully, the servants poured them each drinks into what Roh presumed was the correct glass.

Roh tried the amber liquid in the goblet first. Two sips, and it already made his head fuzzy. He saw Dasai watching him closely.

"If all goes as it has, we should be able to last the winter here before they assault our position," the Patron said. "You'll have until then to find some record of how to stop these people. It's been done before, when the Dorinah insect-witches were turned back. They nearly spawned their way across this continent during the same rising that swept us here. It was the Dhai who were turned away that time."

"We're better at dancing than fighting now," Roh said, and then covered his mouth. Perhaps he was a little drunk.

"Yes, let's speak of happier things," the Patron said. "Do you dance the three genders?" the Patron asked.

"Our five and your three," Roh said. "Yes, I dance them. I was one of Ora Ohanni's best dancing students."

"I have a party of dancers in residence," the Patron said. "There is a particular piece that requires six female roles, and only four of my dancers are comfortable with those steps. They are mostly variations of kanik and morasha forms, with some vonov, which is much more fluid. Difficult to learn but satisfying."

"Oh, I know those! They're–" Roh began.

"I do not want this project to interfere with your work, Ora Dasai," the Patron said, speaking over Roh. "Three hours in the mornings, perhaps. The performance is the day of Para's Ascendance. After that, she begins her descent from this world once again. We will begin to feel her presence less and less with each passing day."

"I'm certain it will not impact his work," Dasai said. "I only hope he can bring you pleasure."

Roh had a difficult time hiding his surprise. After years of saying no and keeping Roh bound up in boring classes and shuttered away from everything, Dasai was going to let him join other dancers for Para's Day of Ascendance? He wondered if the trip to Saiduan had made Dasai a little mad.

Dinner ended several hours later. Roh was nodding off into his dessert liquor when Dasai told him it was time to go. The Patron had talked a long time. Roh thought he would regale them with tales of battles and conquests, but mostly, he talked about building bridges and roads that halved the time it took to reach remote outposts. Roh found all the talk about taxes and the overseeing of government officials tedious.

The servant, Ko, reappeared to lead them back to their rooms.

"May I take your arm, Roh?" Dasai asked. "It is a long walk."

"Of course," Roh said. He offered his arm, and Dasai took it. They walked several steps behind Ko.

Roh said, in Dhai, "Why did you agree to have me spend time with the dancers? You never let me do anything."

"The Patron does not make requests. He orders."

"It all seems so rude," Roh said.

"It's meant to be," Dasai said. "Imposing one's physical presence, one's desires, on another is a demonstration of power. It's meant to remind you that your body belongs to the Patron of Saiduan."

"How can people live like that?"

"One learns."

"I couldn't live like that."

"Couldn't you?" Dasai said. "I am not so sure."

"You knew he'd ask me about dancing. It's why you brought me to dinner. You want me to tell you if I learn anything, don't you?" Roh said. "You want to know what they're saying about us."

Dasai stared at the back of Ko's head. "We are being kept together like animals," he said, "to ensure we learn only what the

Patron has to tell us. Your presence elsewhere gives us a better idea of how things are moving around us. You understand?"

Roh didn't want to use the word "spy" out loud, even the Dhai word, so he didn't. "I understand," Roh said.

"And besides," Dasai said, "if things go badly here, you may need more friends."

"Why would things go badly?"

"Sometimes ignorance is a blessing. Revel in your ignorance just a bit longer."

When they arrived back at their quarters, the others had already finished supper and gone to bed. Kihin waited up in their shared room, paging through a book of Saiduan poetry.

"What was the Patron like?" Kihin asked.

"He talked a lot about taxes."

"Sounds like dinner with my family," Kihin said.

"Both of you need to sleep," Dasai said, rapping on their door. "Kihin, I want you to act as escort to Rohinmey in the morning. He will be beginning dancing classes."

"Dancing?" Kihin said, but Dasai was already walking to his own room.

"What were the other scholars like?" Roh asked.

Kihin yawned. "Dull. Very serious. They have an odd scholar, though. Luna. He's one of those ataisa, like Driaa." They spoke in Dhai, and Kihin used the Dhai male-passive pronoun for Luna, not the Saiduan ataisa pronoun, which Roh thought was interesting. "He's Dhai but bound to Saiduan. He's... interesting."

"Kihin, have you seen many women here?"

"It's odd, isn't it?"

"I didn't think it'd bother me that much. I know they try to separate people here. But it feels very strange."

"I expect we'll get used to it."

Roh wasn't sure that was something he wanted to get used to.

Through the door, Roh heard Nioni's voice. Roh fell asleep to the sound of Dasai and Nioni talking in low voices.

Later, Roh woke to the sound of Chali's raised voice, and
before Dasai hushed him, Roh heard him say, "—death for every
one of us if they catch you out at this, Ora Dasai."

After that, a door slammed, and Roh heard nothing more.

24

Traveling across Dhai unnoticed was not as difficult as Lilia imagined. The spaces between the clans were toxic, contaminated, crawling with poisonous plant life. Most people took the Line, riding inside the shining chrysalis that traveled along the tirajista-trained cables linking the temples and holds. The few who took carts stayed on the roads. And they always traveled during the day, unlike the night-traveling sanisi who urged Lilia on.

Taigan bought another bear – with no small amount of grumbling at the trouble Lilia had caused him – and escorted her across the Dhai valley to the pass at the Liona Stronghold. The stronghold was as old as Dhai, a massive construct of parajista-shaped stone wrapped in vines and tirajista-trained trees that clawed at the sky. The pass cut through the jagged mountain range separating Dhai from Dorinah – more a canyon than a rolling path – and the stronghold spanned the rent in the mountain range at its narrowest point. The stronghold was far vaster than Lilia thought possible, even from the illustrations she saw in books. She had thought the Temple of Oma the largest structure in Dhai.

"I can't believe we built such a thing," Lilia said. She looked forward to a bath and a meal that didn't involve Taigan trying to press her into eating dead animals.

Taigan snorted. They were alone on the road. It was nearly dusk, and most people had stopped at the way house eight miles behind them. "Gifted tricks build great things," he said. "But they can be torn down as easily as anything else."

"How can you say that? It's been standing five hundred years. The Dorinahs never once got over it."

"Your Dorinahs have far greater priorities," Taigan said, "and far fewer gifted people. It's not your petty militia they fear, but your ability to call on the satellites."

"So, you're saying the Dhai are *good* at something?" Lilia said.

"No," Taigan said, and began to lead the bear off the road.

"Where are you going?"

"Around Liona," Taigan said.

"But… they interview any Dhai going in or out. If they don't have a record that you left, you can't get back. They'll think I'm an exile."

"You won't be returning," Taigan said. "Or have you forgotten your oath to me?"

Lilia gazed up at the hulking stone of the hold and felt a renewed burst of fear. She had agreed to leave Dhai forever. Twice now.

"We're going around," he said.

"You can't go around the pass," Lilia said. "It's… impossible."

"It's not impossible," Taigan said. "Simply not pleasant. You'll need warmer clothes. Or perhaps I will cart you there in the belly of a bone tree."

"I'm not afraid of you," Lilia said.

"It will give me time to train you privately," he said. "Some place no one will get hurt."

"I would never hurt anyone," Lilia said, but then she remembered Gian.

"It's not other people I'm worried about," Taigan said.

Taigan couldn't say how one spotted the difference between a person who could channel the satellites and a person who couldn't. The old woman who'd mentored him spun great stories around seeing some bright essence about a person, but he had never seen it. Most teachers, he suspected, did as he did – probed at a person with the breath of the satellites and looked for resistance. Those who could channel had a natural inclination to resist the power of the stars. Many had drawn on that power from their birth – a function as innate to them as drawing their first breath. If one was lucky, the child might be able to draw on the same star as those who tested them. Then they could see the breath of the star when the child drew on it.

But this girl, this little scullery girl... she resisted his every effort. Perhaps she was too old to train. Or simply not as skilled as he had hoped. He had a week to break her, provided the way across the mountains progressed as well as he expected. But as he watched her huff her breath into her cupped hands that morning in the mountains, shivering despite four days of concentration exercises meant to take her mind away from such things – he didn't think it would be enough. He began to wonder if it was worth it to find her mother, if all she had passed on to her daughter was this poor display.

Worse, he had caught a scent on the wind of someone following them. He suspected the only people who would follow them were those who thought the same about the girl as he did. And that meant invaders.

The girl looked up at him from her hands and made a moue. "What is it?" she said.

"Nothing," he said, and rose, somewhat painfully, from his crouch near the cold fire pit. "Let's go through the songs again." His gut churned. The twisting of his insides had begun. Already his male organs had tucked themselves back up into his body, and his chest had begun to swell. He hated the change, every time, no matter what he changed into. Soon he would retch and bleed, and then he suspected it would be time to switch his pronouns again. He was already thinking of himself as ataisa – someone in between. It still gave him some comfort to match his physical sex to a gendered pronoun, even if he longed for some term more unique to him and his constantly changing body. There was no word in any language for him, not truly. Sometimes he wondered if it meant he didn't exist. If he lived outside history. His body was Oma's to do with as it willed. Oma gifted him this unpredictably changing body and mind, which could not be killed and hardly aged.

He had yet to see how either gift served any use to anyone. Some things, he resolved, had no purpose, no matter what the seers said. Maralah needed omajistas who could open gates, but that was not his best skill.

No, all he was good at was not dying.

"I'm making good progress, aren't I?" Lilia asked. Her mind was tangled with Saiduan songs. Taigan told her the songs were supposed to help her concentrate and build things with the breath of Oma, but they were just nonsense sounds to her.

Taigan grunted. He was grumpier than usual, and even less responsive, since they had trudged into the mountains. The air here was colder and drier. After two days of ascent, the plant life thinned out. The mountains were a rocky wasteland – jagged, sometimes porous rock shot through with hunks of twisted metal. When she asked Taigan where the metal came from, he'd looked at her strangely and said, "They don't teach you that?"

"What would they teach me?"

"Ignorant parasites," he had muttered.

When they passed far grander things – massive slabs of soap-slick stones as tall as Lilia, shaped like hands or mossy, grotesque faces – he did not even glance at them. Lilia stared a long time at them, though, and traced the spidery writing on their bases with her outstretched fingers.

"Do you think these are older than Faith Ahya?" Lilia asked.

"Who?"

"The first Kai. Do you think she saw these things when she came here from the slave camps in Dorinah?"

"I should not be surprised that your primary political and religious figure was a slave," Taigan said.

"We were all slaves, once," Lilia said.

Taigan said something biting in Saiduan and yanked at the bear's lead again. With Lilia riding and Taigan walking, they traveled very slowly over the rough terrain.

"Do you want to ride the bear for a while?" Lilia asked.

"No. You're too slow."

"If you're such a great healer, why don't you fix my foot?"

"A sound idea," Taigan said. "If you'd like me to chop off your leg and then spend three months legless while it grows back. We have no time for that. It's an inconvenience, not life-threatening."

"But you could fix it," Lilia said. "The tirajistas say they can't, because the bone is ruined, not just flesh."

"Most things can be fixed," Taigan said, "if they're organic. Perhaps if you're a better student, I'll chop your leg off someday."

"You make everything sound so kind," Lilia said.

"But there is one thing we should take care of," Taigan said. He reached up and took her wrist.

"What did I tell you about asking?" she said.

Taigan's grip was firm. He recited one of the songs he had taught her – the Song of Unmaking. Her skin prickled where he touched her.

"Stop it," Lilia said.

Her skin burned.

She shrieked.

Taigan released her.

Lilia rubbed her wrist. The burning stopped. Her skin looked the same. "What did you do?"

"I removed your ward," he said. He squinted up at her. "Yes. You'll be a bit easier to remember, now. I suspect you had few friends at the temple." He picked up the bear's lead again and started walking.

"Roh was my friend," Lilia said. "He could always see me."

"Some parajistas have the ability to see through or break wards," Taigan said. "In truth, it's impossible to bind a parajista with a ward. The pattern simply will not bind with their blood."

Lilia considered her wrist again. "How did you do it? You just unraveled it?"

"The ward was created using the same symbol burned onto your skin," Taigan said. "Any omajista could see it. You could too, if you'd only open yourself to the star's breath. I suspect she meant for you to unravel it. Your first task. But I fear you're not as gifted as perhaps she hoped."

"You mean the trefoil with the tail? That's the symbol?"

"Yes. The ward was sewn into your skin using that pattern as the base. It was just many trefoils bound together, all hooked by their tails. Wards are easy enough to unravel if you know what symbol was used for the base."

"This is like being blind," Lilia said. "I can't see any of these things."

"Work harder," Taigan said.

"Would you tell me to work harder to see if I was blind?"

"Better to say that you should not be surprised to be blind if you continue to close your eyes."

Every morning, Taigan ran her through a series of stretching and concentration exercises, not unlike those she started her mornings with at the temple in Ohanni's dancing class. She found most of it boring, the same way she did in the temple.

"You're not actually making any progress," Taigan said. They sat around the remains of a fire, the charred ends of sappy crackling brush covered over in ash. It was the only thing that burned well in the mountains.

"Then why are we still doing this?" she said.

"Because you're incompetent," Taigan said.

"That bone tree might have a different opinion."

Taigan stood. Lilia started. She clenched her fists and prepared for the worst, but he only sighed and said, "I have a story for you."

"A Saiduan legend?"

"Something like that," Taigan said. "A problem. A puzzle."

"I'm good at those," Lilia said.

"Let's say there's a man who does tricks. Not the sort someone gifted does. Do you have these sorts of tricks in Dhai? Sleight of hand?"

"Yes, of course. We play all sorts of strategy games, too. Screes, kindar, bendi-"

"Fine, fine," Taigan said. "There are two men in a small village. Like most people in their village, they are illiterate."

"You're saying they can't read? Everyone can read."

"No, not everyone can read."

"Every clan has schools."

"They are Saiduan. Not Dhai. We are a very large country. We cannot school every child."

"That's very sad."

"Be that as it may," Taigan said, and she could already hear the rising irritation in his voice. "A younger man approaches an old man and asks him to pick a stone from a bag. He asks the old man to write a symbol on the stone. Any symbol he likes but preferably one of great power. The young man puts the stone back into the bag, hands the bag to the older man, and instructs him to find the stone he marked. But the stone is not in the bag. The young man tells him he can find the stone one mile from their village, in the belly of a bladder trap. When the older man goes off with the other villagers, they dig up the bladder trap and find the stone, with the same exact symbol the older man wrote on it, deep within the flesh of the trap. How did the young man perform the trick?"

"What does this have to do with magic?" Lilia asked. "Was he a tirajista?"

"No. The whole village was full of ungifted, I told you. Not one could draw on the satellites."

"That's not very realistic."

"Not in Dhai, perhaps. But in Saiduan and other places, it's quite typical."

"The men lived in the same village together? All their lives?"

"Yes."

"Where were the women?"

"What?"

"You said they were all men."

"It's just what one says."

"What did they do for a living?"

"What does that matter?"

"Details matter."

"Let's say they were fisher people."

"Were the men in on this together? Or was it just the young man who knows how the trick is done?"

"Just the young man."

Lilia pondered that. "If I was old and I didn't know any letters, what letter would I know? What symbols? I don't know. That just doesn't happen in Dhai."

"So, you give up? Just like you give up learning to channel the satellites?"

"You're not giving me enough information."

"You can't even think through a proper problem," Taigan said. "Perhaps that's why Oma's breath eludes you."

"Your litanies and songs don't go anywhere," Lilia said. "There's no... no *problem*."

"The problem is you're shaping up to be a very poor omajista."

"Just because you want me to be something–"

"Here's a problem for you," Taigan said. He scuffed away the large stones on the ground before them and drew a circle in the dirt. Then he placed three sets of six stones facing one another. It looked much like a game board. "We have two opposing forces here," Taigan said. "The line of stones closest to you is the defending force. The line closest to me is the offensive. You have three legions of mounted cavalry, two with long-range weapons, and one infantry. I have four mounted cavalry and two infantry. If I move my mounted cavalry forward–" Taigan pushed four of his stones toward her. "How would you respond?"

"This is a war game. We don't play war games."

"Then pretend we're throwing bread at one another," Taigan said. "While riding bears."

Lilia contemplated the stones. It was like a game of bendar, she decided. "I move one of my ranged fighters to flank you on the right and meet your cavalry with mine." She took her two infantry stones and one ranged fighter stone and positioned them on the left flank of the cavalry. "I meet your exposed infantry with my ranged fighters, clear them with my infantry, and once they are out, have them come at the cavalry from the rear, with the support of the ranged fighters."

Taigan scrutinized her. "You said you didn't play war games."

"We learn *about* war," Lilia said. "I studied all the great Dhai battles from before our exile. They made me better at strategy games. I won against my friend Roh all the time. I even played Oras and novices sometimes."

"You're serious?"

She shrugged. "I studied a lot of things."

"You never mentioned this."

"I studied anatomy, too, and agricultural science. I studied magic, and astronomy, and plant biology. I didn't clean sinks *all* the time."

"You are serious about everyone in Dhai knowing how to read?"

"When you forget your history and where you came from, you might forget where you're going. That's what Ora Gaiso always said."

"How old are you?"

"Sixteen, almost."

Taigan shook his head. "Too old for magic," he said. "It's a shame. You looked much younger."

"What are you saying?"

He kicked the stones away. "Only that I wish we'd found you ten or twelve years ago, so we could have shaped you into something useful."

Taigan sat above the camp several nights later, perched on a massive boulder that still retained the suns' heat. Below, the scullery girl tossed and turned in her bedroll. By all counts, she should have been so exhausted that sleep came easily. But her stamina was better than he expected for a cripple.

He saw a swarm of long-tailed swallows dive toward him in the semi-darkness. He held out his hands and dismantled them. They broke apart into the wispy tails of Saiduan characters. He smelled burnt bread and something more pungent: mold, rot.

Over the last few days, he had run the scullery girl through a number of famous battles, using stones as markers – battles the Saiduan had fought against the Dhai while they warred for the continent for a thousand years. Taigan considered himself fair at strategy, and he had the advantage of already knowing both the best and actual outcomes, but the girl seemed to have a knack for it. He played through multiple scenarios and watched her trounce him in three out of every five. This from a pacifist with no training. What could she do with instruction? With actual knowledge on the field?

The Saiduan characters unfurled into Maralah's message, a response to the update he had sent her two days before. It was a much shorter, simpler message than he expected.

We have enough war heroes. I need an omajista. Break her or kill her.

Taigan stirred the characters with a breath of wind for a long time, watching them swirl and pull apart until they were completely illegible. Then he crawled down from the boulder and walked back into camp.

"Was that Saiduan writing?" Lilia asked.

"Yes," he said.

"Was the symbol the man wrote on the stone a Saiduan character?"

"What, in the riddle?"

"Yes, the one about the illiterate men."

"Yes, the symbol he wrote was a Saiduan character."

"It was his name, then," Lilia said. "If you're illiterate, you still have to sign documents. Agreements. Papers. Those sorts of things. You do those in Saiduan, just like here. We've had treaties with you. So if you were illiterate, the one symbol you would know for sure, the one with the most power, was your name. The young man knew that."

"And how did he get it into a bladder trap, then?"

"He lived in the same village with the older man," Lilia said. "He planned the trick a long time before, when he was a child. He wrote the man's name, the symbol, on the stone and planted it many years before. Then he chose that same man for the trick. He knew that man would write the one symbol he knew. His name."

"Is that what you've been up thinking about?" Taigan asked.

"I tried to think what one symbol everyone would know," Lilia said. "Something that was the same across Saiduan and Dhai. We'd have to know our names. To sign public records."

Taigan grunted.

"See, I'm doing well," Lilia said, and rolled onto her side.

But he needed a gifted young girl, not a clever one. He had been a clever girl once, and Oma, Lord of Heaven, knew how that turned out for him. He scratched at the wound at the base of his spine.

Taigan suspected being clever would not turn out any better for her than it had for him. He sniffed the air. Their trackers were closer. Another day, and they'd be upon them. He needed to decide how much of the girl to leave to them.

At midday, Lilia stopped to gather water in the trickling gully of a streambed that looked like it was once a huge clay pipe, as big around as Lilia was tall. The water came from a massive hole milled from the side of a sheer rock face that stretched on and on, covered in scraggly trees and vines Lilia had no name for. She was tired, and Taigan had been surly all morning.

Taigan regarded the cliff face as Lilia rubbed at her sore rump. "Where now?" she said, gesturing to the cliff. "It'll take a long time to go around."

"We go up."

"We can't climb that."

"Up," Taigan said. "Draw on Oma, as I've taught you, and propel yourself up."

"Taigan, I'm–"

"Up," he repeated, and raised his hand. A whirlwind of air threw dirt and small stones at her. Taigan kicked up and grabbed hold of the tiny crevices and spurs of the rock. He jumped up the rock face like he weighed nothing – a feather pulled by a string, leaping from point to point, sixty feet up the face of the cliff.

Lilia watched him, breathless, as he came to the top. He crouched. Peered down at her. "Your turn," he called.

"You know I can't!" Lilia said.

"You will," he said, "or you'll die down there." He moved away from the edge of the cliff. She lost sight of him.

"Taigan? Taigan! You promised to take me to my mother!"

"Fly, fly little bird!" Taigan called, his voice growing distant.

"Taigan!" She moved up against the wall. She saw nothing that looked like it could hold her weight. She screwed her courage and jammed her good foot onto a small spur beneath her. She tried to lever herself up. The spur broke. She fell.

"I'll play your stupid game," she muttered. But not as he would expect.

Lilia led the bear over to a nearby rock. She climbed up onto the rock and slid onto the bear.

Left or right? She looked back at the streambed. The broken pipe curved to the right. If whoever had built this pipe built them the way they did in Dhai, the pipe would be going downhill. She would go north, following the cliffside until she found a way across it, and then come back south until she either found Taigan or found where Taigan waited for her. If he had waited.

She heard the call of a bird, close, and urged the bear forward. In places, the way was impassable. She had to crawl around large boulders and knotted trees. The bear looked behind them often, snuffling, and she worried about predators. She found shelter that night in the arms of a tree, and tied herself tight so she didn't fall off. In the morning, she went on, stopping for water when she found it.

After two days, the long curve of the cliff tapered away. She crawled up the loose stone and shale, grabbing at knotted roots and bushes. At the top, she yanked on the bear's lead and urged it to follow.

She rode the bear the rest of the way, heading south again, back to the place where Taigan had abandoned her.

It was midday when she heard Taigan say, "That was clever but wrong."

Lilia started. Taigan dropped from the draping of a cluster of dense trees, twenty feet above her. He landed neatly in front of Lilia, sending up a little puff of dust, agile as a cat.

"I'd rather be clever," Lilia said. She slid off the bear.

Taigan walked past her, to the lip of the cliff. He gazed at the streambed below. "Three days I waited, expecting you to fly back," he said. "Then I realized what you'd do and came to meet you. You really are just a plain little scullery girl, aren't you?"

Lilia dropped the bear's lead and met him at the edge of the precipice. "I'm sorry I'm not what you thought I was," she said.

"I don't understand why you're unteachable," he said. "Perhaps you're too old. That was a concern. The ones I've worked with before were still children, and most were from Dorinah. They had more discipline, and more..." He stared intently at her. "Fear. It made them easier to train."

"You know you're fighting Dhai, don't you? Another kind of Dhai."

Taigan sighed. "Yes. Some of us know. Why do you think I came to Dhai to find omajistas? What better way to fight the enemy than with the enemy himself?"

"I'm sorry," Lilia said. "I'm just not what you think I am."

"It's a pointless exercise," Taigan said. "I'm losing time. The world is losing time."

"But my mother–"

Taigan's palm thumped hard into her sternum. Lilia lost her balance. Tipped over the cliff. Her ankle knocked a jutting spur of rock. Pain. The freedom of falling. She had a moment of abject terror. Shock.

Taigan's dark form, the edge of his coat fluttering in the wind. Gazing down at her, receding, falling away and away and away... This is a long fall, she thought. It's a mistake. He'll stop it.

"Fly, fly little bird," Taigan called.

Her mother used to call her that. There were three intonations in Dhai, and "Li" with the third intonation meant "bird."

But she had always been broken, for as long as she could remember.

And broken birds didn't fly.

Lilia pinwheeled her arms, clawing at air that whistled around her; a pretty, perfect song.

Songs. Trefoils. Oma.

If she could just–

She grabbed at all of it as she fell.

Her fingers found only air.

Lilia opened her mouth to scream–

Jutting branches and twisted tree limbs splintered beneath her. Snapped her ribs. Raked flesh. Crack and heave. She broke through the low canopy of stunted trees at the base of the cliff and crashed into the sandy streambed below. She landed on her right side. Her right shoulder fractured beneath her. Her right arm snapped.

She rolled another few feet into the soft ravine, sliding to a halt among heavier river stones at its bottom, her blood smearing the rocks.

Lilia saw her own twisted arm, her hand folded back unnaturally, fingers grazing her wrist. Her mouth filled with saliva. Screaming. She wanted to scream. Blackness juddered across her vision.

Fly, fly little bird.

25

The bloodstained tents of Zezili's army were an ugly harbinger for the dajian camp spread below them in the muddy valley. Massive fences and temporary housing had been allotted to this group for at least a century. Zezili sat at a makeshift table outside her tent, gazing across the valley as the dajians lit their fires and put out their laundry and belted out prayers to Para in the little green space at the center of the camp. She imagined these dajians as some monstrous horde of invaders, led by the sneering face of the Kai she had met on the other side, but her imagination failed her. The dajian camp here was enclosed by stout adenoak fences and peppered with guard towers staffed by local enforcers. Technically, these dajians belonged to the Empress herself and were available for rent to neighboring farms that relied on their labor twice a year for harvest and planting. The rest of the time, they served as parasites and brood stock, ensuring there was always another generation of laborers at the ready. Zezili thought the whole thing was a mess, but she liked cheap food, and dajian labor made that possible.

Every dajian she killed now reminded her of her country's impending starvation and destruction. Surely the Empress understood the implications of these deaths?

Monshara approached Zezili in the dawn quiet – Zezili heard the squish of her boots in the turf and the huff of her bear first – leading her mount behind her.

"I have a delivery to make," Monshara said, patting the leather canister at her hip: the map she'd received from the other side. "I'll be back in the morning. You'll have clearance from the towers by then to enter the camp?"

Zezili grunted at her and returned to her breakfast. The morning was chilly and her tea was weak. Summer's balmy evenings were well past, and low autumn was upon them. The season also brought fog that sometimes blanketed the world for miles in every direction, so thick it was like breathing soup. The mist below was nothing compared to how it would be later in the month.

Monshara seemed to take the grunt as an affirmative and moved on past Zezili toward the rocky, scorched road.

Thoughts of fog put Zezili in mind of her childhood, and she remembered that her mother lived not far from this camp, in a little town called Saolina. Her mother, who knew how to make mirrors. Zezili dumped out her cold tea.

"Jasoi!" she called.

Jasoi stood outside her tent, throwing her dagger at a twisted stump littered in knife wounds. She had a good throw, and more often than not, Zezili found herself eating something from the pot that Jasoi had picked off with her dagger earlier in the day.

At Zezili's call, Jasoi turned. She yanked at her helm and swore. Her long hair had gotten tangled in it again.

"Cut it off," Zezili said.

Jasoi pulled her helm free. It took a hank of reddish hair with it. Zezili had never seen hair that color on anyone but a Tordinian. Jasoi sheathed her dagger.

"You're just jealous," Jasoi said. She still ended her sentences with a rising intonation and slushy consonants; a typical Tordinian accent, though she had been in Dorinah for two decades.

"No, I'm practical. You should have buzzed your head when you got lice."

"It wasn't a problem."

"Eight hours in a chair getting insects picked off my head is a problem," Zezili said.

"What did you want, Syre?" Jasoi said, tucking the helm under her arm.

"You have the legion," Zezili said. "I'll be going into Saolina this morning."

"Yes, Syre."

Zezili kicked awake one of her pages – some rosy-cheeked kid from Daorian – and had Dakar groomed and saddled. Some days, she suspected Dakar was better groomed than she was.

She took the main road into Saolina, three hours of riding past sprawling farm holds bursting with children and dajians. The popular refrain in the cities was that the farmsteads produced rice, yams, and the entire country's children. City women tended to have the number required to avoid taxation, but country women often had twice as many. Children were cheaper than dajians and tended to be a good bit more loyal.

Zezili's mother lived in a modest three-story brick house built around a dead bonsa tree that was at least as old as Dorinah. Curtains of weeping moss trailed from the skeletal branches. When Zezili knocked, the house dajian said her mother had gone to the salon. Zezili rode on, down into the central spiral of the city. At the end of the winding road was the Temple of Rhea. The way was lined in artisan and market shops.

She reined in Dakar outside the salon, a nondescript building faced in marble with a painted red awning. She tied up Dakar and pushed inside.

Like most salons, Saolina's was a buzzing hub of activity. Zezili found salons a little beneath her station these days – she had dajians to do her hair – but for most of her life, her mother brought her here twice a week to have her hair trimmed, rolled, curled, and heated. Four women and one man sat in the waiting area, drinking tea and gossiping about local politics. The man was conservatively dressed and seemed to belong to two of the women, sisters from the cast of their faces. The air smelled of burnt hair, boiled agave, and pomade.

Zezili moved past the curtained waiting area and into the long rectangular room where a dozen hairdressers worked nimbly at the shoulders of their clients – twisting, clipping, rolling, and burning hair. The lacquered silver mirrors that stretched across both long walls were a familiar design, each infused with the emerald essence of Tira. Zezili walked past the open-air stations to the back, where gauzy curtains gave the clientele a bit more privacy.

"I've got a question for you," Zezili said.

Her mother raised her gaze from her own image in the mirror and squinted at Zezili. Her feet did not quite touch the floor. She scrunched her plump, lined face as if she'd tasted something rotten. "A year of silence, and you come to me for favors?" She clucked her tongue and waved at her hairdresser. The hairdresser was as old as her mother – pushing toward sixty. Zezili had known her since she was a child.

"We'll need a private room, Haodatia," Zezili's mother said, and then, to Zezili, "won't we?"

Haodatia ducked her head and went to prepare a room. Zezili's mother sat solidly in the padded seat, half her hair dampened with agave and rolled into tight curls at the front, bound in string, and the back knotted in triangles of paper that had already been heated to set the curls. The un-papered portion of her hair hung down to the middle of her back, waiting to be rolled and sewn into place with the rest. Zezili found the elaborate hairstyles exhausting, but her mother hadn't let her cut her hair until she was fourteen, due to concerns about how it would upset their social standing.

Now Zezili stood before her in a dirty padded tunic, her stringy, tangled hair pulled back into a simple tail, blood and dirt smeared across her boots. If the whole town hadn't known who she was, she expected she'd have been booted from the city limits the moment she began down the spiraling road to the temple.

"You should grow out your hair," her mother said. "You look like a peasant."

Zezili chose to ignore that and her mother's challenging stare. They gazed at one another in the mirror until Haodatia returned.

"It's ready, mistress," Haodatia said.

She led them to one of the two private rooms at the rear of the salon. The wooden partitions were latticed at the top, letting in air and light but muffling conversation. Haodatia had lit two additional lamps to give her light to work by.

Haodatia took up another set of paper triangles and began looping the next roll of her mother's hair.

"I hear you're murdering slaves now," her mother said. "How uplifting."

"How do you destroy a mirror?" Zezili asked.

Her mother raised her brows. "Really? You came all this way for that?"

Zezili gestured to the green-glowing mirror in front of them. "You made all of these," Zezili said, "and more besides. I thought I'd come to the expert."

"You're talking about infused mirrors?"

"No," Zezili said, "the kind I can bash in with a sword. Yes, mother. Infused mirrors."

"My daughter has a tongue," her mother said.

"She is spirited," Haodatia said, "like her mother." She reached for the heated crimping iron set in a bowl of coals on the counter.

"Once it's been infused," her mother said, "they don't break. You know that. But why do you care now? You never took interest in my art."

"I was in the area," Zezili said. "Humor me."

"I have humored you a good deal, girl."

"Before it's infused, you could destroy it, right? Same as any other mirror?"

"Certainly."

"What if it was really big?"

"Big, what does that mean? Be precise, Zezili."

Zezili wanted to tell her it was as big as the Temple of Rhea in Daorian, but suspected her mother wouldn't believe that.

"Big as a building," Zezili said.

"Ha," her mother said. "A building." She scrutinized Zezili's face in the mirror. "Well, it's fairly easy to destroy such a thing before it's infused, but that would likely require help. A fairly skilled parajista could break it, or perhaps you and half your legion hacking away at it."

"But once some parajista or tirajista infuses it, that's it? No one can take it out?"

"Take it out? Are we targeting mirrors now on our military campaigns?"

"It's important," Zezili said.

"Indeed." Her mother pursed her mouth, deepening the creases around her lips. She dyed her hair white to match her weathered face when she came to the salon. Zezili saw long white streaks in it, too bold for natural color. Elder women commanded more respect.

"Once it's infused, the only one who can break it is the woman who created it," her mother said. She lifted a finger and pointed at the greened mirror. Zezili watched a tiny crack appear on the bottom right of the glass. It spidered up along the edge of frame, ending abruptly halfway up the face. Her mother pulled her hand away. "It's certainly possible another who could channel the same satellite could do it, but it would take longer. A woman's patterns, the way she folds together the metal and power of the satellite, are unique. It would take another tirajista two or three weeks to unravel this mirror."

Zezili stared long at the crack in the glass. She had never wanted talent; channeling the satellites was a rare gift among Dorinahs. Her mother's station would have been far more advanced if she'd been more powerful. As it was, she could do a few tricks and infuse weapons and other items, but Zezili had never seen her shape trees into boats or grow and strip orchards with a glance. For the first time in many years, Zezili thought it might be a useful thing. The mirror had still been under construction when she went through. It was possible it wasn't infused yet. But if it was... Breaking the shadow mirror would require someone to open the gate – one of Monshara's omajistas – and a parajista to break the mirror. Or maybe an omajista could make a portal and break the mirror, too? Zezili didn't know enough about how any of it was done yet. And she certainly didn't have those types of people in her social circles. In truth, she didn't have much of a social circle. All she could bring were the bodies to fuel the gate. At least she understood the bodies part.

"Thank you," Zezili said, and turned away.

"Look at that, Haodatia; she thanks me!" her mother said.

Zezili waited until she was clear of the salon before thrusting her helm back on. Being in town made her suddenly self-conscious of her hair. She hated that.

As she began to untie Dakar, she saw Haodatia running after. Zezili paused.

Haodatia handed her a folded piece of lavender paper. "Your mother wanted me to give you this," she said, and touched Zezili's sleeve. "It was good to see you again, Zee."

Zezili grunted at her and turned away, taking the paper with her. She saw Haodatia's tentative smile wither. The hairdresser went back inside.

Zezili unfolded the paper and read her mother's neat script:

> *Anyone making a mirror that large would require a very talented jista. Our best is Isoail Rosalia. She lives above the traveler's house outside Lake Morta, doing special projects for Tulana. Tell her I sent you. She owes me a favor.*

Zezili crumpled the note and stuffed it into her coat.

She'd need to burn it later. Lake Morta. There was no dajian camp anywhere near there. It was remote and, this time of year, would already be cold. In another month, snow would start to block up the passes around the country there, and she'd have no way in or out until late spring.

Zezili gazed along the clean, neat streets of Saolina. Women stopped under the awnings to chat. Lines of children sat outside the schoolhouse, eating hasty lunches of rice and dried fish.

Dajians cleaned out the bubbling fountain of azure-colored stones in the square while traffic of all sorts – yellow carts pulled by bears and dogs, rickshaws, and the occasional ridiculous tirajista-trained organic tricycle – wove their way around the fountain, up and down the blue stones of the street. She loved her country. Loved it fiercely just the way it was, even when it hated her. Her Empress told her murdering dajians would save all of this, but she had heard that before when her mother said that murdering Zezili's father would solve all of their problems. "We'll have a fresh start," her mother had said. "You can forget he had anything to do with you. You're only mine now. A real Dorinah." But even without him working inside the house and around the grounds, even after he was many years dead and burned, she thought of him still, and how his face was so like hers, and how she could see his eyes staring back at her when she looked into a mirror.

They had not been able to maintain her mother's country estate after that. Her mother had tripped on a stair that should have been mended long before, and broken her arm, and lost her livelihood. A woman with only one good arm wasn't called on as often to make mirrors.

Zezili thought about those consequences, about the ripples, and wondered how powerful were the ripples she made with the hundreds of deaths she was cutting out across Dorinah. Who would clean the fountains? Mend the stairs? Harvest the food? And how long would it be before they came for women like Zezili, too? She was not so insulated as the Empress, maybe. She could see it because she had lived in the country her whole life. She knew the economy relied on dajians, and she knew that there were plenty of women in Dorinah who would happily burn her with them, as if she weren't a human being at all.

She thought of the day her mother fell and how it changed everything. She thought of how that day would look for Dorinah, when it woke up from the genocide of its dajians and found itself economically ruined... while a storm of invaders burst through the mirror connecting their worlds.

Zezili glanced back at the salon. She had hundreds more dajians to kill in the morning, and she needed to come up with a real plan on how to stop the madness of it all without forfeiting her own life.

26

The clan leaders arrived by dog, by bear, by foot, by cart, by boat, by Line. They assembled in the council house of Clan Osono for food and tea and polite conversation. The tension in the room chilled Ahkio. It took all his courage to smile and greet each clan leader and their companions.

After they settled in, Ahkio shut the windows in his room on the second floor of the council house and turned to face Liaro. Clan Leader Saurika had had the rooms cleared for him; it was a spacious chamber overlooking the square.

Liaro sat in the low divan at the center of the room, legs crossed, arms draped over the back of the divan. "I'm going to be a terrible audience," he said.

"That's why I want you to listen to it," Ahkio said. "If I can convince you I'm competent, maybe I can convince them."

"I know you too well."

"Thank you for the vote of confidence."

"Well," Liaro said, waving a hand. "Get on with it."

Ahkio cleared his throat and began to recite the speech he'd prepared to give the clan leaders.

Liaro interrupted. "That's enough," he said.

"I haven't even started."

"Exactly," Liaro said. He came over and stood next to Ahkio. "You look like you're at your sister's funeral. And that's over. Back straight. Chest out. And stop hiding your cursed hands.

They've all seen them a thousand times. Nobody cares."

"I need to be serious."

"You're plenty serious," Liaro said. "That's the problem." He stood straight next to Ahkio, feet slightly apart, shoulders back. It was a supremely confident stance, the one Liaro adopted every night they socialized in the Osono council house, charming women and men alike with an easy smile. Ahkio, by contrast, stayed upstairs with Caisa, going through all of his sister's and Yisaoh's books and papers, uncovering old temple maps and ciphered communications that made his head hurt.

"Oma," Ahkio said. "I'm not you."

"Listen," Liaro said. "I've seen you on your own, trying to charm people. You're terrible at it. Far too serious. Nobody wants a brooding leader. They want somebody they can relate to. Somebody they can laugh with and have a drink with."

"No one wants that. They look at me and see a child."

"Your sister smiled a lot," Liaro said. "Mostly when she was pulling something over on them. When it was time to be serious, she was serious. It's not just about trusting you. It's about liking you. They think you're sucking at Nasaka's breast, and I don't blame them."

"Thank you for that thought."

"You don't need jokes in this speech," Liaro said. "But you do need to be more relaxed and less closed. You ever wonder why the women you courted were more likely to come home with you when I was on your arm? It wasn't my good looks. It's because people like to laugh. They don't want to be with somebody who's been mourning dead people his whole life. You understand?"

Ahkio tried to tuck his hands under his arms. Liaro took his arms and pulled them back out. "Deep breath," Liaro said. "Look up. Not at the floor. It doesn't look confident. Don't be upset. This is what you asked me to do."

"I know," Ahkio said.

"If it was easy, you wouldn't have asked. Now come on. Do the speech."

Ahkio met his cousin's look. "Thank you," he said.

"Don't get soft now," Liaro said. "I didn't like sleeping without you, either."

He and Liaro had shared a bed – on and off – since they were twelve. Ahkio had never gotten into the habit of sleeping alone; it was half the reason he spent so much time asking women to come to bed with him. The idea of sleeping in a big bed alone was... lonely.

"And thank you for understanding," Ahkio said. "About Meyna and Rhin and Hadaoh."

Liaro's mouth made a thin line. "I'm not happy about it, but I know why you did it," he said. "Just... don't burn any more houses down behind you. They will hate you for turning your back on kin. It's unforgiveable."

"All right," Ahkio said. "Here's what I'm going to tell them."

"Just keep in mind," Liaro said, "they're not going to remember the words. They'll remember how you made them *feel*. Make them feel something."

Ahkio took a breath, and began, "We have reached a point–"

"You're looking at the floor again."

The last clan leaders to arrive were Hirosa of Clan Badu and Tir Salarihi's apprentice, Isaila, acting for Clan Garika. With her were three members of the militia, come to tell Ahkio that Tir, Alais, Gaila, Moarsa, their children, and their children's children had been successfully escorted to Asona Harbor. They had gone willingly.

"And Meyna?" Ahkio asked.

"By the time we came to escort them, they were gone," the plump leader of the squad told him. "Cleared out their house here. I don't expect you'll see them again."

Ahkio could have sent the militia out after them, could have set them to tracking Meyna and her husbands to ensure they left the country. Instead, he thanked the squad and dismissed them. Liaro said he was too serious, but more often than not, Ahkio worried he was too soft.

Ahkio seated the clan leaders in the broad common room of the council house. Most brought their apprentices. The loose group drank tea and smoked Tordinian cigarettes and pipes, and the gazes they fixed on Ahkio were clear but wary.

"I would like to speak to you about Tir Salarihi Garika," Ahkio said. "There are rumors I would like to put to rest. And a way forward I'd like to discuss with you."

On the other side of the room, Nasaka slipped in. She stood at the back, leaning against a broad window frame. Ahkio wondered if she'd timed it just this way, to break his concentration. He had not called her from the temple and wondered what she was doing here.

"We have reached a point in our history much discussed but never experienced," Ahkio said, and then wondered if that even made sense. Liaro hadn't critiqued his words as much as his delivery. He pushed on, hoping he didn't botch the rest too badly. He tried hard to ignore Nasaka. Teaching ethics often required the gift of persuasion, but persuading a child and persuading a clan leader were two different things entirely. He straightened and stood with feet slightly apart, the way Liaro had. "Our gifted Kai, my beloved sister, has been transformed, far too early and before bearing children. I regret that I am not here to introduce you to one of her gifted daughters, a woman who could lead us through what will be difficult times. I was never intended to lead you. Many of you know I would have preferred it never came to this."

He paused, gauging his audience. When he was nervous, he talked fast. Keeping a measured tone was especially difficult when half the audience looked bored or angry, as this one did. Then he saw Liaro enter at the back of the room. Liaro leaned against the back wall, on the other side of the door from Nasaka. He nodded at Ahkio. Grinned.

Ahkio mustered up his courage and said, "Nearly any Dhai here could stand against adversity. I have watched us take on great challenges and conquer them, from the Pass War to hundreds of Saiduan blockades of our harbor. But Faith Ahya, the mother of our people, said that if you ever wanted to test a person's character, you should give them great power. You may think I'm asking you to trust me with power. I understand the fear and uncertainty in that. The Book will tell you it's Oma's will, that as the child of the Kai, I am divine. But I know what is within my power and what is beyond it. You. Each of you together make up the real power in Dhai. I am only your arm, the focus of your will. What you decide here today will shape the future of our country. I give my life to you, and my title to you, and our country's future... to you. That's what it is to be Kai. And no matter what you have heard or feared, it is your future I wish to help shape, if you will allow it."

His hands did not tremble. He stood a little taller in the end, because he realized as he gazed at the open faces before him that he had them.

"Now let us discuss the future of Dhai," Ahkio said as he took his seat among them, "as equals, the way Faith Ahya and Hahko imagined."

They spent the rest of the day in discussion. As afternoon turned to evening, Ahkio was finally able to excuse himself and find out why Nasaka had invited herself to his meeting.

"What do you have for me?" he asked her.

She drew him out into the fading light of the courtyard. "Ora Almeysia is talking. Are you ready to see her?"

"You brought her here?"

"I am, as ever, your servant," Nasaka said.

"Sarcasm does not become you," Ahkio said. "Let me get Liaro."

"I strongly suggest you speak to her alone," Nasaka said.

Ahkio glanced back at the council house. In truth, he didn't want to wade back into the storm in search of Liaro.

"Take me to her, then."

Nasaka led him to the outskirts of the clan square, where two militia waited for them. For a moment, Ahkio feared Nasaka was leading him off to some bloody death, and his pulse quickened.

They followed the skirted women into a tangled clearing. A cart stood at the center of it, wrapped in transparent webbing. Six Oras made a broad circle around the cart. A sizable escort for a single old person, even an Ora.

"What did you do to her," Ahkio asked, "to get her to talk?"

"She's been drugged to reduce her ability to draw on her star," Nasaka said. "But that's all. You should be able to speak to her peaceably."

Almeysia lay at the bottom of the cart, hugging her knees to her chest. Her tunic and trousers were filthy. The pungent smell of urine wafted up from her body. She did not look at them but stared straight ahead at the webbing wrapping the interior of the cart.

"There are ways to destroy people without marking them," Ahkio said.

"Read that in books, did you?" Nasaka asked.

Ahkio didn't give Nasaka the pleasure of replying. He focused on Almeysia. "What can you tell me about Yisaoh?"

Almeysia began to mutter. It took Ahkio a moment to realize it was Woodland Dhai she spoke in.

"She's not from the Woodland, is she?" Ahkio asked.

"No," Nasaka said.

"She looks much thinner," Ahkio said. "Are you feeding her?"

"You have a very poor opinion of me," Nasaka said.

"That shocks you?"

"No, but it does waste my time."

"Let me talk to her alone," Ahkio said. "I expect she's not keen to talk to you anymore."

Nasaka took a few steps back. Ahkio waved at her. "Go on. Stand in the circle with the others," he said.

Nasaka narrowed her eyes but obliged.

Ahkio came to the edge of the cart. "You know Nasaka would have exiled you by now," Ahkio said, "or worse, if I'd said so."

She continued murmuring in her singsong dialect. Ahkio tried to puzzle out the words. Woodland Dhai wasn't so different, but the inflections were sometimes confusing. After a few minutes, he recognized what she was saying – it was a passage from *The Book of Oma*, repeated over and over:

"All of life is change. One cannot hold on to past glory or strife. All of life leads to death. When one is not afraid of death, there is nothing that cannot be achieved."

"What is it you sought to achieve?" Ahkio asked. He folded his arms over the rim of the cart and gazed down at her. She looked very old, older than he remembered. Thin and wizened, like some wild crone come down from the Woodlands. Where was the woman who tried to kill him in the Sanctuary? The one who had attacked Roh? Was she just playing at being mad?

"I'm going to tell you something, Ora Almeysia," Ahkio said. "I have exiled Yisaoh's family to the third degree. Unless you can tell me what you've been planning, for however long you're planning it, I will exile your family, too. I will send them straight to Dorinah, or perhaps Saiduan, so they can meet these invaders before we do. And you, well… I know you don't fear for your life. But I'll leave you with Nasaka to do with as she wishes. Those are things far worse than death. Those are things to fear. You won't die unless I speak it, Ora Almeysia, and I don't kill people."

Almeysia quieted. Ahkio waited. Threatening her with a long life spent with Nasaka was the surest way he could think of to get her talking sense.

"The gates are open," she said softly.

"Is that more nonsense?" Ahkio asked.

She pressed her hands to her head. "Keep me from Ora Nasaka."

"I can do that if you'll help me."

Almeysia gave a little sob and said, "They're here to kill you, and me, and others. The Tai Mora. Softening the way. They've already integrated themselves. They could be anyone. Everyone. They could be you."

"That would be a neat trick," Ahkio said. "How do you know what they're called? Tai Mora? Are those the invaders? That sounds Dhai."

Almeysia snorted out something like a laugh. "It doesn't matter now. She has what she wanted. This place, all of you, all of us – we're all dead now."

"I'm very much alive in this moment," Ahkio said, "and I want an answer to my question."

"She has what she came for. She wasn't your Yisaoh, anyway."

"What do you mean?"

"She was the other Yisaoh."

"The... other Yisaoh?"

Almeysia laughed again. "She hasn't told you? Ora Nasaka hasn't told you?"

"What?"

"The other people," Almeysia said, and she uncurled from the bottom of the cart. She got up on her hands and knees and pushed her head toward him, pressing it against the webbing, distorting her features. He saw, then, that her eyes were milky, clouded. She was blind.

Ahkio recoiled.

"The other people we're fighting," Almeysia said. "They're not invaders. They're not foreigners. They're not some violent Dorinah or meat-eating Saiduan. They're *us*. We're fighting *ourselves*."

"How is that–"

"It was Yisaoh's shadow you saw, not the Yisaoh you know. I had to murder our Yisaoh to do it, to let the other one come over, but Tir is clever, very clever. He has three omajistas, did you know that? And they saved Yisaoh's life. She died, for a time, but they brought her back. And now you've exiled her, and we've lost her, and they are not happy, Ahkio. The other Yisaoh is stuck in her world, and she is not happy."

"This is very mad," Ahkio said.

"She's speaking truth," Nasaka said.

Ahkio started. Nasaka stood just a pace behind him.

"I told you to stay back."

"You've taken philosophy," Nasaka said. "There could be billions of other places just like ours, with people just like us, brought close enough to kiss by Oma. That's who we face now. Not foreigners this time. Not Saiduan. People from another version of our world, when our people made different choices."

"How long have you known this?"

Nasaka shrugged.

"*How long?*" Ahkio said.

"Some time," Nasaka said.

Ahkio remembered Kirana's body rising from her death bed. He remembered what she said: "They're coming, Ahkio. The shadows are here."

"How long did you and Kirana know? Really, this time. A real answer. You not only knew Oma was rising, you knew who we fought!" Ahkio stopped shouting. Looked back at Almeysia. "Why did you bring her here? You could have killed her, and I'd never know."

"Because you thought me a liar," Nasaka said. "It's true I've kept things from you. For your own protection. But we must work together now, Ahkio. It's time you knew."

"And any of us could be from the other world?" Ahkio said. "Wearing someone else's face?"

"Theoretically, yes."

"You, me, Almeysia, anyone."

"Yes, but both versions cannot exist in one world at one time."

"Oma's breath," Ahkio said. He rubbed his face. "Kirana was killed because there are two of her. Just like Yisaoh. Why didn't you tell me someone tried to kill Yisaoh? I'd have wasted less time accusing her of crimes!"

"I've been piecing this together," Nasaka said. "It's a complicated tapestry, and I've only now put together Yisaoh's role in it." But she was not looking at him. She was looking at Almeysia.

"Who killed Kirana, Almeysia?" Ahkio asked. "Was it you? Were you doing it on the order of some other Yisaoh, some other Almeysia?"

"We did," Almeysia said. "We all did."

Ahkio moved away from the cart. "Take her back," he said.

"As the Kai commands," Nasaka said.

Ahkio turned away.

"Ahkio?"

"Let me be."

"We have other tasks to tie. Like your marriage. Meyna is exiled. We face a very formidable enemy. You have gathered the clan leaders to unite the country, but you haven't done the one thing sure to bring you a powerful clan's loyalty."

"And you're here because you have a woman in mind? Or two? Or three?"

"She was at your ascension. I meant to introduce you then, but things... got away from us. Clan Sorai holds the harbor, and their clan leader, Hona, has a very smart and capable daughter named Mohrai who is interested in becoming Catori."

Almeysia was a peace offering, then. Nasaka gave him a piece of information now, before Ahkio found it out in Kirana's papers and distrusted Nasaka even further. She must have heard he cleared out Yisaoh and Kirana's libraries. Ahkio hated that they all thought him so stupid – Nasaka, Meyna, Yisaoh, all the rest. But it gave him an advantage. He could take a woman Nasaka chose or wait until she tried to kill one he chose himself. Some choice.

"Set it up, then," Ahkio said. "Bring her here and we'll make a fine show of Sorai's loyalty."

"You won't fight this?"

"We need Sorai," he said. "If these Tai Mora try to invade, it will be through the harbor. This meeting with the clan leaders may not work. If it doesn't... we'll have Sorai, at least."

"Wise choice."

"I'm my mother's son," he said stiffly. Then, "Exile Almeysia to Dorinah. That's my wish as Kai. Disobey it and I'll charge you with treason." He did not turn. He did not want to see her face. But she did not call after him. She did not stop him.

Ahkio made his way back to the clan square. What now? Where to go and who to trust? He could exile Nasaka, but then he would lose all of her knowledge with her. She knew too much to be thrown out; she had made sure of that. The less she told him, the more he had to rely on her. He could only solve so many things through exile or marriage. Right now, he wanted to do violence against a good many people, even knowing it solved nothing. Fighting their own people... Oma. How was he going to handle that?

He went around the back stair of the council house and upstairs, avoiding most of the clan leaders in the common area. He entered his rooms and found Caisa sitting on the divan, laughing with Liaro. Kirana's effects from Garika were spread all around, trunk after trunk of them. Kirana had loved a good many books.

Liaro grinned. "You look like death."

"I'm glad that puts you in fine spirits."

"We were just finishing," Caisa said. "Liaro invited me to dinner."

Lovely, Ahkio thought. That was just what he needed – his cousin and his assistant starting some torrid affair. "Enjoy it," he said. "Any progress here?"

"Still no progress on the ciphered papers," Caisa said. "Funny book here, though. Dorinah romances. Didn't think much of it, but she has a lot of... odd notes in the margins."

Ahkio took the slim volume from her. It appeared to be bound in snakeskin. The embossed title on the front was indiscernible, the ink long since rubbed away. He turned to the front pages. Inside was his mother's sister's name, scrawled in sloppy characters: Etena Mia Sorai. The book's title wasn't in Dhai, though. It was in Dorinah and read: "Fifteenth-Century Dhai Romances."

"She liked reading these," Ahkio said, tracing the title with his fingers. He'd learned Dorinah as a child in the camps. "We'd sit with stacks of these while our mother went out."

"Nice binding for something in a slave camp," Liaro said.

"She's rebound it," Ahkio said. The Dorinahs wrote all sorts of stories about the Dhai: their history as written by their captors.

He opened it to the first page and found another line scrawled at the bottom, this time in his sister's neat, formal handwriting. It read:

Remember all the roads.

"Roads to where?" Ahkio said.

"It gets weirder," Caisa said. She stood. Liaro scrambled up as well and pressed past Ahkio.

"I'll meet you downstairs," Liaro told Caisa.

Caisa pulled on her coat and went after him. She paused in the door and smiled.

"What is it?" Ahkio asked.

"You're getting better," she said.

"I'm glad you think so."

"When did you give up?" she said.

"Give up what?"

"Ever going back?"

"Back to where?"

Caisa's smile faded. "Oh, I'm sorry. I was mistaken."

"No, what did you mean by that?"

"Nothing. I misspoke. Goodnight, Kai." She pressed thumb to forehead and left him.

Ahkio shook his head and stared at the book. Everyone was going mad. He paged through and read the scrawled notes in the margins. Not just his sister's handwriting but Etena's, too – it matched the scrawl of her name on the front. The notes were in some kind of shorthand. It took him a moment to work out that they must be in the Kai cipher.

He sat down and picked up a bleeding pen, the sort made from the stamens of claw-lilies, and turned over one of Kirana's stack of temple maps. She had an inordinate number of them, mostly of the six levels of basements beneath the temple proper that contained the great bathing rooms, massive storage rooms, and the old garrison.

As he worked out the first of the margin notes, he noticed a familiar symbol from the reverse side of the map. He turned the map over.

It was a map of the lowest level of the temple, roughly circular, just like every other layer, divided into a labyrinth of rooms that spiraled out over the page like a small city.

At the center of the labyrinth was a square with a double circle inside. Where had he seen it? The Assembly Chamber table. The map of Dhai. That was the same symbol on that old map, inlaid in the table about the same time Faith and Hahko took up residence there.

He assumed the symbols for the temples were some holdover from Dorinah, something the Dhai had used instead of writing. Many would have been illiterate when they came over the mountains. But it was odd to see it replicated in the map, because outside the Assembly Chamber table, no one used them anymore.

Ahkio turned the paper back over and finished translating the first margin note, which was in Kirana's handwriting.

The sentence made him pause. He must have made some mistake. He translated the next one, the one at the bottom of the page, in Etena's handwriting.

His breath left him. He stared at the page. Everything he thought he knew fell apart.

Yisaoh was right. He was not as clever as he thought.

Kirana had written:

The Temple's heart is barred to me, Etena. She says she will only speak to a Kai. Why close all the roads to me?

And Etena's reply:

Because if you can open the way, so can your shadow.

27

Zezili sat at the back of the public house outside Ladiosyn, writing a response to Daolyn's letter about her house finances. Zezili's sister Taodalain had asked for a small loan – they always ended up being gifts, but she still called it a loan – and Daolyn needed Zezili's permission to grant it.

Give her no more than 50 dhorins, she wrote, and hesitated before continuing: *I will be at Lake Morta later this month. If she has any other urgent requests, have her send post to me there.*

Zezili sealed the letter with a bit of noxious gonsa sap and called over one of the lazy pages at another table to run it to the post general. As the girl opened the door to leave, Monshara came in. The girl held the door open for her, and the girl's eyes were big as apples. Ever since Monshara's people opened the gate on the slaughtering field, Zezili's women had all taken a reverent shine to her. Oma was on everyone's minds now. Zezili heard the talk at every village and town. Seeing that bloody gate open was enough to make even a nonbeliever zealous. Zezili had prayed to Rhea eight times since the gate opened, expecting Oma was close enough that she might even hear Rhea respond. But no. Things were just the same. Rhea was quiet. Waiting.

Zezili ordered another drink. Monshara sat across from her.

"I'm still not used to the liquor," Monshara said. "Can you get me watered wine?" she called to the house matron.

"What do you need?" Zezili asked.

"Do you play cups?" Monshara asked, nodding at the stack of three round wooden cups at Zezili's elbow – detritus from her afternoon of imbibing.

"The card game?"

"No, the gambling game," Monshara said. She took up the cups and set them upside down on the table in a neat row.

Monshara opened her hand to reveal a small silver coin. On it was the head of some monarch, but not the Empress Zezili knew. Monshara placed the coin under the middle cup.

"Now tell me where the coin is," Monshara said, and began to push the cups about the table in a series of figure eights.

"You must be very popular at children's parties," Zezili said.

"Humor me, Syre. It's been a long day."

Zezili idly tracked the cups. She had played games like this often and knew the trick of it.

When Monshara ceased her cup spinning, Zezili pointed to the center cup.

Monshara lifted it. As she did, Zezili lifted the other two cups as well. There was no sign of the coin beneath any of the cups.

Zezili dropped the cups. They clattered loudly. "Shocking," she said.

"It surprises me very little that you have no friends," Monshara said, retrieving the overturned cups.

"I just don't care for games made to part stupid people from their money."

Monshara put the cups back on the table, upside down. "I suspect your choice was right the first time." She lifted the center cup again. The silver coin appeared beneath it.

Zezili snorted. She took up the coin and examined it. The writing was Dorinah. "Freedom from tyranny and want," was written along the edge. The portrait was of a bold-nosed woman with large lips and a noticeable overbite. Her mane of hair was knotted and beribboned in intricate bows.

"Is this your empress?" Zezili asked.

"Was," Monshara said. "She was killed fourteen years ago. The country was scoured soon after." She gently took the coin from Zezili's hand. Her fingers were warm. "You used to like–" she began, and stopped.

Goosebumps rose on Zezili's arms. Hearing about somebody else with her face still chilled her. "Whoever that person was you knew, she wasn't me," Zezili said. "No more than the empress on that coin is mine."

"I have no illusions," Monshara said.

Zezili stared at the coin again. "How's it possible things are so different there compared to here? How did you lose to those slaves?"

"They were never slaves," Monshara said. "They have always been powerful. We just made different choices over there. Small choices that grew large over time." She shrugged. "I'm not a philosopher."

The bar matron brought over Zezili's three fingers of hard lemon liquor and Monshara's watered wine.

When the woman left, Zezili asked, "What do you want?"

Monshara played idly with the coin, flipping it across her knuckles like some cheap backstreet conjurer. "Can we not sit and drink together?"

"Considering your people are about to wipe the world of mine? I see no need for us to be friends."

"My people?" Monshara pocketed the coin. "The Tai Mora are not my people."

"I think you've done a pretty good job of being Tai Mora." Zezili leaned back in her broad-backed chair.

"I came to you with a warning."

"From your masters?"

"From me. I know your mother lives in Saolina. I heard you visited her."

"You *heard*, did you?" Zezili expected the woman had a number of little birds among Zezili's women, especially after the business with the gate, but she was as yet uncertain how many.

"I can suspect what you visited her about."

"Can you?" She took a long swallow of her drink.

"I didn't survive the end of my people because I was slow," Monshara said. "No doubt your mother had interesting things to say about how she would build a mirror, maybe even one that could focus Oma's power. I think you should forget all that."

Zezili forced a laugh. "Forget? Forget walking into that star-blasted wasteland you call home? If that's what you people will make of this world–"

"Not my people," Monshara said firmly.

"They bleed," Zezili said.

"And they kill," Monshara said. "They've killed you once. And I... don't want to witness that again. That's why I'm warning you instead of stringing you up myself."

"How did you know me?" Zezili asked. "The other me?"

"It doesn't matter. Whatever you're planning, the Kai is eight steps ahead of you. Let's finish these last few camps. Then you can go back to your empress, and I'll go back to mine."

"But that's not what's really going to happen, is it?" Zezili said. Monshara gulped her wine. "Truly? No, probably not."

"They haven't told you their full plans."

"You thought you'd torture it out of me?" Monshara laughed. "I'd like to see you try. They only tell me a piece at a time. I didn't know I'd be working here with you until the day we traveled over."

"But you saw their battle plans. She gave them to you."

"You really think they'd give over something like that to a woman who could read Dhai?"

"You can't read Dhai?"

"Of course not."

"What the Kai turned over to me was likely in some cipher," Monshara said. "I can't even say with absolute certainty that it was an invasion plan. It wouldn't be the first time the Kai sent me on a fool's errand, telling me I had something important that turned out to be garbage. It's how she tests loyalty."

"And you passed?"

"She put me with you, didn't she?"

"You make it sound like that was a prize."

"It was…" Monshara finished her wine. "It was what it was."

"Who did you deliver that map to?"

"You think it's like that, do you? You think we'll have some drinks and I'll betray the Kai? You listen, Zezili–"

"You keep using my name like you think I forgot it."

"I'm reminding *myself* of it," Monshara said. "The woman I knew was much more compassionate than you are. Merciful. And hygienic. You're… something very different."

"Thank you."

"Zezili," she lowered her voice, "leave this thing about the mirror alone. If you interfere, I'll report it." She pulled the silver coin from her pocket and placed it on the table. "This woman on the coin, she was *my* mother. You understand?"

Zezili stared at the coin.

Monshara stood. "You can keep that," she said. "I'll see you in the morning. It's a long way to Janifa from here, so I expect you should turn in soon. Can't go off killing people with a belly full of liquor and no sleep."

After she left, Zezili reached across the table and picked up the coin. The figure looked nothing like the empress Zezili knew – the bronze-skinned, cant-legged woman with the big yellow eyes and wasp-like waist. *The Book of Rhea* said that Empress Casanlyn's line had crossed into Dorinah from Rhea's seat a very long time ago when Rhea's world and their own came together. Her people came bearing great gifts of fertility and abundance to the people of Dorinah. Zezili always thought the Empress was the remnant of some eastern race, but now she wondered if her empress was from another world altogether that had failed to cross over completely during the last rise of Oma. On the other side, they had no bronze-skinned god leading their country. Empress Casanlyn's people had never crossed over to that world. Never tried to take over. Never toed a hole in Dorinah big enough to hide in. They had only Monshara's mother, and she had lost.

"But she is *my* empress," Zezili muttered, and left the coin on the table. She bought another piece of paper from the bar matron and began writing a letter to Empress Casanlyn.

The dajian camps in Janifa lay on the other side of the country, on the coast. A week of hard travel brought Zezili's angry, spitting legionnaires to within shouting distance of the eastern sea. Her women were wearying of blood, and she could feel their frustration. They bickered more. Got into bloody fights among themselves. Brute slaughter was bad for morale. Only the most sadistic took any pleasure from this game. The rest were ready to go home. She began to consider rotating out these women with a fresh group pulled from the primary legion.

The farther east they went, the hillier the way became. They passed through hills tiered with rice paddies, little dajians working up to their shins in the shallow water. They passed fields of ragged brown sunflower stalks, and spent two days in the coastal town of Jovonyn, where a late-autumn masque was held. Jasoi danced drunkenly with Monshara all night, and Zezili pretended not to notice Jasoi coming out of Monshara's tent the next day. Zezili found the mardana men of Jovonyn intriguing and spent a night herself entwined with the young bodies of three boys who could not have been a day over sixteen. What they lacked in experience they made up for in stamina.

They climbed steep hills, and Monshara asked to stop for a day and explore colorful caverns and the great ruins of the city that had been razed by the Saiduans a thousand years before. Zezili watched her picking through the remnants of old temples and fountains and other, stranger structures. A good deal of twisted glass littered the streets. Monshara and the four legionnaires Zezili sent with her came back with cuts on their hands and faces.

Every night they camped, Zezili lay awake in her tent, listening to the squeal and cry and crackle of the camp all around her. She waited for a letter.

Finally, as they camped outside Janifa, the letter came. Zezili broke the royal seal on the purple envelope and read:

Dearest Zezili,

I am well aware of our friends' intentions. You will do all they ask and more.

With all sincerity,

Empress Casanlyn Aurnaisa of Dorinah, Eye of Rhea, Rhea's Regent, Lord of the Seven Isles.

Zezili burned the letter.

The next day, she slaughtered six hundred little dajians so sick and starved, they could barely raise their hands. The Empress had stopped sending out rations to the camp. If Zezili did not kill them, they would starve anyway.

Zezili spent that night getting drunk at a mardana two miles away. She stumbled back into the bar area after vomiting for the second time to see Jasoi waiting for her at her card table, looking nervous among so many half-clothed young men.

"What you want?" Zezili slurred.

"Syre Zezili," Jasoi said, bowing her head stiffly. "I have news from your house."

"My house?" Zezili said, and moved away from the table. She took Jasoi to a darker corner of the room where the tables were empty. "What's happened?"

Jasoi pulled a leather wrap from her coat, unfolded it, and produced a wax-sealed letter. *Syre Zezili* was written in Daolyn's neat hand, and it was sealed with Zezili's house seal.

"Why you rush this?" Zezili slurred as she opened the letter.

"Monshara said to give it to you right away," Jasoi said. "Any news from your house must be urgent, she said."

Zezili read the letter. Muttered an oath.

"I must go," Zezili said. "Jasoi, you'll have to take First. Tell Monshara... I had to go. Emergency at my house."

"Your house is a week away," Jasoi said. "You aren't leaving the legion to–"

Zezili said, "Can make it in four days on my own. Have to go." Zezili hurried outside into the cool air, trying to will herself to sober up.

As she mounted her dog, she glanced once more at Daolyn's letter before bunching it up in her fist and stuffing it into her coat:

> *Tanasai Laosina is dead. Your husband is missing. You must come home immediately.*

28

The yellow eye of the filthy, feathered black raptor blotted out Lilia's vision. Lilia huffed out a sound of distress. Pain rocked her anew. She'd only closed her eyes a moment, just a moment... The feathered raptor hopped back and flexed the claws at the ends of its winged arms. It opened its hooked beak and hissed at her. The wormy red tongue lashed out. Smacked her cheek.

Lilia fought fresh waves of pain with every breath. For hours, she had watched a tanglevine creeping toward her bloody leg exposed through her torn trousers. She saw red welts on her ankles now, in the bright light of the moons. Out in the sandy creek bed, she was completely exposed.

The raptor was a karoi, one of the four kinds of nighttime scavengers. This one stood as tall as her thigh. A pack of them could tear the flesh from her in a few hours, and unlike their daytime counterparts, they didn't always wait until their food was dead before they started eating it.

Lilia watched the bird. Her tongue felt large and thick, her throat parched. The moons were up and Para had set. She had spent twelve hours enduring the pain in her torso and increasing numbness in her limbs. She was so thirsty. Death would be welcome. But being ripped apart... no. Not that. Fear, panic, terror... Now she lay exhausted, staring dumbly at her broken right wrist. The blood had clotted. If she didn't reset the bone soon, she might lose her hand. She may have already. But the one time she had tried crawling back into the trees to find a broken branch, the pain was so intense, she blacked out.

And that left her here.

The raptor hissed.

Lilia watched it lever its long tail. Most bones in the tail were articulated, like the spine, but not the bone at the base of the tail. It was as sturdy and straight as any splint.

She closed her eyes. Flexed her good hand. Waited.

She heard the scuffle of the karoi's claws in the sand. Its wingtips brushed her arm.

Lilia shot out her hand. Gripped the karoi's neck. Pain jolted through her broken body. She screamed. The raptor drove its beak into her cheek. It flapped its wings and raked at her face and hand. Lilia tried to get up. Kept her grip on the bird's neck. She felt the neck snap.

A mistake, moving. She was too broken.

Her stomach heaved. Darkness swam across her vision. The bird screamed and screamed.

Blackness took her.

Finally.

But she had beaten the bird.

"You know the price." Not her voice. Someone else.

Lilia woke to the smell of wood smoke. The hungry claws of a bone tree dangled in front of her, and at their end – the hooked beak of a karoi. She realized the claw of the bone tree was not attached to a tree; it was just a severed limb from one, hanging now from the end of a long stick driven into the ground.

She tried to roll over. Pain blossomed across her chest. She hissed. Tried to raise her left hand. It was bound from shoulder to wrist, wrapped securely around a long, straight branch neatly cut in two. Pain stabbed up her shoulder.

"Drink," the voice said. She knew it.

Lilia could not raise her head. The pain was too much. But the speaker bent over her. Long dark hair brushed her cheeks. The clawed wounds burned. Her face felt puffy.

Gian brought a warm cup to her lips; it smelled of poppy and everpine.

Lilia drank.

"You'll heal faster with a tirajista," Gian said. "We don't have one at the camps, so I'm taking you to a friend, but–" She looked behind her, and Lilia saw they were in a low cavern. It smelled of damp beneath the smoke. "We're being followed. And I don't know how much longer I can keep us hidden."

"How did you find me?" Lilia rasped.

Gian nodded at the karoi beak. "I followed the birds," she said. "They circled for hours, I expect. Had to beat six of them off you."

Gian pulled the cup away. The warmth spread from Lilia's throat and stomach, engulfing her throbbing torso. The edges of the pain blurred, retreated. The absence of pain was shocking. Like freedom.

"Followed me," she said.

"Yes," Gian said. "I could ride a bear just fine with this leg, and there were plenty in the woodland who needed taming. You didn't think I'd give you up to some Saiduan, did you?"

"Pushed me," Lilia said.

"Did he? I hoped you'd run from him and fallen. Why was he so angry with you?"

"Wanted me to fly."

"I expect he did."

"Gian," Lilia muttered. "I'm sorry." Speaking was becoming more difficult. The world was swimming, warm and pleasant. The tide of blackness would take her again, and she was glad.

"You saved my life," Gian said. "Nothing to be sorry about. Except going back on your promise to me."

"Won't go to your people," Lilia said. She tried to move again, but the darkness was taking over. It was so nice. "I promised... my mother."

"I keep telling you you don't have a choice about that," Gian said. "I wish you'd stop being so stubborn. I just hope I can get you to my people before... before we end up with what's behind us."

"You know the price." That voice, again. Gian's? No, this was another. "She lives, then?"

An old woman bent over her. Lilia stared down the length of her own body, covered over in a hemp cloth.

"Where... how long?" Lilia asked. "Gian?"

"I'm here," Gian said. Lilia saw her outlined in the doorway. Lilia was not lying on the floor but set up on some kind of slab or table. Above her, she saw a great vent in a nest of dead boughs. The seams between them were filled with living stranglethorn and purple-blooming fire vine. It was the sort of house only a tirajista could make.

"We're farther up the mountain," Gian said. "This is Nirata. She's a friend from... where I'm from."

"Friend! Ha. We are kin," the old woman said.

Lilia was aware of the muzzy promise of pain, as if it lurked there at the edges of her fingertips.

"I did the best I could," Nirata said, "but I'm afraid we need to move you now."

"But I'm–"

Nirata drew the hemp cloth from Lilia's body. Beneath, she was naked; thin and knob-kneed, with great yellow bruises pinwheeling across her chest.

"Give me your left hand," Nirata said.

Lilia raised her left arm. A knife of pain hammered up her torso. She cried out. Her arm only moved a few inches.

Nirata took Lilia's left hand. Lilia remembered seeing the broken wrist, the mangled fingers. It was still bruised. She saw puckered red scars where the bone had splintered through the skin.

"Rotate that for me, child," Nirata said.

Lilia tried. She could not bend it back. But it did come forward a little, with great effort. And pain. Sina, why was there so much pain?

"Make a fist."

"I... can't," Lilia said.

"You can."

Lilia tensed her fingers. They would not meet her palm.

"We don't have time," Gian said. "Can she walk?"

"It's not the walking that worries me," Nirata said. "Eight days is not long enough for a woman with a descendent star. If you gave me eight weeks, I could heal her properly."

"Your star isn't descendent," Gian said. "It's rising. I expected more."

"I'm a woman with a great many stars," Nirata said. "Oma knits flesh more easily than bone."

"Eight days?" Lilia said. "That long?"

"Should have been longer," Nirata said. "You won't have much movement in that shoulder. Your collarbone was broken. It may still hurt to breathe. Avoid further injury to your torso, too – you broke seven ribs. It's a wonder none of them punctured a lung. Your ankle was broken, too. Take my hand. Let's get you up on that now."

Lilia gripped Nirata's hand with her good one. Nirata helped ease her off the table.

"Hurry," Gian said.

"Hurrying gets us mistakes," Nirata said. "I've already made far too many here."

"Give her the poppy."

"No," Lilia said. She tried to stand. Leaned heavily on Nirata. Both legs hurt now. Her good ankle had been mangled in the fall. She wondered what she looked like. She touched her face. Felt puckered, still-healing flesh where the karoi had pecked at her. As she stood she noticed something dangling from her neck. It was the karoi beak, tied on a long string.

"What's this for?" she said.

"For luck," Nirata said. "Gian kept it for luck. You know all about luck, don't you, Gian? The karoi are lucky. To be eaten and to live, that is a boon, child. Gian was eaten, once, but I pulled her from the jaws of death. Just as she's done for you."

Gian held out a hemp tunic and trousers. "Let's get her dressed."

"Where are we going?"

"Nirata is opening a gate," Gian said. "It's a faster way to get to the camp. The people following will overtake us if we try to walk out."

"A... gate?" Lilia remembered the field of poppies and the tears between the worlds. She remembered the amber sky. Why did they want to take her back if bringing her here was supposed to save her? "You won't be going?"

Gian did not look at her. "No."

"Gian knows the price," Nirata said. "Let me help you dress, child."

"All right," Lilia said, because she could barely raise her left arm to stuff it into the tunic.

Nirata dressed her. They led Lilia outside, into a cold, brilliant morning. Lilia smelled mountain everpine. The living stick-and-vine shelter behind them was just an outbuilding next to the proper house, a soaring construction built into the bubbling bark of a massive weeping tree so large, they stood on the broad back of just one of its roots jutting out from the mountain.

As they walked into the light, Lilia saw Nirata gaze up toward the larger house, as if they had an audience. Lilia saw nothing at the windows. She felt a deep unease.

"Stand here," Nirata said, and released Lilia.

Lilia tottered. She grabbed at a broad, broken branch behind her for balance.

"Are you ready?" Nirata asked Gian.

Gian came forward. She knelt in front of Nirata.

Lilia saw movement from the house. A small child, maybe five or six, stood in the now open doorway.

Nirata drew a blade from her hip, a simple dagger meant for

eating and chores. But the blade was freshly sharpened, shiny. She tilted Gian's head back.

Lilia realized what was going to happen. She remembered her mother's bloody dress, and the dead riders, and the tear in the world. Was it the blood that opened the way between the worlds? Blood witch.

"Gian, don't–" Lilia said.

Nirata drew the blade across Gian's neck. Blood gushed.

Lilia's stomach heaved. "No, no, no," Lilia said. "I saved you, Gian. I saved you!"

"Gran?" the little girl called from the house.

The girl ran toward them. Gian's body jerked and trembled in the pooling blood.

"Go back inside!" Nirata called. She had dropped the dagger. She held Gian's body in her arms. Blood stained her hands and arms to the elbow.

"Is she all right?" The little girl hesitated, not a dozen feet from them.

Lilia gripped the karoi beak that dangled against her chest. Nirata's arms were full.

The girl came forward. "Let me help!"

A price, Lilia thought. There was always a price. Gian chose death to get Lilia to the other side.

But Lilia, too, had a choice.

Lilia sidled toward the girl, shuffling behind Nirata. The girl was just a pace away. Another day, another girl, seeing the woman who raised her covered in blood. It was like a circle, like a sign.

Lilia held the karoi beak so tightly her hand hurt. The girl was just an arm's length away now. Gian's eyes were glassy.

Lilia reached out with her good arm and snatched the front of the girl's tunic. The girl kicked her, and the two of them fell. Lilia's heart thudded loudly. A child, a child, she's just a child... But Lilia wrapped her bad arm around the girl's neck, and jammed the karoi beak against her throat with the other, hard enough to draw blood. The girl screeched.

Nirata turned. Gian's body fell from her arms.

"Let her go," Nirata said. Cold voice.

"I can kill her before you stop me," Lilia said, jabbing the girl's neck again. She was trembling so hard against Lilia's body that it made her teeth chatter. "Try your gifted tricks, but I will choke her or stab her first, or toss her off this tree altogether."

"Gian just sacrificed her life to save you."

"And she still will," Lilia said. "Get me to Dorinah. The capital." She didn't know where she would find her mother, but if she was some important person there like Gian said, she would live in the capital.

"Impossible."

"It's not," Lilia said. "If you can open a gate between worlds, you can open one across the same world. Don't try any tricks. I know the difference. The sky is different there."

"I can't just whisk you anywhere you want to go in Dorinah." Nirata looked behind her, at Gian's body. "We're losing time."

"Dorinah," Lilia said. "Any part, then."

"There is only one soft spot in Dorinah," Nirata said, "and it's nowhere near the capital. You'll be killed before then."

Lilia tightened her grip on the girl. "Dorinah. You aren't going to use me like a game piece anymore."

"So you'll use my granddaughter?"

"The way you want to use me?" Lilia said, and her voice broke. "Dorinah. Now."

"You'll only have a few seconds," Nirata said. "Let her go."

"When I'm through the gate."

"There won't be time–"

"When I'm through the gate!" Lilia said. The girl cried out. Lilia held her so tight, she feared the girl would stop breathing. Now Lilia was trembling, too. Monster, she thought. I'm a terrible monster.

A time to mourn, and a time to act...

"Are you prepared to kill a child?" Nirata said. "A little girl like you?"

"This isn't my world," Lilia said. "What do I care?" It sounded more certain than she felt. She was not a monster, not yet. Was she? She had grabbed this child, a child not her own, without permission. She was threatening harm, she was...

"Dorinah!" Lilia said. The little girl's blood trickled down the length of the karoi beak, onto Lilia's hand.

Nirata raised her arms. The air grew heavy. Lilia tightened her grip again, fearing betrayal. Nirata would try and rip the girl away with some tornado of air or seething plant.

The world wavered. Lilia's stomach dropped.

Gian's body jerked. A great gout of blood poured from her torso. The little girl squealed and squeezed her eyes shut. Blood rushed up into the air, coalesced. A black shimmer wet the sky. And then...

The air tore open.

Lilia saw a thunderous white plain of snow surrounded by vast mountain peaks. The sky was dark. Purple lightning seized the clouds. Was the sky different? She couldn't tell through the cloud cover.

"If you've tricked me–" Lilia said, inching her way toward the portal.

"I have not," Nirata said. "Give me my granddaughter. Hush, Esao. You'll be all right."

Lilia limped to the edge of the gate. Peered through. Cold air buffeted her. "Where is this?"

"The center of Dorinah," Nirata said. "The only soft space in that vile country."

"Why is there snow?"

"It's Dorinah," Nirata said. "You think all the world is as temperate as Dhai? Hurry." She looked over her shoulder. Lilia wondered if there were more people in the house. "I can only keep it open a few moments."

Lilia took a deep breath. She clung to the girl and stepped through.

"No!" Nirata said, and reached for her.

Lilia stumbled into the other side, into ankle-deep snow.

Nirata grabbed the little girl's arm.

Lilia released her.

The gate shut.

Nirata screamed.

Blackness.

Burnt meat.

What remained of the little girl's body fell into the snow at Lilia's feet. Lilia heard a terrible cracking sound. The girl's head and half her torso – including the arm Nirata had taken her by – were missing. Her remaining limbs jerked limply in the snow. Lilia vomited.

She stepped back – one step, two. She heard the groaning again, beneath her. She looked up. A great forest ringed the snowy plain. Cold bit her.

And then she realized where she was. She had been delivered onto a frozen lake.

The ice beneath her gave way.

Lilia plunged into bitter cold blackness.

I chose wrong, she thought.

29

Roh got along with most people. He considered himself very friendly. But the stately old Saiduan dancing teacher, Ghakar, pretended he could not understand Roh's accent, and the Patron's dancers ignored Roh entirely for the first half hour he watched them from the archway every morning.

Ghakar's instructions were biting, spoken far too quickly for Roh to fully understand. A musician kept time at the other end of the hall on a large drum. There was no singing in Saiduan dance pieces – and no poetry, unlike most Dhai performances. It was just painstaking movement set to music. And this piece was interspersed with snide comments from the other dancers about cannibals and maggots that Roh knew were meant to insult him. When Ghakar did not intervene, Roh decided to ignore them.

After three hours of insults and getting shouted at in Saiduan for not lifting the correct foot, Roh still managed to smile and thank Ghakar before they left.

Ghakar turned sullenly away from him. The others pushed past. One even shoved him. Roh clenched his fists and smiled harder.

When they were gone, Kihin said, "So, if they hate us, why did the Patron want you to dance?"

"Because he can," Roh said.

"Then I'm glad Ora Dasai asked me to keep an eye on you," Kihin said. "Because these people aren't very nice."

"I want to figure out why the Patron would ask me at all. Is he trying to shame the others? Is one of them an old lover? Is he angry at Ghakar?"

"So you did think about it."

"I'm not dumb enough to think everything's about how pretty I am," Roh said.

"I think that came out less humble than you hoped."

They walked down the sinuous corridors of Kuonrada to the archives. After seeing the order and simplicity of the rest of Kuonrada, the archive room looked like a haphazard mess, an afterthought. Massive black lacquered bookshelves wrapped the enormous chamber, full to bursting with stacks of paper bound in twine, rotting leather books, and dusty heaps of journals bound in everything from fireweed cord to metal rings. The aisles between the shelves were obstructed by fallen books and records, some of them so fragile, they had scattered into papery bits upon hitting the floor. Along the wall near the door were massive chests of books and records that looked like recent additions. At the center of the room, three tables were rooted to the floor with iron hoops. A mismatched collection of chairs ringed the tables.

Roh saw Chali and Nioni arguing softly among the stacks. Dasai and Aramey worked at one of the tables with two Saiduan men that Roh took to be scholars. Another young man made his way to a separate table with a small chest of records. He was slender and very pale for a Saiduan. It took Roh a moment to realize he must be Dhai. His hair was shorn short, like a slave, but he didn't have the flat forehead of those who'd been born into service. Was he from Grania? Had he been captured? A little flutter of fear made Roh falter.

Dasai looked up at their arrival and introduced Roh to the Saiduans. For the last week, he'd spent all his time dancing and none in the archives. Short, balding Bael was the youngest – Aramey's age – and the other looked to be a contemporary of Dasai's. His name was Ashaar, and he wore his hair long and braided with red ribbons.

"You'll act as runners today," Dasai said, and handed Roh a scrap of paper. "Get acquainted with the catalogue at the back."

"There's no librarian?" Roh said.

"This is what's left from three cities," Dasai said. "The librarians from those are dead, and Bael is acting as record keeper for the collection. As you can see, he is otherwise engaged. We are spread thin, Roh."

"Sorry," Roh said.

Dasai waved a hand at him and called Kihin over to return a massive book covered in what looked like some kind of reptile's skin.

The day became long and tedious. After, Roh was covered in dust and broken scraps of paper, delicate as ash. The day's work pointed them toward two primary texts mentioned in secondary texts. One was a history of Isjahilde, a city far to the north already overtaken by the invaders. It was supposed to be written by a Dhai scholar nineteen hundred years before, just a few decades after the Saiduan completely conquered the continent. The other was called World-unmaker or World-breaker. It was listed six times in an account from a long-dead sinajista as the primary source for information on how omajistas manipulated the way between spaces.

"So, these people aren't coming from boats," Roh said.

"No," Dasai said. "I suspect the Saiduan already know that. Somehow they're moving between... spaces. Great distances. Movement over great distances is one power Oma is known to bestow. We need to find out how to prevent them from doing it."

Roh hovered over Dasai's shoulder as he read one of the passages aloud, "The loss of this world lies at the feet of the Dhai unmakers who failed to save it and the Saiduan unmakers who destroyed it. We who remain have undertaken a great task: to purge the World-unmakers from history and deny the Saiduan victory over another that they have achieved over us."

Dasai sighed. "I will read the rest," he said. "But it doesn't look promising, if there was a conspiracy to destroy the records we were looking for long before we began our search."

"What's the point of all this?" Kihin said. "The Dhai lost last time. How do they expect we'd know how to win this time?"

"Patience," Dasai said. But Roh didn't hear much confidence in his voice. "We'll look for the other texts referenced here. I'll begin a list."

After dinner, Kihin climbed into his bunk above Roh and said, "I bet the other scholars won't work with us because we're Dhai. You saw they didn't let Luna eat with us."

"Luna's that other Dhai, the... slave?" Roh said.

"Yes, Aramey told me," Kihin said. "Luna was a Woodland Dhai. Some Dorinah raiding party caught him on the coast and sold him off to the Saiduan."

"You best be using hir correct pronoun in Saiduan," Dasai said, in Saiduan.

"I'm not an impolite person," Kihin said, also in Saiduan. "I'm aware of hir pronoun."

Roh sighed, and said in Dhai, "Ora Dasai, why would the Patron bring us all this way and then not have us all work together? Do they want to save this place or not?"

"That's a matter of degree," Dasai said.

Roh turned. Dasai stood in the doorway, leaning on his cane. "How did the dancing go?"

"They all hate me," Roh said. "The same way all the scholars hate us. I thought all those stories were a long time ago. Why do they still hate us?"

"Give it time."

"Time's something we don't have," Kihin said, "if omajistas are dropping people into Saiduan."

"Why don't the Saiduan do things that make sense?" Roh said. "None of this is logical at all."

"Logic?" Dasai said. "People do not take actions based on logic. We make choices based on emotion. Every one of us. Then we use what we call logic to justify our choices. People don't do things that make sense."

"I'm very logical," Roh said.

Dasai raised his brows. Roh saw a rare smile touch the corners of his lips. "You are one of the most impulsive people I know," Dasai said, "and I have trained hundreds of novices and scholars."

Kihin snickered.

As the long, cold days in Saiduan continued to pass, the dancing did not get any easier. Roh moved from the more familiar forms to the vonov, which, as the Patron had told him, was much more fluid and required a closer proximity to the other dancers. Despite the fact that the rest of the keep was drafty, an hour into practice, they all danced shirtless, and Roh found he moved with and among a throng of wiry, beautiful dancers. He did not allow himself to dwell on that until after he finished a set, and then he gazed out at the dark-eyed, dark-skinned men and was slightly breathless, too warm. He had to avert his eyes, temper desire.

One of the dancers, a sloe-eyed man called Abas, pressed a hand to the small of Roh's back after one of the sets. Roh started. He was trying to get used to the casual, nonconsensual touching, but it still bothered him.

Abas said, "You are not so hopeless, boy. Does that chaperone never leave you?"

"I've been told I'm dangerous without a chaperone."

"You should smile more often," Abas said. "You could light the world with a grin like that."

While the dancing progressed, the work in the archives did not. Roh spent more and more of his time with the dancers, especially Abas. Abas showed him around the hold one cold afternoon and said, "You have a special love of sanisi, do you not?"

"Is it that obvious?"

"You watch them like a hungry puppy," Abas said. "It makes me jealous."

Below, Roh saw two fighters who appeared to be dancing, the only sound the scuff of their boots on the stones. They were sanisi, and they had drawn a sizable crowd of spectators.

"Who's that?" Roh asked.

Abas came to the rail. "That is Ren Kadaan Soagan and Shao Maralah Daonia."

"I've heard of her," Roh said.

"I expect you have. She's the Patron's most trusted general."

"And Kadaan?"

"Her best student. Not many men apprenticed to her, in the beginning. But he was smart. He saw her for what she was."

"Or she saw something in him," Roh said.

"Perhaps it required intelligence from both of them," Abas said, and showed his teeth, an exaggeration of a smile that Roh had seen many Saiduan flash publicly. The real smiles came in private. Roh cherished those much more.

The two sanisi moved in patterns too complex for Roh to follow, but the movements were fast enough for him to recognize that they were anticipating one another's forms. Roh knew that feeling.

"You see Kadaan?" Abas said, and Roh heard the affection in his voice. "See how they keep pace with one another? A spar like this, between these two, can last hours. Kadaan is the best of them. He is not yet twenty-five and has killed forty-three of the invaders. He gained us many weeks in the northern cities. It's sad they will destroy each other."

"What do you mean?"

Abas shrugged and pushed away from the rail. "It's how it's done. She has lived a long time. Most think the only reason she still lives is because of the war. We lose too many sanisi. But before that... yes, Kadaan would have killed her, I'm sure. You haven't seen it among the dancers yet, but we do it, too. The boy who had my place before me? He fell from this rail, here." Abas rapped the railing. It came nearly to his chest. "You can see it would not be so easy to fall unaided."

"You took his place?"

"Times were different. War has changed us. Now... well, now we have a Dhai dancing with us because we are so few.

Things move quickly, don't they?"

"It's a good thing you changed with them."

Abas gazed down at the sanisi again. "Some," he said. "Not all."

That night after supper, Dasai and Nioni gathered in the sitting room and went over the day's work. Luna and Kihin sat up in the room Kihin and Roh shared, arguing about old Dhai verb tenses. Roh sat in the main room on the armrest of one of the chairs and listened to the older men talk.

"I cannot, in good conscience, force any of my scholars that far north," Dasai said, "and I certainly doubt my own ability to survive such a journey."

"Someone has to go," Nioni said. "I'll take them if I must. The records here are incomplete, and Bael says there was an untouched archive farther north. If we find nothing here, we'll have come all this way for naught."

"This may be all there is," Dasai said. "It's possible the invaders have already destroyed what they came for."

"Then we've come all this way for nothing," Nioni said, "and you know my time is precious." Aramey hushed him.

Chali sighed. "We've hardly begun."

"What do you think, Rohinmey?" Dasai asked.

"I think there's a reason empires aren't made by old men."

"No," Dasai said, "but they are certainly *maintained* by old men." He waved a hand. "Enough for tonight. It's too early to give our tongues to the cat. We have time yet."

"And when we run out of time?" Chali said.

Aramey looked stricken. Roh imagined them all as great frozen bodies caked in ice and buried in some snow drift.

"There is time," Dasai said. "Roh, take my arm and help me to my room, please."

Roh took his arm and escorted him to his chambers. Dasai had been slowing down as the days passed. Every step he took looked painful. He complained often and bitterly about the cold, despite wearing warmer clothes than all of them.

"The dancing lessons are going well?" Dasai asked as he slipped off his shoes.

"They're good," Roh said, pulling back the blankets from Dasai's bed.

"A clipped response," Dasai said, "from one once so talkative. You could once iron my head with your chatter."

"I don't know what to say. We get along all right. They're vain, but most dancers are like that."

"I don't like you wandering about the keep on your own," Dasai said.

"I'm not alone," Roh said. "Kihin goes everywhere with me."

"You think I'm blind as well as arthritic? I know he doesn't go *everywhere* with you."

"I can take care of myself."

"I'm just an old man," Dasai said, pulling the blankets up over himself. He settled back on the pillows. The spill of his white hair trailed down one shoulder. "Go on, now, and sleep tonight. I want you to continue practicing your defense forms with Kihin. You've grown lax in that."

"Ora Dasai, you've already got me dancing three hours in the morning and running errands all—"

"Obviously, such activities do not keep you well enough occupied," Dasai said, "if you have so much extra energy that it must be expended running after dancers in the dark. I would prefer you employ such energies in something useful."

"Yes, Ora Dasai." Roh walked back to his bedroom. Luna and Kihin were still talking.

Luna looked much younger in the low light, slender and spry; his eyes were big and nearly black, the lashes long and delicate like a child's. Luna slid off the bunk and said, in slightly accented Dhai, "I should go."

Roh sat down at his desk to write a letter. It was time. He hunched over the low desk, working through the Kai cipher in his head.

"What are you writing?" Kihin asked.

"Nothing," Roh said.

It was true. For all the scribbling, the only thing the note really said was:

Ora Dasai has found two texts. May be omajista guides. Says many records related to training omajistas may have been purged. Will write again when we find one of those texts. Invaders progress about the same. Patron says they will stay here through the winter.

But Roh had not had time to look for anything at all while dancing in the dark. His mornings in the archives, he merely acted as a runner, and Dasai didn't talk about how much he learned from the book. Roh hadn't read any more himself. Chali chided him for it, but Dasai seemed to prefer it. Dasai wanted him to get something of use from the dancers, he knew, but the more dead ends they ran into, the more resolute Roh became in why he was really here. He wanted to be a sanisi, not a spy. Because as hard as he tried, all he could think of was Abas's smooth skin, and whirling sanisi in the courtyard, dancing with air and death.

30

"Did you sleep?" Liaro asked from the doorway.

Ahkio peered up at him from the stack of temple maps on the tea table in his rooms. Para was well above the horizon, and a hint of the double suns already kissed the treetops. He'd lost track of time. "No. Did you?"

"Not really," Liaro said, shutting the door, "but I suspect I had a lot more fun than you did. What's this?"

Ahkio turned the pages over. "A very old conversation between my aunt and my sister."

"You mean Nasaka?"

"No. Etena."

"Really? Well. That's interesting. You know you have a bunch of clan leaders downstairs who want to keep talking government today."

"I'm aware." Ahkio rubbed his eyes. "I'm going to bathe and change. If Caisa comes in, tell her to leave these pages for me today. I'm in the middle of something."

"Does this tell you what Kirana was up to in the temples?"

"I don't know yet. It all makes me feel a little mad, to be honest." He stood and pulled off his tunic. He'd confided in Liaro about the invaders and made him swear not to tell anyone else, including Caisa. He wasn't sure how the country would take it. "There's something you should know, though."

"It gets better, does it? Have our mothers escaped Sina's grasp and come spiraling back to life?"

"I've agreed to get married."

"What?"

The look on Liaro's face gave him pause. "Are you all right?"

"I... I thought Meyna was exiled."

"She is. I'm marrying Clan Leader Hona's daughter, of Sorai. Probably by the end of the week."

"You say that so casually."

"Is that a problem?"

"Did Ora Nasaka put you up to this?"

"I have to make hard decisions, Liaro. What did you expect? We'll need the harbor."

Liaro sat on the bed. "So we're not getting married, then?" His tone was light, but Ahkio knew better.

"You know I'd like nothing better. You also know that's not likely with a male Kai. A woman Kai like Kirana... she could have as many husbands as she wanted. It's harder to determine parentage, with a man."

Liaro guffawed. "You expect a Sorai to keep to one man?"

"She can take female lovers. It's not unheard of."

"You make like you've thought this through, but you haven't."

"Liaro, I'm tired. I don't want to fight."

"She was Ora Nasaka's choice, right? Ahkio, Ora Nasaka doesn't at all mean for you to carry on the blood of the Kai. She's setting up Clan Leader Hona's family to take the seat. Who knows whose baby it will be?"

"I wouldn't care, Liaro. I'd be distantly related to just about any child, from any combination of parents."

"You gave up so easily."

"If you knew what I did, you'd understand why I gave up on this point."

"Just like you give in to everything."

"That was mean."

"It's the truth."

"Get some sleep, Liaro. I'm not going to fight with you." He grabbed a clean tunic and went downstairs to the bathing room.

After that were breakfast and more polite talk with the clan leaders. He didn't get a break until midafternoon, and by then, his mood had soured completely. He called for a halt to the meetings for the rest of the day and went out to the clan square for a fresh breeze.

He found Caisa there, sweating through defense forms, and asked if she wanted to spar. An hour later, she had thrown him to the stones eight times, and he was exhausted and soaked in sweat. He peeled off his tunic and tossed it aside. Asked her to go again.

She gave him a long look, one he recognized, but he ignored it. If she meant to woo him, she would fail at it. That was one fight he did not want to have with Liaro.

This time, he threw her, so hard he heard her shoulder crack against the stone. She rolled away and came up clutching at her shoulder.

"I'm sorry," he said. "Are you all right?"

She shook her head. "Give it a minute. Are *you* all right?"

"Yes, I'm sorry. Just working some things out."

"There are more productive ways to do that. Write an opera or something."

"Do you want me to call a physician?"

"No, it's fine."

He picked up his tunic and went to the fountain to wash up. Who was he to tussle with a novice? What he really wanted was to pick up a sword and run Nasaka through with it, because she was only going to trade him the answers he wanted for some horrible thing she wanted.

Ahkio undressed and dumped a bucket of water over his head. His clothes, bunched about his feet, got soaked, but he didn't care. They would need washing anyway. As he turned, he saw Ghrasia Madah standing a few paces away, staring at him.

Ghrasia came up into the council house from the rear entrance. The day was warm for high autumn, and the bad news she carried made it all seem that much worse. She had more dead bodies to bring to the Kai's attention, and a recommendation she already knew he was going to resist.

She found Caisa flirting with Liaro near the hearth of the main room of the Osono council house. Caisa was bathed in sweat and laughing uproariously at something Liaro said. Ghrasia remembered how delightful it was the first few years she dressed in a red skirt and called herself a member of the militia. She recognized the girl's easy confidence and open face. Chances were very good that Caisa had yet to kill anyone. She didn't truly know what the sword meant yet. It was just an ornament, like a particularly fine pair of earrings.

"Have either of you seen the Kai?" Ghrasia asked.

Caisa sobered. "He's out training in the courtyard." She rolled her shoulder. "Nearly dislocated my arm. Tell him to take up poetry or something. He needs to relax."

"I'll talk to him," Liaro said, standing.

"Don't," Ghrasia said. "I need to speak to him first."

"He should be by the fountain," Caisa said. "That's where he was headed."

Ghrasia stepped into the Osono square and walked purposely toward the fountain, where Ahkio was stripping off his tunic. Her steps faltered as he pulled off his trousers. She stopped there for half a breath as he leaned over and splashed his face with water. Ghrasia tried to work some sense into her head and some spit into her mouth. He's just a young man, she told herself, but it had been a good long while since she saw a man with the proportions of some passionate sculpture dripping naked beside a fountain.

"Am I keeping you from the fountain?" Ahkio said.

She started. She hadn't noticed him turn his head. Her gaze had been... elsewhere.

"Not at all," she said. "I wanted to speak to you."

"I'm just going up to change," Ahkio said. "Come up."

Ghrasia weighed her response. Her hesitation must have disgruntled him, because after a short while, he simply pulled on his wet trousers and threw the rest of his clothes over his shoulder. He began to walk into the council house.

She made her decision. She followed.

He opened the door to his room. Ghrasia expected to see a number of hangers-on there – she had seen him trailed by students and merchants and members of the clan leaders' families since their arrival. There did not seem to be a moment where he wasn't meeting with someone over a meal. But save for heavy furniture and riots of book-filled trunks and stacks of paper, the room was empty.

Ahkio went to the wardrobe. "What is it you wanted to discuss?"

"I've had small squads running patrols across the clans," Ghrasia said, "in response to the recent murders and rumors about strangers." She shut the door, turned back.

Ahkio had pulled off his wet trousers and begun to dress in the dry ones.

She realized her voice had trailed off. She cleared her throat. Heat bloomed up her face. Somewhere above them, captured within Sina's soul, Javia was laughing. How old was he? Nineteen? Twenty? Even her husbands would laugh. She preferred experienced, quick-witted men, not pliable young ones.

"I apologize," he said, and yanked on his tunic. "It didn't occur to me–"

"Not at all," she said. "I have just been... more tense than I anticipated."

"I had a lover once who said desire is like–"

Ghrasia suspected he was about to quote *The Book of Oma* at her. That indignity would be too much. "The patrols," Ghrasia said.

"Have they found something?"

"I had them map out where each of the murders occurred – such as the ones at Kalinda Lasa's – and follow-up with the local militia and safety ministers," Ghrasia said. She stood on the other side of the tea table from him.

"You found a pattern," he said.

"They did, yes." She pulled a square of paper from her tunic pocket and unfolded it onto the tea table. She had to push some of the other pages out of the way. They looked like temple maps, and she wondered why he'd have any interest in those. "I know your sister's death was strange. Since then, we've seen more. I purposely sought a connection, thinking it may circle back to these invaders the Saiduan are fighting. Before you take a country, you send small groups of scouts to soften the way."

He sat across from her and leaned over the map. Dhai was a narrow sliver of a country, bordered by the sea to the north, mountains to the east and south, and Mount Ahya and the woodlands to the west. The fifteen Dhai clans were demarcated by a series of dotted lines, some of which intersected. Clan territories weren't about claiming land so much as organizing family groups. It helped reduce the chances of dangerous inbreeding, which had become an issue in the country's early history. Clans Sorila, Saiz, Saobina, and Raona clung to the south. Progressing north from there were clans Badu, Garika, Daosina, Taosina, and Osono. Farther north still, the clans of Mutao to the west, then Alia, Adama, and Nako, and finally Daora and Sorai on the coast.

Ghrasia made a circle at the edge of Clan Garika territory. The spot was already marked with a red dot. "This is where Kalinda Lasa, the way house keeper, was killed along with three still unidentified men." She circled another spot on the edge of Clan Osono. "And here's where Clan Leader Saurika found the body of a young shepherd named Romey."

"Romey?" Ahkio said. "Romey Sahina was one of my students in Osono."

"Yes," Ghrasia said. She pointed to another mark in Sorila, near the woodlands. "This was the woman found at the bottom of a mine," she said. "I suspect you may also know her name. She was a member of the Kuallina militia. Fouria Orana Saiz. She and two of her squad members were found here, Alasu Carahin Sorila and Marhin Rasanu Badu."

"Fouria," Ahkio said. He touched the dot on the map. "I remember her, yes. She passed through Osono the day Nasaka called me to the temple. The others, too – Alasu and Marhin were there. They spent the night with Liaro and me before heading back to Kuallina."

"They did not make it back to Kuallina," Ghrasia said. "They've been missing for some weeks."

"What were they doing in Sorila?"

"That's an excellent question," Ghrasia said. "I hoped you might know. Only Kalinda Lasa was found in a place one might expect – her place of business. Romey did not work as a shepherd. His family were weavers. And that squad... should not have been in Sorila."

"Is there a connection between these people we're not seeing?" Ahkio said.

"That's what I've been trying to determine."

Ahkio circled the Temple of Oma with his finger. "If you include Kirana, all these deaths occur around Clan Raona. Have there been any deaths there?"

"No," Ghrasia said. "It may simply be coincidence. I just want to make sure I'm looking at every option. If we have agents inside our country and we're invaded by a larger force, they could sabotage the harbor gates, poison water supplies, or simply continue to assassinate key citizens."

Ahkio pulled the map closer. "I kept thinking Kirana was a singular case. But... all these unnatural deaths. If three were already killed at Kalinda Lasa's..." He traced the rough circle the deaths made around Raona. "What's in Raona?" he said. "They cultivate rice and wine."

"And sparrows," Ghrasia said. "They raise most of the sparrows used by the temples."

"That doesn't bring much commerce–"

"No, but it's key here," Ghrasia said, and took the map back. "If you have a diverse number of agents and needed access to sparrows to relay information, Raona would be a strong base."

"If you worked with the local militia to identify strangers requesting sparrows–"

"We may get one or two of them in for questioning," Ghrasia said. "It could help us track the others."

"That's a start," Ahkio said.

"I'll need the help of a half dozen Oras," Ghrasia said. "By all counts, these people are gifted."

"Nasaka can help you with that."

"This brings up another issue," Ghrasia said. "Right now, I have no authority in the clans. I oversee the militia posted at the Kuallina and Liona strongholds. But working with local militia in places like Raona is... challenging."

"I'm sure they'll be accommodating."

"The clans don't like centralized authority," Ghrasia said. "But being so decentralized makes us vulnerable."

"What are you suggesting?"

"I think we should organize the country's militia under a single hierarchical structure."

"Out of the question," Ahkio said.

"You have over a dozen clan leaders downstairs working on changing the government right now. Why not change this?"

"We are not a dictatorship."

"This is nothing of the sort." His implication offended her. She couldn't keep the heat from her voice.

"I only hold this seat because the clan leaders haven't thrown me out of it," Ahkio said, "and they only hold theirs because the people haven't thrown them out. But what citizen can overthrow an armed militia? You might as well tell me to train Oras in martial combat."

"*The Book of Oma* was written five hundred years ago. It was a different time. They didn't face what we do."

"They had already faced it and lost," Ahkio said. "In the face of that loss, they changed, and that's the reason we're still here."

"That's a very loose interpretation of the Book."

"And in times of great strife–"

Ghrasia made a face. "Please don't quote the Book," she said, and began to roll up the map.

"Did Nasaka put you up to this?"

"Ora Nasaka? No. She is not the only person in this country speaking sense." Sense of a sort, at least, Ghrasia thought.

"So, she did speak to you?"

"I know you and Ora Nasaka don't often agree," Ghrasia said carefully. "I wouldn't trust her to care for my own child. But her shrewdness has preserved this country during terrible times."

"I have confidence in your ability," Ahkio said. "You held back the Dorinahs during the Pass War."

"With volunteer militia sent from every clan, yes," Ghrasia said. "There may come a time when we need more than volunteers."

"When that time comes, we'll have far larger problems than the size of our military," Ahkio said. "When children are throwing roof tiles at invaders, there's another conversation we'll need to have. But not yet."

"I've heard the reports from Saiduan," Ghrasia said, standing. "I had an obligation to bring it up."

"And I appreciate that."

"We'll have this conversation again."

"Find the assassins first," Ahkio said. "Nasaka has already put the harbor on alert. It's our most vulnerable point. Clan Sorai is managing security there. We're bound together by something far greater than empty titles, Ghrasia. That's blood and tradition. We can overcome this without becoming like our neighbors."

"You are very optimistic." He sounded like something from a book of inspiring speeches.

"I have to be," Ahkio said. He, too, stood. "I'll see you out."

"Do we want to capture one alive?" Ghrasia asked.

"If possible. Yes. I'd like to interrogate them and try to come to an understanding. We may be able to find out why they chose to kill who they did."

Ghrasia made her way to the door, and Ahkio followed her. She paused with her hand on the knob.

"There's something I wanted to be clear about," Ghrasia said. "You know how the Pass War really started?"

"The Dorinahs attacked the Liona Stronghold," Ahkio said. "Then they blocked our harbor. A campaign of aggression."

"That's what they teach," Ghrasia said. "Those are the songs. It wasn't like that." It had been a long time since she told this story. But he was Kai, and young, and needed to hear it. "Eight hundred Dorinah-born Dhais from the slave camps came to the gates of Liona pleading for mercy. They said legionnaires were following. But we couldn't let them in. That's the policy. They tried to climb the wall, but that's impossible.

"They called up to us in Dhai. Called their family names. Their clan names. But I knew the rules. We didn't expect the legionnaires would follow. But there they came, two thousand women in chain mail, bristling like bone trees. They trapped the Dhais between them and the wall. They marched in and smashed them. Bled them at our feet.

"Somebody on the wall got upset. They fired on the Dorinahs. Then we all did. I don't know how many we killed, but we must have killed someone important. *That's* when they blocked our harbor. When we were too frightened to save our own people, we murdered others."

"It must have been a difficult decision."

"This isn't the Pass War," Ghrasia said, "but we risk making the same mistakes."

"We have rules at Liona," Ahkio said. "If you hadn't fired on the legionnaires—"

"Spoken like an Ora," Ghrasia said.

"Or a Kai," Ahkio said. "I may not like the morality of those policies, but I understand them."

Ghrasia flexed her scarred knuckles. "I'll find the assassins," she said, "but this is all going to get bigger, Kai."

"One more thing, Ghrasia. When you find these assassins...

when you speak to them… don't be surprised if they look like us. If they speak like us. There's a reason they've been so difficult to find."

Ghrasia frowned. "And will you tell me the reason?"

"In time," he said, and opened the door.

Ahkio married Mohrai Hona Sorai in the Osono clan square amid a brilliant stir of falling leaves, big as plates, and a cascade of tiny white seedpods carried on the stormy wind. He remembered her hands were soft, and she had a kind mouth, and when she stood next to him, her mother stood a little straighter, too.

They married with every clan leader in the country in attendance, even if a few of them huddled in the council house behind them, surly that it was not their clan he joined through marriage. Liaro drank with them inside. Ahkio did not blame him.

Nasaka came in from the temple, acting in her capacity as Ahkio's closest kin, and bound their hands in brilliant blue grass and lemon flowers.

After, Ahkio led Mohrai upstairs to his cluttered rooms. Caisa had tried to tidy the trunks and stacks of paper, but even now, married and bound to Sorai, his mind was on the work more than the marriage.

"I expect you'll want me to go home in the morning," Mohrai said. She dressed in violet; orange flowers were pinned in her hair.

"I expect you have lovers to get back to," he said.

"Has Ora Nasaka spoken to you about that?"

"It's not necessary," he said. "I need Sorai's loyalty. Is that less than romantic?"

She smiled. A lovely smile that reminded him of Meyna. "My family has held the harbor for two centuries, Kai. I'm aware of what this match means. I just wanted to make sure you were, too." She began pulling the flowers from her hair. "I've spoken with Ghrasia Madah about the murders she's investigating, and Ora Nasaka told me about the invaders. I expect my family to be kept in conversation as things progress."

"You will be. Anything else?"

"I have two lovers, both from Sorai. I'd like permission to continue to court them."

"You have it."

"And you?"

"And me what?"

"Lovers?"

"Just my cousin Liaro. And that's... what it is."

"Of course. I see no conflict there."

"Let's sleep," she said. "I've never seen a man look so haunted. You made a good choice, Kai. Ora Nasaka has your best interests at heart. My family is with you. I am with you."

Ahkio stared at the stack of temple maps. "Let's hope it's enough," he said.

After Mohrai went back to the harbor, Ahkio finalized a draft of the revised Dhai constitution. The clan leaders set their signatures on it, and he took it up to his room to stare at it. They would sit with him at council four times a year, rotating the location of the meeting to a new clan each time, and debate matters of state. Clan leaders would continue to be elected by their clans, and each clan had the same weight when voting motions into law. The Kai line was still hereditary. Oras still chose the Kai from among the Kai line.

But there were more limits. He could request no taxes without their permission. Could conscript no militia without approval. Much of the Kai's role throughout history was simply as a religious and political leader, someone to help negotiate contracts with neighboring countries and serve as arbiter for clan disputes. Very little of that had changed. Much of the stipulations written in were indicative of the clan leaders' fears of his attempts to overstep that traditional power. He suspected the ever-widening influence of the Oras inside the clans had caused the distrust more than anything else. If they believed he was Nasaka's son and not his mother Javia's... they had every right to fear how Nasaka would use him.

Liaro yawned and stretched in bed. The bed covers were a tangle. He had been out most of the night with Caisa and some of the younger novices and militia, helping with a joint bridge building project at the edge of Osono where a walking tree had smashed much of the bridge's foundation. He spun a long, drunken tale about fencing with a tree the night before as Ahkio helped him into bed. Sometimes he wondered if he needed an assistant on hand just to care for Liaro.

"You don't look drunk enough for a man stuck in a political marriage," Liaro said, peering at him. He squinted at the light from the windows. "What time is it?"

"Midmorning," Ahkio said. "I was surprised you came home alone."

"You being Kai isn't helping," he said. "Everyone I talk to is afraid of you."

"Me?"

Liaro sat up and shrugged. "Well, your wife. I suspect she's trying to make dead certain she'll be the only one carrying an heir."

"I'm not foolish enough to challenge her claim," Ahkio said. "It's fine, Liaro. She and I came to an agreement."

"Good. Let those women fight over whose baby is Kai. Either way, it will be yours."

"I'm cheered that it's me in this seat and not you."

"Cheered by that, are you?" he said, gesturing to the revised constitution. "Looks like the same old story to me, though."

"Most people don't actually want power," Ahkio said. "They want this illusion of power."

"Is that from the Book?"

"I'm paraphrasing, yes."

"You need some better lines, Ahkio." Liaro pulled on his tunic. "Have you heard from Ghrasia yet? It's been over a week since she left for Raona."

"No. I needed to tie up things here before we joined her."

"You want to go to Raona? Where there might be assassins killing people across Dhai?"

"Just get Caisa up here."

"Fine, all right. Do this, Liaro, run here, wear this, dance around, Liaro." He slipped on his shoes and headed downstairs.

Ahkio went to the window. What did it feel like when someone tightened a noose around your neck in Dorinah? Was it like this? A sense of dread and powerlessness? He'd untangled the notes his sister and Aunt Etena had written in the book, most of it related to philosophy, but the conversations about the soul of the temple bothered him. He couldn't get that symbol out of his mind. What way was barred? Why?

Caisa entered and announced herself. "You asked for me?"

"I want you to ensure that all of the clan leaders leave today," Ahkio said. "It may be some time before we gather in one place again."

"Is something wrong?"

"I need the Oras and militia attending me to pack up," he said, "we're going to meet Ghrasia Madah in Clan Raona."

"Where you think the assassins are? Is that wise?"

"I really do need to keep you and Liaro apart."

31

The weeks in Dorinah passed slowly, coldly, for Zezili's husband, Anavha. He spent most of those autumn days sleeping. He slept because he could dream when he slept – dream he was a pirate like the ones that pillaged slaves from the Dhai coast, or the man in one of the romance novels Zezili's sister Taodalain bought for him, saved from assassins and kidnappers by a handsome legion commander like Zezili. With so much time spent sleeping, he kept himself out of trouble. The dajians avoided him. Daolyn sat up and read him Zezili's letters when they came. It was his quiet, stifling life. Every day the same, waiting for Zezili's return, waiting for news of the outside.

Low autumn lengthened to high autumn, then low winter. One cool evening, he passed time with Daolyn in the sitting room. A squat stove brought in from storage warmed them, but Anavha still wore a coat over his under-tunic and girdle. He was preparing to pull out yet another crooked seam in his embroidery when a heavy knock sounded on the front door.

Daolyn set aside the garments she was mending and stood. Anavha followed her. He paused in the doorway of the sitting room and watched her cross the yard to the main gate.

"Who's there?" Daolyn called.

"Tanasai Laosina!"

"Syre Zezili isn't here," Daolyn called. "I've told you, she no longer permits you within her house."

More voices filtered in from outside. Anavha heard the sound of dogs barking, the jingle of tack. Tanasai had not come alone.

"Open this fucking door, you fucking dajian, or I'll fucking burn it down, you hear me? You think I won't fucking burn it down and cut you open from slit to tit?"

Daolyn hesitated another moment, then pulled back the iron latch.

Anavha thought she was mad until he saw Tanasai enter, and behind her, half a dozen women in chain mail wearing infused weapons and helmets. If Daolyn had not opened the door, they would indeed have forced it open.

"Where's my bloody cousin?" Tanasai said. Her voice was slurred. The others were snickering and stumbling over one another.

Anavha stepped out of the sitting room and hurried across the courtyard toward his room, trying to stay in the shadows.

But Tanasai saw him.

"There's my cousin's bauble! Come here, boy!"

Anavha ran into his room and shoved his weight against the door, but Tanasai wedged herself in the doorway. Three more women tried to squirm in behind her. They stank, not just of alcohol, but of themselves. They must not have washed for weeks.

"Come here, pretty," Tanasai said. Her damp hair clung to her flushed face, the skin so dark her freckles were no longer visible. She grunted and pushed at the door. Anavha stumbled back, fell. His head hit his mattress. Tanasai stepped inside. Her women slunk in behind her.

Tanasai reached for him. The other women laughed.

Daolyn pushed inside. She grabbed at the last of the women entering the room and said, "The Empress herself will punish you! This boy was her gift to Zezili. She will punish you if harm comes to him!"

The woman took Daolyn by the hair and slammed her head into the doorframe twice. Daolyn's body made a dull thumping sound as she hit the floor.

"Let me see you," Tanasai said, leering at Anavha. "Let's see what my near-cousin thinks she's keeping from me."

They stripped him naked and pushed him onto his belly. Tanasai grabbed hold of his hair, jerked his head back, hissed in his ear, "This is what you're made for? You forget that?"

She reached beneath him and tugged at his flaccid penis. "What do you think, my women? Think he needs this?"

"No!" one of the women yelled. "Take it off! Leave Zezili with a proper girl!"

"Looks like he doesn't know what to do with it!" another said, and the others cackled.

Tanasai pressed her big body onto his. She sucked at her thumb and parted the cheeks of his ass. Shoved her thumb inside him.

He cried out.

"No virgin here," Tanasai said into his ear. Her spittle flecked his face. "Let's see what else we can get up in there."

Tanasai let go of him. She reached for the dagger at her hip.

Anavha clawed at the floor. He twisted upright and grabbed at the ring of his dressing table drawer. Tanasai laughed and moved closer.

Anavha jerked open the drawer. It pulled free of its runner. The force of his own momentum and the quick release of the drawer sent the contents clattering to the floor. His container of powder thumped his chest, sent a burst of gold dust into the air. He sneezed. Kerchiefs scattered.

And there was the kitchen knife on the floor beside him; his cutting knife. He took it without being sure what he was going to do with it.

Then Tanasai threw herself on top of him.

Her bulky body pinned him to the floor. She let out a huff of breath, like the wind had been knocked from her. The sordid stink of her breath roiled over him.

Anavha felt wet on his fingers.

"Huh?" Tanasai mumbled.

Anavha kept hold of the knife. Tanasai pulled herself off him. She stood, tottering.

When she was clear of him, a thread of blood spurted from her wound, spraying Anavha's face. He held up his bloody hands. Dropped the blade.

She dabbed her fingers in the wound, into the gush of blood.

"Oh," she said. Her face grew pale.

The women behind her fell back, skittish.

Tanasai fell to her knees. The wound continued to gush dark blood. Tanasai toppled against the chair in front of the dressing table.

"Fools," Tanasai muttered. Her eyes rolled back in her head. "Fools. Get me something."

But the women were retreating. One or two, then the rest. Their bootsteps sounded in the courtyard. Whispered voices. The dull hiss of leather and armor, the clink of chain mail.

An affront to Zezili's possessions was an affront to Zezili. They no longer had a near-cousin to stand behind.

Anavha watched the blood leave Tanasai's body. It pooled about his naked feet.

He pulled himself away from her. She spat blood at him.

"They'll kill you... for this. You're... Rhea's now," Tanasai said. She made a hissing, gurgling sound, like a cough or a sigh.

Then she was still.

It took Anavha some time to move. He crawled toward Daolyn's crumpled body. She was breathing but not conscious. An ugly black bruise was forming on the right side of her face. He went to Zezili's room where the big tub was and ran some water. He washed his hands and face. His hands were trembling.

He had done violence. He had done violence against a woman. She had died. Would those women call the enforcers? Or the priests? Karosia Soafin had already been called in once because of something he might have done. This... this was much worse. Zezili was away. She could not protect him from Karosia, or the enforcers.

But he could go to her.

Once he made the decision, it seemed so easy, so obvious. He would go to her. She wasn't far, if her letter to Daolyn about visiting Lake Morta was true. The lake was just a three- or four-day journey away, southeast. He had been there before during high summer with Zezili. The dog Zezili let him use was still in the kennels. The dajians would put on the tack. He would pack food. He would... But he would be a man traveling alone. Someone would stop him, ask for his papers, his chaperone. He might be able to pass as a woman, though, if he wore a coat and hood, left the girdle behind...

Zezili would understand.

He walked to Zezili's wardrobe. Her clothes were too big for him, but he managed to tie on women's straight-legged trousers and an under-tunic. He found a dark coat with a hood. He would have to wear his own boots. Bring gloves. It would be cold at the lake. Daolyn kept a little petty money in a box in the high cupboard in the kitchen for everyday things. He retrieved this, pocketed it, and went back to where Daolyn lay. He put a pillow from his bed beneath her head and draped her with his own quilt. The dajians had gathered in the doorway to the kitchen and stared at him as he moved about. He did not speak to them until he was dressed and walking to the door.

"Care for Daolyn," he said. "Tell her I'm coming back with Syre Zezili."

He shut the gate behind him. One of the dajians saddled his dog, silent and obedient as the mount. As the dajian handed over the reins, Anavha saw her brand in the light of the kennel lanterns. A raised scar of tawny flesh, Zezili's initials branded onto the back of her hand.

He remembered his own mark, Zezili cutting her initials into him. You are mine. I own you.

He got up onto the dog and whistled him forward.

Zezili arrived at her estate four days later, well after dark. She let Dakar's reins fall. The dajians weren't expecting her. She pounded on the gate and called for Daolyn.

The door opened. Pale light spilled onto the walk. Daolyn held a lantern. She had a yellowish bruise along one side of her face.

Zezili pulled off her helm and pushed past her. "What's happened?" she said.

"Your near-cousin ordered entrance," Daolyn said. She called for dajians to tend to Dakar and shut the gate after them. "Half a dozen women arrived with her. They asked to see you. When I said you were not home, they turned on Anavha."

"Where is he?"

"I do not know," Daolyn said, and Zezili saw her flinch. "The women assaulted me. When I woke, your husband and the women had gone. Tanasai was dead in your husband's room."

"Did the other women take him? I will have them hunted down for thieves! If they've so much as *touched*–"

"No, I spoke with the dajians. They said your husband went alone."

"Alone?"

"Took one of the dogs."

Zezili let out her breath in one long puff. "Did you alert the priests, the enforcers, any of the others?"

Daolyn shook her head.

"Good girl. And the body?"

"Outside, in the barn," Daolyn said.

"I must think," Zezili said. She walked to her room, unshuttered the lanterns. She paced. Daolyn hovered in the doorway.

"He read your last letter," Daolyn said. "He may have gone to Lake Morta to find you."

"Why'd you let him read that?"

"I read him your letters," Daolyn said. "You did not say to keep correspondence from him."

Zezili swore. The journey had been wearying, and what she found here at the end of it only deepened her exhaustion. Her near-cousin had come here with the intent to use or perhaps harm one of Zezili's possessions. If it had been Dakar, and Dakar bit Tanasai, killed her even, could the dog be faulted? No, that argument would not hold, not if the priests were called into the matter. No priest would speak of mercy for an act of violence,

316   THE MIRROR EMPIRE

committed by a dumb beast or no. Would he be foolish enough
to travel all the way to Lake Morta?

"Did he take money?" Zezili asked.

"A bit from the petty jar," Daolyn said. "Not enough for a sea
passage."

"The roads are not safe for an unescorted man. He will not
have gotten far."

"Should I alert a hunter? Someone to track a missing man?"

"No. His disappearance coincides with Tanasai's. A hunter
would figure that out. She might ask questions." Zezili stopped
pacing and stared at her shuttered window. "He would not leave
me," she murmured. "Get me pen and paper. He may have gone
to my sisters, seeking assistance. I'll have Taodalain and her wife
make discreet inquiries at the mardanas. Quickly, go!"

Daolyn moved into the dark courtyard.

Zezili crossed to her window, opened the shutters. The room
was cold, but the outside air was colder and spilled onto her face
like a slap.

She could send letters to her sisters and go to Lake Morta
herself. It was on the way back east to the coast. She owed an
explanation to Monshara, though, and perhaps the Empress.

Daolyn returned. Zezili penned the letters to her sisters and
Monshara. But as she began the letter to the Empress, she could
think of no words to justify her actions. She had deserted her
post to run after her absent husband, a man who had committed
violence against a woman. If she did not get to him first, he
could be killed or sold into slavery. If the Empress never knew,
if Monshara kept the confidence... a few days more. Monshara
could slaughter that camp without her, and Zezili could join them
at the next. It's what she wrote in her letter to Monshara.

As she handed off the letters to Daolyn to post, she was
suddenly drenched in a sheen of cold sweat. If she did not get to
Anavha before the local enforcers... if the Empress found out...
but those were a fool's fears. She would sort this out the way she
always had.

Zezili went to her desk and opened a handful of correspondence Daolyn had yet to forward to her, many of them addressed from Daorian. Three were letters from her sisters, likely relating gossip or asking for more money, and another was from Syre Kakolyn.

Zezili broke the seal on Syre Kakolyn's letter. There was a signature at the bottom that was not Kakolyn's. Kakolyn had her second pen all of her correspondence, as she herself could not pen a word much beyond her own name.

Syre Zezili,

I heard about your campaign to purge the camps, which is not unlike my own enigmatic campaign. I was just dispatched to the S. Sanctuary by the Empress to eliminate the Seekers.

I thought it a strange order. How were we going to kill our own satellite-wielding assassins? But she sent a bunch of foreign magic-users with us. I wanted to relay this to you because when we got to the Sanctuary, the Seekers were gone.

That means we have magic-wielding seers the Empress wants dead running around, led by your old friend Tulana. Keep a watchful eye. Send word if you have it.

I remain,

Syre Kakolyn Kotaria

Zezili set the letter aside. Killing Seekers? How much more madness could the country take? Zezili's legion would be worthless against the Tai Mora without the aid of Tulana's Seekers. Zezili opened one of the missives from her sister Taodalain and read about the news from Daorian. She skimmed most of it until she came to a particular passage:

Already, Daorian has seen increasing violence against both private and publicly owned dajians. The Empress has denounced

them as having caused a wave of infertility in Castaolain,
and linked their indulgences to increasing food prices. I have
enclosed some papers from Daorian, sheets circulating to this
effect, blaming dajians for numerous ills, including an outbreak
of yellow pox in eastern Kidolynai. I heard news of your legion
purging the dajian camps. Does this mean the reports of the
dajians' role in these matters are true?

Zezili pondered both reports and looked through the papers
Taodalain had sent. They were poorly printed, sloppy, on low-
quality paper, and full of propagandist ranting. Monshara had
told Zezili to stay out of things. Told her she knew nothing and
understood less. But even Zezili could see that eradicating the
entire country's labor would result in famine and strife. The Tai
Mora would coax them into destroying themselves.

And no one stood in their way.

Zezili moved, of habit, toward Anavha's room. She stopped
halfway across the courtyard, realized her error, and turned back
to her own room. No, she could not summon him from sleep.
Tanasai had stolen him from her.

She got into bed, alone. Daolyn had turned down the sheets,
but not warmed the bed; an understandable oversight, considering
the circumstances. Zezili lay awake, staring at the canopy hanging
from the posts of her bed, listening to the stillness of the house.
The fountain had been turned off for the winter. She heard
laughter somewhere. The dajians' quarters, likely. She closed her
eyes and saw a tide of blood, a field littered in dajian bodies.

She pushed back her blankets and walked across the courtyard.
She pushed open the door to Anavha's room and unshuttered
one of the lanterns by the door. Whatever mess had been done
by Tanasai, there was no immediate trace of it. Anavha's bed
was made, his dressing table in order. His dog-eared copy of *The*
Book of Rhea lay at his bedside table. Zezili walked to the book,
pressed a finger to the hard leather cover, and moved away, to
the dressing table.

She leaned over and looked at the bottles of scent, the containers of gold powder, rouge, and kohl. She opened the big standing wardrobe and gazed into the interior. It smelled heavily of everpine and the musky scent of Anavha, mixed with saffron and lemon grass. She tugged at the white sleeve of one of his coats. She had the ridiculous urge to press it to her nose and inhale the scent of him lingering on the clothing.

Zezili curled her lip, disgusted at her own sentiment. She left the room, closed the door. She would have Daolyn lock it until Anavha's return.

She walked back to her room, went to the window, and stood leaning out into the air, inhaling cold like a drowning woman first tasting air, her head thrown back, fingers gripping the sill.

She wanted her husband. She wanted the world back the way it was. She wanted the Tai Mora dead and their mirror smashed to dust.

32

Anavha was lost. He had passed the previous two nights in dodgy way houses along dark roads. The dog was hungry; whenever Anavha dismounted, it pushed its nose into his hand. He hadn't shaved in three days, and his face itched. Daolyn would have had time to alert the priests and the enforcers by now, and he trembled to think of what would happen if they found him before he found Zezili.

He got back onto the dog and turned it round the way he had come. He had no idea what direction that was. Didn't the moons rise in the west where the sun set? He had located himself by the cobbled road in the beginning, but he didn't know a lot about roads. He had never seen a map of Dorinah, and his schooling had been limited.

He urged the dog down a dirt track. He clung to the dog with numbed hands and prayed to Rhea to help him find the right way. The moons moved across the sky. His dog halted once, to sniff at the frozen body of a big spotted rabbit lying in a ditch.

Anavha nodded off in the saddle sometime later and woke to find that the dog had paused again at the edge of a vast snowy expanse ringed in jagged mountains. He thought perhaps he had come to Lake Morta at last, but it was too small and not the right shape. Where on Rhea's face was he?

Anavha saw a flicker of light on the other side of the crooked lake. His dog barked. The sound echoed eerily across the lake.

Anavha whistled the dog forward. They followed the snowy path around the circumference of the lake.

It was another hour before Anavha reached the porch of the inn, but by that time, the thought of finally finding Zezili had invigorated him. He would need a bath, a shave, a change of clothing. He could not allow her to see him this way.

He slid off the dog's back, so sore he could barely walk. No one came out to greet him. He pulled his hood low over his face and walked up to the porch, tried the door. It was open.

He walked into the common room. The light was bad; most of the lanterns had been shuttered. Candles threw shadows. A woman sat behind the bar counter, reading a battered copy of a book he recognized called *Guise of the Heart*, a romantic political thriller set in Daorian a century prior. Taodalain had loved that book.

The stout woman put the book down. Candles drooled great runnels of wax along the edges of the bar. The weather was too cold for flame flies.

Anavha stayed a step away from the light.

"A little late, isn't it?" the woman asked. She could have been his mother with her big squared shoulders and disgruntled mouth.

"I would like a room, if that's all right," Anavha said, careful about the pitch of his voice. "Maybe a bath. And… my dog is outside."

The woman nodded at an arched doorway near the stair. "Bath's through there. How many nights?"

"One, I think. Is Syre Zezili Hasaria here?" he asked. He could not keep the trembling from his voice.

"No Syres here, child."

"Which lake is this, matron?"

"Which lake?" she said. "Are you so lost? This is Lake Orastina."

"Is that close to Lake Morta?"

"Morta's another day south of here. Where are you coming from?"

"I'm sorry," he said. "I just need a room."

The woman demanded payment. Anavha fumbled through his purse for the correct amount and paid over the last of his money. He hadn't realized how expensive things were. The woman handed over a key.

"You'll have number eleven, last door on the left, second floor."

The tubs in the bathing room were separated by painted wooden screens. He bathed in privacy and wondered what to do next. Another day along snowy roads sounded horrible.

Warm, clean, and exhausted, he made his way upstairs with the hood of his coat pulled up. He fumbled with the key. None of the doors were numbered.

He put his key into the lock of his room at the end of the hall and waited for the click, but the door was unlocked. He pushed it open.

There was already someone in the room.

Anavha thought he had interrupted some scene of sexual congress. He must have chosen the wrong room. The blankets of the large bed had pooled around the floor at the foot of the frame. A large woman lay half on and half off the bed, naked. A naked man sat astride her, big hands gripping either end of a silken cord twisted around the woman's long neck. Her face had taken on a violent purplish cast. The head lolled back. The eyes bulged, and the pool of her black hair puddled across her bare shoulders.

Anavha did not move. His mind reassembled the images.

The man standing above the woman glanced over at Anavha. He was lean and angular, strong, square jaw, dark stubble, shadows under the eyes. His hair was tangled, short at his shoulders, auburn-brown. Anavha saw the stringy mass of a black wig on the floor. The light of the lanterns rippled along the length of his muscular body: wide shoulders, powerful forearms, a chest too broad to have ever worn a girdle, a torso so firm Anavha imagined he could throw fruit at it and watch it bounce off without any perceivable disturbance of flesh. Men in the mardanas did not look like that. Anavha most certainly did not look like that. The man could have been a creature from another world.

The man's gaze caught Anavha's, held him. The man let go of the silken cord. The woman's body slumped. The man stalked toward Anavha, took his arm. Jerked him into the room. He kicked the door closed.

"Whose are you?" the man said softly, a deep voice rendered all the more ominous by the hushed tone.

"Syre Zezili," Anavha said quickly. "I won't... I don't... Zezili's coming for me, she–"

"What are you to her?"

"Her husband," Anavha said.

The man released him. Anavha fell to the floor. The man began to dress, covering – bit by bit – his fantastic body, the sort of body only seen on Saiduan statues lining old roads in Daorian, their faces and genitals defaced. He wore straight-legged trousers and an embroidered tunic – women's clothes.

"I'll go," Anavha said. He made to stand, but the man, dressed now, crossed to him in three long strides and gripped his arm again.

"You'll stay," the man said.

"I won't say anything, please... Zezili will come for me. She knows I'm here. You don't want Syre Zezili Hasaria after you!"

The man cuffed him.

Pain burst across Anavha's face. Black spots blotted his vision.

The man crouched in front of Anavha. He took him by the collar of his coat and leaned into him. He smelled of sex and himself, a sharp, bitter scent like the inside of an empty wine barrel. His skin was the bronze-brown of a Tordinian, his eyes a gray wash.

"You're going to be silent," the man said.

Anavha opened his mouth. "What will you–" but the man had the silk cord in his other hand. He stuffed a kerchief into Anavha's mouth and knotted the cord around his head. The cord was so long that he could twist it around Anavha's hands. The man pulled the cord taut and knotted it well. Anavha's fingers were numb. His mouth hurt.

The man opened the window. A blast of cold air stirred the room. He hauled Anavha to the window.

Anavha tried to struggle. The man's grip tightened. The man opened the window that looked out onto the snowy roof of the verandah. He pushed Anavha out. Anavha slid to the lip of the roof and faced the yawning darkness of the drop. He managed to claw himself to a stop with his bound hands, just in time to see the man leap easily over the sill and onto the roof beside him. The man kicked Anavha once.

Anavha lost his hold on the tiles and fell. He tried to cry out but gagged on the kerchief. He landed on his side in a powdering of snow. The air rushed from his lungs.

Before he caught his breath through the clotted kerchief, the man landed beside him. He dragged Anavha out to the kennels. A big black dog was already saddled and harnessed. The man whistled to it. The dog came forward, sniffing and snarling.

The man hauled Anavha up in front of him onto the dog. The man's body was warm and tense behind Anavha. One strong arm held Anavha against him. The other gripped the reins.

Anavha expected to see Zezili stride out onto the road, draw her sword, hamstring the dog, and cut open Anavha's assailant with one clean strike.

But the dog was trotting off at a quick pace, the road streaking behind them. Clouds covered the moons completely. It began to snow.

Anavha was already sore from days of riding, and being jarred in the saddle as the dog leapt forward at a clipped pace was agony. He imagined blisters forming on his thighs.

The hours stretched. Anavha's whole body hurt. The snow continued. The dog was padding now not across a road but winding through low-lying everpine trees. Anavha's feet and hands were numb.

They stopped sometime well after dawn in a ring of everpine trees. Anavha's captor tossed him out of the saddle and onto the snow as if Anavha weighed no more than a rag doll. The man unsaddled the dog but kept its harness on.

The man unpacked food from the saddle bags and fed the dog dried meat. Anavha followed his captor's progress until the man squatted before Anavha, reeking now not only of himself, but of dog.

"You going to be silent?" the man asked.

Anavha tried to nod.

The man unwrapped the silk cord from Anavha's hands and mouth. He pulled out the wet kerchief.

Anavha's mouth was unbearably dry. He sat up painfully and rubbed at his numbed hands. Red welts marked his wrists.

"It won't be long," the man said, turning away from Anavha. He handed Anavha a small piece of bread and an onion from his pack. Anavha tried to hold out his hands to receive the offering, but his fingers wouldn't work.

The man set the food in front of him and walked back to his seat in the snow. He continued eating.

Anavha tried scooping up some snow. The snow felt good as it melted in his mouth. He sat quietly.

"You say your wife will come after you?" the man said. He was looking at Anavha as he ate.

Anavha nodded.

"I don't doubt it," the man said. He had a strange accent, one Anavha could not identify, but he figured it must be Tordinian, since he looked so much like one. He continued to gaze at Anavha. Uncomfortable under the close scrutiny, Anavha looked away.

"We're two weeks from Tordin," the man said. "Someone else will decide what to do with you once we cross the border."

"I won't say anything," Anavha said softly. He had seen this man kill a woman. It was like sitting with some sort of dangerous animal. But then, Anavha had also killed a woman. Did that make him like this man? Anavha hugged his knees to his chest. He was terribly cold. We're just animals, he thought. The enforcers will find us. Zezili will cut both of us open.

"It's not a matter of what you will or won't say," the man said.

"Who are you?" Anavha asked.

The man smiled, but it was a tight, forced smile that did not touch his eyes. "They'll know me as Natanial Thorne of Yemsire."

Tordinian after all, then. And he had killed a woman in an inn in Dorinah.

"You work for the King of Tordin," Anavha said.

"I work for a lot of people," Natanial said, "but yes, he's the one who'll decide whether or not you're useful."

"Zezili will come for me," Anavha repeated with conviction. Zezili would always come for him.

Natanial wiped his hands on his trousers. "I certainly hope so," he said. "You're worth a nice penny, I'd wager. Get some sleep now. We have a long day ahead."

Anavha lay on his side, hands bound. He didn't think he could sleep, but it came eventually. He started awake not long after and froze. Something stared at him from across the remains of the fire. A creature moved in the undergrowth. He heard the huff of its breath, and saw its eyes reflecting the moons' light.

"Natanial?" Anavha whispered. But he could not see Natanial. He began to tremble.

The beast crept into the moons' light. It was a giant, mangy wolverine, wild and slavering. Anavha had only seen the things in the papers, drawn up to accompany a story about some horrific mauling. Anavha tried to sit up.

The wolverine growled and pounced.

Anavha shrieked. He rolled just in time, so the beast latched onto his arm instead of his neck. Jagged needles of pain burst through his arm. A blood-red haze cloaked Anavha's vision.

The undergrowth shivered again. Anavha screamed. Natanial leapt toward him, metal sword raised, as the wolverine shook Anavha like a straw pillow.

Natanial's sword struck the wolverine. The wolverine released Anavha, and snapped at Natanial's sword instead.

Anavha shook so violently, his teeth chattered. Blood soaked his arm, his torso. He saw a bubbling gush of it pumping from his arm, and felt suddenly light-headed. The air around him grew heavy. He saw a blinding sheen of glittering red mist boil down from the sky and cling to his body like a lover.

It was happening again.

"Help me," Anavha said.

Natanial skewered the wolverine with his sword. Looked back.

"Please," Anavha said. He could not keep the panic from his voice. The mist collected his blood into a syrupy whirlwind. The air condensed. He felt a terrible pressure.

Then the world opened up.

"Fuck," Natanial said.

And Anavha fell into the void.

33

The world outside lay hushed under a heavy curtain of snow. Darkness ate the mornings and the evenings. One day soon, Roh knew, daylight would be but a moment between sunrise and sunset, turning day into one dusky evening. Winter's grip was relentless.

Inside Kuonrada, in a small cramped room brimming with preening dancers stepping through bad brazier lights, Roh decked himself in a long skirt and billowing trousers. His eyes were rimmed in kohl, shadowed in green, his lower lip painted red, his hair lengthened with braids of human hair. It was the Festival of Para's Ascendance. Today was the day the world's parajistas would reach the full measure of their power. Or, at least, the day the stargazers had given as their best guess. After today, Para was in decline. Roh and the others who shared his star would lose just a little bit of power every day. Roh expected he would feel different today, but he had not yet tried to draw on Para. He was a little afraid to.

Abas caught him gazing at his own reflection and said, "You could almost be a dancer."

Roh smiled. It was the closest Abas would get to saying he'd become one of them. They waited with the other dancers outside the massive eating hall at the center of the hold. The hall was a stir of voices and low laughter. It was a great honor to dance at any festival, but for Roh, this one meant a great deal. It marked the end of something. There would be no more dancing after this. No more distractions.

The Saiduan celebrated and mourned the day as well with a dance that Roh had at first thought was a little strange. It was the story of the Dhai and their annihilation of the Talamynii. When Roh asked Abas if this was the dance they usually did for this celebration, Abas said no – on Para's Day of Ascendance, they chose more uplifting pieces. But the Patron had requested this one specifically.

To remind us we're not so different, Roh thought, but he dared not say that out loud.

When they were announced, Roh and the dancers purled into the room. Roh took note of the room as he swept in, aware that he would not have time to measure it properly again until after the dance. There were three long tables adorned in sinuous carvings: the heads of snarling men, fanged wolves, and other creatures Roh only knew from books. The high table stood on a dais of pale stone. Seated at the lower tables were dozens of northern soldiers with purple ribbons at their collars. A dozen lower-ranking sanisi sat with them, marked by their infused blades and dark clothes. The Dhai scholars were there as well, though Roh's gaze did not take in individuals, merely the blur of their paler faces. At the high table was the Patron. Sitting with him were the most prized of his sanisi. Slaves removed empty dishes and replenished the bread. Roh saw more women among the servants than he had in all these weeks in Kuonrada.

And then Roh was dancing.

Roh lost himself to it. He was no longer himself but one of the Talamynii fighting foreigners from a distant shore – fighting the Dhai, the empire that had once stretched from Saiduan all the way south to the opposite pole, before the middle of the world sank into the sea. Abas was not his friend but his enemy, a shadow, his face a stony crag of cruelty; he played the Dhai emperor. Green eye shadow licked the faces of the dancers playing Talamynii from eyelid to eyebrow.

Roh's people were overwhelmed. They retreated to the hearth, ducking and cowering as the sanisi approached. Abas was supposed to pull one of the other dancers, Taralik, from the stir of others before the sanisi put them to the sword. Taralik was to be the last living Talamynii, all that remained of the brown, green-eyed race the Dhai had purged from this continent four millennia ago.

But as Roh and the other Talamynii crouched by the hearth, Roh watching as the paint melted from the faces of his fellow captives, Abas's hands fell not to Taralik's shoulders but Roh's.

Abas pulled Roh from the condemned. Behind them, the dancers playing the Dhai circled the Talamynii, and the Talamynii gave great cries. Roh and Abas continued to regard one another, Roh breathless, Abas's gaze filled with mirth.

The dancers portraying the Dhai pulled back from the circle of Talamynii who lay motionless on the floor behind Roh and Abas. The dancers playing Dhai moved into the final set, ending in a uniform pirouette that became a long bow of the body toward the long tables.

There was a long silence before the Patron stood to thank the dancers. The audience tapped their plates with their long soup spoons.

"My captive for the night," the Patron said to Abas, "do bring yourself and your chosen to my table."

Roh glanced at Abas. Abas gave him a trifling smile and held out his hand. Roh took it.

Abas led Roh up the purple carpet to the high table. He passed Wraisau and Driaa sitting at one of the lower tables. Wraisau stood as he passed and slapped his shoulder. Roh jumped, and they all laughed. Servants brought two extra chairs to the dais. Three women – wearing torques, and belts of silver loops – hung back behind the Patron. They held silver basins of water and wine. The feasting was over, so the drinking had begun. The women did not speak, but their kohl-ringed eyes took in Abas and Roh with something more than polite interest. Roh saw calculated study in those gazes, measuring the two dancers for what they were worth.

Roh met their gazes and noticed, with a start, that one of them had green eyes. She was dark-skinned as a Saiduan, yes, but there were the Talamynii eyes. If one measured the death of a people in blood, it was never complete. What the Dhai had eradicated was the Talamynii culture, their memories, their dreams. As Roh gazed at the Patron, he wondered what parts of his own people had been erased when the Saiduan murdered them in droves and exiled them from the continent.

The servants set the chairs just behind those at the Patron's elbow. Roh gazed long at the sanisi at the high table. The sanisi sitting to the left of the Patron was not as tall as the others, even sitting down. He had a mass of inky, oiled hair knotted back in a braid like a rope. He did not look at Roh or Abas but continued to talk in a low voice to the sanisi at his right, whose beardless face and manner of sitting made her Shao Maralah Daonia, the woman he had watched spar in the courtyard. She had a lined, weathered face that put Roh in mind of the creased leather spines of old books. She looked far older than forty. He saw silver hairs in her mane of black.

The Patron motioned for Abas and Roh to sit. The Patron smelled heavily of aatai liquor and cloves and some sort of lavender oil that made Roh's eyes water.

"Abas," the Patron said, gesturing to the imposing sanisi at his right, a tall but very young sanisi who could not have been much past twenty. "You're familiar with my eldest son, Shas Chaigaan Taar?"

"I am," Abas said, inclining his head to Chaigaan. Chaigaan had the same build and broad cheekbones as his father. Roh had heard all but seven of the Patron's sons were dead at the hands of the invaders. He wondered why this one was spared. Because he was a sanisi?

"You did not choose the prettiest of the dancers this year, Abas," Chaigaan said. "I always thought Mhor the prettiest."

"No," Abas said, "I chose the best."

"We have different tastes," he said, and laughed.

The laugh attracted the attention of Maralah and her conversation partner. The sanisi at the Patron's left glanced back at Roh. There was nothing immediately compelling about him. Next to Maralah, he was dark as fired clay. His lean face was lightly bearded. His eyes were a deep blue-black. A long scar began just behind his left ear and disappeared beneath the collar of his tunic. The hilt of his infused blade stuck up along his left shoulder.

Roh chanced a look at the backs of the other sanisi at the high table and saw that they, too, remained armed in the presence of the Patron. They were sworn to the Patron, but to trust all of them, all sixteen, at such a table... The Patron owned these people: blood, skin, bone.

The sanisi at the Patron's left looked once at Roh, dismissive, then turned away. But Maralah gazed long at Roh. Her flat, squashed nose looked as if it had been broken many times.

"Surely this isn't one of our scholars?" she said.

Roh felt like one of the servants, one of the women standing behind him: completely visible, displayed overtly, an interesting possession.

"It is," the Patron said.

"You are using him most... wisely," she said.

"He is Ora Dasai's assistant," the Patron said, and to Roh, it sounded as if he was trying to justify himself. "Rohinmey Tadisa Garika. Rohinmey, this is Shao Maralah Daonia, Blue-Blade Soul Stealer and Sword of Albaaric. Beside her is Ren Kadaan Soagan, Shadow of Caisau."

Roh stared at Kadaan, who had emptied a glass of wine and now turned back to Roh and the Patron. He should have recognized him as Maralah's sparring partner.

"Rohinmey?" Kadaan said. "A soft, Dhai name and a mouthful. I think their names get longer over the centuries as they look to configure new ones."

Maralah turned away from Roh, another dismissal. "Perhaps each time they eat one of their dead, they add a name," she said, and laughed. She seemed a little drunk.

"Nearly as grotesque as Dorinahs," Kadaan said. He picked up another glass of wine, turned, eyed Roh. Kadaan dipped a finger into his wine cup. "Tell me, what does that mean, your name? Rohinmey. What does that mean in Dhai?"

Roh hesitated. Abas and the Patron and his son watched them with amusement. Maralah turned to her other dinner companion, and said something that made him snort.

"I would ask you what Kadaan meant," Roh said, "but I've done my studying."

"Have you? I've never met a dancer with a mind that matched his body."

"You haven't met many Dhai," Roh said.

"I've killed a great many Dhai," Kadaan said. "You all look the same."

"I've killed a great many bugs," Roh said. "It doesn't mean I understand them any better."

Maralah coughed into her glass and shook her head. "They don't know, Kadaan."

"Don't they?" Kadaan frowned. "I suppose that's wise."

"What don't I know?"

"You know little of… death," Kadaan said.

"Death is less extraordinary than a sanisi would have people believe."

Kadaan finally chuckled. "I tire of foreigners cluttering our table."

Roh sat back, only a little wounded. He looked longingly down at the table where his friends sat. Luna and Kihin were lost in conversation. Aramey and one of the Saiduan scholars were locked in a heated discussion. Only Chali appeared melancholy. He brooded over his clean plate and empty liquor glasses. After a moment, he caught Roh's look and smiled wanly.

Roh saw someone moving behind Chali, a spry man with dark hair and a pinched face. He was not a Saiduan, from the look of his tawny skin and small stature; he looked like a Dhai. He did not have the shaved head of a slave, though he wore a short coat and trousers as the slaves did. Roh saw more movement at the corner of his eye. Another man, similar to the first, walked along the opposite wall. Roh had not noticed them during the dance. Seeing those two, he became aware of others – four more ahead of the first, five ahead of the second man on the opposite wall. They walked without any particular urgency, weaving among the slaves, pacing themselves with the ebb and tide of the crowd. They were making their way toward the high table. The other dancers sat around the lower tables, laughing and joking with soldiers and lower-ranking sanisi. No one paid any heed to the men along the walls. Were they some underclass of people Roh hadn't seen before? One he hadn't read about?

Kadaan was looking at him again. The first of the unknown men reached either end of the high table. Kadaan followed Roh's stare, and said, "What are you looking at, boy?"

"Those men," Roh said. "Who are they?"

"Which men?" Kadaan asked.

"The ones there," Roh said, and pointed. He felt a chill. "Don't you see them?"

Kadaan looked again. Something in his expression hardened. The first of the men reached the ends of the dais and mounted the steps.

Roh felt the hair on the back of his neck stand on end. The tips of his fingers tingled.

The men advanced across the dais. A woman stepped past them. Roh watched one of the men slide his hands behind his back. Roh felt Abas lean over, put his hand on Roh's knee.

Abas snickered, said, "Roh, did you–"

Roh started to speak–

–and Kadaan pushed himself up, brought his hand back over his shoulder, and gripped the hilt of his infused blade. The blue breath of Para surrounded him.

Kadaan's piercing yell, merging with the hiss of the blade, "Ohkair!"

Maralah moved first. Hers was the only order of movement Roh was certain of afterward. She and Kadaan leapt up as if attached to a string, like they knew one another's movements three heartbeats before they began. She fell back out of her seat, tucked into a backward roll, and Kadaan leapt over her, hurling a twisted skein of blue mist at the nearest attacker. Only then did the other sanisi move, a fraction of a second later than Maralah, a full second after Kadaan, but enough time for the strange men to note their detection and leap for the Patron at the center of the high table.

Everything changed in the space of a breath.

Someone clipped Roh's ear; he felt the kiss of a glowing blade. Then he was on the floor, gasping. Abas lay against the wall, the skin over his skull split, oozing blood. His eyelids flickered.

Roh looked over at Abas's broken chair. One of the women lay heaped next to Abas. A dark pool was forming beneath her. Roh's head spun. A slow spread of blood moved over the stones toward him. He was shivering. Someone was next to him, making rasping sounds, the way Lilia did when she had trouble breathing, only these sounds were wetter, choking, as if he did not drown on air but blood.

Roh tried to see who was making that sound. The Patron's chair was overturned, empty. Crumpled beneath the table was the inert form of his son, the sanisi. Chaigaan lay four feet from Roh, cheek pressed to the stones, staring at Roh with wide, glassy eyes. It was dark beneath the table, but Roh saw a wet, glistening mound heaped against the sanisi's belly – the spill of his insides, leaking onto the floor. Roh's hands were sticky with blood; the blood of the Patron's son, flowing along the runnels in the stone, mingling with the blood of Abas, and the dead woman, bleeding past Roh.

He heard muted cries, the scuffle of boots, leather, and above that, the hissing of infused weapons. He looked under the table, toward the main room, and saw wispy tails of Para's breath streaking through the air. He tried to find Kihin and Dasai, Nioni, Chali, and Aramey, but he saw only a mass of fighting figures, a stir of fleeing slaves.

Roh crawled toward Abas and cradled Abas's head in his lap.

Abas murmured something but did not move. Cold sweat stung Roh's eyes. He heard the rasping breath of the Patron's dying son.

Roh choked. He clutched at his stomach and pulled away from Abas. He wouldn't vomit. Not here. He looked back under the table and saw a way through. It was three feet from the top of the dais to the floor. He was too small to drag Abas. He had to wake him up or leave him. He lay on his belly beneath the table. The dying sanisi was whispering now, something that sounded like a prayer.

Someone cried out. Blades burst and hissed.

A man grabbed hold of Roh's ankle. Dragged him out from under the table.

Roh gurgled a cry. He clawed at the stone with his bloody hands, kicked out.

The grip relaxed. Roh tried to hop away, too late. One of the strange men gripped Roh's shoulder and brought one hand back. A blue blade flashed – it sprouted from the man's wrist like a living thing. Roh crossed his arms. The air around him grew heavy, condensed. He recited the Litany of the Gale.

He tensed. Not himself but the blue particles of Para's breath. The air around him pulsed, contracted. He expelled the breath from his lungs and pushed the wall of condensed air outward.

His attacker shivered. His blue bonsa weapon lodged in the coagulated air.

Roh parted the air and caught the man's hand in a deceptively simple grip. He twisted. The weapon wrenched free.

The misty blue breath around him dissipated. The man reached through the broken defense and jabbed toward him, impossibly fast, a kill strike. Roh saw the strike just as the man formed it. Roh pivoted. He still gripped the man's hand in a crippling hold.

Roh stumbled over one of Abas's arms. He fell to his knees and pulled his attacker down with him.

He saw something moving at the corner of his eye. A blue weapon flashed. The length of a sanisi's infused blade arced across Roh's field of vision, neatly splitting the man in two. For one still moment, the man grinned at Roh. A thin line of blood appeared across his face. Half of his head slid away.

Roh still held the man's warm hand, his grip welded to the flesh like a vise, terrified to let go, his body still telling him that to let go meant death.

Blood gushed. The body tottered, balanced upright only by Roh's grip.

A figure bent over the leaning body. Clad in black, spattered in glistening blood. A lean face, an ugly scar. For a long moment, Roh did not recognize him.

"You can let him go," Kadaan said.

Roh's fingers were numb. The dead man's hand felt cool. Roh let his grip relax. The corpse fell to the floor.

Kadaan's infused blade hovered over the still body, black with blood. As Roh watched, the blood seeped into the branch. A single drop escaped from the tip, dripped to the floor.

Kadaan held out his free hand to Roh. "Up," he said.

Roh couldn't move.

Kadaan gripped his hand, pulled him up. Roh found his footing. He was too shocked even to protest Kadaan's grip.

"That was the last," Kadaan said as Roh looked back to either end of the table. Fewer sanisi moved among the dead, perhaps only a half dozen standing. How many had been seated at the table?

"My friends," Roh said, "where are my friends?"

"The dancers are out."

"No," Roh said, "the Dhai."

Maralah stepped up behind Kadaan. She wiped the blood from her weapon onto her trousers. "That could have gone worse."

Kadaan spit on the floor. The spit was bloody. "Anyone tell you you can see through hazing wards," Kadaan asked Roh, "or were your Dhais not interested in telling us that?"

"What do you mean?"

Kadaan sheathed his weapon. "More than wards," Kadaan said, looking back at Maralah. "He saw them clearly. I had to look twice. I felt them before I saw them."

"No simple ward could get them this far into the hold," Maralah said. "The boy can see through complex wards, too. That's a pretty skill."

"Where are the physicians?" Roh knelt next to Abas.

Kadaan crouched beside him. He gripped Roh's elbow, not unkindly. "What does a Dhai boy know about fighting? Those were some interesting tricks for a coward."

"Dhai aren't cowards," Roh said. "I'm going to be a sanisi."

"Are you?"

Kadaan's face was a hand's breadth from Roh's. Roh knew the sanisi wasn't even ten years older than him, but so close, Roh saw something dark and vast in his gaze – a knowledge of things Roh had yet to grasp, let alone understand. He felt suddenly very small.

Kadaan barked at one of the sanisi to get a physician.

"The Patron's son," Roh said, glancing under the table.

Maralah nudged Chaigaan's hand with her boot. "Gone," she said.

The sanisi still lingered about the table, inspecting the bodies of the dead men, when Chali came up. He asked, and then hugged Roh tightly. He helped Roh wrap Abas's head. Chali assured him Abas would be fine. Then he went back down to help the others, the sanisi and petty soldiers alike, until the Saiduan surgeons arrived.

Roh sat on the steps leading up to the dais, waiting for Dasai to send someone to fetch him. The sanisi would not permit him to leave the hall alone, and Chali was helping the physicians.

Kadaan passed near Roh. Roh watched him.

"You do not look much like a boy," Kadaan said.

Roh wrinkled his brow.

Kadaan stepped over to him. He picked up a chalice from the table. He wet his finger in his wine, reached out. The sanisi's wet finger touched Roh's lower lip.

"This doesn't seem to suit," Kadaan said. He leaned over and took Roh's chin in his hand.

Roh sat absolutely still.

Kadaan pressed his mouth to Roh's, so both his lips covered Roh's bottom lip. The gesture was so startling that Roh was afraid to move for fear the sanisi would cut him in two. Kadaan's tongue licked away the smear of red on Roh's lower lip.

Kadaan still leaned over him. When he spoke, his voice was low. "You have a gift, boy. Without that gift, we would all of us be dead tonight. I don't mean to forget that."

Kadaan left him.

Roh stared after the sanisi. He did not move again until Kihin shook him.

"Roh?"

Kihin's face was stricken. "Tira! Is this your blood?" Kihin was staring at Roh's hands.

"No, no," Roh said. "None of it's mine."

"We need to get back," Kihin said. Roh saw Aramey standing behind him.

"Ora Dasai?" Roh asked.

"He's fine. He sent us back for you. Me, Aramey, and Ora Chali. Ora Nioni is just outside the door. We were afraid–"

"I'm fine," Roh said. He stood. He bit his lower lip. "Kihin?"

"What?"

"Why did those men look like Dhai?"

34

Taigan couldn't say when she decided to go back for the girl. For two days she walked west, back to Dhai, feeling nothing but the churning of her insides and the throbbing intensity of a blinding white migraine that forced her to bed down in the dirt, in the dark, for six hours until it passed. When she emerged from the duff and bracken, she squatted to urinate, and pissing was painful and bloody.

Sometime in the last few days, Taigan had decided it was time to change the way Taigan thought of himself... hirself... herself... yes, herself, again. The gods had a grim sense of humor, because though she could knit her flesh and bones and organs back together at will, she had never learned to cure something as simple as a cold or a urinary infection. "They are not of your body," the old woman who trained her once said, "they are in your body. Interlopers. You must wait for them to pass." But a skilled tirajista could cure pox and blight and every sexually passed disease from Dhai to Saiduan, so why couldn't she?

She knew there were holes in the old woman's knowledge. A people couldn't pass two thousand year-old training skills down without losing a great deal. As Oma rose, perhaps Taigan would come into the knowledge on her own, the way she had learned her body denied death, the way she learned it also denied a fixed physical sex more than most. Some days, she wished the change would halt halfway through and give her some aspect of both sexes in both mind and body so she could feel more confident in calling herself ataisa. Most days, though, she was just Taigan – all sexes and none. It amused her to play with the language of self.

Her beard had thinned many months before, and what remained was soft and downy but did not recede any further. Her breasts were almost noticeable now, so she bound them. It was a relief they never got bigger. She could still pass for male. People made assumptions in Saiduan when they saw a lone figure on the road dressed as she was. Assumptions made her life easier.

Some days, she envied the omajistas who could open gates. At least they knew what they were. Or would know, once she found them and told them. But the gifts Oma bestowed upon her often felt like curses. What use was there for a person whose body and mind shifted with the seasons?

Taigan spent her second night within the welcoming arms of a bonsa hybrid, a gnarly, twisted thing that grew like a bear's claw from the side of a rocky mount. She woke sometime during the night to voices and watched a small family camp in the ravine below. They lit a fire. She saw their faces in the warm glow. Two mothers, perhaps an aunt, a father or two or maybe an uncle, and four young children. Taigan often found it difficult to sort out Dhai family relations. Things became complicated very quickly.

They were exiles, or perhaps Woodland Dhai come to carve out an existence in the less toxic mountains. Despite having less virulent plant life, living this close to Dorinah had its own dangers for Dhai. Taigan imagined this family would fetch a fine price in the slave markets there. In Saiduan, the two women alone would net a very fine purse. Taigan began putting prices on them and imagined the sort of things she would buy. But after a time, that no longer amused her, and she found herself caught up in their light banter and storytelling. One of the mothers brought out a stringed instrument from a battered case. She sang in a low, clear voice. The others joined her.

Taigan wondered if their lives would be any different here during the coming darkness. Perhaps they could escape it, this plucky little family with the bright eyes and soft mouths. Taigan had often thought about running away to some icy, mountainous island and waiting out the next twenty years of madness. But going too far down that line of thinking caused the ward on her back to burn. It incited the headaches. She was a bound thing, tied by Maralah's string, the same way these people would be if she sold them off into someone's household.

After the singing, the family banked the fire and bedded down. Taigan listened to two or more of the adults making love in the tall grass near the camp. She heard soft laughter and the low sounds of desire and need and release. How strange to be Dhai, she thought. How strange to have a family that eats and sings and laughs and makes love as if it were nothing.

Their desire provoked hers, and she moved her hand between her thighs. But the fullness of her bladder and the promise of the pain she would experience on emptying it dampened her spirits. Instead, she folded her hands across her belly and closed her eyes.

Taigan found herself running through the details of the last great campaign the Saiduan fought against the Dhai. It was a battle every Saiduan military member learned, from line soldier to war minister. It was the last great battle of the long war. Two forces met outside the great city of Aaraduan, then known as Roasandara.

The Saiduan bear cavalry had been outside Roasandara since dawn, just northwest of the city, waiting for the Dhai. They numbered ten thousand. Forty thousand Dhai – a mix of infantry and tirajista companies – came down and met them on open tundra. They fought for less than an hour before the Saiduan cavalry gave ground, withdrawing to positions closer to the city. Two more divisions of Saiduan infantry – including a command of tirajistas – were coming up from the south and were within hearing distance of the fighting. Two Dhai generals, their names blotted from history, rode toward the battle at the head of their units. Seeing the small Saiduan infantry, they attacked their right flank.

Taigan had not shared this battle with the scullery girl. It was one she wanted to put before her, to see how she'd solve it. Before Maralah sent the letter. Before she learned the scullery girl could not fly. Perhaps it didn't matter anymore. They were fighting Dhai again. A fitter, smarter Dhai. They would not act like their ancestors, so in truth, it shouldn't matter now how some old conflict was resolved.

Taigan's bladder was heavy again. She slid down the tree and squatted off to the side. She gritted her teeth and bore down. It felt like pissing blood. She knew from past experience it would be two or three days more before the pain eased and the infection cleared. Until then, blood and fire.

As she pulled up her trousers, she heard a noise nearby. She froze. Though she wore all black, the moons were out. She would be visible. She stepped closer to the tree to blend in with the dappled shadows. She opened herself to Oma, like reaching through a thick, sticky gauze, and recited the song that helped her tether its power just beneath her skin, ready to shape the misty red haze as she saw fit.

A small figure climbed into the clearing. It was one of the children from the camp below. Taigan let out her breath. She released Oma; it was like expelling some syrupy weight.

The girl stopped short. Looked right at Taigan.

Taigan thought to call on Oma again and strike her dead. But her heavy bladder and sour mood made it all feel like too much effort. She raised a finger to her lips, thinking it a universal sign for quiet, but the girl spoke anyhow. Taigan wondered how any of these Dhai survived in the world.

"I saw you in that tree," the girl whispered.

"You saw shadows," Taigan said.

"No," she said.

"Would you like to hear a story about a battle?" Taigan said.

"From very long ago?"

"Yes. Two forces. The Dhai and—"

"Are you a ghost?"

"A... ghost?"

"One of the souls that got free of Sina. Come to haunt us."

"No. Are you?"

She laughed. "No, of course not."

"You should go back to your family. There are terrors in these woods."

"You're not terrible," the girl said, "you're a person."

The girl's fearlessness made Taigan breathless. She tried to remember a time when she did not fear people and they did not fear her. Her birth had been strange, and during her formative years, before she began going through the changes, her sexual organs – let alone her sense of herself – never fit into the three neat boxes her people had for them. Unsure of what to call her, they labeled her ataisa, but that never felt right, either. She wondered, looking at this little girl with the orgiastic parents, how different her life would have been if she were raised in Dhai instead of Saiduan. Not Dhai as it used to be, not the Dhai that taught the Saiduan to hunt and kill and enslave, but the Dhai as they became. The Dhai that made this girl and the one Taigan had pushed off a cliff.

"Go home," Taigan said, and walked away.

When dawn touched the sky, and Para's fiery blue essence flooded the world, Taigan was still walking. It wasn't until then that she realized she wasn't going west, back to Dhai, but east, back to where she had left the scullery girl.

By the time she reached her, Lilia would have been without water for four days. It was quite possible Lilia hadn't even survived the fall. Taigan had spent a lifetime doing as others told her. The oath she broke to her Patron, the betrayal that lost her the title of sanisi, had shaken her more than she realized. Before the betrayal, before she was Maralah's instead of the Patron's, she acted on blind faith, following the call of Oma, the Lord of the Dawn, the Lord of Awakening, the Lord of Change. It was not Maralah who moved her now nor her Patron, but her rising star, her bloody, glorious god.

She stopped to urinate again, braced against a tree, and hissed out a prayer to Oma to relieve her from pain and want and confusion, and to deliver calm and clarity.

Her star was rising.

It was the scullery girl's star, too.

Oma help them both.

35

Snow bathed the world in pearly silence. Zezili found something very comforting about that as she walked Dakar across the clean stretch of silent white. Few travelers were on the roads to Lake Morta this time of year. As dusk fell, she finally saw the approaching stretch of the vast lake. Blessed by Rhea, all said, it was a lake full of stories – and tourists during the summer. But the peak of summer travelers had passed, and the first snows were on the ground.

The road took her around the lake. The falling snow began to taper off. Clouds roiled across the black sky, revealing the moons and the tiara of satellites that circled the largest moon, Ahmur. The world seemed to glow.

Zezili saw no tracks on the road, but the snow was new. It didn't mean Anavha hadn't gone this way. Unescorted men were generally picked up very quickly. Her fear was that someone had already found him and turned him in to the enforcers.

She could see the spill of light from the inn on the other side of the lake, a sprawling hulk amid the snow.

Dakar halted suddenly and let out a low whine. He turned his head toward the flat, snowy expanse of the lake. The teeth of mountains called the Cage reared up behind the lake, chewing at the dark sky. Scraggly everpines peppered the mountains.

Zezili kneed her dog and whistled at him to move forward. He twitched his ears toward the lake.

"What's out there?" she asked, patting the dog on the shoulder. The dog yelped.

The quiet stretched. Dakar yelped again; a cry that echoed.

"What-" Zezili began.

She felt the air shudder. Heard a great *whumping* sound, like a massive ripple of air.

Then a dull thumping came from the lake.

Once. Then again.

She doubted her hearing. Was it some kind of echo? The echo of their passing?

Zezili dismounted. She knotted Dakar's reins to a tree. She strode down a snaking path to the lake, her coat flapping behind her. She heard ice cracking. The sound rolled across the bowl of the lake.

Outside the cover of the trees, the flat lake caught the moons' light like a mirror. The lake glowed milky blue. Zezili walked out onto the ice. It creaked beneath her. She peered across the lake and saw a fissure opening at its center. The snow trembled. A chunk of ice broke up from the lake and skittered across its surface.

Zezili moved faster, toward the heart of the lake. "Who's out here?" she yelled. Her voice echoed, loud and eerie.

Something was coming out of the lake.

Zezili crouched where the cracks in the ice originated, and saw hunks of ice floating on open water. She got down onto her belly and slid forward. She saw a pale, clawed hand striking at the black water.

Then a head emerged, and a torso.

There was a woman in the lake.

Zezili should not have been surprised, not here, on the glowing ice of this twice-cursed lake, not after everything that had happened since she got the Empress's order to start killing dajians, but she was struck dumb with horror as she watched the woman pull herself from the icy depths of the frozen lake, hand over hand, from freezing water to powdery snow.

The woman gazed up at her, not so much a woman, Zezili realized, as a young girl. She was dark of hair and eye.

Zezili took her under her arms and dragged her forward onto the ice. "Stay flat on your stomach," Zezili said. "Don't stand or you'll drown us both."

Zezili grabbed the girl's arm and pulled her away from the broken ice floe. She dragged her clear of the long cracks around the scar. Then she stood and took the girl with her. The ice continued to groan. Zezili's stomach knotted. The inn was not far, but if she, too, fell in the ice, she'd have to leave the girl behind.

She huffed out a sigh of relief when she stepped onto solid ground again. She picked up the girl, surprised at how light she was. The girl clung to her like a sodden puppy. Zezili glanced over her shoulder at the wound in the ice. A soft wind buffeted her face, drew the clouds back over the moons. The lake fell into darkness.

By the time she reached Dakar, it had begun to snow again.

The girl's eyes fluttered.

"Where did you come from?" Zezili asked.

The obvious answer, of course, was the lake. But that was absurd. Zezili pulled off her coat and wrapped it around the girl. In the darkness, it was difficult to make out her features. If she bore some resemblance to a family Zezili knew, it might give her a clue as to why she was out here. Most likely, she was some desperate person trying to murder herself. Zezili had no patience for that sort of thing. Death always came soon enough.

Zezili commanded Dakar to sit. She pulled the girl up in front of her and wrapped her arms around her. She was a little thing, no more than a hundred pounds.

The girl murmured something.

"What's your name?" Zezili asked. "Who's your family? Did someone push you into the lake?"

The girl didn't respond. Zezili whistled for Dakar to increase his pace. The girl had begun to tremble violently, which was good. When she stopped shivering, things would be bad.

It took another twenty minutes to get to the inn. Zezili called out for help, and a meaty innkeeper came to the door carrying a flame fly lantern.

"Found a girl in the lake," Zezili said. "You have a physician here?"

"No, but I have a tirajista," the innkeeper said.

"That's not much help."

"She is if you've brought something from the lake. Come in."

Zezili tied off Dakar and took the girl into the inn. The innkeeper led her up to a room that already had a fire lit. Zezili lay the girl down in front of the hearth. One of the innkeeper's dajians came up to help her strip off the girl's wet clothes.

In the light of the fire, Zezili noted that the girl was a bit dark for a Dorinah, and she had the low forehead and broad cheekbones of a Dhai, covered in strange puckered scars, as if someone had taken an ice pick to her face. Not all with Dhai features were dajians; if this girl's mother had claimed her as Zezili's had, she would be free. Being marked like that made self-murder an even more likely reason for her jaunt across the lake, though. When they undressed her, Zezili saw old bruises mapping across her legs and torso, as if she'd been abused by some foul master. A runaway dajian was a more likely scenario than some parajista catching her up in a vortex and throwing her in the lake.

They wrapped the girl in a large blanket.

"Is this the girl?" said a woman at the door.

She was an older woman, forty at least, with long, lustrous black hair and the same broad Dhai cheekbones as the girl on the floor. But this woman was more clearly Dorinah, pale and gray-eyed, with a high forehead and bold nose.

"Found her in the lake," Zezili said. "You're the tirajista?"

"I am," she said, and waved away the dajian. She knelt beside the girl. Put her hands to the girl's cheeks.

Zezili heard her mutter something, and a warm vortex of air moved over Zezili's hands where they met the girl's body. Zezili pulled away. That was a parajista trick, not a tirajista. As

Zezili watched, the water on the blanket evaporated, and the girl's skin began to regain some color.

"I came here looking for my husband," Zezili said. "He thought I was coming to Lake Morta."

"And why would you do that?"

"To find Isoail Rosalia. Are you her?"

"May I ask who you are?"

"Zezili Hasaria."

"Your reputation is well known."

"My mother is Livia Hasaria."

"Of course," the woman said. "I'm Isoail, but we've seen no men here since the leaves fell. What did your husband want with me?"

"I expect he thought to find me here. My mother recommended you."

"For what, may I ask?"

"She said you're the best jista in the country."

The girl on the floor opened her eyes. Zezili glanced down at her. "You alive?" Zezili asked. "You best get your papers together. What were you doing out there?"

But the look on the girl's face reaffirmed that she had no papers. Zezili had seen that look of terror on many dajian faces. She sighed. "Listen, girl–"

"Mam," the girl said in Dhai. Zezili realized she was looking not at her but at Isoail. "Mam!" The girl grabbed at Isoail's dress. "I promised."

Isoail took the girl's wrist as if to push her away.

"I thought you were dead," the girl said. "But I promised I'd find you. I promised. I did it. I'm not a coward, Mam." She began to weep.

"Is she yours?" Zezili asked.

Isoail shook her head. She pulled the girl's fingers free and said, in Dorinah, "I don't know this dajian. Call the enforcers."

After the girl was sedated, Zezili went downstairs for a drink and information.

It was still early enough that the innkeeper had hot food on order. Zezili ordered some and asked the innkeeper if an unescorted man had arrived at the lake.

"Man? Rhea's tears, no," the innkeeper said. "You pursuing a runaway? I didn't think that was up to the legion."

"He belongs to me," Zezili said. "I'd pay well for his return." She gave his description. "You hear anything of him, contact me at the Hasaria estate outside Daorian. Easy enough to get post there."

"I'll remember," the innkeeper said, "though I expect you'll be disappointed. The weather's worse this year than usual. I'm not sure a housebound boy could survive it."

"He had some currency," Zezili said, and wanted to add that he was very pretty, but the idea of him using his prettiness to survive angered her, so she let that go unsaid.

"I'm sure he'll turn up," the innkeeper said. Zezili didn't like the sympathy in her voice.

After eating, Zezili ordered a warm brandy.

"Anything else before I go to bed?" the innkeeper asked. "I've given you a room on the second floor, end of the hall. There's a shared privy. You have your own sink, though."

"Thanks," Zezili said, and slipped the key into the pouch at her hip. "I'll be fine for the night." She found a broad, comfortable chair by the fire in the dining room and sipped the brandy. She was at Lake Morta. Anavha was not. She was uncertain what to do next except drink.

The innkeeper left her a lantern by the chair and put out the rest of the lights in the common room. She bolted the door. Zezili wondered if she had any security out here. Surely she had some hulking swordswoman around to deal with rabble?

Zezili sat in the semi-darkness, drinking and considering her next move. A sane woman would go back to Monshara. A sane woman would forget about a runaway man. But every time she thought of Anavha lost, her chest hurt and her vision blurred.

As she watched the banked coals of the fire flake and fade, she heard a sound from outside. She thought at first it was just the

wind, but the wind became words. A muttering voice. Clunking
on the porch. Then rapping on the door. More muttering.

Zezili went to the window.

"Don't open it."

She glanced back. Isoail was coming down the stairs, her long
skirt caught up in one hand. She carried a lantern in the other.

"You heard it from up there?"

"I expected it," Isoail said. "You already pulled one thing from
the lake tonight. They come in pairs now."

"What do?"

Isoail shuttered her lantern and stood with Zezili at the
window. In the light from the moons, Zezili saw a hunched,
hooded figure standing on the porch. It leaned against the door.
As Zezili watched, the figure brought up its hand. Knocked again.
Then began to scratch at the door.

"What is it?" Zezili said, low. "If it's dangerous, I can kill it."

"I could kill it just as well," Isoail said. "Listen to that language.
Do you know it?"

"No," Zezili said.

"Then let it be," Isoail said. "Sometimes when something comes
through, it triggers another event. Other things... come after."

They watched the figure in silence for some minutes. Zezili
saw a hank of pale hair escape the hood. An older woman, then,
or an Aaldian? The figure snorted. Laughed. A small, childish
giggle that made Zezili's flesh crawl.

After what felt like hours, the figure shuffled off the porch and
waded back toward the road.

Zezili glanced over at Isoail. "Who was it?"

"Something from the lake," Isoail said. "Not all of them are as
docile as that dajian upstairs."

"I don't understand."

Isoail took up her lantern again. "I'm surprised at that," she said.
"I heard rumors that you've been eliminating dajian camps at the
Empress's order for some weeks. Has she not told you why?"

"I have a good idea why," Zezili said. "I've been on the other side."

"Have you?" Isoail sounded genuinely surprised. She unshuttered her lantern. Her face looked garish in the sudden light. "Then surely you understand."

"What, you think she was from that other world?"

"There's more than one other world," Isoail said. "Some even less friendly. We're still determining how many."

"Who's 'we'?"

"The Empress requested a coterie of Seekers to monitor occurrences here at the lake ten years ago," Isoail said. "It's always been a holy place. It's only very recently we understood why."

"So, you're Tulana's?"

"All Seekers answer to Tulana."

"People come through?" Zezili asked. Isoail was isolated here. She must not know about what happened at the Seeker Sanctuary.

"A good number of them," Isoail said. "We're not sure why here. It requires less effort, less energy from Oma, perhaps."

"Why was that one dangerous?"

"Some come from a world very like ours with similar people. That's likely the one you visited, correct? A world very like ours, with people who share our faces?"

"Yes," Zezili said.

"Others are... much different."

"How?"

"That's... I'm not sure that's something I can speak of without breaking an Imperial order."

"What *can* you tell me?" Zezili gestured to the chairs by the fire. "You know I've been there. I'm working with one of them."

"I'm afraid I know little that will help in your campaign," Isoail said. Isoail took a seat. Zezili sat across from her. "We both have our orders from the Empress."

"I expect you won't tell me all of yours."

"No," Isoail said.

"So, how do you stay in residence here without raising suspicion?"

"I do tirajista demonstrations in the summer," Isoail said. She smiled wryly. "I'm particularly sensitive to Tira, and Para, of course."

"A double channeler? That's rare."

"Yes."

"No wonder you got stationed out here."

"I'm sure you understand the burdens we all bear to maintain the empire," Isoail said. "All the intrigue becomes tiresome, though. I go to the Seeker Sanctuary twice a year to renew my license. In blessed years, the Empress has no other task for me but my research here."

"No family, then? No children?"

Isoail leaned back in the chair. She seemed amused. Her eyes sparkled. "Do you?"

"And mark them with this face? No."

"My parents both bore some dajian blood, from very far back," Isoail said. "But my mother was free. She claimed me, even after my father tried to call me some terrible Dhai name, Navarra or Nava." She shrugged. "So I am free. It's very easy to pass, especially here. All they see is a jista."

"So it wasn't your face that steered you away from children."

"No," Isoail said. "I had a child once. After a difficult pregnancy. The midwives told me to flush it, but I was stubborn. Then the last few months, it started to kill me. Poisoned my blood. So they cut me open." She made a cutting motion across her belly. "Pulled out a deformed mass of twisted limbs. That might have been all right, but they botched the surgery. I didn't realize how badly until I tried to conceive again. No luck."

"Midwives often have very sound advice," Zezili said. "Surgeons' skill is less."

"I was young," Isoail said. "I thought I knew better. If I'd chosen to end it before it went bad, perhaps I'd have had other children. But I did not. So here we are."

"Yet you have strange little dajian girls calling you mother," Zezili said.

"I'm not her mother," Isoail said softly. "Most likely she mistook me for someone else."

Zezili picked up her brandy and drank too much of it. It warmed her stomach and softened her doubts. "When girls like this pass through these… tears in the lake… Could people here travel through them? Go after them?"

"If they were in the same area, yes. Ah, yes. You're thinking of your husband."

"He meant to meet me here."

"Many things can happen to a man on the road."

"My husband is loyal. He meant to meet me here. If he's not here, it's possible he's on the other side, isn't it?"

"Many things are possible. But why would you think that?"

"He… there was an incident at our house. I thought it meant nothing at the time. Thought it was some trick. But maybe, with all these people showing these gifts now… maybe he opened a door by accident."

"Ah," Isoail said. "That is… something."

"Have you ever tried to go to the other side, through one of these doors?"

"I'm more than a double channeler," Isoail said. "I thought for a good long time that's all I was, until I saw the disturbances here. I could see them – the red breath of Oma. I shouldn't have been able to."

"Triple? Ha. End times, indeed. I can fairly feel the fiery eye of Rhea."

"Who can say what will be rare in a year's time? Maybe all jistas will be able to call on Oma in addition to their ascendant star. We don't know. Oma hasn't risen in two thousand years. Everything is strange now."

"You figured out how to open a gate."

"Yes. I tried to copy some of the patterns I saw on the lake. But it always opened to the same place, some blasted vista, and I could never pass through. It was like trying to get through a window made of steel."

Zezili nodded. Isoail couldn't pass over because she did have a double, then. Someone on the other side, possibly working with that... other Zezili to build the mirror? And if Anavha was there, too... She took another drink. Saw the head stamped on Monshara's coin again. Monshara had lost her world and become a frightened tool, but Zezili was no one's slave.

"There are things coming into this world that shouldn't," Zezili said. "You know that. You see it. I think there's an easier way to stop them besides just pulling wreckage from a lake or murdering dajians at their order."

"If you're about to talk treason, I won't hear it."

"Not at all," Zezili lied. "Have you ever built an infused mirror? One as big as a building?"

"That would be something," she said, "but no."

"If you had, could you destroy it?"

"Destroy an infused mirror?" Isoail said. "Yes. You unravel the pattern. Each channeler has a distinctive pattern. I'd know if it was mine."

"My mother said you're the best at what you do," Zezili said. "The best in Dorinah at making infused mirrors. So, if we apply the logic of dual forces, that means your other self over there, she's probably going to be good at building mirrors, right?"

Isoail shook her head. "That's a large stretch."

"You can help me stop them, Isoail."

"That's treason."

"There's a mirror they're building there to keep open the way between worlds. Once it's infused, their armies will spill through. Help me stop it."

"I love my Empress."

"So do I," Zezili said. "But she's not loyal to you. Do you know what she has Syre Kakolyn doing?"

"I haven't any idea."

"Purging Seekers from Dorinah. Seekers like you. She cleared Tulana and Sokai and the rest from the Seeker Sanctuary."

"That's madness. Why are you here, really?"

"You can check out that story," Zezili said, and stood. "Then if you want to help me, you let me know. I leave in the morning, but I'll be at a camp in Aloerian for a week or so, if you want to join me."

"The Empress would never–"

"I didn't think she'd wipe out two million dhorins worth of dajians, either," Zezili said. "It sounded fine, at first, but the more you think about it, the more the whole thing unravels. The Empress is planning something with these strangers, something that isn't meant to benefit Dorinah."

"If you mean to betray–"

"I don't," Zezili said, and she found the conviction in her own voice very comforting. "Ask about your Seeker Sanctuary. Ask where your friends are now."

Zezili went to bed. She lay awake for hours, staring at the spiders crawling across the ceiling, each as big as her palm. She should have known Isoail would have a living double on the other side. If she couldn't destroy the mirror, perhaps she could still help Zezili find Anavha. They could open a door here, and Zezili could spend... how long? How long would she look for him, before her Empress gave her up for dead or had her friends over there murder her for treason?

No. If the Empress destroyed her, she wanted to take something with her.

When she finally slept, Zezili dreamed Anavha was scratching on the door, his head covered in a hood of fine spiders' silk. When she woke, a hooded form stood over her. Fear seized her. She grabbed the sword next to her bed.

Isoail threw back the hood of her coat. She looked pale and distraught in the early morning light.

"They came for the girl," she said, "and brought me a message by sparrow, from the Sanctuary. It had died on the way. A tirajista with the enforcers kept it in tissue paper."

"And?"

"I want to know what the Empress really has planned for us."

"I thought you might," Zezili said. "But if we're going to destroy the new world they're building, we need to figure out how to get there."

"How would I know where this mirror is?"

"You don't have to know. I know where it is."

"Do you?"

"Right here," Zezili said. "You said you always open a door to the same place? You say the easiest place to come through is here? Maybe the easiest place for you to build a gate to over there is the best place for them to put a mirror, too."

"That is a great leap in logic."

"I'm full of leaping today. But the bigger question is how we get you over there when your other self is still alive."

"We don't have to get me over," Isoail said.

"Why not?"

"The girl," Isoail said.

"What, from last night? What about her?"

"The girl could break the mirror if she knew the pattern."

"Why?"

"She may not be my daughter here, but there... well. I went over our conversation many times last night. You believe I was the one who made this mirror, this great gate, over there. If that's so, I can untangle it. And so can a very close blood relation, if they are gifted and know the pattern I used to create it. Sometimes they are able to see the pattern and unravel-"

Zezili threw off her blankets. The room was cold. "Let's get her, then."

"We can't," Isoail said.

"What do you mean? She's in the next room!"

"Did you not hear me?"

"I'm half asleep, Isoail."

"The enforcers came for her this morning, before I woke. That was six hours ago. I don't know where they took her. There are eight camps within a few days' march of here – north, south, east, west... they could have gone any direction."

Zezili grabbed fistfuls of her own hair and grunted. Isoail could open the gate. The little dajian could destroy the mirror. And Zezili could use the ensuing chaos to find Anavha. Rhea had handed it to her all in one night, and she'd tossed it away.

Zezili stood. "Come with me."

"Where?"

"I'm purging every last one of those camps in the coming weeks," Zezili said. "The girl's bound to be in one of them."

Zezili swept into Monshara's tent completely sober. She was cold but already had her helm under her arm and her gloves off. It showed a measure of trust, she thought.

Monshara stood bent over a field table with a steaming cup of tea clasped in her hands. Her hair was knotted atop her head in a loose tangle. A heavy woolen scarf that had once been blue and was now a washed-out gray swaddled her neck. If she was surprised at Zezili's appearance, she did not show it.

"I expect the purging of the last camp went well," Zezili said.

"Has your husband been rounded up and whipped? I understand that's your way."

"It's cultural, not personal."

"Indeed. Your desertion was reported."

"You knew where I was and why. We share command. I answer only to the Empress."

"She isn't pleased. Nor is the woman I answer to."

"I've spoken with my Empress personally," Zezili lied. "She understands." She pulled a piece of paper from her belt and unfolded it on the table. It was a rough sketch of the girl from the lake. Isoail knew an artist in the neighboring town who created it based on their shared memory. She'd passed it on to enforcement offices along the way, but to the enforcers, every dajian looked alike. "She's asked me to find a dajian thought to be hiding in one of these final camps. We'll need to circulate this before we run each purge."

Monshara set down her tea and squinted at the page. "What's she done?"

"I didn't ask. You and I only follow orders, remember?"

Monshara leaned toward her. "If you think I'll forget your desertion–"

Zezili thumped her helm on the table. "If you think you're my superior, you're sorely mistaken," she said. "My business is my own and I answer only to the Empress of Dorinah. *My* Empress. So watch your tone and do as she tells you."

Zezili snapped up the page and her helm. She walked out.

Monshara called after her, "Don't think that's the end of this, Zezili."

"We have a lot of killing to do," Zezili called over her shoulder, and slid her helm back on. "Best give your full attention to that."

She had four full weeks, she guessed, before Monshara confirmed her story was hash. What happened when she found out, well... the world was ending anyway, wasn't it?

36

"I should have told them the boy could see through wards," Dasai said. He stood on the great wall of Kuonrada and gazed north. The days were getting shorter and colder. He huddled in a thick coat, but his feet were cold and his knees ached. It had been months since he woke without pain. He was a hundred and twenty-eight years old and felt a hundred and fifty.

"Not even the boy knew," Nioni said. "It was still best left unspoken."

"There it is," Dasai said, and pointed to the shimmering amber blur in the sky. A flash, a moment, and it was gone. The wrong color for the northern lights.

"I thought it would be more dramatic," Aramey said. He sat next to Nioni on the cold stone of the ramparts.

Dasai had yet to find another part of the hold where he felt he could speak freely. Most of the hold's lookouts staffed the great spiraling thorn of the watchtower that grew from the center of the hold. Even so, he'd had Nioni construct an air bubble around them here to muffle sound. He had spent much of his youth in Saiduan. It's why his bones hurt so much now.

"In a few weeks, the snow will be bad enough that it will be too late to send the boys home," Nioni said. "We should do it now, before the Patron takes any more interest in how Rohinmey or any of the rest of us fit in his wider campaign. I'm dying, but these boys have their whole lives ahead."

"I know you meant to protect him, Ora Dasai," Aramey said, "but *this* much interest could harm him. And us."

"If things go badly here, the Patron's interest in that boy may save him," Dasai said. "Rohinmey is many things but not stupid. You see how much he impressed those sanisi? They are taken with him. If they love him, they love us. It's relationships that save us in the end. If I have to manipulate people to achieve that, I will."

"You need to tell him," Aramey said.

"I will discuss Rohinmey's ability with him," Dasai said. "He and the boys may require it on the way home. I admit I wished his brother had the talent he has. Ora Chali has a less passionate disposition."

"That's not always an asset," Aramey said.

Nioni sighed. "Ora Chali has ambitions."

"I wish to see him achieve them," Dasai said. "So does Ora Nasaka. They must go back."

"Tomorrow, then," Nioni said.

"Not until we've prepared for our escape north," Dasai said. "Ora Nasaka trusted my memory of what lies waiting for us in Caisau. Caisau is already under the sway of the invaders, but two of my colleagues are still in the city. We need our sinajista before we proceed. She is at least another week away. We hold until then."

"If Rohinmey hadn't seen those men–" Nioni said.

"If he had not, we would be dead," Dasai said, "along with the Patron. Or we'd be sold off among his possessions to his successor. The terror and madness that sweeps across Saiduan when a Patron is killed would have ended our task before it began. Now we can get to Caisau and wake the creature there. We must merely endure more intense scrutiny."

"Are we going to tell the boys who the invaders really are?" Nioni asked.

"We continue to do what the Kai sent us to do," Dasai said. "Until it is time to do as Ora Nasaka and I planned. I made inquiries about the books mentioned in that text from the Dhai scholar. I have an old colleague who may have found one of them for us. Let's wait to tell the boys about the invaders. It's too much."

Aramey folded his arms. "We are putting a lot of faith in old books."

"All of my faith is in a book," Dasai said. "*The Book of Oma*. Books have great power, Aramey."

"Only as much as we give them," Nioni said. "The Saiduan are hoping for a book of miracles."

"We may have one," Dasai said, "but I prefer to keep a number of switches in my basket."

"I hope it's worth sending the boys out for it," Nioni said. "If they're caught–"

"They won't be caught," Dasai said. "It's still festival season. The Saiduan have a festival every week during the winter, even now. Especially now. They have very little to hope for. Sending the boys out to enjoy themselves won't seem amiss."

"I'm just very uncomfortable with this," Nioni said. "These are Saiduan we're betraying."

"I know that better than anyone," Dasai said, "but now is a time for calm." For the second time in as many weeks, he questioned his decision to bring Nioni here. He needed men he could trust who could speak Saiduan, and whose families were large enough that they could afford to lose them. And Nioni was dying of stomach cancer. He would not survive the year. Aramey, his large-hearted husband, had wanted to die with him. Their situation was ideal for his purpose. But he worried they did not have the strength for what needed to be done.

"We'll wait," Aramey said. He pointed to the sky. "I just worry they won't."

Dasai found Kihin and Chali working in the sitting area outside their shared quarters. The group had turned it into a library and study space. Dasai saw stacks of books from the archives on Saiduan culture and ethics, all books the Saiduan librarians only agreed to part with because they had copies.

"Where's Rohinmey?" he asked. The slaughter in the banquet hall had occurred the day before, and Roh had been sick most of the night. The endless vomiting told Dasai that the boy's queasy stomach likely had to do with food poisoning or some stomach ailment instead of fear or visceral terror. He had almost hoped the killing had sobered the boy instead of invigorating him. But Dasai understood the sort of boy Roh was early on. The Kai had not.

"Still in bed," Kihin said.

Dasai walked to Roh's room and opened the door, announced himself.

"I'm awake," Roh said. He sat on the bottom bunk, huddled close to the fire. Two candles burned brightly in iron lanterns.

"What are you reading?"

"Saiduan stories about the Dhai," Roh said. "Did you know Grania was once part of the larger land mass of Saiduan? The whole continent stretched unbroken from here down to Hrollief."

"I did," Dasai said.

"When the breaking came – they called Oma's rise last time the breaking – it unleashed huge forces across the world. It broke up the whole continent. Imagine how that must have been. It was so powerful, it broke *continents*. There were earthquakes and terrible storms."

"Yes," Dasai said, "and very powerful omajistas who knew that breaking up the continent would break up the Dhai's line of supply. Not all of these phenomena associated with Oma's rise are caused by Oma. The gods grant us many gifts, and they guide us on how to use them, but they make no moral judgments on the use of those powers. What one woman believes is evil, another thinks is for the greater good of her country."

"I just didn't realize how big Dhai was," Roh said. "We learn a lot, but not… not all the things they have here."

"There is fear we may become as we once were," Dasai said. "No one wants us to be those people again."

"We would be so powerful–"

"We would be murderers and dealers in flesh," Dasai said. He feared this boy sometimes, feared what someone so passionate, with so much gifted potential, would become. "We have chosen another path."

"Sorry," Roh said.

"Let me tell you a story about a slave," Dasai said.

"Ora Dasai, I'm sorry—"

"Quiet, now. Be respectful for a moment of your exhausting life, please."

"Sorry."

"There was once a Dhai slave owned by the Patron of Saiduan. Not this Patron, but the one four Patrons before this one. He was captured very young, when the fishing boat his mothers took him out on was overtaken. This slave was a dancer like you, and a powerful sinajista. He was so powerful that for much of his life, he was paired with a flat-headed slave with greater talent who prevented him from tapping into his full abilities."

"They just stayed together day and night?"

"Yes," Dasai said. "He became very close to the Patron, and the flat-headed slave did, too. One day, the Dhai slave seduced the flat-headed slave and drugged him. Then he crept to the Patron's rooms and tried to burn him in his bed. But the Patron was protected by powerful wards. He woke unscathed and had the Dhai slave's legs broken."

"Did the Dhai live?"

"He did," Dasai said, "but he never danced again. And he could no longer fight. If he was going to improve his circumstances, he needed something other than brute force." Dasai pointed to Roh's head. "He needed to use his wits."

"Did he escape?"

"He did," Dasai said, "many years later, when the Patron's family was killed by usurpers. He convinced the new Patron that he was a free Dhai. And, having no use for him, the new Patron released him. He walked one thousand miles to the harbor in Alorjan and rejoined his family in Dhai."

"That's a sad story," Roh said. "But why tell me?"

"Because you may find yourself in a very bad position, Rohinmey," Dasai said. "If things go wrong, I do not want you to fight. I want you to live."

"He lost years of his life, Ora Dasai," Roh said. "I couldn't live like that."

"You'd be surprised what one can endure," Dasai said. He watched the boy's face. He looked young and fragile. Dasai imagined listening to some old man tell him not to fight. To just endure. To have his legs and will broken time and again. Foolish old man, Dasai would have thought then.

"Ora Dasai, did you know I can see through wards? That's what the sanisi said I did."

"It was known to me, yes."

"Why didn't anyone tell me?"

"You're a young novice. We preferred to wait until you had more... discipline."

"What does it mean? I don't actually see any breath around them. I just... see them."

"Some parajistas can see through wards. It means you can see things that others wish to keep hidden."

"I thought I was just smart."

"Being smart takes effort," Dasai said. "I suspect that seeing the things you do requires little effort."

"Can I get better at it?"

"Perhaps. But not here. I have other tasks for you."

"Like what?"

"You're to stay away from the dancers," Dasai said, "and the Patron, and the sanisi, during our final days here. I want you working only for the archive project now. We have much yet to accomplish."

"Ora Dasai, I still–"

"This is not a negotiation, let alone an argument," Dasai said. "Tomorrow, you and Kihin and Luna will travel a few hours south with a text we've uncovered. You'll meet a man named

Shodav, an old colleague of mine. You will give him a book to translate. In return, he'll turn over a book to you to bring back in its place. I want you to deliver it to me. Discreetly. If anyone asks, you're simply going there for the Bone Festival, to see the wolf dancing and meet with a friend of mine to discuss Saiduan grammar. Understood?"

Roh grinned. "Yes, Ora Dasai." Dasai found it wearying that the boy was so excited at the prospect of deception. I was young once, he reminded himself, but that did not make him feel better. He should have left the boy in Dhai, Sina take the Kai.

Dasai eased to his feet, leaning heavily on his cane. It was like the world itself wanted to suck him back into it, yanking painfully at his bones. "Good night, Rohinmey."

He shuffled to the door.

"Ora Dasai?"

"Hm?"

"Were you a very good dancer?"

"The very best," he said.

37

Ghrasia Madah preferred fighting blinding-trees to questioning skittish Raonas. But she had three dead sparrows in her pocket and a description of the man who'd returned them to the clan's primary dealer three days before. It was the best lead on the men who might be assassinating people in Dhai that she had had in days, and with a lead that fresh, she knew she had to work quickly, even if it meant spreading her people beyond the clan fence to suss out the stranger.

She walked with a young parajista named Halimey, a big-eyed, plump-cheeked young man who put her in mind of her own daughter. The militia was stretched thin, and the Oras she brought with her were even thinner. She had started out breaking them into teams of four – two militia, a parajista, and another Ora whose star was descendent. But the ground they had to cover around Clan Raona was substantial, and time was short. With no other leads beyond the vague description of the stranger, there was nothing to report to the Kai. The Kai, not Ahkio, she had to keep reminding herself. Because when she thought of him as Ahkio, it stirred up her memory of him at the fountain, and that stirred up a good many more feelings best left shuttered up. She'd gotten word of his marriage a few days before. A fine political match. She wished them much success. But she had far larger concerns.

"So, you haven't seen anyone with that description?" Ghrasia asked the matronly woman on the steps of her gill-topped home.

Best Ghrasia could figure, the house was actually a tirajista-trained mushroom, very old.

"I'd remember a stranger like that with yellow eyes, missing three teeth," the woman said. "I'll remember your faces a good long time, too, and they aren't half so colorful."

"I'm sure," Ghrasia said.

"You don't look the way I imagined," the woman said, and Ghrasia regretted introducing herself with her full name. Sometimes, it opened more doors. But on occasion, it did get her into trouble. "Thought you'd be taller. And have larger arms."

"I hear that a lot," Ghrasia said.

"I expect so."

"Thank you for your time," Ghrasia said.

"Feed this boy something," the matron said. "He looks too thin."

"I'll do that," Ghrasia said.

Once they were clear of the house, Halimey snickered. "Feed me, Mother!"

"Call me that again and I'll fix you up a proper mud pie," she said. He could have been hers, though. He wasn't more than eighteen or nineteen.

"Delicious!"

"Next one's two miles farther on," Ghrasia said. "You want a rest?"

Halimey glanced up at the sky. The suns were winding down toward the horizon. "If we're going to finish one more before dark, we better press on."

"Then hurry on, now."

Halimey hopped after her. Ghrasia was tired, but knowing they only had one more house for the day gave her the extra bit of energy she needed to push forward.

"Why is it you don't dance?" Halimey said. He fished around in his pocket for one of his scorch pods and threw it off into the brush. It made a loud popping sound.

"What?"

"They have dancing at the council house every night," Halimey said. "Everyone goes. Clan Raona is happy to host us."

Ghrasia had her own impression of just how happy Clan Raona was to have them. The local militia had spent much of its time since their arrival running around, curbing spurious storefronts, like the ones selling tax-free liquor and at least one illegal butcher shop, whose existence alone made Ghrasia's stomach lurch. It took four days to assure them she was more interested in the sparrow buyers than in collecting taxes. Tax collection was not the business of the Liona militia.

"You can dance for both of us," Ghrasia said.

"Was it some terrible accident?" Halimey said. He tossed another pod. Another pop.

"What?"

"Was it because you were dancing and some bear attacked you? Or did you fall into a wine barrel while doing a Garika jig? My sister once–"

Ghrasia laughed.

"Ah," Halimey said. "You see? You do laugh."

"I laugh a lot when I'm not tracking assassins, Halimey. I'll leave the talking to you, then."

Halimey chattered on for the rest of the long walk while Ghrasia kept watch for creeping vines and floxflass. The temperatures were cool but still mild. It didn't snow much in Dhai, which contributed to the problem with the plants. They never experienced a hard freeze.

As they neared the end of the road, the low whine of the mock cicadas went suddenly quiet. Ghrasia came up short, but Halimey walked on. She heard something crashing far off – the sound of a small herd of walking trees. She listened for a while, but they seemed to have stopped.

Halimey paused ahead of her, looked back. "What is it?"

"Just worried we'd run into some walking trees. They've stopped now, probably to bed down for the night. The suns are setting. Hurry, now." She was jumpy, she knew. It had been a long, boring day knocking on doors.

The last homestead of the day lay at the end of a winding path overhung in mossy bonsa trees and weeping green bamboo. The house was thirty feet up the side of a bonsa tree, built on the ledge of a massive calcified fungus. It looked like a fairly large working homestead. Broad, tirajista-trained vines snaked up the surrounding trees. They supported open-mouthed grub boxes that collected the fat parasites that fed on the trees. Dorinahs considered them a delicacy, and they were among Dhai's chief exports. Walking trees liked them, too. No wonder there was a herd of them so close. They likely sensed the wriggling worms in the cages.

"Hope you aren't afraid of heights," Ghrasia said.

"I'm a parajista," Halimey said. "I could fly if I wanted to."

They walked up the narrow stair to the porch of the house. Ghrasia saw two more buildings linked with the main house, hugging up to the side of the tree. Outside the clan fences, the safest places to live were the trees, especially as a grub farmer that would draw herds of walking trees.

She reached for the door handle. The door was locked.

Ghrasia reflexively reached for the hilt of her sword.

"What's wrong?" Halimey asked.

"Locked," Ghrasia said.

Halimey reached up and knocked. "They're grub farmers," he said. "Anyone who lives outside a clan fence is a little odd. Lots of semi-sentient things crawl around out here."

The door opened.

"I'm Halimey Farai Sorila and this is Ghrasia Madah. We're from the Liona militia and–" He stopped.

The man at the door was about Halimey's height, thin, with a shadow of a beard and matted black hair. His eyes were not gray or brown but yellow. His lips were parted, and Ghrasia saw the gap on the right side, where three teeth were missing. How the matron they last spoke to had not seen this man living just two miles from her home...

"We're looking for a woman about your height," Ghrasia interrupted. "She has long dark hair, about here," Ghrasia said, putting a hand to her waist. "Maybe forty-odd years old, high forehead, sloping nose, plump like my friend." Ghrasia realized she had described Javia, the former Kai.

"No one like that here," the man said, squinting. "What did they do to bring the Liona militia all the way out here?"

"I'm afraid we can't discuss it," Ghrasia said. If this man was a foreign assassin, she needed three more Oras and half a dozen militia on hand. She could have Halimey call them up once they were out of sight of the house, post a watch overnight, and overtake him in the morning with a mounted force.

"Thank you for your time," she said.

Too late.

Halimey made a choked sound of distress. He groped at his throat and tumbled backward. Ghrasia grabbed his coat. A massive force thumped her from behind. The railing broke. They fell. Ghrasia had a long, sickening moment of freefall, just enough time to wonder how much it was going to hurt. She released Halimey. Relaxed her body. Bent her knees and prepared for impact.

She landed hard on the balls of her feet. Pain jolted up her legs. The air rushed from her lungs. Halimey thumped beside her. Ghrasia's right ankle throbbed, but she felt no shattering pain. As she struggled to breathe, the assassin leapt from the railing and fell slowly to the ground beside her. She yanked at her sword, still gasping.

The assassin stepped on her scabbard. She followed his look to Halimey. Blood flecked the boy's mouth. He had fallen hard on his right side. She could tell from the angle of the arm pinned beneath him that it was broken. A parajista could only fly if she was not wrapped in the powerful grip of another parajista.

"You wanted to talk," the assassin said. "It would be impolite not to invite you inside."

He yanked Ghrasia's sword from its sheath. The everpine branch curled around his wrist. He ran Halimey through with it.

Ghrasia cried out. The man plunged the blade a second, a third, a fourth time into the boy's prone body.

She turned over and clawed forward, ignoring the pain in her ankle. The assassin grabbed the knot of her hair and yanked her back.

"Not you," he said. "You're a gift to the dogs. The great Dhai hero. Even I have heard that name."

He thumped Ghrasia over the head with the butt of her everpine sword. Blackness pooled across her vision. She lost her balance, collapsed. She was suddenly weightless, wrapped in a skein of air and propelled into the sky so quickly, she blacked out.

When she came to, she was lying on her side on a scuffed floor in front of a wooden fence. Her hands were tied in front of her with stout fireweed cord. Her ankle and head ached. What was a fence doing inside a house? She looked through the fence and saw a line of small kennels, like one would use for an adolescent dog. The room was mostly dark. A thin line of light came in through ventilation slits high up on the ceiling. The stink of the place was overpowering. It smelled like urine and old feces and unwashed bodies. Ghrasia gagged.

She heard a thump and looked to the other end of the room. The assassin sat at a broad, bloody table. The remains of Halimey's body littered the floor, tangled in his blue tunic and trousers and gray coat. The assassin was hacking up hunks of the boy's leg on the table.

A massive wave of terror seized her. Ghrasia tried to sit up. She punched it back down and breathed through it. She heard a soft whimpering sound from the kennels.

"They haven't eaten in days," the assassin said. "They're very hungry."

Ghrasia tried to think of something clever. The door lay between her and the assassin. She saw a large, intricate padlock on it, the sort that only came on crates from Dorinah. No one used that type of lock in Dhai. They required an exacting series of actions to remove them, pushing sliders and rotating pins in the correct order.

"How long have you been here?" Ghrasia asked. Talking made her head hurt more, but she suspected not talking would ease the headache far sooner than she wished.

"Many years," he said. "My brothers and I."

"Where are your brothers now? They help you farm this place?"

"There are a dozen of us," he said. "We have worked in Raona longer than you could imagine. You are not the first to find us. Only the most famous."

He raised his cleaver. "I am a good boy. Loyal to the Kai. But she did not say we'd be killing our own people. No, she did not say."

"Kai Kirana is long dead," Ghrasia said.

"Your Kirana is dead, yes. Not mine."

Something moaned from the kennels. It didn't sound like a dog.

"They all made me the messenger," he said. "Passing their notes to one another. But I'm more than that. Stronger." The cleaver came down. Bone crunched.

Ghrasia flinched. "That boy was a friend of mine," she said.

"He was weak."

The assassin threw a hunk of Halimey's thigh over the fence. It landed with a wet thud on the floor. She heard more whimpering from the kennels. An excited stir of movement.

Dirty, matted figures burst from the kennels. They loped out on all fours, sniffing and snarling behind long matted hair. Dirt and feces and dried blood covered their bodies and the tattered remains of what could have been some old tunic or sack mended for the purpose.

The three creatures descended on the thigh, howling.

Ghrasia's gorge rose. Their fingers dug into the meat.

The creatures were human. Or had once been.

They fought and snarled over their prize. Great pools of twisted flesh made puckered scars around where their eyes should have been. They were young, in their teens, perhaps. Living exclusively on human flesh in such conditions might have stunted them, though. For all she knew, they had lived this way for a century.

"I'm freeing them," the assassin said. He threw another hunk of Halimey over the fence. Another frenzy ensued. "They know now that they are just animals. Weak beasts, to be cared for and to serve a superior people. I am training them, you see. The way you will all be trained to serve us."

Ghrasia left herself then. It was a strange, detached feeling, like watching some other little woman holed up in a tree house with a madman while children feasted like wild dogs on the desecrated remains of her companion. From the outside, it was easier to understand what she needed to do. She focused on Halimey's coat and the bulging pocket of scorch pods.

"It must have taken great strength to live here all alone," she said, looking away from the coat.

The assassin reached for another of Halimey's limbs, disturbing the coat. He slapped a long, tattered arm onto the table. She listened to the chewing, crunching sound of his captives gnawing on what he'd fed them.

"Strength beyond measure," he said. He peered at her. "You'll do, I think."

"How's that?"

"I've been wondering what to do with you," he said. "Feed you to them… or make you one of them. What do you think? The great Dhai hero, one of my dogs."

"I expect that will make you very happy," Ghrasia said. "Are you going to blind me with your bare hands? I suspect there's a better way to do that."

"Oh, there is," he said. "I'll show you."

He moved toward her. Ghrasia tensed. She had no defense against him. He was gifted and she was not. If she moved quickly enough to cause him serious pain, she might be able to break his concentration, but she would have to be fast.

The assassin grabbed the lock on the door. Ghrasia tried to watch the sequence of pins and knobs he manipulated, but he stood in front of the lock, his back to her. The lock clicked. He opened the door, then shut it behind him. Ghrasia waited a breath, long enough to hear his footsteps on the stairs leading to one of the other houses – she wasn't sure which level she was on – and then she crept across the room to Halimey's butchered body.

The things behind the fence snarled at her. One flung itself at the fence. Ghrasia worked quickly. She grabbed two fistfuls of the scorch pods from Halimey's pocket with her bound hands and smashed them against the floor with all her strength. The heat was nothing, at first – an inconvenience.

She heard the assassin's footsteps on the stairs.

Ghrasia murmured a prayer to Oma.

The scorch pods burst into flame beneath her hands. She smelled burning flesh and clothing, and rolled away, fearing she was on fire. But when she looked up, she saw it was Halimey's coat that was on fire.

The creatures on the other side of the fence bayed and howled.

Ghrasia threw herself against the door, fingers seeking the padlock, her range of motion limited by her bonds.

The assassin's steps on the porch quickened. He pushed against the door.

Ghrasia clicked the padlock into place.

The fire licked at Halimey's coat, warming the collection of pods inside. They began to crack and hiss. Flaming pods popped from the pile, arcing across the room. The creatures were screaming now. Smoke began to fill the room. The floor caught fire. One pod landed in a creature's hair. It began to smoke. They screamed and screamed.

The assassin pounded on the door. Ghrasia scurried back into the far corner of the room, away from the fire. She kicked at the fence.

The door blew off its hinges with such force that it burst apart the fence for her. Ragged splinters knifed into her right side. She cringed away.

The assassin's burst of air and shower of kindling only fueled the fire. Ghrasia choked on smoke. His captives were running around in mad circles, squealing.

The assassin turned toward Ghrasia. He carried an awl in his hand.

One of the creatures bounded onto the top of the door and across the broken fence. It leapt onto the assassin's back and clamped onto his throat. He cried out and flailed. The second creature came after the first. They began to tear him apart.

Ghrasia crawled past him and pushed herself out the door. She came up short, reeling at the drop off the porch. They were in the topmost of the three buildings that wound up the tree. She inhaled a gasp of fresh air. With her hands tied, she couldn't mount the ladder. She looked down at the roof of the building below. Ten feet. Her ankle was still sore, possibly only twisted. If she landed on it again, it was possible she'd break it.

The assassin roared behind her over the sound of the flames.

Ghrasia saw more fire licking up the outside of the building. She gritted her teeth and thrust her hands into the fire. She smelled burning flesh as the flames seared her hands – and her bonds. Pain throbbed. She twisted her hands until the singed cord snapped.

The assassin fell out the door, clawing his way toward her. His creatures were still hooked into him, bloody and beaten. One's arm looked dislocated.

Ghrasia jumped onto the ladder and climbed down, hissing through the pain of her scorched hands. She slid the last few feet and stumbled onto the porch of the second house. She pushed inside and saw the room was dominated by a large table. Various types of plants lay dissected on its surface. She smelled rotting flesh, too, and found bits of birds and rodents mortifying in cages hung from the ceiling. She heard a rustling sound and saw a line of twelve tiny cages set along the floor. A single Dhai character was painted on the outside of each – initials. Inside the cages were sparrows. Tirajista-trained sparrows could be compelled to return to the same locations – or even the same person – time and again.

What had he said about his brothers and being a messenger?

She heard the assassin screaming. Heard him trampling down the ladder.

Ghrasia bolted from the room, favoring her injured ankle, and slid into the lowest house. She banged open the door. So long as she stayed out of the assassin's sight, it would be harder for him to net her in some cone of air.

She hopped down the front stairs and rolled onto the bare ground. She kissed it. Looked up at the long lines of grub cages running up and down the big trees. Under the cover of the bonsa trees, it was almost full dark, but she could see their outlines in the dappled shadows.

Ghrasia climbed onto the vine at the base of the bonsa tree and began kicking over the worm cages. They dropped to the ground and burst. She followed the long line of the vine, spiraling up and around the tree, staying out of sight of the assassin. She could hear him screaming at her from the ground.

Then she heard another sound.

Ghrasia pressed her back to the tree behind her and held her breath. Her injured hands burned as if they were still on fire.

A crashing, keening cry came from the woods. She felt a blast of air nearby. She clung to the tree and prayed the assassin was too injured to concentrate properly.

Hungry walking trees burst into the sea of wriggling grubs like a sentient tide. Their limbs moaned and creaked. A lashing tendril whipped the tree she hid up on, narrowly missing her face.

The assassin screamed. The air felt heavy. Ghrasia heard bursting trunks. Shattered branches.

The air pressure normalized.

The massive tide of walking trees continued to pour into the homestead, greedily snapping up the grubs with sappy tendrils and dropping them into the toxic bladders that hung from their crowns.

Ghrasia let out a single agonized sob.

She lay there all through the night while the walking trees fed. A few hours before dawn, the walking trees moved on. Ghrasia waited until there was enough light to see by and then gazed down into the wrecked clearing. She saw dozens of trampled grubs and the remains of a bloody, smashed body.

Ghrasia made her way back down the vine. She approached the body hesitantly, until she saw that its entire torso had been mashed in by the feet of the trees. It made her bolder. She stood beside the assassin's pulverized body. Then she went over to the house and picked up a rock. She wanted to mash his face in. His yellow eyes, shot through with blood now, stared blankly out at the tree she had spent the night in.

She lowered the rock. If she mutilated him now, was she any better than him?

Ghrasia looked back up at the house. The topmost house had burned down to its foundation in the night. The bonsa tree it clung to had fared much better. It was scorched and the nearest leaves had turned black, but the fire had burned itself out after that.

She made the painful walk back up into the second house, the one with the cages. She opened the door and held her breath.

The sparrows were still alive.

Ahkio was speaking with Talisa, clan leader of Clan Raona, in her private quarters when Caisa burst in.

"Ghrasia Madah to see you, Kai."

"Where has she been?" Ahkio said. He half expected to hear Clan Leader Talisa had shuttered her up in some gaol for two days while she completed her tax-free trading. Ahkio had never seen a clan openly thwart so many national prohibitions.

"You see," Talisa said, "she's quite fine. Ghrasia Madah can handle herself quite–"

Ahkio didn't wait for her to finish. He followed Caisa outside, pulling on his coat as he went. He saw Ghrasia limping into the town square alone. He came up short. She was covered in soot and blood, and there was some kind of… creature following a hundred yards behind her. It almost looked human.

"Ghrasia?" Ahkio said.

Her face was grim but otherwise unreadable. Her hands looked raw, burned, and his stomach clenched. He knew what that felt like.

"Oma, Ghrasia, what's happened?" Ahkio said. "I arrived yesterday and they told me you'd be back by dark. And what's... what's that?"

Ghrasia glanced back at the creature following her. "It's a long story," she said.

"I'll get you a physician," he said, and glanced back at Caisa. "Can you call someone?"

Caisa ran off.

Ahkio held out his hands to her. He wanted to touch her, but was terrified to ask. He dropped his hands. "Tira, what happened?"

"I know where the assassins are," Ghrasia said, "every last one of them. But you need to tell me who we're fighting, Ahkio."

38

Roh and Kihin met Luna out in the chilly courtyard of Kuonrada. They borrowed bears from the kennel boys with a note from Ora Dasai, marked by Keeper Takanaa. The bears were bigger than Roh was used to and didn't have the forked tongues of the bears in Dhai. Their feet were broader, their coats shaggier.

The little party traversed the slippery ways of Kuonrada, through the walls of the keep, to the threshold of the massive city wall. As the bears stepped onto the road, Roh gazed over the broken, craggy landscape of snow and ice. He hadn't been outside the hold since he entered it many weeks before.

Kihin had the book Dasai had tasked them with delivering bundled up on the saddle behind him. "Fresh air, at least?"

"And fun," Luna said. "You'll like the Bone Festival."

"It sounds... different," Kihin said.

"You don't kill people during it, do you?" Roh said.

"Roh, that's very rude," Kihin said.

"It's a fair question," Luna said. "Did you know that when the Dhai ruled here" – he made a sweeping gesture across the wintry landscape – "they used to feed the Saiduan to bears during ascendance ceremonies?"

"I get it, all right," Roh said.

"Let's go," Kihin said. He hung back with Roh as Luna urged his bear forward, and said, "Try, just this once, to not talk so much. I'm surprised none of those dancers killed you."

"We got along very well," Roh said.

"I bet," Kihin said.

"What's that supposed to mean?"

"Nothing, just… try to be nice."

"I'm always nice!"

"Politic, then."

"I don't know what that means."

Kihin sighed. "Just… let me do the talking this one time."

"I'm not sure you're a very strong speaker."

"Roh…" Kihin made a sound of distress. "Just… be quiet."

"Are you coming?" Luna called back at them.

"Yes!" Kihin said, and patted his bear forward.

The cold outside was vicious, even bundled up as Roh was. His eyes stung, and he could have used another layer over his ears. He slowed his pace after a while, and Luna slowed next to him. Kihin took longer to catch up. They came upon the village a few hours later and left their bears with a stir of others in a broad pen. Luna led them to a bowled half theater dug into one of the hills. The circular space in front of the theater was penned and gated. Blood colored the snow.

The three of them sat shoulder to shoulder, pressed close to the other spectators. Roh stood up when the wolves were brought in, muzzled and hobbled, growling. He had never seen a real wolf before and didn't know what to expect when Luna told them they would see "wolf dancing." The three in the ring were big brutes, thick in the shoulders. Their eyes were unsettling, not yellow but a peculiar sort of gold that made Roh shiver. Unlike dogs, the wolves were a uniform black from nose to tail tip. They were physically bigger than dogs, more muscular, not sleek enough to saddle, even allowing for the shoulder-saddles used on all dogs.

"That's Shodav," Luna said. "The one Ora Dasai wants us to meet." He pointed to a stir of brightly colored figures approaching the pen from the sidelines. There were five men, Shodav the tallest and oldest. The others looked like children or adolescents, thin and young. They were not dressed for the cold. The headbands and short trousers, ornate belts and streamers of ribbons at their elbows were ornamental, not practical.

"Aren't they cold?" Roh asked.

"It's like a battle frenzy, Shodav says. Keeps them warm," Luna said.

The dancers leapt up on top of the wall ringing the circle and raised their arms to the crowd. The audience stamped their feet and hollered at the dancers. Roh strained to see around them. Luna elbowed someone.

The dancers jumped into the ring as a purple-clad man hit a gong. The sound reverberated in the cold air. The wolf handlers pulled off the wolves' muzzles and jumped out of the ring.

The wolves snarled and leapt, and so did the dancers. The wolves paced the five dancers as a pack. The dancers leapt clear of them. A small boy gave leverage to his companion, who jumped up over the back of one of the wolves, spun, and landed neatly on his feet as the smaller boy sprang out of the path of the wolf.

The wolves snapped at the dancers careening over their heads and snarled at the tumbling boys. When one boy caught too much attention, Shodav jumped forward to call away the wolf.

After the dance, Luna brought Roh and Kihin around the back of the stage and introduced them to Shodav. Shodav, despite the cold, was covered in sweat. His hair hung down his back in a spiral of braids twisted through with tiny bells and brightly colored string. He grinned at Luna. He was missing his front teeth.

"Hello, maggot," Shodav said. He collected Luna up into an embrace.

"Hey, stop!" Luna said, laughing. "I'm not that little."

"Only just," Shodav said, returning him to the snow. He took in Roh and Kihin. "What, are you collecting a set?"

"These are my friends," Luna said. "Roh and Kihin. They're from Dhai. They brought a book to translate, from Ora Dasai."

"Ah, Ora Dasai. Business."

Shodav led the party back to his house. There were only three rooms in the house and one hair-stuffed mattress on the floor.

They sat around a low table on cushions, like Dorinahs. The little stone house was well furnished with intricate hangings and rich carpets. It stank of sod and incense. Shodav made them tea.

"I expected Ora Dasai to come himself," Shodav said.

"He told us to bring you this," Kihin said, pulling the book from the bag at his hip.

Shodav unwrapped the book from its cloth binding. Turned the first page. Roh saw a blank piece of green paper inside, the sort that official messages in Dhai were written on. But it was blank.

"Ah," Shodav said, considering the page. "You're to take this, then." He went back into the bedroom and returned with another book. He pushed it across the low table toward Roh.

Roh looked at the characters on the front. They weren't any language he knew. He opened it. The script was unintelligible.

"What's this?" he said.

"Talamynii," Shodav said. "Ora Dasai will know where to find the proper translator for it."

"So, what's in here?" Roh asked.

"A record of the Talamynii in your country, I believe," Shodav said. "To be honest, that's only a guess. It was the best match for the criteria Ora Dasai gave me."

When all the tea was drunk, Shodav bid them farewell. They rode back out of town and came to a river crossing at dusk. Kihin and Luna rode up onto the glittering ice together ahead of Roh, heads bent toward one another. Roh lingered behind, watching them talk. The wind picked up, pelting him with icy snow. He shielded his eyes.

Roh heard a noise and pulled his hands away from his face.

Luna wasn't there anymore.

Kihin was off his mount, bending toward a splashing form in the dark water. A jagged hole had opened in the ice.

Kihin's bear roared and let loose toward the other side of the river.

Roh urged his bear forward. He dismounted and ran to the

river's edge. The crack opened up from the riverside to the gash where Luna and his mount had disappeared.

Roh slid out onto the ice on his belly. He reached the edge of the hole as Luna's hands lost their grip on the ice.

Luna was carried under.

Kihin screamed, in Dhai, "He's gone under! He's gone under!"

Roh looked at the great sheet of dark ice. He saw nothing of Luna. He edged closer to the riverbank and stood up. He began sliding along the surface.

"The current has him," Kihin said. Roh heard despair in his voice.

Roh slid farther along the ice. A face pressed up at him from beneath the ice. A bubble of air had formed between the ice and the river. Luna clutched the underside of the depression.

"Here!" Roh said.

He pounded at the ice.

Kihin slid next to him. He hit at the ice. Flakes splintered away.

Roh saw Luna's fingers slipping. His face disappeared back under the water.

Roh yanked off his gloves and spread out his fingers. He concentrated on the ice, and the air beneath it. He murmured the litany for an explosive air burst. Blue mist suffused his fingers.

He ruptured the ice with a great exhale.

The circle of ice blew apart, revealing Luna's face to the sky.

Kihin caught Luna by the collar. Roh pressed and pounded out the ice until Kihin could pull Luna's limp form from the hole. Roh was dizzy and his breath came hard, as if he had run a great distance.

They grabbed hold of Luna and pulled him back onto the bank, into the snow. He lay limp.

Kihin turned Luna onto his side. They pounded his chest and tried to push the water from him.

"He's too cold, it's not—" Roh started.

Luna vomited water.

"Luna!" Kihin said.

Luna began to shiver. His eyes rolled.

"Make a fire," Roh said.

"With what?" Kihin said.

Roh gazed toward Kuonrada. The darkness was deep now.

"I'll go for help," Roh said.

"Ze's going to freeze," Kihin said, in Saiduan. He cradled Luna in his arms.

Roh looked back at Luna, then again at Kuonrada. He said, in Saiduan, "Here, get hir feet dry, wrap hir in blankets. I'll take hir up on my bear and carry hir back. I can try to keep hir warm."

Kihin pulled off Luna's boots. He rubbed Luna's feet dry and put his own dry boots onto Luna's feet. He kept Luna's stockings on.

"Be quick," Kihin said. "I'll freeze out here."

"I'll come back," Roh said.

With Kihin's help, Roh pulled Luna up onto the bear with him. He put his arms around Luna and took the reins.

"Will the ice hold?" Kihin asked.

"It better," Roh said. He navigated the bear back up toward the place they had crossed that morning, a dozen yards upstream. He whistled to the bear. "Fast," he muttered. "Like the wind."

The bear shambled out over the ice. Roh nearly lost his grip on Luna. Luna shivered and clutched at the blankets.

They cleared the river and loped out toward the curve of the road.

Roh kept up the pace as long as he dared, but the bear was starting to balk. He slowed. An hour to the keep would be too long. He'd have to ask the garrison to bed Luna down. Even that might be too late.

The road was utterly dark. He navigated by the lights of Kuonrada. He was still some way from the gate, moving up toward the curve of the hill, when he saw the dark rider.

His heart stuck in his throat. He felt a tingling across his shoulders. The rider was tall, cloaked all in black. Was it one of the invaders?

Roh gathered himself and prepared to call Para, though his hands trembled and his body shook.

The rider's voice: "Have you found your way back, puppy?"

Roh let out his breath.

The dark rider's bear loped to him, the shadow of a sanisi, not... something else.

"Kadaan," Roh said.

"You expected someone else?" Kadaan said. "Your Ora Dasai said you were late. My Patron has an interest in where you are."

"Luna fell into the river. Ze's going to freeze. Kihin's back there without boots."

Kadaan reined in next to him. His knee touched Roh's. "This is what happens when Dhais are left alone," he said. "You see it?"

"Kadaan!"

Kadaan placed a hand on Luna's forehead. The air around Roh condensed, felt too heavy. The blue breath of Para cloaked Kadaan's body and then encircled Luna. Luna glowed blue for a long moment. Then his shivering ceased.

"That will do for a time," Kadaan said. "Get hir back and get hir warm. I'll find your friend."

Kadaan whistled his bear past.

Roh turned back. "Kadaan!" he shouted.

Kadaan turned.

"Thank you," Roh said.

"I do not do this for you," Kadaan said. "I do this for my Patron. Best not confuse my intent."

39

They trussed Lilia up like a beast, slung a blanket over her, and put her across the back of a dog. Her skin was rubbed raw; she was jostled painfully, and rode that way for all the daylight hours and several more after dark. She offered no resistance. After a while, the enforcers stopped goading her.

She had fulfilled her promise to her mother, some other woman's mother, a shadow-mother. And her mother didn't want her. Lilia really was no one, a ghost, caught somewhere between this world and another. Despair had overcome her. She looked at the world through a black well of darkness.

They arrived at the camps the evening of the sixth day. Lilia smelled the camps before she saw them. She didn't think that any smell could overpower that of the dogs, but the camps stank like a mass grave. They passed through a gate onto muddy ground that put Lilia in mind of a churned-up dung pile. The women did not untie her. They pushed her off the dog and into the cold mud.

Lilia landed on her stomach and choked on slushy mud. She rolled over onto her side. From the gate ran stone walls capped in iron spikes. The wooden gate was wound in sharp metal. The enforcers shut the gate.

Dirty figures squatted around campfires just outside makeshift shelters of old wood, stitched hides, and tangles of bonsa and everpine branches. Ice crusted the ridges of the muddy ground.

The smell of the fires could not overpower the stench of unwashed bodies, and something fouler, more terrifying – the cloying stink of rotting flesh.

Three men crouching under the awning of the nearest shack were already looking over at her. Others had stopped along the outer edges of the camp to look – outright or surreptitiously.

Lilia saw something in their faces that scared her. It roused her from her misery. Motherless or not, if she did not move now, they would devour her. She twisted her hands behind her back and tried to tug at the loops around her ankles with her fingers.

These are Dhai, she told herself. There's nothing to be afraid of. There will be people from the clans here, novices sent into exile. They'll be–

The men were first to move.

They started toward her like a pack of curious dogs. Then, some of the other spectators were moving: two matrons with sticks and a gaggle of scrawny children.

Someone grabbed Lilia's ankle. She kicked out, but there were hands on her, pulling at her hair, her clothes.

She tried to curl up, bowed her head to protect it. One of the women tugged her short coat off as far as she could until Lilia's bound hands prevented her from taking it. Then the pack of them, the men, the women, the children, and more stragglers, unknotted Lilia's bonds, tore at them with teeth and fingers.

They pulled the ropes free. One of the women yanked the coat from Lilia's body. The woman tried to run with it. One of the men gripped the sleeve, pulled. The woman hit him with her stick. The children took Lilia's boots.

She was free, but Lilia's feet and hands were numb from days of poor circulation. The other woman grabbed hold of Lilia's tunic. Cold mud bit her bare skin. The tunic came free. She kicked out at one of them; hit him in the jaw with her bad hand. Pain rocked up her arm. The third man returned without the coat and held her down while they stripped her of the last of her clothes. The men bunched up her pants and linen and ran back into the camp.

Lilia staggered to her feet and fell. It was the first time she had tried to stand in two days. She rubbed at her bare skin and the new bruises forming over her old ones.

Her despair was deep. But so was the cold.

She crept toward the outer edges of the dwellings. She wrapped her arms around herself for warmth. The men watched her as she moved. Her feet and fingers were numb. She huddled against the flimsy side of a shelter, shivering.

The smell of urine was strong; someone was using the space between the shelters as a latrine.

The temperature dropped as night lengthened. Lilia scooped up some of the mud and slathered it onto her body. She had read of someone doing that in a Dorinah novel, only they had mixed fat with the mud. Soon enough, the mud would freeze and dry and flake off.

People passed her many times, but the only light in the camp came from the smoky fires, and she was so covered in mud that many did not even glance at her. She dozed sometime in the darkest hours of the night and woke to find two men near her, the same men who had stolen her pants. She froze under their gazes, their outlines just visible – she remembered their forms and their smell. She waited, thinking they had made a mistake, thought she had something else they could steal.

Then the men grabbed hold of her, yanked her painfully up. They were big men. She twisted and bit at them, but they pulled her farther into the camp. They were laughing and joking, crude jokes. Lilia let out a long scream. The man holding her cuffed her. She tasted blood.

He had a good hold on her, and his companion was just behind, ready to grab her up if she squirmed away. The man who held her had a ratted tongue of black hair circling his head, and a heavy beard.

She let herself go lax and fell back into him with the full weight of her body. He stumbled again, not expecting her submission. Her head fell back onto his shoulder. She looked at the folded flesh of his ear.

Her gorge rose.

Lilia took her assailant's ear in her mouth and bit down, hard. The man screeched. He released her and jerked away. The top of his ear came away in Lilia's mouth.

Lilia staggered back onto her own feet. She spit the man's flesh out, tasted blood. She made to run and fell into a stout woman. The two of them collapsed, a tangle of limbs. The woman had a heavy blanket around her shoulders.

Lilia tore the cloak away from the woman and ran through the clutter of houses. She ran past banked fires, skirted around a refuse pile and what she suspected was a corpse. She ran and ran.

Her chest felt tight and her breath was heavy. She darted left, then right again, and slowed her steps. She heard voices behind her and kept walking. She twisted the ends of the cloak over one shoulder, knotted it at her hip. Her legs were trembling.

Breathe.

Breathe, Li.

She had no mahuan powder here. An asthma attack would kill her.

Lilia slowed her pace and slunk deeper into the camp. She wandered until the graying of the sky found her at a large rectangular building propped up in a cleared square of trampled mud. The building's entrance had no doors. Lilia saw the carving of a great eye above the mouth of the entry. Faint light trickled from two lanterns set high up on the interior walls.

Lilia lingered at the entry, expecting to look inside and see altars to the gods, a Sanctuary. Instead, she saw battered benches facing a raised stage. The floor was smooth dirt. She walked to the other end of the room and squeezed into the corner between the raised stage and the wall. She rested her head in the crook of her arm, meant to doze, but she must have slept, because she dreamed.

She dreamed of a cold stone hall, not the sinuous circular halls of the temples but a long, straight hall built on the assumption of sharp lines and angles. She went to the windows and gazed down from a great height across a black city. She saw a jumble of jagged buildings capped in snow, peaked roofs carved with grotesque faces at the eaves, above the doors, all of them laced in a fine, powdery snow. The snow collected in immense drifts along the streets. Tall stone walls ringed the city, three walls deep. The city sloped downward to the wide bay, a bay ringed in old, old mountains, their tops worn smooth, blanketed in white. The bay was a rolling landscape broken by the jutting pillars of ice jams along the coast. Farther out, the bay was a tumble of dirty ice floes and black water, seething with something else: ships. A hundred – a thousand – ten thousand? More than she could count. From her vantage, Lilia saw movement outside and inside the walls, an immense black tide of figures. She caught the smell of smoke.

She turned away–

And looked into her mother's face.

"Isn't it beautiful?" her mother said. She wore a long robe of white. Her skin glowed with a faint luminescence, like Faith Ahya was said to glow. Her black hair was knotted with white ribbons. "You were meant to lead them."

Lilia woke so suddenly, she knocked her head against the wall. She yelped. Cold morning light seeped in through the doorway. I didn't come this far to die in Dorinah, she thought.

That woman hadn't been her mother. What she had done didn't matter. Lilia rubbed her wrist, where the ward had been. She was alone now, but in truth, she'd always been alone. She would die alone in the mud if she didn't act.

From the stoop, she gazed out at the hovels ringing the meeting house. Figures tended fires. She heard the low wail of a child.

She went to the first woman she saw, a stout, middle-aged woman who bent over a banked fire.

"Pardon, mother," Lilia said. "Do you know anyone looking for a healer, a midwife?"

"You look more like *you* need a healer," she said.

"I'm a temple-educated Dhai," Lilia said. "I can read and write, Dorinah and Dhai. Do you know anyone who needs letters written or read?"

The woman turned her attention back to her fire. "Move on."

Lilia went to the next fire. She asked every woman if they needed a healer, a midwife. These people knew nothing of her, and there was some freedom in that. It meant she could be anything. Their language was a strange patois of Dhai and Dorinah. Lilia picked it up quickly. She could be a good mimic, when she needed to be.

"A healer or midwife?" Lilia asked.

"Go on," another woman said. She wasn't much older than Lilia, and she had two young children at her skirt, another at her breast. "We got Emlee for all that."

"Where can I find Emlee?"

The woman pointed. "Go to the place with the purple awning there, left, then a right when you see the orange flag. House with the big dead snapping lily out front."

"Thank you," Lilia said. She turned away. Her feet were numb. The sky was gray, brooding, threatened snow.

She found the healer's house after doubling back twice. An old woman ducked out almost immediately, nearly knocking Lilia over. Her face was a map of wrinkles in a face of mottled flesh the color of river clay. The woman's hair was a tangle of white knotted atop her head with ragged black ribbons. She held a stout staff of adenoak and wore a sturdy but well-used dress, Dorinah cut, practical, very long at the sleeves and hem. The hem was soaked in mud.

"Are you the midwife?" Lilia asked.

"Midwife, healer, sorceress. I'm all that and more. Do you have need of skill?"

"I was educated in the temples."

"I can tell that in your talk," the woman said. "Ah. You're looking for work. But they don't teach herbs, medicines in those shiny temples, do they? Can you tell stories? Are you gifted? Eh, probably not; the enforcers would have culled you out, but sometimes... Well, what is it?"

"My mother was a midwife and herbalist. From the Woodlands. And I know lots of stories."

"Do you now? We'll see. You coming?"

"Now? Yes, oh, yes."

Emlee pushed open the hide door of the low-lying plank house. The house's seams were stuffed with mud and grass. Lilia stepped inside to warmth. Her body throbbed.

"We have a straggler, Cora," Emlee said.

A stout young woman sat at the fireside, nursing a baby at her breast. Her hair was pulled back from a sharp, wolfish face; she looked at Lilia as if she would devour Lilia whole.

"Don't have room for another one," Cora said.

"We have any water? She's filthy. And listen to that breathing! Where's my wax wraith?"

"There were some bad people at the gate," Lilia said tentatively.

"Gate trash," Emlee said. "Parasites are always hanging around the gates. I assure you the rest of us are quite civilized. Cora, did you hear me? Where's Larn?"

"Fucking that priest and asking favors of his women," Cora said. She got to her feet and pushed her big baby onto her hip. The baby squirmed, began to whine. "Him and those women set up in Tolda's hatch, and Larn's got enough gossip in her lungs to trade over for bread."

Emlee grunted. She rested her staff near the door, said, "We'll talk about that later. This is... what's your name?"

"Lilia."

Emlee raised her brows. "Haven't heard that name in some time. Thought no one named girls that anymore. Clean up now. I've got a full list today. I've three cases of yaws and enough coital diseases to last me two lifetimes. You think I have all day, temple Dhai?"

Lilia dropped her filthy blanket. Cora brought out a pan of tepid, mostly clean water. Lilia sponged herself off as best she could. She wiped at her thighs and saw tendrils of blood leaking back into the pan. She had not wiped her face. She looked down between her thighs, saw a smear of blood. She pressed her fingers between her legs. They came back red.

"I'm bleeding," Lilia said. It sounded stupid to say it out loud, but seeing the blood reminded her of her bare, scarred arms, and the power that could be called with blood.

"Get her something," Emlee said. She had settled by the fire and was stirring up some rice.

Cora handed over a wadded rag. "I'll find you some linen and a belt," Cora said.

Lilia tied on the linen belt that secured the clean rag between her thighs. She dressed in a long skirt of Cora's, too big and too long for her. The tunic they gave her was also too big and made of itchy wool, but it was warm. Cora loaned Lilia her shoes and stuffed them with straw to keep them on Lilia's feet.

"The sick wait on no one but me," Emlee said. "Up, up. Let's go now. See how useful you are."

Cora handed her a sticky rice ball as Emlee pushed her out the door.

Lilia walked after Emlee, wolfing down the rice. Emlee strode purposefully down paths, around refuse. She called to those sitting around the fires, knew the names of all the dirty children, at the breast and apron strings, and the others, the orphans who ran in packs.

Emlee greeted two young women sitting outside the awning of a lopsided hide tent. One of them carried a twisted bundle of firewood. Both women looked relieved to see Emlee. Emlee introduced Lilia. They led them inside the dim tent.

"Have you seen yaws before?" Emlee asked.

Lilia shook her head.

They stooped over a young man who lay in a corner of the tent. He turned his face to them.

Lilia's stomach lurched.

Something had chewed away the center of the man's face. Where a nose and upper lip should have been was an open wound of flesh, leaving the top of the mouth open, the lower teeth visible. His left eye was lower than the right, drawn down into the wound that was his face.

Emlee handed Lilia her pack of supplies. "Open that up," Emlee said. "Get familiar with it."

Lilia sat down behind Emlee as the old woman settled beside the faceless man. Lilia unrolled Emlee's pack of supplies. She had two dozen vials of herbs and mixed concoctions, none of them labeled. She had several kinds of scalpels, a mirror on the end of a metal rod, a small file-saw that Lilia could hold easily in the palm of her hand, and a length of clean gauze wrapped in a thin paper that smelled of everpine.

In the days that followed, Lilia became intimately familiar with the contents of Emlee's kit. She learned the names of all the potions and how to mix them. Emlee brought her to births and deaths. Lilia saw cancers and gonorrhea, dysentery, gangrene, syphilis, and diseases she had no name for but the ones Emlee gave them: orange fever, billicks, sen rot, and skin ulcers and lesions that ate away arms and faces and feet. They treated frost-bitten drunks, women whose insides had been cut out by Dorinahs and left ill-treated, men who had been castrated and become infected, urinated blood and pus – when they could urinate at all.

Lilia worked silently, like a shadow. She did not lose her stomach until the day they were brought to a woman who had been carried to Emlee's doorstep. She had a swatch of dirty, bloodied bandaging up one leg and wrapped about her torso. She stank of dead flesh.

Emlee reached forward to take off the bandaging. Lilia saw something moving beneath it. When Emlee drew the bandages clear, she revealed the woman's gaping wound: a shiver of writhing maggots seethed inside the rotting flesh. The smell of death thickened the room.

Lilia's skin crawled. She stumbled out of the tent and vomited her breakfast into the latrine gutter. She crouched with her head down for several minutes until her stomach stopped heaving.

Then she went back to Emlee and knelt beside the woman.

"Found her in a ditch at the rear of the camp," Emlee said. "They only throw the traitors there."

"Traitors?"

"Dajians who worked for the Empress," Emlee said.

"Why would the Empress send them here?"

"Because they betrayed her," Emlee said.

"Wait. So they are traitors to the Empress, not to us?"

"Us?" Emlee frowned. "Child, those who betray the Empress also betray us. We're her people."

"But you're... you, all of you–"

"You're a temple Dhai," Emlee said. "You wouldn't understand. But you will."

Lilia gazed across the comatose woman to the open door and the camp beyond. She found something to replace her numb despair then. It was rage. Rage at all of this, at this world, at a place that could create all of this sorrow and madness, at a place that could throw her and these people away like filth.

She bent over her patient and gently pulled the woman's matted, dirty hair from her face. Lilia's fingers froze.

She knew the woman's face.

It was Gian.

40

"I said I would tell you when it was time," Maralah said. "It's time."

"The Dhai are keeping information from us," the Patron said.

"And we're keeping information from them," Maralah said. "They have yet to ask if we're fighting Dhai."

Maralah, Driaa, and Kadaan stood with the Patron at the top of the keep, in what had become their makeshift war room. The space wasn't meant for it. Best Maralah could surmise, it had once been a luxurious retreat for some very old Patron's favorite wife. Silver and gold gilded passages from the *Lord's Book of Unmaking* graced the ceiling. The passages were a selection of love poetry to Oma written by a sixth-century scholar included in one of the appendices of the Book.

The chamber also had a breathtaking view of the surrounding countryside. Maralah suspected that before it was tarted up, its original purpose was a military one. Village elders always told her that time was a circle and everything came back around again. It was strange to see how literal that had become.

"I tried to keep them close by having one of their boys dance," the Patron said. "It reminded me of happier times. But I suspect they mean to betray us, if they have not already."

"Five little Dhai? We can deal with five Dhai," Maralah said. "Especially one that just saved you from men that looked just like him."

"They let my son die."

"That was my failure," Maralah said. "Kadaan and I were seated at that table for that purpose. I failed you, Patron, not the Dhai."

Kadaan did not look at her. In meetings such as this, with the Patron's mood uncertain and conditions rapidly deteriorating, she preferred to be the only one to speak with him, even if he had called up all three of them. Some part of her expected he would ask the other two to kill her, and invite Kadaan to take her place. It was a fight she had prepared for these many months by sparring with Kadaan in the courtyard and sending Driaa off on assignments. Kadaan was faster, but Maralah had more experience. All that remained was for the Patron to give the order.

"Why else would they bring a boy who could see through wards and not tell us?" the Patron said. "Why would Dasai bring him to my table? I know Dasai's history here."

"I don't know why they failed to mention his talent," Maralah said. "But to be fair, we failed to mention they were fighting themselves." The Patron had been drinking more of late. Rumor had it he had not visited his wives in some time, not even the formidable Arisaa, who had borne his most beloved sons and given him sound advice when he was in these moods. When Maralah's counsel could not keep him balanced, Arisaa's usually could. She made a note to have Driaa stop by Arisaa's quarters after this meeting. Arisaa did not care for Maralah, but she would tolerate Driaa.

"We must not act on fear," Maralah said.

The Patron choked on a laugh. "Fear?" he said. "Fear? This is about respect. They disrespect me in my own house. I've had their correspondence monitored all these weeks, and I believe it's been telling as to their intentions."

"A valid precaution," she said.

"But not one you suggested."

"No," she said.

He began to pace along the wall of windows. His long coat was dirty at the hem. His boots were scuffed, and his hair needed washing. Seeing him like this, she was reminded of a story of the last days of the Empire of Dhai, when a group of sanisi finally penetrated a room much like this one, where the city's magistrate, her family, and their bodyguards made a final stand. They were mad, broken people, the sanisi wrote, with big bug-eyed faces and wan complexions. They had eaten their own children. What remained of their little bodies was spread out on the stones, washed and neatly butchered with skinning knives and cleavers. Maralah wondered what she would be driven to do at the end.

"They have found something," the Patron said. "It's been too long with no progress. They *must* be sending all the information they have back to Dhai."

"That may be," Maralah said, "but it does not change our position. The invading armies are marching south from Caisau. They've burned out four villages and routed much of my brother's regiment. He's bringing what remains here. It isn't enough to hold Kuonrada. We need to retreat south to Harajan."

"After Harajan is Anjoliaa," the Patron said, "and once they have us against the sea, we are done." He ceased his pacing and stood motionless, looking north. From this great height, Maralah thought she could see smoke from some burned-out little town. She had given her brother's regiment permission to burn out the farms between Caisau and Kuonrada as they retreated, taking what they could for themselves and leaving nothing behind for the invaders.

"They should have stopped their advance," the Patron said. "You said they would stop as the season deepened."

"It's madness to march in this weather," Maralah said. "If I led them, I would have stopped two weeks ago. They'll freeze in their tracks."

"Then the weather will devour them."

"That is my hope," Maralah said, "but they do not seem to heed the cold. They could make it here before the worst of the weather and turn us out. Then we'll get caught in the weather during our retreat. It's just luck now."

"This is the place," the Patron said softly. "This is the place they'll write about."

"What?"

"We make our stand here," he said. "In Kuonrada."

"Patron, I must protest–"

"That's my decision," he said.

"We discussed this before we retreated from Caisau. When the time was right–"

"You are my general," the Patron said. "You are not Patron. That is my burden."

"We could last out the season in Harajan."

"That's what you said about Kuonrada," he said. "Yet here we are, retreating again. What would my predecessor say to this? What would Osoraan have said to this?"

"Former Patron Osoraan would not have survived this long," Maralah said. "He would have broken his armies against them in some vain and glorious gesture early last year, and all of us would be dead. It's what he did when he assaulted us. It's why we won."

"We?" the Patron said.

Maralah grimaced. "It's why *you* won, Patron."

He jabbed a finger at her. "This is where we stand, Maralah."

"Then this is where we will die."

"It is a good place to die."

Maralah bowed deeply. She clenched her teeth so hard her jaw hurt. "Then I will die beside you," she said.

"When your brother arrives, give him the order to hold this position."

"Yes, Patron."

"You may go. All of you."

Maralah took two steps back before turning away. Kadaan and Driaa waited until she turned before also retreating. They cleared the doors. Kadaan shut them. They were heavy doors, amberwood banded in steel. But Driaa put up a bubble of air around the three of them anyway. Maralah's ears popped.

"Do you want me to call back Soraanda's command?" Driaa asked. "They've already started the retreat to Harajan at your order."

"What do you think, Kadaan?" Maralah asked.

"I think we can last another year if we retreat to Harajan," he said.

"Driaa?"

"I didn't want it to come to this," Driaa said.

"No one does," Maralah said.

"We have no one for the seat," Kadaan said.

"The Patron will stay on the seat. My brother will be here in four days with his army," Maralah said. "I can convince the Patron to… retire. For a time."

"You'd put him into a slumber?" Driaa said.

"When peace arrives, we will wake him," Maralah said. "I'm no betrayer, Driaa. No oath-breaker. I told him I would protect him. That's what I will do. My brother and I will lead the armies. Start speaking to those you know to be allies. When it happens, it will happen very quickly."

"You must expect some resistance," Kadaan said.

"His star is descendent," Maralah said. "It won't take but a few moments. But I want to make sure the people left in the hold are ours first."

"When do we begin?" Kadaan asked.

"When my brother arrives. I want Para below the horizon," Maralah said. "Parajistas who side with him will be weaker."

"So will those parajistas who side with us," Driaa said.

"But we'll know what's coming," Maralah said. "Sometimes that makes all the difference."

41

When Roh arrived back at the hold, he handed over the Talamynii book to Kihin and went down to the infirmary to visit Luna. Two green-robed orderlies were helping Luna dress. They pulled Luna's soiled robe off, revealing his small breasts. Roh was used to Dhai, where everyone chose what gender they went by. He wondered, for the first time, who had decided Luna was not "he" or "she" but "ze." Was it the first person who owned Luna, or Maralah, or someone else? But that, it turned out, was a terrible train of thought, because then he had to acknowledge that every single person he'd meant in Saiduan had had a gender decided for them. They had no choice in it at all.

The orderlies tucked Luna into bed. Luna saw Roh and beamed.

"It's not often you get saved by a sanisi," Luna said.

Roh sat at the edge of the bed. "I wanted to see if you're all right."

"Kihin's already been up," Luna said. "He worries."

Roh didn't think Kihin was much of a worrier. "I only wish it was me who got to ride all the way back to the hold with Kadaan."

"I bet you do."

As Roh left the infirmary, Abas surprised him in the hall. Abas cried out in delight and asked to hug him. They embraced. He had a handful of other dancers with him.

"I heard you flushed out Kadaan, the Shadow of Caisau," Abas said. "Maralah and Kadaan are fighting again, come see. We've missed your happy face."

"Abas has missed your face more than most," one of the other dancers, Rasandan, said.

The dancers walked out to one of the large secondary courtyards at the center of the hold. Roh stood at the edge of the circle in the sanded snow of the courtyard while sanisi and slaves, kennel masters and blacksmiths, soldiers and clerks, crowded behind him.

The sanisi moved too quickly for Roh to understand how Maralah got the better of Kadaan during their first bout. Like any strategy game, the error seemed to lie somewhere behind them, one wrong move that set all the others in motion.

They began the second dance. Maralah stepped back at the edge of the circle and raised her right foot. Kadaan kicked her foot with his as she moved to strike, caught her off balance, and forged a way through her defenses. Maralah staggered, rolled. Kadaan landed two jabs at her back, then a thumb at her neck, not a strike but a press, a call for yield.

"Yield!" Maralah said.

Kadaan stepped back.

Appreciative calls came from the audience.

Kadaan and Maralah clasped one another's forearms. Maralah leaned in to say something to Kadaan.

The crowd began to disperse. Abas called for Roh, but Roh walked out into the circle, where Kadaan was buckling on his baldric. Maralah pulled on her coat.

Maralah looked up when she saw Roh. "Your puppy's here," she said.

"How do you know he's not yours?" Kadaan asked.

"The dancers are always yours," Maralah said. She walked past Roh and back into the keep.

"Are you going to teach me to move like that?" Roh asked.

"Why are you so persistent, puppy?" Kadaan said.

"You're the one who followed after *me*, remember?"

"Pacifist," Kadaan said.

"I'm going to be a sanisi," Roh said lightly. "Why do you think I came here?"

"Youth," Kadaan said. "Foolishness." But Roh saw humor in his face as he turned away.

After, Roh tried to slip back into the archives unnoticed, but Nioni caught him on the stair.

"Ora Dasai wants to speak to you," Nioni said. "In his quarters."

Dasai's door was open. The old Ora sat on the couch with a pile of correspondence.

"I wasn't far," Roh said. "I just went into the-"

"I'll be sending you home in a few days, Roh. I've written a letter to your parents. They will expect your return."

"It's still winter," Roh said. "No ships will be going to Dhai!"

"There is a ship that leaves every year at the beginning of Siira to bring us Saiduan steel. You and Kihin and Ora Chali will return with it."

"I think you should ask the Kai first, before you send me back. And... and what about Kihin's exile? What's he going to say when you send Kihin back?"

"He will most likely be glad to see Kihin alive. If Kihin perishes, it could make things very difficult with Clan Leader Tir, exiled or no," Dasai said.

"Ora Dasai, I don't understand—"

"Then let me make it clear," Dasai said sharply. "Shut that door."

Roh did.

"You are an asset to Dhai," Dasai said. "You're a fighter. You can see past hazing wards. You think these sanisi are interested in you for your own sake? No. They are owned body and soul by the Patron of Saiduan. We are nothing to them. Dhai is nothing. And those creatures that stepped so easily into the great hall of Kuonrada are going to be descending on Dhai. Your place is Dhai. I am getting you away from here before the Patron demands that you stay. Because if he demands it of me, I will have no choice but to honor him. Do you understand now?"

"No. Who were those men in the banquet hall, Ora Dasai? Where are the invaders coming from?"

"You're willful and arrogant," Dasai said. "That will either save you or ruin you. I hope I'm no longer living when you find out which."

"Ora Dasai, you can't–"

"I can. You're dismissed."

Roh spent his evening penning letters and watching the light fade from the world outside. What would happen if he went back to Dhai? Would he spend the rest of his life telling this story, about dancing with the Saiduan and talking to sanisi and then... farming in Dhai?

Kihin returned from the archives a few hours after dark. The suns only appeared in the sky four hours a day now.

"Has Ora Dasai told you?" Roh asked.

"Yes," Kihin said. "It doesn't matter. I'll be gone before then."

"What do you mean?"

"You should know something, Roh," Kihin said. "Luna and I are going to run away together."

"What? Where?"

"To Dhai, eventually," Kihin said. "Someone needs to stand up to the Kai."

"But," Roh tried to wrap his head around what he knew of Kihin. "I didn't think you–"

"We're in love, like Hahko and Faith Ahya. You'll see. We'll remake the country."

Roh wasn't sure what to say.

"Be happy for us, Roh," Kihin said.

"I... all right," Roh said. "Have you talked to Ora Dasai?"

"We're not going to ask permission. We're just going to go. I wanted to tell someone. Before we ran away. So my father knows I'm not dead. But don't say anything yet. Luna has to get well. I didn't tell anyone about you sneaking off with Abas. Please keep this secret?"

"I will," Roh said. "Just be careful, Kihin."

"Ora Dasai always thought it would be you who ran off. He's going to be really surprised."

Surprised wasn't the word Roh would use.

Kihin went to bed.

Roh lay awake another half hour. Even Kihin was making his own fate. But Roh's world was spinning back to Dhai again, back to some orchard, the life of a farmer. And he didn't know how to stop it.

Roh woke from a dream of sparrows. They swarmed his body, pecking at his flesh, tearing away strips of meat until they flayed him alive.

Kihin shook him. "We're summoned, Roh," he said.

"What? By who?"

"The Patron's summoned us," Dasai said from the doorway. Nioni and Aramey were behind him, arguing.

Roh rubbed his eyes. "But why—"

"Come, get Ora Chali," Dasai called. "We have sanisi waiting on us."

Roh threw off his blanket. He slipped on his boots and ran into the common room, expecting to see Kadaan. But the three sanisi weren't familiar.

"Is this all of you?" the eldest sanisi asked.

Chali stumbled into the room, pulling on his coat.

"He's the last," another of the sanisi said. "Let's proceed."

Roh's stomach knotted. Why did the Patron want to see them? He glanced at Dasai. Had he shared the book they got from Shodav with the Patron yet?

The sanisi led them on a winding route through Kuonrada, down narrow corridors and up twisting stairwells. They went up and up. Finally, they came to an amberwood door banded in iron. The sanisi in the lead opened it.

They walked into a broad room with a stunning view of the tundra and the hulking mountains in the far distance. The room itself was lush, dominated by a massive bed. Roh saw Saiduan writing on the ceiling, and around the tops of the walls, all in gold. Despite the bank of windows, the room was warm. A fire crackled in the massive hearth opposite the windows.

The Patron stood with four more sanisi at the center of the room behind a long, narrow table. The table looked out of place. It was battered and nicked, made of hard, black wood. On the table was a single piece of paper.

As the sanisi herded Roh and the others forward, Roh tried to make out what was on the paper, but it had been turned over.

"Stop there," the Patron said. Roh was within spitting distance of the table. The Patron looked weary. He spread his arms and leaned toward them.

"I will give you one opportunity to speak the truth," the Patron said. "Then I will begin killing you."

Nioni let out a little cry.

Roh looked at the sanisi's faces. He didn't know the four in the room, either. Eight sanisi felt like a lot of trouble for a handful of Dhai.

"My Patron," Dasai said, pushing his way gently to the front of their group, "we would be most pleased to answer any question you have of us."

"Which of you wrote this?" the Patron turned over the paper.

Roh winced. It was the letter he had written to the Kai, the ciphered letter that, on the surface, looked like nothing more than banal talk of the weather and how terrible the food was, but once untangled with the cipher said... well, not much more. Only that he had not found what he was looking for. He thought it would be obvious who wrote it, but as he stared at the page, he saw that in tearing open the letter, the signature had been smeared and part of it ripped away, leaving no record of its creator.

Roh opened his mouth to tell the Patron everything – about the Kai cipher, the book they'd gotten from Shodav–

"I wrote it," Dasai said.

Roh started.

"You?" the Patron said. "Did you think me a fool?"

"Not at all," Dasai said. "I accept full responsibility for this correspondence and accept whatever justice, vengeance, or mercy you choose to grant me."

"Do you understand what it is to rule a people?" the Patron said.

"I do not," Dasai said.

"Ruling a people means you are responsible for them," the Patron said. He slowly made his way toward the front of the table. "It means that when they suffer, you suffer. When you retreat, they retreat. It is a heavy burden."

"I cannot imagine," Dasai said.

"No, you cannot," the Patron said. "My intelligence officers know a ciphered letter when they see one. Give me the cipher."

Roh reached for Dasai's sleeve. Dasai moved his arm away, turning it into a shrug. "I'm afraid I can't share the cipher with you," Dasai said. "It is not mine to gift. But I can tell you the correspondence did relate to the number of Saiduan here in Kuonrada. The Kai wished to understand how thinly your forces were stretched, so that we may assess the threat the invaders will pose to us. We know they will come to our shores soon."

"I invited you here," the Patron said, low. "I fed you. I clothed you. I invited you to my own table!"

Dasai handed Roh his cane. Roh tried to meet his look, but Dasai's gaze was downcast. Dasai slowly, and with great effort, began to get to his knees. Roh offered his hand. Dasai leaned on him. The old man grimaced. Once he reached his knees, he extended the full length of his body before the Patron and lay prostrate.

"I am yours," Dasai said.

Roh watched Aramey and Nioni. They looked at Dasai with expressions of naked horror. Kihin and Chali stood close to one another. Roh thought Kihin was trembling. Chali met Roh's look, eyes wide, and gave a single shake of his head. Roh knew that look, that gesture – shut up, he was saying. Don't run into this. Don't make a mess of it.

Roh gazed at the sanisi. He called up the litany he would need: a vortex about the size of the room, a vortex whose heart he and the other Dhai could stand safely within for... as long as he could hold them.

"I will not have traitors in my house," the Patron said. He made a cutting gesture with his hand.

The sanisi beside the Patron stepped forward. They took hold of Chali and pushed him against the table.

"No, no!" Roh said. Kihin grabbed his tunic. Held him back.

The sanisi made Chali put both of his palms on the table.

"You're the lucky messenger," the Patron said to Chali. "You are spared for one purpose. You will go back to your scheming Kai and tell him I uncovered his treachery and meted out justice. Tell him his spies are all dead, and I look forward to seeing these invaders destroy his country as they have destroyed mine." He gestured to the sanisi.

They cut off Chali's hands. Chali screamed.

Roh tried to charge forward, but a blue curtain of Para's breath came down in front of the table.

"Remove the messenger," the Patron said.

The sanisi dragged Chali from the room screaming. Roh heard his screaming from the hall. Blood leaked across the room.

"This is not necessary," Dasai said. "These are children–"

"Kill them," the Patron said.

Roh pulled on Para, so much, so quickly, his head buzzed and his skin burned.

A wall of air thumped into his chest. He was flying. Roh smacked hard into the far wall. The breath left his body.

The blades came down quickly. They took Dasai's head from his body. Roh saw a great gout of blood. Nioni and Aramey were run through by the sanisi flanking them.

Kihin bolted between them to the doors, toward Roh. Roh clawed toward him, gasping for air. The air around him trembled. He recited the Litany of the Palisade to create a shield of air to cut off the sanisi from him and Kihin.

Kihin slammed into another wall of air. Not Roh's. Roh heard Kihin's head crack on the floor. Saw blood. The sanisi descended on him. Black coats flapped. Blades flashed.

Roh yanked the doors open. Four more sanisi burst in. Roh

scrambled away. It was like something from a terrible dream. He saw Kadaan at the head of them, blue blade drawn. He moved Roh out of his way with a broad motion of his hand, sending a gout of misty blue air his way. It knocked Roh to the floor.

The Patron's sanisi met Kadaan's group with a heavy whump of air and clash of blades and maelstrom of blue haze.

Kihin lay on the floor, bleeding out. The air in the room condensed. It was like swimming through honey.

Roh pulled Kihin into his arms. Blood pumped from multiple wounds in his chest. Roh remembered holding his own wounded belly, the way Kihin was grasping now at his.

"Don't die," Roh said. His voice sounded deep and syrupy in the thick air.

Kihin's blood pooled across the floor. A dead sanisi thumped beside him. Roh flinched.

Kihin struggled. His mouth moved, like a gasping fish. "Please don't die," Roh said. "It's my fault. I'm sorry."

Kihin went still.

Kadaan and two of his sanisi had cornered the Patron. Ten dead sanisi littered the room, more than Roh ever thought could die. They were speaking too fast for Roh to understand.

Roh looked across the bodies of his friends. Dasai, who had escaped this place and then died in it, Kihin, who was spared exile and then run through, and Aramey and Nioni mangled together in a twisted heap, their work cut short. All for nothing. They had achieved nothing.

Roh crawled over to the dead sanisi beside Aramey and Nioni. The man's infused blade still lay in his hand, glowing with a faint blue light.

The voices of the sanisi thundered in his mind.

Roh took up the infused blade. Pain burst up his arm. He saw his skin blister. It was not his weapon, and he suspected it would punish him for it. He hefted it aloft before the hilt could grow around his wrist. A cold litany burned in his mind. He wrapped the weapon in Para's breath and threw it with all his strength.

The blade flew straight and true. It split the sanisi next to Kadaan, then buried itself in the Patron's chest. The Patron took flight. He careened across the room and was pinned to the wall above the bed. He huffed out a great spray of blood.

"Kadaan!" A woman's voice, from the hall.

Kadaan met Roh's gaze. It was a hot, terrifying moment.

Kadaan's blade came up. He jumped onto the bed. He tore open the Patron's shirt. The Patron pushed at him weakly, grunting.

Maralah burst into the room, weapon drawn.

She was just in time to see Kadaan yank the Patron's fibrous, pulsing heart from his chest.

"Lord of Unmaking!" she said.

Kadaan threw the Patron's spongy heart to her feet.

They stared at one another across the long length of the room, the bodies of the sanisi and Dhai between them. Roh dared not move.

"You can't take the title any more than I can," Maralah said, breathless. "Was this your plan all along? Because you won't ascend that seat."

Kadaan leapt from the bed. His weapon was still out. The Patron's body hung behind him, limp. Kadaan pointed to Roh. "I claim the boy as a victory spoil," he said. "He's under my protection."

"You have no victory," Maralah said. "The victory is my brother's. He'll sit this seat before a sanisi ever will."

"I will support Captain General Daonia," Kadaan said, "and you, as I have in all things. But this boy, this one thing, this is mine, Maralah."

Something passed between them. It was a look Roh had seen them give one another in the courtyard, before a spar. Roh realized he was trembling. Waves of pain still ebbed and flowed across his hand, fire.

"So be it," Maralah said.

Only then did Kadaan sheathe his weapon.

"How long do we have?" Kadaan said.

"My brother's army is at the gate," Maralah said. "You've made things much worse. We'll have to purge the harem now. The nursery. I'll have Driaa activate our people below. And you," – she narrowed her eyes – "you meet my brother with me at the gate. Come. Now. Leave the boy."

Maralah ran out of the room.

Kadaan came to Roh's side. His hands were smeared with the Patron's blood. He took Roh by the shoulders. His look was intense.

"I'm sorry I–" Roh began.

"You belong to me," Kadaan said. "Do you know what that means?"

"No," Roh said.

"It means if they hurt you, they hurt me. If we are successful downstairs, that may mean something. If not, and I'm dead, well... someone else will try to claim you. If that happens, run. Go to Anjoliaa. Find a ship to Dhai."

"I can help you downstairs. I'm a fighter, I–"

"Stay here. No matter what happens. This murder, what you see here? These bodies are nothing compared to what is about to happen below. Stay here, puppy."

"But my brother–"

"You can do nothing for him now."

"I need to find Chali."

"Go now and you'll die with him," Kadaan said.

"Why did you protect me?" Roh said.

"If she knew it was you who killed him..." Kadaan shook his head. "By law, you'd be Patron. And she would have killed you for it."

"Instead, you own me? Is that better?"

"One can escape slavery," Kadaan said, "but death is permanent."

"You can't keep me from going after Chali," Roh said. "You try it. You try to–"

"You won't run," Kadaan said.

Roh pushed past him to the door.

"If you run," Kadaan said, "if you die with your brother, you'll never learn to be a sanisi. And that's what you want, isn't it? More than anything. Even now. It's why you came to watch me fight. It's why you came to Saiduan. You are not a boy of books."

Roh pressed his hands to the door. His eyes filled. He wanted to call on Para and burn himself into nothing. He had made his own fate, and this is where it led him. To die with his brother... or become a Saiduan slave. He said, "Why, Kadaan?"

"You remind me of someone."

"Someone you killed?"

"Nothing so romantic," Kadaan said. He came up behind Roh and gently pressed his hands to Roh's shoulders. "I'm sorry," he said, "but this is what can be done now. What happens after is up to you." He released Roh and slipped out the doors.

Roh went back to the center of the room and stood amid a pool of blood and bodies. He sagged to his knees. He was shaking so hard, his teeth chattered. He was better than this. Stronger than this. He took a deep breath and forced himself to look at Dasai's headless body.

Dasai's head lay beneath the table. The letter Roh had written to the Kai had fallen to the floor beside Aramey's body where it lay with Nioni's, just to the left of Dasai. The letter was speckled in blood.

Roh crawled forward and took up the letter. "Why did you do that?" Roh whispered to Dasai's still form. Roh still believed he could have talked the Patron down. He could have made up a better story. He could have been witty and charming. Somehow, he could have made this all right. He thought of Chali's horrified face. Saw his brother's hands still on the battered table, forgotten.

Roh felt something tugging at his trousers. He jerked his leg back.

Aramey's bloody fingers reached for him.

Roh dragged himself forward and took Aramey's hand. "You're alive!" Roh cried. "We'll find Chali and-"

"Caasa Mingaaine," Aramey said, and his fingers went lax. He lost consciousness again.

"Who is that?" Roh asked. He shook him. "Who is that? Aramey?"

Silence.

It took another hour for Aramey to die.

Some part of Roh died with him.

42

Lord General Rajavaa Daonia expected to hear a good many horrible things from his sister Maralah. She had been the harbinger of terrible news since he was three years old, when she told him their mother had drowned herself in drink and again in the icy river that bordered their equally icy village.

When he saw her face as she descended the thorny spiral of the stairwell in Kuonrada's drafty main hall now, he recognized the look. The year before, she had borne the same look when she told him that their village had been inundated by foreign invaders with the faces of Dhai. They had butchered what remained of their extended family, including the grandparents who had raised them after their mother's death.

Maralah was an ugly woman, which was a blessing in her chosen profession, but he still winced when he saw the look on her ugly face. Perhaps it reminded him that he was less handsome than he believed. Or perhaps it just made her death-look more distasteful. He had seen far more distasteful things in the field these last four years, but that face... that face still made him cold.

They met at the bottom of the stair. His best friend and second, Morsaar Koryn, stood with him. Rajavaa rested the flat of his hand against his hip, and canted his pelvis forward. It was a southern affectation he had picked up at parties with titled lords in the south. Maralah turned her nose up at him every time he did it. But if it annoyed her now, she gave no sign.

"Let's hear it," he said.

"Alone," she said.

"Anything you can tell me–"

"Alone," Maralah said.

Rajavaa sighed and waved Morsaar away. The man grimaced and gave a little bow. Rajavaa knew he'd hear of it later.

"I'll see that the men are settled in," Morsaar said.

"Thank you," Rajavaa said. When he was gone, Rajavaa said to Maralah, "I'm exhausted; can we make this–"

She took his arm, and pulled him to her. She lowered her voice.

"You're about to become Patron of Saiduan," she said.

He stiffened.

She continued, "Alaar is dead."

"Whose hand?"

"Yours."

"Who, Maralah? This has your smell on it." The Patron's minister of war had been killed six seasons before, and that left the Patron with Maralah as confidant. Rajavaa always wondered if that was her doing or just happy circumstance.

"One of the sanisi."

"An oath-breaker? Didn't you cast out the last sanisi to break his vow?"

"Taigan's indiscretion was very public. In this case, you and I are the only ones to know. We've kept it quiet, waiting on your return."

"No witnesses, then?"

He saw her hesitate. Her large mouth firmed slightly. Just enough.

"No," she said. "Just me."

Her, the sanisi, and a dozen slaves, more likely. Rajavaa said, "You do have a way of sitting on the seat without wearing the cowl."

"I could never harm Alaar," she said, "but others are not so gutless. He was going to hold our ground here. Kuonrada was to be the final stand."

"We don't have enough to hold Kuonrada."

"I know that. His sanisi know that. I believe he knew it as well. But it's been a long war, and he wanted to go out at a place of his choosing."

"So you killed him."

"No," Maralah said. "You did."

"Milk and tits, Maralah, I can't–"

"We're purging the harem and nursery now, and eliminating the sanisi who will not follow you. I recommend you marry Arisaa, his favorite. She's from Anjoliaa. We'll need them."

"I can't be Patron, Maralah."

"You will," she said. "Who else is there? It can't be a sanisi. He only has two adult sons left, and they're in the far north, already targeted by the invaders. They'll be dead in a month. They have no army. Your force is the largest standing company we still have, and we can grow it as we retreat south."

"It's not the right time," he said.

"When you see what's been done upstairs, you'll disagree," she said. "His family is already slaughtered. If you don't take up this mantle now, this hold will descend into chaos, and what remains of the country with it. Divided, we'll be destroyed in three months. With you to lead us, we could last three years."

"A year at best."

"Three, if you take my counsel."

He narrowed his eyes. "I like breathing too much not to take your counsel."

"Then we are in agreement."

"I can't, Maralah."

"Lords why? You can't tell me you haven't thought of it. I'm handing it to you now, Rajavaa. I held this coup for just the right moment. There are people dead upstairs, my people. I have twenty dead women in this harem and forty children–"

Rajavaa stared at Maralah's bloody boots. She had done it, then. Done the thing she always told him she would. When she was accepted into sanisi training, she told him, "Someday, you will be Patron, and I will be your sanisi." A lifetime ago. It was her idea to leave their village together, to travel to far-off Caisau to become sanisi. He had failed the training – he was not gifted – and joined the military instead. Not because he had a passion for it, but because he needed to eat.

Someday, you will be Patron...

He had never doubted it. He prepared for it. His men loved him. They flocked to him like bees to honey. He loved them like a father, a brother, a lover, a friend. He was all things to them. But he had not anticipated this long war of attrition and what it would do to the country and to him. For the last decade, he had marched them to their deaths each day and drowned himself in drink every night, just like his mother.

"I have the rot, Maralah."

Her grip on his arm tightened. "You don't," she said.

He showed his teeth. "They tell me it's the drink," he said. "Blew out my guts. No way to fix it until Tira's ascendant, and I won't last that long."

"How long?" she said.

"A year, maybe two," he said.

"That's long enough."

"I'll be vomiting blood before the end," he said. He pulled his arm away.

She leaned into him. Pressed her forehead to his, the way she had when they were children. "I can get it fixed," she said. "If I tell you I can fix it, will you do it?"

He choked on a laugh. "You're mad. There's no way to–"

"We have omajistas. I have one out on an assignment who can fix it."

"Lords, you don't mean Taigan?"

"Alaar is dead," she said, "so it's up to you to pardon Taigan. I give you a few extra years, and you spend that time keeping our people together. What's it hurt, if you weren't even going to have those years anyway?"

"You would call him to help even if I wasn't going to be Patron."

"Would I?" she said.

Her tone chilled him. "You insult me," he said. "When have you ever had to threaten me?"

"These are dark times, brother."

"And you need my army."

"Saiduan needs your army."

Rajavaa closed his eyes. He could not bear to look at her face so close. It reminded him too much of their mother's face. He wondered if that was what made it so ugly.

"Call your omajista," he said.

"Come upstairs, Patron," she said, and pulled away.

43

Lilia turned Gian's care over to Emlee long before the woman regained consciousness. She knew it could not be the same Gian, but her heart had swelled at the sight of her, and that frightened Lilia too much for words. A week after seeing Gian again, Lilia sat alone in the meeting house at the center of the camp, huddled in a tattered coat and new mittens Emlee had made her. It was far too late for her to be out alone, but the day after prayer days, members of the camp congregated to drink homebrewed liquor and tell stories. The warmth and camaraderie reminded her of the temple.

As she listened to the drunken rambling of the young man on the stage, she noticed a tall woman walk into the room. She had a bold, regal face and broad shoulders. She was too skinny for her big frame and had the hollowed look of those who had spent some time in the camps. There was something in the kiss of her mouth that reminded Lilia of someone. The woman's hair was a spill of black knotted at the back of her head, very long and well kept.

It was Gian. A thinner, warier version of Gian. She did not have the same confident walk or lustrous skin as the woman Lilia watched die in the mountains.

Gian came over to her. She wore a skirt that was too short for her, and her ankles were muddy.

Lilia tensed. She looked straight ahead.

Gian sat next to her.

"I know you," Gian said.

"I'm sorry," Lilia said. "All the things I did, it didn't-"

"You're the one who saved me," Gian said. Her voice was very soft, much softer than Lilia remembered, and she had a Dorinah accent, the same accent all the Dhai had when speaking the patois of the camps.

Another man took the stage. He told the tale of Faith Ahya's death. Lilia had heard the dajian version before. It was different from the one in Dhai, where Faith died in childbed, birthing the first Kai and ushering in Dhai's five hundred years of peace. In the version here, she was betrayed by her lover and confidant, beheaded and spiked up on the ramparts of Daorian long after her child was born. Lilia did not like the story, not until the end. Because at the end of this story, Faith Ahya flew.

"I'm Gian," the woman said. "You remember me? You and Emlee cleaned me up, my leg. I was half mad, I think."

"Oh," Lilia said. "You aren't Gian."

"But I am."

Lilia remembered what Gian had said about her twin having a double in this world. This was, of course, not Lilia's Gian. It was the twin Gian would have had if she'd been born under a lavender sky.

"I'm sorry. Yes," Lilia said. "Of course you're Gian."

Gian frowned and hunched her shoulders. "I understand if you don't want to talk to me," she said. "It's just that you're a temple Dhai. I thought you must be different."

"Because you betrayed the Empress?"

"It isn't like that."

Lilia gestured to the stage. "You should tell them your story."

"My story is mine," Gian said.

"We're one people," Lilia said.

"You really are a temple Dhai."

"Yes."

"You have yet to tell a story here, either," Gian said. "I know. I've been standing at the back, watching to see if you'll speak."

"Why didn't you come up to me before?"

Gian's color deepened. "I was afraid."

"Of what?"

"This," Gian said.

Lilia shifted in her seat and tried to think of something else to say. "I don't think they'd be interesting, my stories. Mostly, I tell stories about what I've read."

Gian spoke softly into her ear, "I think you could spin a beautiful story."

"I–"

Gian pressed her hand to Lilia's. She had strong hands with long, slender fingers. Just like the other Gian. Lilia stared at their joined fingers.

Lilia withdrew her hand. "You should ask first," she said. "I'm not a dajian."

"I apologize," Gian said. "I want to know the woman who saved me. Most of these people would have let me die."

"Emlee–"

"It's your face I remember."

Lilia looked into Gian's eyes. Dark eyes. The same as the Gian she had watched hack through the undergrowth in the Woodland. It was unsettling.

"Tell me a story," Gian said.

The man on the stage reached the end of his story.

Lilia stood. She had done so much else. Why not tell a story, a real one, instead of pretending?

Lilia walked up onto the stage and looked out over the long rows of benches. She felt different up there. Taller. Stronger. She could be anyone, up there. The three or four dozen people before her looked cold and tired, but their eyes were bright – mostly with drink – and only a few were talking among themselves.

"I once made my mother a promise," Lilia said, "and I still intend to keep it."

It was an easy story. She thought it would make her sound brave. But as she spun out a story of Roh's arrogant swagger and

Taigan's sour sense of humor, she felt like she was telling the story of someone who *could* be brave, if only she let go of all the bloody things that came before her, and forged some path not constrained by old promises.

Lilia finished her story at the point when she fled from the sanisi and started down the road to Kalinda's. She could not say much more, because that's when Gian entered her story. The real Gian.

As she left the stage, Gian's twin walked toward her.

"It was a fine story," Gian said. "Did that really happen?"

"Yes."

"Then how did you end up here?"

"I made a lot of bad choices," Lilia said. "Can we be friends, do you think?"

"I don't know you."

"No one really knows anyone. Do you have a better place to go?"

Gian shook her head.

"Then come with me," Lilia said. "I'll protect you." Which sounded strange when she said it, because she had done so poor a job of protecting herself. But it was something Faith Ahya would say.

Lilia invited Gian home to live with her, though Emlee made faces and Cora turned up her nose. At night, she watched the light play across Gian's fine face but dared not touch her.

Sometimes, she thought of the girl torn asunder by the gate. She knew, gazing into Gian's gaunt, tired face, that despite her horror at the girl's death, she would do it again to save herself, to have this moment. The Oras would say it was the direst kind of selfishness. Oma would eat her; Sina would not collect her soul.

But Lilia had no soul. She wasn't even of this world.

More people began to come to Emlee's door, but no longer solely for the help of Emlee. They asked about Lilia. They asked her to tell stories and mend their flesh while she did it. Emlee told her that storytelling could get her new shoes, more food, vials of everpine to scrub the lice from her hair and clothing. And those things could buy her respect, too. Even more respect than she was earning from mending broken bones and fevers and delivering babies.

So Lilia told stories. All the old stories from the books she read in the temples, and the history lessons she learned from Dasai and Chali. And when she ran out of those, she made some up. She began to ask for scraps of white cloth instead of payment. When she went home each night, she spent an hour sewing the pieces together into a dress, which she kept folded up and hidden beneath her pillow.

Gian listened to all of Lilia's stories, even the ones about Aaldian merchants who led rebellions and dog thieves who became empresses.

"Why did you come to me?" Lilia asked her one night.

"You have a very memorable face," Gian said, tracing the karoi scars on her cheek.

Lilia flinched. "You should ask."

"I'm sorry."

"What happened to your leg? You haven't said."

"There are some stories that don't want telling," Gian said. "Some stories you tell, they make things worse. Not better."

Lilia didn't ask again, even when Emlee confronted her about it some days later.

"That woman's a danger," Emlee said. "They don't dump dajians there for just anything. She clings to you for your reputation and your warm bed. Don't think it's more than that."

"You don't know her," Lilia said. "Or me."

"Better than some man, I suppose," Emlee said. "There's only so much you can clean out of a womb. But you watch her, Lilia. She wants you for more than your quick tongue."

Lilia spent hours combing out Gian's long hair. Gian tried to endear herself to Emlee and Cora and Larn by bringing them food, warm tea, clean water. Larn was still often gone, consorting with the man she called a priest and his priestesses, though Lilia doubted any of them was any such thing. Larn came home from those meetings pale and drawn, and Gian made her tea.

As high winter dragged on, Gian presented her with a gift: eight white ribbons in a little box.

"Where did you get these?" Lilia asked.

"They will go with your dress," Gian said.

"You don't know what the dress is for," Lilia said.

"I know you'll tell me when you're ready to."

Lilia kept the ribbons with the dress and sat up at night imagining that she could fly.

The days spun out. As winter hinted at low spring, the camp began to stir with rumors of other camps. Camps purged by bloody legionnaires.

"There have been rumors for months," Emlee said one night while Cora cooked dinner. "About the other camps. Refugees, sometimes. But they won't kill us all. Who would care for their children? Who would work in their fields?"

"Why don't you leave?" Lilia asked.

Emlee glanced at Cora, who guffawed. Cora said, "And go where? To Dhai? You think they'd let us through the pass? You think it hasn't been tried?"

"They'd let you in," Lilia said.

Emlee said, "My mother died at those gates during the Pass War. This is our place. We will die in it, if we must. Birth is everyone's beginning. Death is everyone's end. Doesn't much matter where you do it."

Lilia left her with a poultice of everroot and strawberry and started toward the dwelling of her next case. She waved to those she passed. They greeted her by name. It was still strange to be seen.

She walked in a filthy, tattered skirt and tunic, on shoes that were no longer Cora's but her own. Gian had combed out her hair and worked it into a whirl of braids knotted in colorful string, the way Gian said she had done the hair of noble Dorinah women.

Lilia heard the muttering slosh of footsteps approaching, and turned to see one of the bands of orphans running toward her.

"There's a man asking for you!" one of the children yelled.

Lilia stilled her steps. The rider rounded a collection of tents just behind the children. The rider wore black. The hilt of a blade stuck through the back of his coat. He called his bear to a halt and dismounted.

"You look terrible," Taigan said in Dorinah. He had a new scar running from his left cheek to his left ear, and there was something different about him, something in his voice and posture.

"So you can fly after all, can you?" Taigan said.

"I can," Lilia said.

"I'd very much like to see that," Taigan said. "There are legionnaires outside the gate. One of them is passing about a picture of you. It won't be long until someone turns you over."

"They won't," Lilia said.

"Won't they?"

"No," Lilia said. She looked at the wide-eyed children and remembered her mother's hands and her mother's face back at the lake, when she said Lilia was not her daughter.

Lilia said, "These are my people. I'm not going anywhere without them."

"The woman with your picture says she's your mother," Taigan said. "Isn't that what you wanted?"

"We'll see about that."

"I think you may be mad," Taigan said.

"No," Lilia said. "I'm a bird. And we're going to fly away from here."

44

Zezili rode Dakar into the camp at the mouth of the pass to Dhai with Jasoi and two pages close at her heels. Isoail and four more legionnaires met them on the muddy field outside the sprawl of stinking tents and blocky housing. Monshara only gave her an hour before every purge to find the girl, and they were already forty minutes into it.

"They say they don't know her," Isoail said, "but their eyes say differently. They also say there's a sanisi in there."

"Dajians will say anything," Zezili said, "especially to legionnaires."

"There's only one more camp after this," Isoail said. "If she isn't there, then we've come–"

Zezili shushed her and pointed. A small group of dajians was moving toward them from the camp.

Isoail sat a little straighter. Zezili felt the air shift. "Gifted are culled from the camps," Zezili said, "and shipped off to your Seeker Sanctuary. The most they'll do is throw stones."

"A well-thrown stone is equally deadly," Isoail said.

Zezili shrugged. She was cold and tired and more than a little sick of Isoail. They had spent all winter slaughtering dajians across Dorinah. Every public-owned dajian from here to the sea was dead. It was just this camp at the base of the Liona Mountains and another farther south, close to the range that separated Dorinah from Aaldia. With every dead dajian and every cold day, Zezili lost a little more hope. She had nightmares about Anavha being swallowed by a great winged beast, and Daorian burning.

A short girl with a dragging walk led the group. With her were a tall, thin woman, a young boy, and a square-jawed old woman. It was one of the most pathetic groups of people Zezili had ever seen. They wore patched, worn clothing. As they approached, Zezili caught a whiff of them on the wind and grimaced.

But the limping girl's face did indeed bear a resemblance to Isoail's drawing. The girl at the front stopped abruptly a few paces from them. She looked up at them with a neutral, unreadable expression. The scars were right, Zezili decided. It was the girl from the lake.

"So, today you decided you're my mother," the girl said to Isoail. "Do you even know my name?"

"We don't have a lot of time to catch up," Zezili said. "You know what you are?"

"I do," the girl said. "Do you?"

"We're going to open a gate," Zezili said, "to another world. Your world. I need you to come with us."

"Why?"

"Because this woman can't," Zezili said, gesturing to Isoail. "Your real mother is still alive on the other side. That's why I can't send this one here."

"My mother is dead."

"I wish that were so," Zezili said. "It would have made this month a lot easier."

The girl knit her brows. "This is some trick," she said.

"Not a trick," Isoail said. "There are people coming here. If you came through the lake, you know that. We're asking for your help to stop them."

"Quite a joke," said the old woman. "Who are you to these people, Lilia?"

So, she had a name. Zezili began to doubt her whole plan. A month of sweating out each night, waiting for Monshara to find her out, and killing squealing dajians all day might have impaired her judgment. What, she was just going to ask this girl to destroy the mirror from her own world? What if she was an agent?

Zezili sighed. An agent looking for her mother, Zezili? she thought, and firmed her resolve.

"Here's what we're going to do," Zezili said. "The people that want yours dead? They told me to murder this camp and all the other ones, from here to the Sagasarian Sea. And I can stop them. But for reasons that might get clearer later, you can help us delay them awhile. Your mother, your real one, built something in that other world that we need to destroy. Your fake mother here thinks you can dismantle it."

Lilia's eyes widened. It was an expression, at least. Better than the grim neutrality she'd been fronting. The girl licked her lips and glanced at the tall young woman beside her.

"How do we get there?" Lilia said.

Zezili let out her breath. She showed her teeth. "You can all come back here with me," she said. "We need blood to power the gate."

"Whose blood?" Lilia asked. She took a step back.

"Not you," Zezili said. "You and your little friends here, we can spare them. We'll just need a few hundred from the camp. They'd have died anyway. I have orders to kill them. What I'm offering you is a chance to live and save the rest. Take it or leave it."

Zezili had never been a good negotiator.

"You're not going to hurt these people," Lilia said.

Isoail sighed. "I'm sorry, child, but sacrifices have to be made. It will take the blood of many just to open a gate and keep it open, but you'll find your mother. Your true one."

"Sometimes, a few have to die," Zezili said, "so a lot more can live. I like my country, little girl. I like having you all around to do the work. We saved you from yourselves. Now I can save you again, but only if you'll cooperate."

"You're not saving me," Lilia said. "You're saving your way of life. It has nothing to do with me, except in how much you can control my people."

"I tried to make this easy," Zezili said. She nodded to Jasoi and the squad of women with her. "Take these ones out of the camp. I'll call in the legion and clean out the rest."

"You need bodies?" Lilia said. "I'll give you bodies." Zezili hardly heard her.

But she certainly felt the blast of heat that knocked her from Dakar.

"No," Lilia said. Her rage had been bubbling since they crossed the camp to meet the legionnaires. Now it burned white-hot, so vicious and hungry that it blurred her vision. Beyond the little group of legionnaires were hundreds more. Row upon row of them. Dorinahs who had been murdering her people forever, for a thousand years or more. They had cast out Gian and corralled Emlee and Cora here. How many uprisings had there been over the centuries? Thousands, surely. But it was these women who put them down. Who kept them slaves.

They would not touch one more.

Something opened inside her. A blazing red haze cloaked her vision. Lilia gasped. Her lungs opened. Air rushed in, more than her poor asthmatic lungs had ever been able to draw – air and something more, something hot and vicious that burned beneath her skin like fire.

Fire.

"You need bodies?" Lilia rasped. "I'll give you bodies."

She breathed out. Pressed her hands forward. She expelled the burst of bloody power from her body.

For a moment, her vision cleared. She dropped her hands. Nothing was different. Was she having some kind of hallucination? Was she ill?

The first line of legionnaires circling the camp burst into flame.

The wave of heat was so intense, it blew Lilia back onto her rump. The legionnaires mounted next to them were blown off their dogs.

Lilia gasped and clawed away from them. Her body twitched and jerked. The heat was intense. It felt like she was on fire. Then,

her vision went bloody again. Her lungs filled. The heat of some
foreign thing, some other substance, some other breath, moved
beneath her skin. She had to get rid of it. She didn't know what to
do with it. Sweat soaked her clothes. The muddy snow all around
them had melted. It was a morass of warm, stinking mud. Where
was Gian? Gian and Emlee and Emlee's nephew Sorat needed to
get away from her. Far, far away. She was going to explode, going
to burn from the inside out.

Lilia turned. Raised her hands. Focused on the line of screaming
legionnaires. Breathed out.

The burning air left her body. Her skin cooled. She huffed out
another breath, a real one this time.

Another burst of fire exploded inside the ranks of the legionnaires.
Women's screams carried across the fence.

Lilia gasped. She needed the safety of the camp. She needed to
get away from the fire. Her body ached. She was shaking so hard,
her teeth rattled.

"Oma protect me and guide me," she muttered, an old prayer,
something her mother had taught her. "Bring light when there is
darkness, show me the shape of the new world, cleanse us in fire
and water, show us the–"

"Lilia!"

Taigan's voice.

She squinted. The bloody haze was coming again. Oma, Oma,
please stop, she thought, please stop.

Taigan slid off his bear and pressed his hand to Lilia's chest.
"The song, Lilia, the Song of One Breath, the one I taught you,"
he said.

Lilia's teeth chattered.

Taigan shook her. "You're burning up, Lilia. You'll murder
everyone here."

"Let them burn," she growled.

Taigan slapped her.

"You will not hurt me again!" Lilia pressed her hands forward.
The air around her grew heavy. Mud splattered. She let forth a

burst of power. It met Taigan's misty red wall of air. Blew back at him, past him, toward the legionnaires who met them in the camp.

The woman called Zezili had made her group lie in the mud and put their hands over their heads. Lilia's wave of heat engulfed their mounts instead. The dogs yipped and shrieked.

"You'll burn us all up and yourself!" Taigan said. "The Song of One Breath. Say it. Feel it. You'll burn yourself out right here and that will be the end of all this bright power. Do you understand?"

"Lord Oma," Lilia muttered, "Lord of mercy, lord of light..."

"Heads down! Stay down!" Zezili yelled. She kept her hands over her head as the wave of heat moved over them. "Isoail! Get me my gate!"

"Are you mad?" Isoail cried. "She's going to burn out. She'll turn us to pulp!"

"Open the gate!"

"You won't get her in."

Zezili peered across the mud to where the girl lay with some tall Saiduan. Her companions had scattered.

"Open it up right behind them!" Zezili yelled. She chanced a look over her shoulder. The air around them was heavy as spoiled milk. She saw the shimmering heat of her blazing women begin to ebb. The cries faded. She heard the roar of a vortex. Monshara would be calling up her omajistas to retaliate now. Zezili had every intention of annihilating this little girl when she was done with her, wreaking vengeance on her for every good woman gone.

But she wasn't done yet.

"Zezili," Jasoi said, "The legion—"

"Keep your shit-soaked head down," Zezili said. "If my women remembered anything, that second wave kept their blighted heads down."

Zezili had spent two decades fighting the gifted and mundane alike. When they went off, it was best to separate and stay low while the Seekers picked them off. It was easy to kill great groups, but destroying individuals took more time and concentration. Winning against magic required fast reflexes and stealth. Hitting hard and unexpectedly was the only way to keep breathing.

She had guessed the girl's ability was latent. She just hoped to keep it that way until she shoved her in front of the mirror. If she hit something hard enough, it was supposed to fall in line. So it was time to hit harder.

"Isoail!"

"Stupid woman," Isoail spat.

"We'll all be dead in twenty minutes anyway," Zezili said. "Open the fucking gate!"

The air crackled. It got so thick, Zezili gulped air like water; it was like trying to breathe molasses. A whirling vortex moved over her, carrying with it a bloody crimson mist that rained across Zezili's body. She kept her head covered, for all the good it did, and kept her eyes on the space behind the girl and the sanisi.

She needed a distraction.

The whirling tornado of blood coalesced just behind the girl and the sanisi. The Saiduan raised his head, his attention fixed on the swirling blood.

Zezili tensed. "You have your dagger on you, Jasoi?"

"Yes, Syre."

"When I say, you hit that Saiduan's neck. You understand?"

"He'll chop me in two!"

"I'll do worse if you don't!" Zezili said. "Throw the knife. I'll take the girl through. You have the legion."

"Syre, this isn't–"

"Take the legion!" Zezili said. "They're my women, and I'm giving them to you until I get back. You understand? Now throw the knife."

"Zezili!" Isoail called.

"Just open it," Zezili said, "and close it behind me."

"How are you going to get back?" Isoail asked.

"Let me deal with that. Jasoi?"

Jasoi still hadn't moved. The gate flickered into existence.

"Curse you to Rhea's seat!" Zezili said. She looked back at Jasoi. She was whispering what sounded like prayers in Tordinian. "Now, Jasoi, or we've lost more than the legion!"

Jasoi pulled her knife from her boot. Bared her teeth. She jumped up and threw the knife.

Zezili hurled herself forward.

The knife hit the Saiduan in the neck.

Zezili spread her arms. She was ten feet away.

The Saiduan clutched at his neck. Blood gushed. He yanked the knife out.

Zezili scooped up the girl under her arms and hurled herself through the winking gateway.

She landed hard on the other side. Looked back. The Saiduan stood. The blood on his neck ceased to flow. As Zezili watched, the wound began to close. He didn't look pleased.

"Close the fucking gate!" Zezili yelled. "Isoail! Close it! Close it now!"

The Saiduan stepped forward–

–and thumped into the invisible film between the worlds. He pressed his hands against the air and snarled. No, he did not look pleased at all.

Zezili laughed so hard, she began to hiccup. She rolled around in the charred dirt on the other side, snickering and hiccupping. "You're still alive over here!" she crowed. "Still alive!"

The gate winked out.

Zezili's mirth left with it. She stared across a blasted landscape of black hills. The sky was a rust-red along the horizon and amber-gold above her. But she saw no tower and no mirror. Fear seized her. She turned and looked across the body of the girl she'd dragged to the other side. The landscape flattened out, shot through with old bones and bits of glittering armor. She stumbled past the girl to a nearby hill. She crawled to the top and gazed across the field. In the far distance, she saw a glint of blue.

The tower. The same one she had described to Isoail. In the valley beyond the tower would be the mirror. Just to the east

– east? – of the tower, a massive black specter stained the sky, oozing black tendrils behind it. The sight of the thing made Zezili's skin crawl. She went back down the hill.

The girl was standing now. Zezili could hear her heavy breathing from almost ten feet away.

"Welcome to the other side," Zezili said. "Follow me." She started toward the tower.

"I'll kill you," the girl said.

Zezili turned. She put her hands on her hips. The girl was hunched over and hollow-eyed. From the sound of her labored breath, it would be a good long time before she recovered.

"This isn't the first time I've fought with a new channeler," Zezili said. "It'll be awhile before you can pull again, and when you do, there's a good chance you'll either burn out like a roaring scorch pod or lose that great gift of yours altogether. Fried nerves, Tulana calls it."

"I'll take you with me," the girl said.

"True," Zezili said. "You might." She pointed to the tower. "You crossed worlds to find the woman over there. You won't give it up now, will you?"

"I'm going to kill you," the girl said, "and everyone like you."

"You're not the first to tell me that," Zezili said. "Are you coming?"

Lilia limped after the legionnaire. Her lungs burned and her body ached. She could barely see straight. She kept seeing the bloody haze flit across her vision. The air here felt strange. She stopped after a few paces to vomit.

The legionnaire, Zezili, urged her on.

She wasn't sure how long they walked until she realized they were following the scent of something. Maybe it wasn't a scent but a… breath. She saw a reddish haze floating on the air. At first, she thought it was her eyes again, but it was a trail of red, not a gauze across her vision. As they walked, the trail got thicker, heavier. Lilia put out her hands, expecting to feel a damp mist, like the blood that had merged to form the gate. But she felt nothing. She even tasted the air.

"What are you doing?" Zezili asked.

Lilia had stuck her tongue out. "The red mist," she said. "Don't you see it?"

"No," Zezili said. "That's what gifted people see. When people use your star to make something."

Lilia shook her head. "I'm not... I... Oh."

"You murdered my women back there," Zezili said, "and it wasn't with air. You've got the dark star in your blood. It's crept in, and it's not going away."

Lilia could see a blue tower ahead of them, at the bottom of the charred rise, and something beyond it. The hazy red trail continued on past the tower, toward a glint of silver-red metal that looked like some massive arch.

"It leads to the arch," Lilia said.

"The mirror," Zezili said. "Come and see what your mother made. It's how I knew she was alive. Isoail said her gates all opened here."

They walked together to the tower. Zezili drew her blade and went inside. Lilia waited in the foyer. Blue and amber tiles glinted from the floor.

Lilia turned away from the tower and walked around to the other side. In the valley below, she saw the full height of the mirror for the first time. It was at least as tall as the Temple of Oma. The border of the mirror glistened a startling ruby red. As Lilia stared at it, she couldn't even think of it as a mirror. It was a looking glass, a window onto another world. Inside the face of the mirror was another sky, another place. She knew that lavender-tinged sky. It was the world they had just come from. And it was where the swirling trail of red mist ended. The tails of red trailed off in every direction, breathy wisps leading out into the hills around the mirror.

And stretching beyond the face of the massive mirror, on and on across the hills for as far as she could see, the ground bristled with thousands... tens of thousands... hundreds of thousands of soldiers. It was the most massive army Lilia had ever seen... the Dhai army. The army in the valley. High red flags flew among them.

Zezili stepped up beside her. "Tower's empty," she said. "We're too late."

Lilia pointed to something at the top of the mirror, a strange, elongated figure that seemed to be moving. "What is that?" she said.

"I don't know," Zezili said. "Rhea's tits. Where are they sending this army? That's not tundra. That's not Saiduan."

Lilia stared at the figure. She watched the twisting strands of red mist that circled around the mirror, snaking up and up, to the captured figure at the top of the mirror. Lilia knew who it was immediately.

"This was a fucked idea from the start," Zezili said.

Lilia pointed to the figure at the top of the mirror. "That's my mother," she said.

45

Seventy-five Oras and one hundred militia from the Kuallina Stronghold arrived in Clan Raona six days after Ghrasia came back to the clan square. Ahkio stood with Ghrasia in the common room of the council house with twelve multicolored sparrow cages and a map of Dhai laid out on the table. Four of the cages were already empty, their sparrows attached to a fine string knotted to the wrist of an Ora, and four militia members and two more Oras were sent out to accompany each of them.

Ahkio hadn't slept the night before. He had sat up with Ghrasia, explaining how the invaders rising with Oma during this turn were not some foreign force, but some darker, different version of themselves. She had poured them both very strong drinks and passed out on the divan in his room. He had sat across from her for an hour, watching the light and shadow move across her face, before going downstairs to sleep in one of the oversized chairs. His back still hurt.

Liaro was out helping a group of day laborers store barrels of oil in the council house's cellar. Ahkio had called for a stop on all unescorted travel and commerce into or out of Raona for the duration of their hunt, which had put a pinch on warehouse space. While the teams went out, an additional force of Oras and militia were moving in from the perimeter they'd set up around the three surrounding clans. They used a wall of air to flush vagrants and exiles from the toxic surroundings of the clans, creeping their circle ever closer to Raona.

Ahkio took a sheaf of correspondence from Caisa as Ghrasia marked a spot on the map as clear. The runner who'd delivered the news was a young woman, maybe twenty, who looked at Ghrasia with such intense awe, it made Ahkio smile. Ghrasia hardly looked at her.

"Thank you," she said. "I'll need a run of this area here, near the old homestead that makes that fish meal. You remember it?"

"I do," the woman said.

"Good, thank you." Ghrasia raised her gaze. "That's all. You're dismissed."

The woman looked disappointed. She turned away.

When she was gone, Ahkio said, "You've made an impression on them here. A far better one than I have."

Ghrasia stared at the map. She moved two more markers forward, representing one of their teams along the perimeter. "It's midday. The other runner should be here by now." She began to move the other markers forward as well. Her hands were still wrapped in salve-soaked muslin, but the blisters had already healed. Raona had an especially sensitive tirajista in residence and a very fine physician. Ahkio suspected she wouldn't even have scars.

"Ghrasia, I–"

"How is the Catori, Kai?"

"Mohrai? At the harbor with her family, of course. Waiting on our orders."

"Good. We need more caution."

"You're one to talk of caution," he said. "You hunted–"

"I was just fulfilling my obligation to Dhai," she said. "Now we will flush them out."

"Have I done something to offend you?"

She finally looked up from the map. "Not at all," she said. "I apologize. A good boy died under my watch. I don't like death. It's my job to ensure there's less of it, not deal it out. And killing my own people... It's a difficult thing to live with."

"I'm sorry," Ahkio said. "I know how... I have an idea of how death can weigh on a person."

"Do you?" Ghrasia said. She peered at him. "Have you ever killed a person, Kai? Do you understand that killing these other Dhai is the same to me as killing you or Liaro?"

"I've sent enough people to their deaths. I agreed to this venture. These deaths are on me as much as you."

"I'm sorry. People say I'm too serious."

"I've heard that a few times myself."

"I'm better at leading people than dancing," she said.

"I'm actually a pretty fair dancer."

"I'm going to get an hour or so of sleep before the next runner comes in. You'll lock this door?"

"I will."

Ghrasia moved past him. Ahkio stepped away to let her pass and caught himself watching her form as she went by. He glanced back at the map on the table. Ghrasia had shared concerns about spies inside the clan square, so they had taken to locking the strategy room, and Ahkio posted a member of the militia at his door each night.

He took his correspondence back to his room. Clan Leader Talisa had given him her own room, and he was not fond of her style. The bed was big enough for four people; not an unusual thing in Dhai, but Talisa only had one spouse. Above the bed was a portrait of the Temple of Para and Talisa's great-grandmother, once the Elder Ora of that temple, and her family – six husbands, four wives, and twenty-one children. Ahkio found it oddly creepy but didn't have the heart to take it down. If Talisa saw that he'd removed it, she might see it as an insult.

Kirana and Yisaoh's trunks of papers were there, too. He'd spent hours with the temple maps and Kirana's strange notes, and still had no idea what she and the Garikas had been up to.

Ahkio started going through correspondence. He found two from Nasaka and left those to last. Buried in with the rest was a tattered piece of green paper with a return stamp made up of

Saiduan characters. He thought for a moment it was from Roh, but the handwriting looked too formal for a sixteen year-old boy. He broke the seal and read:

Kai Ahkio Javia Garika,

With a devastated soul, we remind you that treason against our Empire is dealt with swiftly. Your citizens have been given the full measure of compassion they deserve for committing the crime of deceit against the Empire of Saiduan. Their actions have resulted in the renunciation of their citizenship. They have become assets of the Empire. Their dishonesty invalidates all previous treaties, and we no longer require the assistance of the Commonwealth of Dhai now or in the future.

Know that your betrayal also constitutes an act of war. We show great mercy in meting out justice to your scholar-assassins but sparing the autonomy of your country. We would caution you to remember this mercy in any future interactions.

We remain,

Keeper Takanaa of Kuonrada for Patron Alaar Masoth Taar, Imperator of Saiduan, Father of the Eight-Point Commonwealth, Divine Light of Oma, Keeper of the Twelve Thresholds...

Ahkio did not make it through the other dozen titles.

He sat at the desk as a wave of fear rolled over him. If the scholars were still alive, he needed a diplomatic intervention. He needed to talk to Nasaka about it and the Elder Oras. Five of his own people – people he had put in harm's way – were dead or dying, and he had no way to stop it.

"Stupid," he said aloud. He had sent Roh there. The treaty was his idea. The mess was his. He threw the letter onto the desk. He pressed his hands to his face and sat very still. He would have to call on Nasaka to help him fix this. And he hated himself for that.

For his own inability to manage the issue himself. Would he have to send another emissary there to apologize? Someone else the Patron would kill?

"Caisa?" he called.

She entered. More often than not, she was the one posted to his door. "I need you to pen a letter to Nasaka. Call her here, please."

"Should I call her a boar?"

"What?"

She grinned. "Sorry. A joke."

"Oma's breath," he muttered.

"Liaro thought it was hilarious."

"Have one of the secretaries write it, and I'll sign it," he said. "Something simple." It would be easier if someone else wrote it. Just the idea of writing to Nasaka for help angered him. He should have been prepared for something terrible to happen. The danger was supposed to have been the Tai Mora, not the Saiduan. He'd been so caught up with politics and the mystery of his sister's death that he was losing his grasp on important matters. And it was costing lives.

"Yes, Kai."

Ahkio changed his clothes and went downstairs. The common room was surprisingly empty. Night was beginning to fall. In any other clan, the common room would be packed with people and laughter. Instead, he saw only three militia at a table in the back and a very tired-looking barkeep nodding off into her palm.

In the very back, near the fire, he saw a slender figure nursing a cup. It was Ghrasia.

He walked over to her. "I thought you were taking a nap," he said.

"Couldn't sleep," she said. "You?"

"Bad news," he said. He sat across from her in an oversized chair.

"Seems that's the only kind," she said.

"Yours was good."

Ghrasia sighed. "Maybe."

"How's the girl you brought back? The... feral one."

"Still living in some hidey-hole at the edge of the clan square," Ghrasia said. Her look was so solemn, Ahkio's heart ached. He wanted to hold her, and far more. Ahkio realized that it wasn't a drink he'd really wanted. He had spent much of his life drowning sorrow by spending his time in the arms of others.

"You stopped a monster, Ghrasia."

"I'm worried that catching monsters will turn me into one," she said.

Ahkio stared into the fire. "None of us could do what these people are doing," he said.

"You're wrong," she said. "Any one of us could. You. Me. Liaro. They *are* us, Ahkio."

He leaned forward. "They won't break us," he said. He reached out to her. "May I touch your knee?"

She started. Knit her brows. He felt a little foolish. "I apologize if I–"

"It's all right," she said. "You may."

He pressed his hand to her knee and realized he was doing it to comfort himself more than her. "If there's anyone I know who could come out of this alive without sacrificing her humanity, it's you," he said.

"Did you know I was your mother's lover?" she said.

He pulled his hand away. "I did," he said.

"If I told you I wanted to spend the night with you, would you worry it was because I loved your mother?"

"I... No, I would not." Ahkio did wonder, though, if she would think differently about him if she knew who his mother really was. Would she still stand with him? Would she be looking at him like that right now?

"Is it a mutual desire?" she asked.

Ahkio had to look away from her then. It was still frightening, sometimes, to talk so frankly about desire. But this was Ghrasia, the woman who turned back the Dorinahs at the pass. He should have known she would speak of it plainly instead of continuing to dart around it.

"I'm married," he said.

"As am I," she said.

"I don't expect Mohrai will give her permission for such an affair," he said, "even if your husbands did."

"I'm barren," Ghrasia said, "though I expect that will not dissuade her."

"No," Ahkio said. "Barren with your husbands does not mean barren with me." He wanted that to be the end of it. But he opened his mouth again and said, "Our desire would need to have limits."

"I've heard your wife has an eye on your seat," Ghrasia said.

"She does," he said. "And some days, I have a mind to let her have it."

"Why is it you didn't just turn it over to her? We all knew you didn't want to be Kai."

"Maybe that's why," he said. "I always did like being contrary."

"So, let's pretend I didn't ask about an affair," she said.

Ahkio wanted to touch her again. He was already on fire with images of the two of them together. He'd been dreaming of her for weeks.

"I think I'm afraid of having a happy moment," Ahkio said.

Ghrasia reached out her hand. He took it. He wanted her so desperately, he nearly fell into her lap.

"I'm far more afraid of never dancing again," she said, and led him upstairs.

Ahkio lay awake, staring at the ceiling. He heard voices from the courtyard. They faded before he could make out the words. He thought about Roh and Dasai, and wondered what had become of them. Were they awake, too? Or dead? The moons' light bled in from the window. He had forgotten to draw the curtains and now regretted it. He did not often desire or require privacy.

He went to the window. The air was cold against his bare skin. The fire in the hearth was low. He gazed out at the lighted square.

Saw no one.

"What is it?" Ghrasia asked. She propped herself up on one elbow. She was captivating in the low light. The moons' light made her skin glow. Her hair was unbound and spilled across the sheets. It reminded him suddenly of Meyna. A lifetime ago.

"Thought I heard something," he said. He climbed into bed next to her, drawn back to the warmth of their shared bodies.

She took his scarred hands and kissed them.

He made to pull away, suddenly self-conscious, but she held his wrists. "What really happened in that camp?" she said. She pressed her thumbs to his smooth palms. "I know the stories, but I also know stories lie."

Ahkio pulled his hands away a second time. She released him. He traced the lines of her cheek. "My mother took us to a big refugee camp on the other side of the Liona Stronghold. I still don't know why. She said it was to enlighten people. Maybe she was searching for someone."

Ghrasia shook her head. "Your mother and I... had a falling-out. Soon after you were born."

"She took us with her," he said. "A mad thing, by all accounts. We lived in that refugee camp for years while she met with all sorts of people – farm workers and scullery drudges and servants. I don't remember what they talked about. But there was an uprising in the camp. She was certainly a part of it. How much, I don't know. But when the rebellion came, the Dorinahs were ready."

"They burned the camp," Ghrasia said.

"Yes," he said. He flexed his fingers. "I still remember. There was this legionnaire. She looked old to me, but I guess she must have been young, maybe as old as I am now, and it was so strange. She looked Dhai. Mostly Dhai, anyway. And she torched our house and the houses of those around us. My father went out to kill the legionnaire, but she cut him down."

"I'm sorry," Ghrasia said. "Maybe I shouldn't have–"

"It's all right," he said. He expected his hands to tremble, but they did not. "I didn't know how to use a sword. So I ran back inside the house to find my mother. She was ill. When I got in...

she was burning. Her hair was on fire, her clothes..." He could still smell the stink of her burning hair and flesh, even now. "So I just grabbed her." He held out his hands. "I don't know what they burned the houses with. Some tirajista-created thing, maybe, because it stuck to me. The fire just licked up my arms. My own hair caught fire."

"Did Ora Nasaka really–"

He grimaced. "Yes. Nasaka pulled me out. She left my mother to burn up, but she pulled me out and rolled me in the dirt until all that was left was the pain. Then she pulled out that sword of hers. She made quick work of the legionnaires after that. But she didn't go back for my mother."

Ghrasia pressed her hand to his face. "It's a horrible thing. I'm sorry it happened to you."

"It's done," he said. He pushed out of bed. "I think I'm going to stay up and read for a bit. Do you mind?"

"What is it? A religious text?"

"A book of Kirana's. Some lurid Dorinah romance."

"That will do the trick," she said.

He walked over to his tunic draped on the back of a chair and grabbed the book in his tunic pocket.

"You know what haunts me," he said, "about Dorinah? Besides all the burning?"

"The legionnaire," she said.

"How did you know that?"

"Dhai killing Dhai," she said. "The first time you see it... it breaks the world, a little bit."

Ahkio crawled into bed. He pressed himself against her, savoring the heat, as he opened the book.

"It's odd to see all Kirana's things stacked up here," Ghrasia said, pointing to the trunks. "I've been trying to think of where I saw those maps of the basements before. I just remembered. Kirana requested six of the militia in Kuallina about, oh, four years ago? To help her go through and confirm some maps. They were just like those."

"Why would she need militia to help with that?"

"That's why I remember it. Odd request. I thought there might be a fugitive down there, some rogue novice or Ora she didn't want to tell me about."

"Something she... feared," Ahkio said.

"That's possible."

Ahkio closed the book. "What if I told you I'd heard someone say that Kirana killed herself? Why would a person do something like that?"

Ghrasia touched his hands. "To save someone they love."

Ahkio heard raised voices again. A shout. The noise was coming from the other side of the council house.

Ahkio glanced at the door. He saw light coming from beneath it. The house was abuzz with movement.

Ghrasia released him. "Oma's breath," she muttered, and began pulling on her clothes.

Ahkio lit a lantern. He tucked the book back into his tunic and pulled on the tunic. He yanked the bedsheets straight and grabbed his trousers.

Footsteps sounded in the hall, closer.

Just as Ahkio noticed the edge of Clan Leader Talisa's terrible painting sitting behind the bed – he'd taken it down before taking Ghrasia to bed – the door burst open.

Caisa and Ohanni ran into the room.

Ghrasia was standing by the fire, still knotting her hair back. Ahkio put his hands on his hips. "What is it?" he said. His heart hammered. For fear of being found out or fear of what they had to say, or both.

Caisa glanced quickly from one of them to the other.

"We have one of those foreign assassins downstairs," Ohanni said.

"Alive," Caisa said.

46

"You mean Casa Maigan," Maralah said. They were still mopping up the halls from the coup four days earlier; the Patron's former dining room now served as her strategy room while they took out the three remaining groups of rogue sanisi holed up in the keep. The hold still shook occasionally, caused by dueling parajistas. Dust trickled from cracks in the ceiling.

Maralah stood with Kadaan and his little Dhai ward, Roh, in the dining room. Her brother was asleep in the next room with his mouthy second, and Wraisau and a squad of Rajavaa's own men guarded them. Kadaan had brought Roh to her after discovering he knew something about a book the other Dhai were hiding. It turned out that slaughtering his companions had shaken something loose in him. As much as Maralah abhorred what the Patron had done – it was very unlike him – she had to admit it was effective.

"I thought it was a name you might know," Kadaan said. "It sounded like someone from the north, one of Alaar's women."

"I'm familiar with her, yes," Maralah said. "She was part of Alaar's harem in Isjahilde, inherited from the prior Patron. She was one of those we had to leave behind. And you heard this from one of your Dhai friends?"

"From Aramey," Roh said. The boy stood straight, with his hands clasped behind his back just like Kadaan. Kadaan had dressed the boy in a dark tunic cut in the Saiduan style, and shaved his head. Maralah thought it better fit his new status.

Kadaan had undertaken his scrubbing up with an eye for utility. She appreciated that. It would make things easier on the boy, too, though Maralah was uncertain how much he knew of that yet.

"Keeper Takanaa had your friends' rooms cleaned," she said, "and the contents returned to the scholars."

"There was a book there," Roh said, "written in Talamynii. Ora Dasai said it was very important. I thought maybe the woman's name had to do with the book. Maybe they meant to give it to her? To translate?"

"Indeed," Maralah said. "It was the first book our scholars brought to my attention after the rooms were cleared. I've never seen two men so excited. There was no record of it in the archives. Do you know where Ora Dasai found it?"

Roh shook his head. He met her look when he did it, but Maralah suspected that any boy smart enough to survive the slaughter of his comrades would be smart enough to tell half-truths when the time came for it.

"The issue with the book is translation, as you noted," Maralah said. "Casa had Talamynii roots. Hers was a very old and isolated family. It wouldn't surprise me if they wanted her to translate this book."

"Isjahilde is under enemy control," Kadaan said. "Even if she still lives–"

"We can find other translators," Maralah said. "All this death and politics and tracking down omajistas... You think what we need is in this dusty book?"

"It may be a list of recipes, for all we know," Kadaan said.

"It's not," Roh said. "There were two books mentioned in a text we found from an old Dhai scholar. They were specifically about omajistas. He referenced them as among the first books they tried to get rid of, to punish the Saiduan during the next rising of Oma. This could be one of those books."

"I can't spare many for this," Maralah said. "Take Roh, Luna, and a small team. I need Driaa here, but aside from hir, any of the others can go."

"Where?" Kadaan asked.

"The Shoratau. Tell anyone in there who can translate the book that we'll free them."

Kadaan shook his head. "Trusting prisoners to speak truth-"

"I suspect having a squad of sanisi over them, looking to sniff out lies, will aid in preventing some of that," she said. "So will having two Dhai. Luna knows later Talamynii, though Bael says the ancient is beyond hir. They'll know if anyone is bluffing."

"I'm sorry," Roh said, "What's Shoratau?"

"A prison," Maralah said, "where we put the people we should have killed but thought we might need later."

"It's north of here," Kadaan said. "We won't be able to find a clear road—"

"It's northeast," Maralah said. "You're a small group. You may be able to avoid detection. We'll be retreating south to Harajan. If the weather holds long enough, you still may be able to meet us there before it takes you."

"Yes, Shao," Kadaan said.

Maralah held out her hand. Kadaan gripped her elbow. She leaned in. "It was a good, hard run," she said.

"If you can't keep him on the seat, I expect you to take it," he said.

"A woman on the seat? Then you'll know we're lost," she said, and pulled away.

She watched the sanisi and the boy leave the dining room. Then she sat in one of the tall chairs and stared at the crystal place settings. The slaves had set the table for eight – for Patron Rajavaa and his ministers of finance, agriculture, commerce, foreign relations, health and education, transport and infrastructure, and her, the acting minister of war. She remembered standing here at Alaar's side, more than twenty years before, when he was the minister of commerce and she just a young sanisi bound by oath and blood to the Patron at the head of the table. She did not know what she saw in Alaar then. It went beyond his quick wit and generous but firm hand. She realized it was his willingness to end all the bloody internal wars and rebellions and invest heavily in their gifted arts and infrastructure. Oma was only a century from rising, he had told the table. Every astronomer said it. It was not just myth. It was coming. Saiduan had to be the most stable country in the world, united, strong, to take on whatever invaders Oma brought with it this turn. It was he who reinstated the minister of health and education. After his bloody ascension, they had sat here together to build a fine new country.

Alaar had not been made for war. He was made for peace. Perhaps Kadaan had done her a favor. She could never have killed him herself, even knowing the rules, even knowing it was necessary. She would have secreted him away somewhere – simply sent him into stasis by slowing down his fibrous heart – and brought him back after the tide was turned back and they needed a man with a head for politics instead of a stomach for strategy.

The loss was still painful. Putting her brother on the seat meant she had finally given up on that dream of peace.

"Maralah?"

She glanced up. Rajavaa entered, dressed in Alaar's soft amber robes. Her heart clenched. She stood.

"Yes, Patron," she said.

"I need a woman's guidance on something," he said.

"Then I am not the person to ask," she said.

The Saiduan had six words that described types of snow, and Roh had seen every one of them. He trudged across an icy tundra, trailing after twelve sanisi. They had thrown off their dark garb for white fur coats and boots. They were making for Shoratau, staying far away from the roads and regular paths. The days blurred together, so many that Roh woke one day and felt blinded by the blank stretch of white.

Roh traveled mostly with Luna at the back of the group, spending their rest periods and evenings poring over the Talamynii book.

"Did you tell them about Shodav?" Luna asked early on. It was the first thing Luna said to him.

It made Roh angry that he thought first of protecting Shodav, though it was his own friends who were already dead. Luna's only protecting Shodav, Roh thought, so what happened to Dasai and the others doesn't happen to him.

"I didn't," Roh said. "I said the book was just something Ora Dasai found."

"I'm sorry about what happened," Luna said.

"It's done," Roh said.

"You could have run."

"The way you and Kihin were going to run?"

Luna looked away, but not before Roh saw Luna's eyes fill.

"I'm sorry," Roh said.

"It's all right," Luna said. "It's how it is here. Every time you think you find a way out, they hobble you again."

"Did you love him?" Roh asked.

"Do you love Kadaan?"

"That's a mean question," Roh said.

"Yes," Luna said.

"Kadaan is kind," Roh said. "It could have turned out a lot worse."

"Kihin was a nice boy," Luna said, and did not speak of it again.

Roh and Luna worked on the book until their fingers were numb and the letters all looked the same. "Why do some of these look like Dhai characters?" Roh asked as Luna taught him the few Talamynii characters Luna knew.

"They borrowed from each other a lot," Luna said. "It's pretty rare to see one people take over without picking up a lot from the people they conquered. This is more likely a Dhai book than a Talamynii one – it's the Talamynii that's borrowed, not the Dhai."

Roh turned to the back of the book, where there were simple line illustrations, mostly maps and circles. Without being able to read the characters, the circle figures were unintelligible. But at the beginning of the illustrated section were five symbols carefully drawn on a map with the familiar cross-section of mountains found only on Grania. This Grania, though, had no oceans. The map seemed to go on far past the page. Written onto the map were five familiar symbols. Roh knew them immediately. They were the same ones he had seen on the table in the Assembly Chamber in Oma's Temple: a triangle with two circles; a circle with two lines through it; a coiled curl with a circle; a square with a double circle inside... and the trefoil with the tail. The one Lilia dreamed her mother pressed into her skin.

"I know these," Roh said. "These symbols are in the Temple of Oma in Dhai."

"What do they mean?"

"I don't know," Roh said. "Most of them marked the temples." He traced the trefoil with the tail. The table map had shown that symbol over a spur of land that jutted into the ocean. But on this map, there was no ocean, just flat land. Whatever the trefoil had marked had probably fallen into the sea during the cataclysm the last time Oma rose.

"Symbols aren't good for much if we can't read the book," Luna said.

Roh stared at the map for nearly an hour, flipping back and forth between the pages. The symbols showed up again – this time, each had their own page – later in the section, tucked into a corner on a page with more of the circular illustrations.

"Ora Dasai would know what this meant," Roh said, frustrated.

"He isn't here," Luna said. "So we better figure this out."

"I was supposed to die an old man in an orchard," Roh said.

"I was supposed to marry a farmer," Luna said. "Not everything happens the way it's supposed to."

Kadaan led their small party, and Roh only saw him at night after meeting with Luna, when they shared the same tent, but little else. Roh kept his hat on all the time. His bare scalp itched, and his ears burned with cold.

Roh had never known such a spare existence. They were mired by a windstorm over a frozen river whose breadth spanned a valley. They retreated inland and dug themselves into snow caves. They were stranded for a week, and killed and ate two of the bears. Kadaan cut everyone's rations.

And at night... the nights were the worst. The sanisi and the bears patrolled the edges of the camp for the invaders. Most nights, they found them. Two sanisi died.

Then one morning, Kadaan took Roh to the top of an icy plateau and pointed north.

"There," he said.

Roh gazed out over a white, ice-encrusted plain to the churning crush of ice floes in what must have been a harbor. There was a black spire jutting up from behind a pulsing gray wall. The frozen sea made eerie structures on three sides of the tower, great ice sculptures that clung to the hold as if carved by master craftspeople.

Kadaan sent a man ahead to scout. When he came back, he and Kadaan conferred for a few moments. Then Kadaan waved them all forward. "I'm afraid the invaders got there before us," he said.

As they walked to the tower, bodies became visible within a hundred yards of the walls. The only reason they hadn't seen them sooner was because the snow had claimed them, covering the churned-up ground, the bloody trails of the dying, the detritus of spent arrows and crossbow bolts, the discarded weapons of the dead.

As they neared, the frosty forms of the dead emerged from the snow heaps: a boot heel, the edge of a coat, a clawed fist frozen forever to the hilt of a weapon. The bodies had been so long on the tundra that they didn't look real. They were pasty imitations of people, stiff and grotesque, bloodless.

The bodies reminded Roh of Dasai and Aramey, Nioni and Kihin. He thought of his brother dying alone in a pool of his own blood on icy tundra such as this. I was a coward, Roh thought. A selfish coward. His throat closed and tears came. It was so cold, the moisture froze at the corners of his eyes before it could fall.

"This is different," Kadaan said. "They don't usually leave the bodies. They spirit them off somewhere."

Roh wiped his face and looked up at the ruined gate of the tower. The ironbound door had burst inward, shattered like glass. The edges of the gate that remained fixed on the hinges looked like the remnants of the windows.

There was no movement along the battlements. Just inside the gate were heaps of Saiduan bodies. The walls blocked most of the wind-carried snow, so the bodies remained almost entirely exposed. Crystallized blood, frosty entrails, headless corpses, men shattered in two. Great scorch marks stained the walls inside. The buildings surrounding the keep had been reduced to charred stone, their roofs and interiors carried away by fire.

The sanisi followed the trail of bodies and burned-out homes up into the interior of the tower.

The gate there had been broken open as well, with the same violent force that had torn apart the gate outside.

The party did not speak as they moved through the keep. Dead sanisi littered the floor. Roh wondered at first where they all had come from – wasn't this a prison? Then he realized that people from the surrounding areas must have fled here, hoping it was a place of refuge. Among the dead Saiduan were the shorter, paler bodies of the invaders. The invaders who looked like Dhai. Roh looked from the dead to Kadaan and wondered why no one ever called the invaders by name.

For the first time, Roh understood what kind of battle they were fighting. This wasn't a war at all. It was genocide. It was the complete decimation of an entire people. The invaders were doing to the Saiduan what the Saiduan tried to do to the Dhai, and what the Dhai had done to the Talamynii before them. There would be no middle ground. No peace. No end. Dasai and the others were dead for nothing. Why had he lived? To what purpose?

Luna came up beside him in the cold hallway. "What is it?" he said.

"We have to win," Roh said.

"I'll settle for dying old," Luna said.

"I won't," Roh said.

Roh helped move the bodies out of the main rooms. They were to leave the bodies haphazardly: no stacking, no burning, nothing that so obviously left a trace of their passage. They raided the keep for food, and Kadaan allowed them to light up the braziers but no regular fires. Fires made too much smoke. They covered up the windows of the rooms they used so no light could be seen from the harbor. They posted sanisi at the gate to the keep but left the main gate into the city untouched.

There were only a handful of bears left in the kennels not yet starved or frozen – most of the others had been taken.

That night, Roh sat awake at the foot of Kadaan's bed for many hours, though Kadaan did not come to bed. Luna always slept with the Talamynii book, and he thought about sitting up with him for a while and going over more characters. But he was restless.

Roh moved through the corridors in search of a friendly face. He found Kadaan in one of the ransacked libraries. Kadaan sat near the soft glow of a brazier. The room was bitterly cold. Roh could see his breath. The books were covered in frost.

Kadaan did not look at him, though Roh knew his presence was noted.

"How did they get in?" Roh asked softly, from the doorway.

"If I knew that, we would not see this. There is a good deal we do not know. More come every month. Like roaches. We cut them down, and still they come. Sanisi cannot train their children so quickly." He gestured to the ransacked room around him. "They are coming here for knowledge no one has been able to give them. Maybe we should give up on this book business and take what remains of our people south. There is another continent there. Perhaps we will be welcome."

"You think we're going to die like they did?"

"Does it matter?"

"Yes," Roh said. "I'm supposed to die an old man in an orchard. If I don't, it means the seer was wrong."

"A farmer. Yes." Kadaan laughed. It sounded very strange in the cold, ruined room. "That explains much about your decisions."

"I suppose I should have asked what kind of orchard," Roh said. "A Dhai one? A Saiduan one? Or an orchard on some other continent..."

Kadaan gave a thin smile. "Or an orchard on this world at all," he said.

"Who are the invaders, Kadaan?"

"I think you know."

"They're Dhai."

"Yes. Dhai who live on some other world, where the Saiduan didn't kill them."

Roh let out a breath. "Gods. Why are they killing you? Us? All of us, I guess."

Kadaan shrugged. "I'm not sure it matters. We may be at an end of Maralah's hunt through the archives. Whatever they're looking for wasn't made for us to understand. It's something only some old Dhai would know."

Roh remembered the Dhai-looking characters in the Talamynii book and swore softly. "They're our people. Dhai. They can read all these books. That's why they want them," he said.

"What?"

"I need to talk to Luna. Just... give me a few minutes."

Roh woke Luna from a dead sleep.

"Lord of Light, Roh," Luna said. "What–"

"I need to see the book."

"It's under the bed."

Roh pulled the Talamynii book from beneath the bed and unwrapped it. He set his lantern beside the book and grabbed Luna's sketchbook and a charcoal pencil.

He opened to the inside pages and counted the characters. He put them down in the order of the Kai cipher – two down, four across, three up, over one. He set down each letter, then reversed the order.

Luna pulled off the blanket and knelt next to Roh. "What's that?"

"Kai cipher," Roh muttered.

"What? Really?"

Roh scribbled out what he'd written. It was all nonsense. He groaned and started over. More nonsense. Nothing.

"I just thought..." Roh wrote it out yet again, but the letters made no sense; they didn't form any words he knew. He threw down the charcoal pencil and rubbed his face.

Luna took up the book. "I think that made it worse," Luna said. "Good idea, though. How did you have the Kai's cipher?"

Roh cried. He didn't even realize he was crying until Luna touched his face, and Roh pulled his hands away, and they were wet.

"Roh?" Luna said. "Roh, there's not an answer to everything."

Roh sobbed then. It bubbled up from inside him like some terrible sickness. His shoulders shook. He wrapped his arms around his knees and keened like a child. Nothing made any sense. Nothing was what it was supposed to be.

"Roh, don't cry," Luna said.

"It was all for nothing," Roh said. "Ora Dasai's dead, Aramey... my brother... for nothing."

"What happened to making your own fate? Isn't that what you always say?"

"I did make it," Roh said. "This is it. Freezing to death, at the end of everything, for no purpose."

Luna pulled Roh's hands from his knees. "Living is the purpose, Roh. For however long we have to do it, we live. That's all. That's all there ever was."

"We aren't going to win," Roh said.

"No," Luna said, "but we're going to live."

47

Ahkio stared down at the slight man surrounded by Oras and militia on the council house floor. His wrists and ankles were bound. He lay on his side. Dark fluid oozed from his mouth, his broken nose. His long, dark hair stuck to his sweaty neck. Ghrasia stood between him and Ahkio, hand already on her sword, the hilt wrapped around her wrist.

"We had him talking," Caisa said.

"Is that so?" Ahkio asked the man.

"I can talk," the man said. He sounded like any other Dhai. No trace of an accent. Of course not.

"Why are you here, then; have you answered that?" Ahkio asked. "We could resolve our differences peacefully. There was no need for violence."

"This is where the hunting ends," the man said. He showed dark, stained teeth.

"You're right about that," Ahkio said. "We took your messenger. We'll take the rest of you."

"There are more of us than you can imagine."

"And I'll kill you one at a time."

"Bold words for a pacifist."

"Things change."

The man chuckled. "You think you've cornered us, Kai. But it's us who've cornered you. We've softened the way for an army that will overwhelm your harbor come spring, and you're too late to stop it."

"Ghrasia—" Ahkio said.

But Ghrasia was already looking around the room – the windows, the door.

Caisa took a step back. Ahkio felt a prickling across his shoulders, but that could just as easily have been the presence of the other Oras in the room, keeping the shadow bound. The room went quiet. The air was heavy.

"Did you drug him?" Ahkio asked Caisa. "They're gifted."

"Of course," Caisa said.

Ahkio's ears popped. "Get this man out of here," Ahkio said. "The rest of you, out!"

Ohanni and Shanigan grabbed the man. Hauled him out. A wave of air shuddered through the room.

Then all of the others were moving. Ahkio heard a groan of timber above. A creaking of glass.

The windows of the council house imploded. A spray of glass shot past Ahkio's head. A wall of air buffered his path, but it was not solid. He pushed through it, like walking through water. He came out on the other side, stumbled.

"Ghrasia?" Figures streamed past him.

His voice was swallowed in the groan of timber, the cracking of adenoak beams. The floor shook violently.

"Kai!" Caisa said. "The maps!" She bolted back upstairs.

Ahkio ran after her. He got halfway up the stairs before the whole house groaned and heaved sideways. He fell. Caisa appeared at the top of the crooked stairway, Kirana's maps of the temple under one arm. She'd grabbed four books. She threw them down. Half her face was covered in blood.

The lanterns in the hall were dimming and flickering as the flame flies moved in frantic circles.

Ahkio threw the books out the front door. He had no idea which ones she'd grabbed. He reached for her hand. She stumbled down the steps.

With three paces left to tread, the ceiling collapsed.

Ahkio looked up too late. He tried to cover his head. Dust

misted his face. He took a breath, coughed, opened his eyes.

An arm's length above him, splintered wood hovered in the air. He looked back at Caisa. She lay on her back on the floor, one hand gripping the maps, the other crooked over her head. She had summoned some shield of air to halt the collapse of the ceiling, but Ahkio wasn't sure how long she could hold it. Sweat beaded her brow.

Wooden planking, straw insulation, bits of plaster and broken ceramic tiles littered the floor. Ahkio saw Ohanni and Naori at what remained of the door, calling for them to come forward. The shadow man lay on his side on the porch, cackling.

"Ora Ohanni," Ahkio said, pointing back at Caisa. "Can you keep that ceiling up?"

Ohanni held out a hand toward the stair. The air rippled. He choked on it. Air like soup.

Ahkio grabbed Caisa by the ankles. He pulled her out onto the porch. Caisa coughed out the dust and pushed the maps away from the house. He let her go, and she crawled out onto the stone of the clan square.

"Watch yourself!" Ohanni said coldly. "There are more outside."

The Tai Mora. Their shadows.

All dozen of the assassins? More? Ahkio didn't know. They'd come hunting Ahkio, encircling his people here. Eight steps ahead of him.

Ahkio caught his breath. The air outside choked him. Too many jistas drawing power. He heard shouts from the yard, muted and distorted. Behind him, the ceiling above the stair collapsed as Ohanni dropped her shield of air. The sound was oddly dulled, distant.

The lanterns of the square flickered. Oras stood in the center of the courtyard in a circle, their backs to one another. The militia – including Raona's militia – stood with them.

And on the edges of the flickering lights, at the edges of the square, were the shadows. They bore metal weapons, not the glowing infused brands of the militia. It made them far harder to see in the dark. All around the square, violet, blue, and green bursts of color bloomed against the night as the militia took up arms.

Ahkio looked over at the council house and saw a yawning gulf of black. He looked up at the formerly moons-lit sky. Boiling clouds had rolled over their faces, smothering them in darkness. A heavy wind made the treetops creak, but he could feel none of it in the square in the thick, sticky air.

"How many are there?" Ahkio asked.

"I do not know," Ohanni said. "Ghrasia went to rally the forces we have here, but... Ahkio." She glanced back at the council house. It had utterly collapsed into a splintered mass of shattered glass and broken timber.

"Ahkio," Ohanni said, "If it's all the dozen of them at once, we're lost. They may have... they may be omajistas. We have no defense against omajistas. In the dark, we can't see them. They'll have abilities wc don't and use talent we won't expect."

Caisa took hold of the railing and drew herself up. Her blade, unlike those of the militia, was bare metal, too.

Someone from the circle of Oras cried out.

There came the sound of breaking glass.

One by one, the lanterns in the square shattered.

"Light," Naori said.

Ghrasia's voice, from the other end of the meeting house, "Weapons out!"

And there, in the light of the last lantern, in the instant before it shattered, Ahkio saw Ghrasia rushing into the courtyard, at least a dozen Oras and militia behind her.

The last lantern in the square flickered and died. Someone screamed.

The darkness was complete.

"Stay with these documents," Ahkio said to Ohanni and Naori. "Caisa, come with me."

"I'm here," she said. Her voice said she was very close, nearly at his elbow.

"We need to go around the other side of the council house," he said. "You're from Raona. This is your clan. Can you lead me from memory?"

"I'll try," Caisa said. "Take my hand."

He took her fingers.

"Take me to the door of the cellar," he said.

She led him down the short alley that went behind the council house. His footsteps sounded loud. For her part, Caisa stepped as softly as a cat.

"There are barrels of oil under the house," he said. "If the floor didn't collapse, we can ignite what's down there and give the militia some light." He wondered, briefly, where Liaro was. He'd been the one to move the barrels here. Ahkio hoped he was tucked safely in someone's bed.

Ahkio groped forward for the cellar door. Opened it. They stepped down. Ahkio ran into something. Caisa hissed. Just a chair. The house above had not collapsed into the cellar.

When they reached the far wall, Ahkio said, "Start at the room on the end. We're looking for oil barrels. I'll head down the other side."

He had never liked the dark. It helped if he closed his eyes. He knew these rooms. He had stored things in cellars just like this, worked as a laborer just as Liaro did during long summers in Osono, loading and unloading carts whose owners used the council houses for temporary storage. Ten steps across the first room, six deep. He found the outlines of trunks and crates, a couple sacks of what must have been hasaen tubers. No barrels.

He felt his way over to the next room and bumped into something. He gasped.

"It's just me." Caisa's voice. "They're in here," she said. "They're heavy."

She led him into the room. The barrels were only knee-high but as wide around as Ahkio's arms.

"We need to roll this out," Ahkio said. "Break them open in the stair."

"We could burn down the whole square."

"Better to burn down the square than die in it," Ahkio said. "It's cold and there's no wind. The council house will burn because of the oil. Rolling these outside will take too much time. I can rebuild the council house, but I can't save lives lost. Help me."

She said something that sounded like a curse.

He tipped over one of the barrels and pushed it across the floor to the stairs. As they came to the stairs, Ahkio heard the sound of shouting grow louder. When he looked up in the direction of the sound, he saw bursts of color as weapons met.

Ahkio rolled the barrel into place at the bottom of the stair.

He heard Caisa behind him, rolling her barrel. "Caisa, set it here."

He felt her settle the barrel against his opposite hip. Ahkio unstopped his barrel. He pushed it over. The oil glugged out. He stepped to the other side, fearful of getting his feet in the oil. He had a sudden, terrible image of his body aflame. He took a deep breath.

"Caisa, you have some scorch pods?" Ahkio asked. "I know you smoke. Check your pockets."

"I don't have any."

Ahkio patted his tunic pockets. The Dorinah book, a pen nib. But there, deep in his trouser pockets, were two scorch pods. In his haste to dress, he had grabbed Liaro's trousers instead of his own. Ahkio tore one of the end pages from the Dorinah book and twisted it lengthwise.

He heard Ohanni yelling.

Ahkio smashed the pods and touched the end of the twisted paper to them. He blew gently. A tiny flame flickered. Grew. He flinched in the face of it. Burning the council house had seemed like a fine idea until he lit a flame. Ahkio glanced across from him at Caisa.

But the figure squatting across from him was not Caisa.

Ahkio cried out. The paper fell from his hand and into the oil. The flickering fire licked at the oil and became a gluttonous flame. Smoke stung his eyes. He remembered his mother shrieking.

Ahkio fell back away from the stair. On the other side of the river of oily fire was a wiry, dark-haired man. The man grinned. Caisa's height. Caisa's slender build. His eyes glinted gold.

He spoke with Caisa's voice. "Kai, what's wrong? Not who you expected?" He drew his sword. "Have you not fought an omajista?"

Ohanni screaming, "Kai!"

Light burst up toward the sel oil barrel. Fire licked at the wood. Ahkio recoiled from the heat. Smelled burning flesh. He tucked his hands under his arms, terrified.

He tried to bolt for the stair, but the shadow was over the oily fire in one leap. The man grabbed hold of Ahkio by the collar. Leaned into him. This close, his eyes were like looking into the sun.

"Your victory was going to be a sloppy one," the shadow man said, still in Caisa's voice. "A dozen of us dead? What does that matter? There are millions of us, boy. We will swarm this world like sparrows."

Fire leapt behind them, curled up the length of the beam. Smoke filled the cellar. Ahkio realized he feared the fire more than the man.

The shadow man lifted Ahkio by the collar. The heat was unbearable. Oil caught the floorboards – the close ceiling, the straw insulation, the old wooden timbers, were perfect tinder. The fire ate, crackled, spit. I'm on fire, Ahkio thought. I'm going to burn up. Just like my mother.

The column of fire cast a great, long shadow. The man's eyes caught the light of the flames, like a mirror.

The shadow grunted. Spasmed.

Ahkio saw the glistening blade of a sword protruding from the man's chest. The sword withdrew.

The shadow dropped Ahkio and crumpled.

Ahkio fell onto the burning floor. His breath came in ragged gasps. He sounded the way his mother had, when he'd hooked her under her arms and hauled her burning body from their blazing house. He panicked then. His stomach roiled. He grabbed at his hair, terrified that it burned. But he still had his hair. His face. His hands.

Ahkio rolled away from the burning wood and oil. He rolled until he hit the opposite wall of debris. He uncovered his face. The back of his tunic had caught fire. He took either side of the tunic and pressed the fabric together to smother the flames. The flames went out. His breath came easier. Ahkio stared at the charred fabric. Kirana would tell him to get up.

Get up, Ahkio. Or all this death and madness is for nothing.

He choked on smoke. He saw Caisa ducking away from the shadow man she had skewered, ducking from light to shadow, dancing around flames as the ruined ceiling began to burn, loose bits of straw and char falling like flame flies from the ceiling. The shadow had dropped his sword and punched at her with a dagger now. Caisa's forearms bled.

The shadow's sword was just three paces from Ahkio, ablaze in a puddle of oil. Ahkio yanked off his tunic and wrapped it around his hand. He plunged forward, into the blazing oil, and snatched out the flaming sword.

As Caisa ducked and parried the knife, Ahkio held the sword tight in both hands and swung. Not for the man's head or torso, the places the shadow would anticipate and set up gifted defenses, but his legs.

The man yelled, leaping away from Ahkio's strike, and turned. Ahkio knocked into him with his own body; pushed him over.

Caisa took up her weapon in both hands and drove it into the man's back, pinning him to the floor. Ahkio got as close to the burning wall as he dared. His clothes were smoking. He raised the fiery sword as high as he could and realized what he was about to do.

Murder. At his hand.

He could not bring down the sword.

Caisa pulled her sword free and hacked a second time. Blood sprayed them. Her third stroke freed the head from the torso.

Ahkio dropped his own sword, throwing the flaming tunic with it. "Out!" Ahkio said.

Caisa stumbled over the body. She had one arm clutched to her chest. Ahkio saw more blood there beneath her arm. Her face was drawn.

"Kai," she said. "I'm sorry."

"Quiet, now," he said. "You did well. Let me help you out."

When she consented, he took her in his arms. His hands did not tremble.

They stumbled up the flaming stairs and into the cold, murky air.

Ahkio released her, and Caisa sagged against him. Ahkio felt the heat at his back. He helped Caisa into the courtyard, near the fountain. The fire blossomed up through the house and spread out over the wreckage, an enormous bonfire that licked at the cold sky and sent out a wave of heat and light. Other people lined the square, those living in the houses above their market stalls, those in nearby community houses, some hovering in the shadows, but others…

The fire lit the square. Ahkio saw a stir of fighters. How many left? Twenty? Bodies lay in the square. Militia and Oras. And Raonas. Civilians.

He saw forgotten swords. Shattered glass.

He looked down at Caisa. She was covered in blood and soot.

"I'm sorry," she said.

"You keep saying that."

"He stabbed me going into the alley. Closed the air around me, stabbed. I'm sorry."

"Caisa–"

"Go on," she said. "Fight them now or fight them later." She handed him her sword.

Ahkio shook his head. "I can't."

"They will destroy us."

"Maybe not in the way we think," he said.

The building blazed behind them. He sat with Caisa, watching the fighting in the roaring light. Ghrasia fought a man in a dark cloak, she and two others. There were four Oras behind them. Ghrasia plunged forward. Her blade took the shadow through the gut.

The shadow faltered.

Ghrasia darted forward again. She took him with a solid thrust through the chest, then cut off his head. Then she was moving again, limping toward the last stir of figures.

As she walked, the screaming stopped. The figures stilled. Ghrasia turned. Saw Ahkio. He held out his hand to her.

"Kai," Ghrasia said, running over to him. She was covered in blood. Her hair was plastered to her forehead.

More Oras and militia joined them, pulling away from the bodies of their comrades and the assassins.

"How many?" Ahkio asked.

"We've counted six," Ghrasia said.

"Including the one Caisa killed?"

"Seven," Ghrasia said. "Our strategy for flushing them out worked. A little too well, perhaps."

"How many of us dead? What was the cost, Ghrasia?"

"It's too soon to know," Ghrasia said, "but... fifty, maybe more? Most of the Raona militia and many of my own. And Oras..."

Ahkio stared at Caisa's forgotten sword, lying on the stones between them.

"What are we going to become, Ghrasia?" he asked.

She gazed out at the square. "Dead, likely," she said. "Or very different."

48

"We have one shot at this," Zezili said, "so don't fuck it up." Looking at the filthy, scar-faced girl next to her, Zezili suspected all the girl ever did was fuck up.

"I'm going down there," Lilia said.

"I'd like you to burn up that army as much as anyone," Zezili said, "but they've got omajistas down there and gifted ranks. You see those flags?" She pointed to a collection of red flags painted in blue Dhai characters. "Those are rallying flags for different troops. You talk like a temple Dhai, so start thinking like one. What do those symbols mean?"

"Para, Sina, Tira, Oma..." Lilia said. "There are hundreds of those flags. All those people can't be gifted."

"Why do you think they're winning?" Zezili said. She pulled off her helm. It was embossed with the Eye of Rhea. So were her sword and the collar of her tunic. Looking like one of Monshara's people here wouldn't go well. "There are some clothes in that tower," Zezili said. "Not armor, but red skirts and things, a lot like what your militia wears. We'll wait for dark and head down there. If they ask who we're looking for, we just say we're running a message to the Kai from Monshara. You understand?"

Lilia gazed down at the army. "You think the Kai is down there?"

"I don't give a toss for the Kai," Zezili said. "We're after the mirror. It took them a decade to build it. If we destroy it, it'll take a decade more to replace it."

"They won't need it," Lilia said. "Oma will be in the sky soon."

Zezili grunted. "Bunch of fucking fatalists, you Dhai. Suck up your petty mewling and do something with all that talent before you burn out." She marched away from the girl, back to the tower.

She went upstairs to the dusty trunk she'd found in what looked like a pillaged armory. She began to pull off her armor. She wondered if it was something about the Dhai people that just made them mealy-mouthed little good-for-nothings. Why did she have to pull them all around by the nose?

She shook out a long red tunic and pulled it on. The skirt was bulky and a little short, but it would do. She found a leather belt embossed with the Dhai characters for all four satellites and pulled it on. There was another outfit in there, far too big for the girl, but if she ripped up the tunic and just put a belt on her, they might be able to pass for a while. She found no sword in the trunk or anywhere else in the ransacked room. All she could wrestle up was a broken javelin and what looked like some kind of busted crossbow. But she did find a long coat, perfect for hiding the sword strapped to her back. She drew her belt across her chest and rehung her sheath. As she finished up, she heard footsteps on the stairs and tensed until she saw it was just the dajian girl.

"I have a tunic here for you," Zezili said. She threw it to the girl's feet.

The girl stared at her.

"What?" Zezili said.

"You have one advantage, at least," Lilia said.

"What's that?"

"I think you might look more Dhai than I do."

After the suns went down, Lilia marched toward the camp with Zezili. They followed a beaten path down to the encampment. Lilia had slept several hours back in the tower, the dead sleep of the sick or exhausted, and woke feeling wrung out. She vomited out of a high window. They had no water, and her mouth was dry and sticky.

"Could you stop if we see water?" Lilia asked.

"No time for that."

She remembered Larn telling her that the priests she met within the camp often paid her in clear water. "Are your priests over here?" she asked. "The ones who pay in water? We could ask them."

Zezili turned around. "My... what?"

"Priests?" Lilia said, wondering if she had gotten the word wrong. "Priestesses?"

Zezili laughed. "Oh, you mean Seekers. Dajians are always calling them priests."

"What are Seekers?"

Zezili began walking again. "Dorinah's gifted."

"But," Lilia said, "why would they be in a camp?"

"A camp?" Zezili stopped again. "Tulana's in a dajian camp?"

"Who? I don't know, but–"

"Should have figured," Zezili said. "It's the one place we wouldn't look."

"Why were you looking?"

Zezili shook her head. "Empress is killing our own gifted. For the Tai Mora. The people on this side. They ran off some time ago. Should have figured they'd hide in a camp."

"That's mad."

"It is," Zezili said. "Shit. Good thing I didn't slaughter you after all."

"You would have fought your own gifted," Lilia said.

"Becoming a thing, isn't it? Killing ourselves."

As they came down into the military camp, Lilia tensed. The mass of the army up close was far more overwhelming than from afar. Massive, stinking bears were camped in large rings outside the periphery of the camp. A few blue-clad kennel girls led tall white bears past them. Lilia saw runners and pages. And the troops... they were too many and too different for Lilia to comprehend. She expected they would all be Dhai, but the armor, the hair, the clothing, and the languages – the languages!

– were all foreign. She saw every type of face in every shade of brown – from pinkish tan to the deepest violet-black, and every type of hair in every type of color, from red to white to black, coiled and curled, straightened and dreadlocked. What confounded her even more was that the groups were mixed. People who bore little resemblance to one another wore uniforms that clearly marked them as units. Lilia looked at every standard they passed, noting how many were parajistas, sinajistas, tirajistas… Finding the omajistas was much easier. She could still see the misty trails leading off from the mirror. As she followed those trails, she saw they wended back to groups congregated around omajista flags. Whatever her mother had made, it needed a lot of power to work.

Ahead of her, Zezili's right hand kept twitching. They had expected a challenge, a fight. But blending into this colorful group proved to be easier than Lilia imagined. In fact, as they passed, people tended to glance at them once, lower their eyes, and step away. It took Lilia a long time to realize it was because they looked like Dhai.

Lilia trotted forward to catch up to Zezili. She opened her mouth to talk in Dorinah because she didn't want anyone knowing what they said. Then she realized that might be worse.

Instead, she spoke very low in Dhai. "They will kill us after we break it."

"I expect so," Zezili said. "But you were willing to burn up my legion to save a few hundred sniveling dajians. I figured killing yourself to save forty thousand or so would be fine by you."

"But you'll die, too," Lilia said.

"I like living," Zezili said, "but I don't fancy living as a slave."

"That's very strange coming from you."

Zezili grunted.

As they got closer to the mirror, the troops thinned out. Finally, they reached a barrier of bone-white pillars that jutted up from the charred ground. It completely encircled the mirror. This close, Lilia could see through to the other side. The sky wasn't as dark there. She saw the moons' light glinting across a broad field of amber-colored grass. In the far distance, Lilia saw the winking lights of a house or hold of some type, obscured by a stand of spiky trees.

"Do you recognize that place?" Lilia asked.

Zezili shook her head. "Thought you might."

"No."

"Well," Zezili said. "It's your turn now."

"To do what?"

"To break it."

Lilia gazed up and up, to the top of the mirror where the figure she had first spied still writhed. The body, she saw now, was fused with the edge of the mirror, embedded into it with braided bands of Oma's breath. She gagged, filled with a horror so powerful it left her breathless, just like the day she watched her village burn.

They had not killed her mother. Oh, no. They'd put her to work for them.

"I need to get up there," Lilia said.

Zezili pointed to the edge of the mirror. "See that braided silverwork, there? It's a lattice. You can climb it."

"Climb?"

"Climb," Zezili said. "Or are you afraid of heights?"

Lilia looked at her twisted left hand. She still couldn't close the fingers all the way.

"Beautiful, isn't it?"

Lilia started and turned. Zezili's reaction was more casual. She continued looking at the mirror for another breath.

A solid, swarthy woman wearing a green tunic and long skirt stood a few feet behind them. When Lilia turned, she swaggered forward. "I still admire what you all did here," the woman said in accented Dhai.

Lilia tried to work some spit into her mouth.

"You're welcome," Zezili said. She crossed her arms. "You need something?"

"Funny accent," the woman said. "What is it?"

"Southern," Zezili said, so smoothly that Lilia wondered just how often she lied.

The woman laughed. "It's been a long time since I went below the Granian line," she said. "But I suppose, soon, we'll all sound foreign there." She gestured to the mirror.

"Let's get a drink," Zezili said. "Tell me about your travels below the Granian line. My girl here wanted a few minutes alone to stare at it again. Finds it mesmerizing. I'm tired of it, myself."

"Your girl?" the woman said. "Is she your daughter or your apprentice?"

"A bit of both," Zezili said. She reached out her arm, and Lilia almost shouted at her not to touch the woman without asking. But as she wrapped her arm around the woman, the woman only smiled more broadly.

"Lead on," Zezili said. She glanced back at Lilia. "And you get to work."

Lilia watched the two walk off toward the green flag of a unit of tirajistas. Then she glanced back at the mirror. Up. The figure embedded in it. There was some puzzle here she needed to figure out, but she wasn't seeing it. She placed her hand on one of the pillars. She could see no red mist here, nothing manipulated by Oma. She tried to put her hand between the pillars and found a solid wall of air, though. It was a parajista-built barrier. So, at least two sorts of magic-users would have to work together to gain access.

Lilia began to walk slowly around the mirror. As she passed to the other side, she saw that the reverse face was a flat, solid surface, just like the back of any mirror. She spent a few minutes walking back and forth, taking in the impossible vista visible on one side and the flat pane on the other. She kept walking, trying to keep her gaze on her feet at least as much as on the mirror. A few people at nearby camps stared at her, and she knew that if she made more than one revolution, someone was going to question her. She didn't have much time.

She arrived back at the front of the mirror. Gazed again at the withered figure atop it. Maybe her mother was alive, but from the look of what they'd done to her, it wasn't any kind of life Lilia would recognize. She studied the long streams of red haze braiding up the edges of the mirror. They radiated toward the middle of the mirror.

Zezili and Isoail, her shadow-mother, had thought she could unravel this because she was the daughter of the woman who built it. But why did that matter? What did she have or know that no one else did?

Lilia gazed at her mother's body. Then she stared down at her wrist.

She remembered Taigan pushing her from the edge of the cliff, telling her to fly.

The trefoil.

Litanies and songs focused power, but it was patterns that built objects of power. Specific patterns writ large. Like the trefoil pattern her mother had seared into her skin. It wasn't just a ward of protection. It was a ward that told her how to build things.

Lilia stared more closely at the braids of mist. She concentrated on one of the songs Taigan had taught her, the one for perceiving objects created by power. Then she took a deep breath and focused.

Nothing happened.

What had she done back there with the legionnaires? How had she called Oma then?

I'm afraid, she realized. Back then, I wasn't afraid.

Fear. Fear of death, fear of life, fear of failure, fear of succeeding. Bundles of fear that knotted her insides and tore at her guts. Kept her wound tight, closed off.

She took a breath. Then another. Only fools didn't feel fear; that's what Ora Dasai had always taught. But that wasn't true. Heroes felt fear. Villains did not. She was always afraid to let it go, because if the fear went, so did everything else.

She remembered the burning legion.

She let go.

Opened her eyes.

The braids of Oma's breath were suddenly clearer. It wasn't mist but intricately bound symbols. They were trefoils with long, curled tails. The tails bound them together.

Lilia took a deep breath. Her lungs opened. Her skin burned. She focused her power on the delicate end of one of the trefoils and pushed.

Something pushed back.

Lilia gasped.

Great, clawing figures of trefoil-bound mist gathered her up. Pulled her from the ground. Yanked her forward.

Lilia rushed into the air. She dangled eight stories up, propelled to the top of the mirror. The body there had come alive. It was more a torso, really, with stumps for arms and sightless eyes. Weeping thyme sprouted from the eye sockets, covering the cheeks of the face.

Lilia recoiled. But she was bound tightly from head to foot in Oma's breath. She looked down. A mistake. The height was dizzying. She had fallen from this height once already. Fear riddled her. Oma, she could not fall again. She was already so broken.

The body that was – or had once been – her mother lurched toward her as far as her buried torso would allow. Her mother opened her mouth and made strange garbling sounds. Her tongue was gone.

Tears streamed down Lilia's cheeks. She knew then why her mother pushed her through the gate so many years ago. This is what the Kai meant to do to Lilia.

"I promised I'd find you," Lilia said. "And I did. But you opened a gate for them. I have to close it."

Her mother sank back toward the edge of the mirror. Lilia watched the ropy bands of power pulse and shimmer. Her mother cocked her head. She wasn't sure how much of her mother was in there, or if the Kai had truly made her into something else.

"The trefoil," Lilia said. "I can break it, but you have to let me."

Lilia saw the bands of power begin to grow more sluggish. Her mother grunted. Spasmed.

"Let me go!" Lilia said. "Let me go so I can—"

The breath holding her aloft was suddenly gone.

Lilia fell.

She gasped – air and the breath of Oma, one breath. She envisioned the trefoil with the long tail. She had half a breath to choose – break her fall, or break the mirror? She chose. Lilia pushed her hands forward. She recited the Song of Unmaking and directed the surge at the apex of the mirror. At her mother.

Her mother screamed. The bloody red mist around the mirror's edge evaporated.

Lilia braced for impact.

She landed in a field of succulents. The broad, slime-filled leaves cushioned her fall. She landed amid a tangle of broken leaves and watery plant matter.

Lilia crawled out of the field and saw the white pillars in front of her. Looked back. The succulents had grown spontaneously, just in time to catch her. Her mother's final gift.

She gazed up at the mirror. The surface had gone dark. It reflected the fires of the camp, the flags, and the broken succulents. The infused power that had made it glow was gone. Where her mother had been was a scorched mark.

Lilia heard raised voices behind her, the sounds of a kicked nest swarming. But she walked to the face of the mirror anyway. She stared into her own scarred, grimy face. Her torn tunic, smeared in the guts of succulents. Her matted hair, her forgettable face.

"You will remember me," she said, and broke the face of the mirror with her bare fists.

She brought up her bloody hands as people began to stream toward her. She looked back at them only once. Then she pulled on Oma, a deep, frightful breath, and flayed the first wave of them where they stood.

Blood flecked her face. She brought up her hand and another raw breath of Oma, and tangled together the blood of the dead into perfect trefoils, bound by their long tails. She sang the Saiduan Song of the Dead as she did it. She burned the image of the camp in her mind, the camp at the base of the Liona mountains, where Gian waited for her.

A gate winked open, just big enough to crawl through. Unsure how long she could hold it, she jumped through and released Oma. The gate closed.

Lilia stood in the mud. The moons were out.

"Taigan!" she yelled. She looked back. The camp was intact. No fires. But she could still smell the burnt meat of the legion. "Taigan!"

"Here!" Taigan rode out to meet her from the far fence. "I thought you might return."

"Is everyone safe?"

"They pulled back," Taigan said. "I suspect they worried there were more of you. Where's the legionnaire?"

"I don't care," Lilia said. "Where's Gian and Emlee?"

"Your friends? Where they live, I expect."

She began to trudge toward the camp.

"Where are you going?" Taigan asked.

"It's time to fly," Lilia said.

49

Ahkio walked into the low bedroom of the private home in Raona where Liaro lay. He looked small. Ahkio sat on the edge of the bed. With the council house burned to the ground, the wounded were bedded down in whatever homes would take them.

Liaro reached out a hot, sweaty hand to him and said, "Ahkio."

"I hear you're supposed to live," Ahkio said. He pulled Kirana's book from his pocket. "If I practice reading aloud, I might get better at it, and you might get some sleep."

Liaro laughed. It turned into a cough. "Run a man through, then tell him stories. Sounds very Dhai."

"Ghrasia told me what you did just outside the square. It was brave."

"I tripped over my own sword and fell on it," Liaro said. "That's just stupid. It wasn't even an infused blade."

"But brave that you tried," Ahkio said.

"How *is* your friend Ghrasia?" Liaro said slyly.

"She's as well as can be expected," Ahkio said.

"Caisa told me you took that horrible painting down in Clan Leader Talisa's room before you blew it up."

"I did. Why?"

Liaro leaned toward him conspiratorially. "I wouldn't want all those dour people looking at me while some hero took me to bed, either."

Ahkio's face burned. He cleared his throat.

Liaro smirked. "I knew it."

"Can I read to you or not?"

"You know, I always thought Caisa played for the other side," Liaro said.

Ahkio's fingers lingered over the text. He still needed to deal with Caisa. But not yet. "Which one?"

"Good point. Not ours."

"Don't tell me you're becoming as paranoid as Nasaka."

"I'm just worried," Liaro said. He bunched up his bedsheets in his fists.

"Because you care for her?"

"We'd have been a merry union in another life," Liaro said, "me and you, Meyna and Caisa."

"You never liked Meyna."

"I didn't *dislike* her."

"Let me worry about Caisa," Ahkio said. "I'm good at it."

Liaro waved a hand. "Fine, fine. Read. It's been one person after another jabbering away in here, asking when I'll be ready for cards and bendar."

Ahkio turned to the last story in Kirana's book, titled *Faythe*. It was the story he heard at every Festival of Oma. He should have known it by heart. But as he read the story to Liaro, he found it was not at all the story he remembered. In this version, Faith was a slave from Aaldia. The child she carried was not Hahko's but an enslaved Dhai condemned for thievery in a dajian camp. Faith was not strong and brave and passionate. She was petty and weak and self-serving. The book made Faith into a figure of pity, not worship. Ahkio did not know if he liked it, and could not say if Liaro did, for he had fallen asleep.

Faith lay in childbed to give birth to the first Kai of Dhai. But when Hahko burst in, it was not to claim her child and free her, but to steal the child and proclaim it Kai. Ahkio decided that no, he really didn't like this story.

At the end of the last page of the book, Faith Ahya was still alive.

And though Ahkio had read the story, he was not certain how it would end. He would remain forever uncertain, because the last page of the book, the page following the broken sentence at the end of the final, intact page, recorder of the last days of Faith Ahya, had been torn out.

He had used it as kindling to light the fire that drove back the shadows.

After Liaro was asleep, Ahkio made his way back to the clan square, where the last of the Oras and militia Ghrasia had sent out to net the assassins had returned. They had sent out over a hundred Oras and militia, but he counted scarcely twenty in the square.

Ghrasia stood talking with the group's leader, a grizzled militia man named Farosi Sana Nako.

"Is this all?" Ahkio asked.

"Afraid so," Ghrasia said.

"And the assassins?"

"Here," Farosi said, and pulled back the cover on a cart. Ahkio counted five bodies.

"The full dozen, then," Ahkio said.

"At a great cost," Farosi said.

"Walk with me, Kai," Ghrasia said. She led him across the courtyard and onto a winding lane leading out to the rice fields. He kept his hands in his pockets.

As they walked, he noticed the sightless, feral little girl trailing after them along the weed-tangled road. He hadn't asked Ghrasia if the girl followed her all the time, but he suspected that unless she was inside a building, the girl was always within shouting distance.

"You were right," Ghrasia said.

"About what?"

"Me lording over the militia," she said. "Those assassins did what they did out of blind obedience to their Kai. They made things like that." She nodded to the feral girl. "And if they're what we'll fight... I'd rather we lost than become as they are."

Ahkio stopped walking. She came up beside him. "What is it?" she said.

"You know this was the easiest part," he said.

"May I touch you, Kai?"

"Always," he said.

She put her arms around him. Her head rested just above his heart.

"I know it will get more difficult," she said. "Just swear to me you'll keep us the people we are."

"I swear it," he said. But even as he spoke the words, he remembered standing over the dying man in the blazing council house basement, ready to impale him with his own blade.

"Then it will be all right," she said, and pulled away.

50

Lilia swept into Emlee's house, her bleeding hands wrapped in strips of her tattered red tunic. Gian jumped up from the floor and embraced her. Lilia had missed the smell of her hair.

"You're alive!" Gian said.

Taigan pushed in behind Lilia. He was much too tall for the low ceiling and had to duck.

"What happened out there?" Emlee said.

"I need to see Larn's priest, the one she gets all those nice things from," Lilia said. "The ones who are new to camp. The ones you keep on the side of camp you won't take me."

Emlee and Cora exchanged a look.

"I'm going to find them with or without you," Lilia said.

Cora handed her baby over to Emlee. He fussed.

"I'll take you," Cora said, "but I don't know what you'd want with him. Him and his priestesses are a secretive bunch. Larn has to–"

"I know what Larn does," Lilia said. "Take me to them."

Cora looked up at Taigan. "Him, too?"

"Yes... *him*, too."

Lilia asked one of the orphan packs to guard Taigan's bear. They would make enough of a stir without the bear.

Cora led them through deep mud, around dark hovels stained in smoke, to the far edge of the camp. She pointed to a large round hovel thatched in everpine and mud. "That's the place," she said.

Lilia strode toward the door. Taigan stayed silent.

She entered unbidden. It was dim inside, but she could see the women's seamed faces, their broad frames and hands. An adenoak staff with a jeweled knob at the end rested near the door.

All talk ceased as Lilia entered. Someone pulled back a curtain at the other side of the room. Larn was lit in profile, sitting up thin and disheveled in the bed.

The man who had pulled back the curtain stared at her with dark eyes in a very Dorinah face.

"Who are you?" the man said.

"They're gifted," Taigan said.

"Dorinah's gifted," Lilia said. "Soon to be my gifted."

The faces of the Empress of Dorinah's Seekers stared out at her. "What are your names?" Lilia asked. They told her: Voralyn, Amelia, Laralyn. Their leader – they called her a Ryyi – was Tulana. Tulana sat on a raised bench on the other side of the room, combing out her hair. Their clothes were tatters, their faces smeared in grime.

"And you?" Lilia asked the man.

"Sokai," he said.

"Zezili says hello," Lilia said. "And you're all going to help me. You're going to bind yourself to me, and you're going to come back to Dhai with me."

There was nervous laughter.

But Tulana did not smile. Lilia saw a soft red mist begin to suffuse the woman's body.

Lilia pushed out her hands, throwing her own web of red mist. She bound a skein of Oma's breath around the woman, cutting her off from the satellite.

Tulana's face paled.

Taigan nodded. "That was very good," he said.

"So, you have omajistas too," Lilia said. She kept the woven breath that held Tulana taut. In the back of her mind, she recited the Saiduan Song of Binding.

"I am many things," Tulana said. "Dangerous enough for my own Empress to try to kill me, in fact."

"I can promise I won't kill you," Lilia said. "But if you don't go with me, you'll die here. They have omajistas outside, much more powerful than you or me. They're going to burn us out. They'll come looking for you. But I can get you into Dhai. I can get you over the wall."

"No one gets over the wall," Tulana said. "You could force it, but–"

"No," Lilia said. "Listen."

And she told them her plan.

They stared at her in stunned silence. Only Gian laughed.

"You have grown bold," Taigan said.

"No bolder than a sanisi who pushed me off a cliff," Lilia said sharply.

"They will pound us against the wall," Tulana said. "They will slaughter us like boars."

"They'll do that anyway," Lilia said. "Yes or no?"

"You get us through that wall... then yes."

"Taigan, can you bind them to their word? Can you bind them in blood?"

"What?" Tulana said.

"You can't–" Voralyn spat.

"This is not–" Sokai said.

Lilia's voice rose. "You will bind yourselves in blood, or we're done."

"No," Tulana said.

So Lilia left them.

Taigan followed after her, said, "What are you trying to do, raise some kind of army?"

"They'll come," Lilia said with conviction. No one opened the gates of Liona, she knew. To get home, she needed to do something extraordinary.

Lilia went to the meeting house at the center of the camp. She took the stage. The whole camp was already abuzz with what had happened at the gates. They had begun to collect in the meeting house.

"I'm leaving for the pass," Lilia said loudly.

"You're mad!" someone yelled back.

"Maybe so," Lilia shouted at him. "Maybe so! Listen, I'm going. If you stay here, you're dead. I cannot protect you like I did yesterday. You understand? We're going home, or not at all."

"It's not our home!" someone else said.

"That's where you're wrong," Lilia said. "It's the home of every Dhai. They will open those gates to you as your kin. I swear my life on it. Will you join me or burn here?"

She tried to jump off the stage, but her bad leg made it difficult. Taigan offered his hand. Lilia took it. They walked back to Emlee's house. Lilia announced she was leaving.

"I have known no other home but this," Emlee said. "I will not smash myself against your wall."

"It's different this time," Lilia said.

"Why?"

"Because you have me."

"You are powerful, girl, but you aren't a god."

"We'll see about that," Lilia said.

Lilia held out her hand to Gian. Gian took it.

"Are you with me?" Lilia asked.

"Yes," Gian said.

People collected behind them as they made their way to the western gate. Hungry people. Big women and thin old men, and the orphans, some of them almost adults, but most of them young and small and scared.

Lilia waited until the dusk came and she was certain no one else was coming.

And as Taigan approached the gate to open it, Lilia saw Tulana stepping from the crowd of houses. Amelia, Voralyn, and Laralyn walked behind her. Sokai took up the rear of their procession.

Lilia glanced over at Taigan. Taigan popped the lock with a simple burst of air.

Lilia and Gian went through. The others followed.

The western gate was unguarded. Most of the legionnaires had withdrawn.

They walked all night, hungry and cold, stopping to collect hasaen tubers as they went. Lilia had not eaten a full meal in some time, and she was light-headed. The stronghold was a two-day walk. She was glad then of the small group. They would have moved more slowly with the others.

Taigan trotted back up behind Lilia and Gian. They led the column of ragged Dhais and dajians and Seekers.

"There are more following," he said.

"Who?" Lilia asked.

"There's smoke to the east," he said. "They've burned the camps. There are surviving Dhais following."

"And legionnaires?" Lilia asked.

"Not yet," he said, "but they will come."

They pushed on.

Night found them inside the mouth of the pass. At its widest point, the pass was nearly a mile across. Lilia knew it tapered to its narrowest point at Liona, two hundred yards across.

The trees became shorter, the path steeper. Finding a comfortable place to sleep that night was impossible. Lilia slept from sheer exhaustion and woke cramped and aching, her body pressed to Gian's. She was so cold, she didn't think her body could move, let alone stand, but she got up. Her body sometimes amazed her. She could keep going long after she couldn't.

At midmorning, the first of the later refugees caught up with them. Lilia recognized Pherl, the man with yaws whose nose was still a gaping hole, though some of the flesh had grown back over his missing upper jaw. His sisters were with him, Sazhina and Tal, Tal trailing behind, carrying her child. Someone else's child clung to her apron strings. Their faces were smeared with soot.

"What happened?" Lilia asked Sazhina.

"The legionnaires came," Sazhina said. "Sent fire first. They came in under the smoke."

Lilia saw the lights of Liona long after dark. She didn't know what time it was. The night was clear and cold. The moons were brilliant. They lit the rugged pass in a garish light. The lights of

the stronghold glinted from behind the massive wall, a crown
of square turrets topped in toothy parapets. The wall itself, even
from so far away, was imposing.

As they neared, Lilia realized how big the wall was. Just one
stone was as tall as she was. The beaten dirt road they traveled
upon broke itself against a small gateway just tall enough for
someone Lilia's height to enter. It was not a wall meant to be
breached. It was not a wall for idle travelers.

The steps of the refugees slowed as they approached the wall.
Lilia stilled a dozen yards from it and gazed up. The height was
staggering. Three hundred feet tall, easily. She could just make
out dark figures patrolling the top.

Her resolve trembled.

"Tears of the goddess," Gian said. "You don't mean to get us
through *that*?"

"At dawn," Taigan said.

Lilia looked behind them. More ragged figures trailed after
them in the moons' light, far more than had begun the journey.
And there would be legionnaires behind them. Soon.

"Where are the Seekers?" Lilia said. "We have to do this now."

Tal sent the child at her apron to look for the Seekers.

The girl brought back Tulana and Sokai and the others.

"Are you ready, dajian?" Tulana asked.

"Take off your coats," Taigan said.

Lilia watched the Seekers line up with their naked backs to Lilia
and Taigan. Voralyn was cursing. Tulana's face was unreadable.
Amelia cried. For a moment, just a moment, Lilia felt sorry for them.

Taigan saw Lilia watching them, said softly, "Would you like
to cut?"

"Yes," Lilia said. "What's the mark I put in?"

"Your name," Taigan said.

"My name," Lilia said. "Of course. Like the boy with the stone.
Names have the most power."

Lilia cut three neat Dhai characters into each of them, between
their shoulder blades.

Taigan said to Tulana, "Do you swear to remain loyal to Lilia Sona of Dhai, to aid her in every way, to keep all oaths and promises, to not deal falsely with her or her kin or play her false at pain of a death at your own hand?"

"I swear," Tulana hissed.

The others swore and were cut. The air around them was heavy, electric. Lilia could not tell if any of them were working against Taigan, trying to unbind the flesh and blood Taigan manipulated to bind their bodies to their words. If they did, Taigan said nothing of it, and Lilia saw no red mist massing around Tulana. Lilia watched the way Taigan braided the red mist so she could replicate the ward in the future. It was an intricate thing, like a piece of prose poetry set to music.

When Taigan finished, Gian cleaned their wounds.

Lilia sat awake with Taigan on a mass of rough-cut stones. They gazed up the height of the wall. Taigan passed her a pipe of sen leaves. She took a few puffs, choked on the smoke, handed it back.

They sat in silence for a long time. Finally, Lilia asked, "Why did you come back for me? You left me to die, Taigan."

"I wanted your opinion on the battle at Roasandara, the one fought two thousand years ago," he said.

Laughter bubbled up. Lilia choked on it. She laughed so hard, she doubled over. Tears streamed down her face.

Taigan said, "Should I pound your back? Are you dying?"

His serious tone made Lilia laugh harder. She remembered being broken at the bottom of the ravine, the karoi pecking her apart, piece by piece. She thought of the dead child severed by the gate, the burning legionnaires, the burst mirror, and how she had killed her own mother.

"If you wanted my opinion on a battle," she said, "you should have turned around sooner."

"No," Taigan said. "I came back for you at just the right time."

51

Zezili was getting happily drunk when the world exploded.

She supposed she should have expected who it would be shaking her awake the next morning while she slept off the drink and violence of the night before in the cold, crooked roots of a tree stump.

She rubbed her gummy eyes and saw Monshara standing above her. "You're predictable, at least," Monshara said. "You want to go in chains back to your Empress, or take a dog and walk in on your own two feet?"

Zezili gazed up at the rotten sky of Monshara's world. "It was worth it," she said.

"We'll see," Monshara said.

By the time Zezili was delivered back to her own world, put back into her proper clothes, and escorted back to Daorian by Monshara and two of her omajistas, Daorian was already wreathed in red, the color of mourning. Great red banners flanked the tower gates, the spires of the distant keep. The city people had put out red kerchiefs in their windows, hung them from the snow-heavy awnings of their shops. Zezili wondered who died. Then wondered if it was supposed to be her.

People knew her by her armor, the plaited skirt knotted with the hair of dajians, the image of Rhea holding a sword over a dead bear etched into the breastplate, outlined in flaking silver.

Her helm had no plume, ending instead in a curve of metal like a snake's tail. The people came out to see her, muttered about her on their doorsteps, pointed. Some saw her and hid. Two old women made a ward against evil as she passed. It told Zezili something of the Empress's silent ambiguity regarding her station that they did not spit at Zezili or curse her. It helped that Monshara hadn't bound her.

It was a small kindness, Zezili supposed.

The city waited on the Empress's judgment.

Zezili reined her dog within the courtyard of the keep. Monshara and her omajistas slid off their bears. A kennel girl darted out from the warmth of the kennels and took the reins of Zezili's dog without looking Zezili in the face.

Zezili reached up a hand to her dog's ears and rubbed at the base of them. She pressed her cheek to his and pretended he was Dakar. She had lost her husband and her dog. She had betrayed her Empress. It was the end of all things.

The dog licked her face with his hot tongue. She pulled away only to find that she had gripped the hair of his collar in both hands. She slowly uncurled her fingers. She turned away and walked up the loop of the outdoor stair and into the foyer of the hold. She glanced back at Monshara. "I can get the rest of the way myself," she said.

Monshara swept her hand forward. "You should have listened to me," she said.

"I don't listen to anybody," Zezili said. "Not anymore."

Saofi, the Empress's secretary, was waiting for Zezili outside the audience chamber. She played with the eyeglass at the end of her chatelaine.

"She's been expecting you," Saofi said.

"You have too, no doubt," Zezili said.

"Your fate and mine are linked," Saofi said. "So yes, I have an interest in this outcome."

At first, Zezili wasn't sure what she meant. But of course, everyone knew about the purging of the dajian camps by now. The privately-owned dajians knew it was only a matter of time before the bloody swords came for them, too. And for me, Zezili thought. Us.

Saofi went inside the audience chamber to announce Zezili. Zezili felt oddly calm. She had been courting this day for some time.

The secretary reappeared. Her expression was blank. "She'll see you," Saofi said. Saofi gripped the outer handle and leaned back with all her weight, pulling the door wide.

A chandelier of crystal shards and flame flies hung from the ceiling. A purple carpet stretched the length of the hall to the raised dais at its end. Atop the dais sat the silver throne of eighteen hundred years of Dorinah rule, the throne usurped from the first Patron of Saiduan's fiftieth son, constructed in the far north of that country two thousand years before by silversmiths whose like Zezili had never encountered.

The Empress did not sit on the throne but stood near it, surrounded by her enormous green-eyed cats, each as tall as Zezili's shoulder. The sight of them sent a prickling up Zezili's spine. The Empress herself was a tall, striking figure, slender, with knobby arms and legs that were often canted at awkward angles. Her face, neck, and hands were smeared in a bronzer that gave her the color of dark honey. A blotch of red marked her lips. Her black brows and brilliant yellow eyes were smudged in kohl, and her hair – most of it her own – added another foot to her already extraordinary height. She dressed in a pale white dress with bone corseting that gave her the figure of a stick insect. The elaborate hooping under her gown created a wall of material belling out from her narrow frame, a distance that would have to be crossed before one touched her.

Zezili squared her shoulders. She concentrated on the length of purple carpet, but as she walked, her gaze was drawn to the Empress's cats. They sat quietly watching her, their faces as inscrutable as the Empress's.

Zezili walked to within a yard of the cusp of the Empress's belled white gown, stared at the hem, and got down on both knees before her. She took off her helm, set it beside her.

The cats wound closer. A dozen, more? She imagined them chewing on her body, saw claws rend flesh.

She bowed her head and moved the tangled mass of her hair, baring her neck. One of the big cats lay down beside her. Its tail caressed her legs.

A delicate hand alighted on the base of Zezili's neck. The fingers were cold.

"I charged you," the Empress said, her voice like a sigh.

"I did as you bid," Zezili said. "All but one of the camps is cleansed, and I'm sure Monshara can take care of the last. I obeyed you in all things."

"You darkened their way. You interfered," the Empress said. Her fingers dug into Zezili's hair. "Worse, you may have hurt my other plans." She took her hand away and beckoned to the cat lolling beside Zezili.

Another of the cats hissed.

"I find myself uncertain what to make of you or do with you." The Empress sat in her silver throne, the fantastic menagerie of beaten silver rods and spires twisted into grotesque faces.

"Perhaps this was my fault," she said. "I expected pure obedience. Look at me."

Zezili raised her gaze from the carpet. She did not know what she expected to see in the Empress's face, but looking up, she saw an unchanged visage, unmarked by feeling, grief or fear or anger. The Empress was, as ever, a blank bronze canvas, with the long, regal neck and supple form of her kind, the startling eyes.

"I do have a platter for your head here." She patted the silver throne. "But my cats are not hungry, they say."

Zezili looked at the cats. They stared back at her.

"There is another use for you," the Empress said. "One for my sisters patiently waiting for Oma's rise. You see, the Tai Mora are not the only world brought closer now. Our alliance with the Tai Mora was for convenience only, until the world of my sisters was close enough to wake those of us left behind. I will charge you with the sacred task of preparing for their awakening.

You will prepare your legion in the spring and travel to Tordin."

"But... Empress... I thought I'd be feeding bugs in the dirt. I know what I did." She wanted to say more; it bubbled up inside her, a mad anger she'd held back these months. "I can't follow you any more. I'm not your slave."

But the Empress continued as if Zezili had not spoken. "I will send mercenaries with you from the outer islands. Three thousand Sebastyn pike men, five hundred Jorian archers. You understand?"

Zezili stood. Her knees ached. Cold sweat had gathered along her spine. She had not expected she would be allowed to rise. She had not thought past kneeling upon the carpet.

"You know I can't obey you any longer," Zezili said.

"I know you think that," the Empress said. Her tone was light.

The cats were uncurling from the floor. Zezili had never known such fear. But the fear of going back to her servitude was far worse.

"I cannot serve," Zezili said. "Me, the dajians, the other Dorinahs. We're all the same to you. I know that now."

"I know you think you've turned your face from me," the Empress said. "You think you've found some other path. But we'll change your mind. You'll know, when we are done, who it is you belong to."

Her cats crept up alongside Zezili and blocked her from the door. They circled her.

"My cats can be very persuasive," the Empress said. "You understand?"

"Yes," Zezili said. And she did.

The cats pounced.

Zezili did not have time to bring up her hands.

52

Ahkio welcomed Nasaka to Clan Raona three days after the massacre. What remained of Ahkio's caravan was nearly packed up and ready for the journey back to the Temple of Oma. The air was cool and wet; the suns had beaten back the high winter frost so fiercely, Ahkio worried low spring would come early this year. Far too early.

Nasaka wound her way past the snuffling bears and carts and somber militia. Ahkio met her in front of the charred ruin of the council house, near the fountain, where Caisa was filling water bladders for their trip.

Ahkio had a ledger full of Kirana's temple maps under his arm, and a letter from Mohrai's family at the harbor. Spring had not yet broken in Saiduan, she said. But the watch houses were staffed double. His concern now was encouraging clans to begin rationing early without inciting panic.

"So, you've slaughtered some people," Nasaka said, "and lost us sixty-five good citizens."

Ahkio wondered at that greeting. Some people, he decided, would never change. "I sent you a message over a week ago," Ahkio said. "You took your time."

"There are a great many tasks that need management and minding in order to run a country," Nasaka said. "It's not all blind, heroic bloodbaths."

"We'll need to speak about Ora Dasai's mission," Ahkio said.

"I've had some news I wanted to speak to you about. In person."

"Indeed. It may be time to for us to speak of that in full."

"You heard, then?" Ahkio needed people closer to Nasaka, someone who could intercept correspondence. He had begun to think like Kirana, he realized. Like a Kai.

"I summoned you here because I need to tie some things up at the temple," Ahkio said. "I'll be taking the Line back, but I need you to accompany my caravan. On foot."

Nasaka narrowed her eyes. "What's this?"

"You're my political and religious advisor. Aren't you? I'd like you to travel overland and report back. I need to assess our readiness for war. I can rely on your discretion?"

"Ahkio—"

"Good. Ghrasia's been summoned to the Liona Stronghold on an urgent matter, so I can't have her do it. I'm sure you understand how important this is, without her to help."

"If you want a few days to yourself at the temple, you could have asked."

"I need a woman on the ground here who can assess this threat."

"I could give you Elaiko and—"

"That will be all," Ahkio said. He gestured to Caisa, who'd finished filling the bladders. "Let's call Liaro and go."

She slipped on her pack and leapt forward.

Ahkio left Nasaka with grim company in Raona. Caisa and Liaro accompanied Ahkio on foot to Kuallina, though Liaro's pace was slow, to account for his fresh but healing injuries. Kuallina was a hulking fortress at the center of Dhai, a tirajista-trained construction built for defense. From what, Ahkio wasn't certain, as it was many days' walk from both the harbor and the mountain pass that Liona guarded. It was a massive relic from another time, just like Liona, and the temples, and the twisted Line that carried people between them.

They stepped into the shimmering organic chrysalis that rode the corded Line, and the attendant parajista wished them luck at Oma's temple.

"I wonder if she knows how much we'll need it," Ahkio said.

"I'm still worried this is a dead end," Caisa said.

"Kirana didn't think so."

Liaro said, "I'm already feeling a bit like some secret explorer. Think we'll fall off the map of the temple basements all together? Uncover old artifacts? I'm hoping to find a cure for hangovers, myself."

Ahkio's arrival at Oma's Temple incited a flurry of activity. With Elder Ora Gaiso dead in the attempted coup and Ora Almeysia banished, he found new faces occupying their places. Younger, less predictable Oras with unknown family connections. He had Caisa note their names. They would need to study them, find their weaknesses, and exploit family ties.

Late that night, he woke Liaro, Caisa, and Una, the gatekeeper, and gained access to the temple basements. The first floor below the temple were the baths, great stone basins of fresh water heated by the beating heart of the temple; low ceilings, steam, and luscious night-creeping plants ran all along the warm walls. Many of their flowers were in bloom, great white-and-violet fingers that filled the air with the smell of honey and roses.

The four of them carried flame fly lanterns through the cloying heat. When they dropped to the second level, the warmth was gone, replaced by a dry chill that reminded Ahkio that spring threatened to warm the world.

"Ora Nasaka doesn't like people going down past the third basement level," Una said as she cleared the bracken trap from the door leading to the third subfloor.

"Ora Nasaka doesn't like loud voices," Liaro said, "or butterflies. I expect she strangles kittens in her spare time."

"You're a rude boy," Una said. She patted her nest of hair and huffed down the long corridor of storage rooms. The doors here were marked in old Dhai characters, labeling rooms for rice and rye storage, dried hasaen tubers and fiddleheads, honey and salted greens. When they reached the fourth level, Una refused to go any further.

"Did you ever go down here with Kirana?" Ahkio asked her.

"Kai Kirana only came down here by herself," Una said. "You'll pardon, but the former Kai was a strange bird."

Liaro rolled his eyes. "Pots and kettles."

Ahkio raised his lantern so he could see the look on her face. He saw fear more than cunning. "Wait here for us, Ora Una."

Her chin trembled. "An hour, Kai. Then I call down the militia."

Ahkio plunged ahead, Caisa at his heels, Liaro grumbling behind. The store rooms went on forever. When they reached the sixth floor beneath the massive temple, Ahkio told Caisa to wait in the stairwell.

"But Kai–"

"If we're not back by the time your flame flies settle, have Ora Una call for Nasaka."

Once he and Liaro were out of Caisa's sight, Ahkio pulled out Kirana's map of the lowest basement. There were no proper rooms here, just massive, tangled vines made out of the same stuff as the temple's skin; they reminded him of tree roots. He had to squeeze among them. Soon, his hands were covered in grit and mucus. He sneezed often.

"I hope this isn't a fool's run," Liaro said.

"You have something better to do?"

"Caisa and I can fill time."

"You'll break your stitches."

"It'd be worth it."

Much to Ahkio's relief, the final mapped level of the temple was a finite space. He circled around the outer edges of it twice and had to double back and follow the map again. He knew he was closer the third time, because the fleshy roots grew warmer; the air felt less congested.

He peered through a viny tangle marked on the map, and saw, on the other side, a small clearing and a massive stone slab.

"Well," Liaro said, "not a snake chase after all."

"Stay here. I'm going to go through."

Ahkio reached through the tangle and set the lantern down on the other side. Then he squeezed into the narrow space between two roots. Halfway through, he got stuck. His ribs caught.

Liaro grabbed his legs and pushed from the other side. "Let your breath out," he said.

Ahkio let out his breath. He pulled while Liaro pushed.

He slid onto the other side of the tangle, falling inelegantly onto the gritty floor. Scrambled up. Grabbed the lantern. The towering circular slab wasn't quite stone. He pressed his fingers to it, and it felt slick and chalky. The face of it was inlaid in blue and red stones. Above, twisted vegetation and the temple's thrumming roots held it upright. He tried to walk around it, but the mass of living plant flesh was too tight there for him to pass.

There were no Dhai characters on it, no writing at all. It was not until he stepped all the way back and raised the lantern higher that he saw the stones were arranged in a familiar shape – a double blue circle inside a red square.

"Is it some infused thing?" Liaro called.

Ahkio tried pressing the stones. He kicked gently at its base. Nothing happened.

Kirana had been gifted, and it wouldn't surprise him if whatever he needed to do to this slab to get a reaction involved having a gift. It was the one thing he lacked. He wished that he'd brought Caisa all the way down. He would need to go back for her.

Ahkio set down his lantern and turned the map around a couple of times. There must be something he wasn't seeing. Kirana spent time down here with these maps. It wasn't as if this object was wholly inconspicuous. So, what was it supposed to do?

He pulled the Dorinah book from his pocket, the one with the ciphered phrases. He had tucked a sheet with the translations inside. Mostly, Etena and Kirana had debated philosophy and Garika politics. They talked about lovers and old Dhai battles. But there was that exchange:

The Temple's heart is barred to me, Etena. She says she will only speak to a Kai. Why close all the roads to me?

And Etena's reply:

Because if you can open the way, so can your shadow.

Ahkio faced the slab again and gazed up the face of it into the darkness, where it seemed to merge with the roots of the temple. His mother had said the temples were living things. Living things had hearts.

It felt foolish to yell in the darkness, but he was out of ideas. "I'm Ahkio Javia Garika," he said, "brother to Kirana Javia Garika, and I am Kai of the Dhai."

His voice echoed.

Kai. Yes. He was Kai, and Kirana had believed he would get this far, for good or ill.

But nothing happened. The slab remained unchanged.

"Any other ideas?" Liaro asked.

Dead ends. Ghost trails. Kirana was killed by the invaders, the assassins he murdered in the square, just like the others. Trying to make it more than that would lead him down a path to madness, the way they all said Kirana had gone. He was trying to unpack riddles on top of riddles, and he had a country to secure.

But Kirana said she killed herself, and that only made sense in the context of who the invaders were. There was something down here she didn't want her other self to be able to use. Something she had to die to ensure only her successor had access to. Not her shadow. And not Nasaka.

The only way for her to raise another Kai, one recognized by a living temple, was to die.

Ahkio sighed. It had made more sense in that warm bed with Ghrasia than it did in this oppressive dark. He leaned forward. Pressed his head against the stone—

—and tumbled forward.

He landed hard on his side. Lost his breath. It was like falling through soup, as if the slab were some gauzy webbing. His face and hands felt sticky. He'd bit his lip. He tasted copper.

A warm glow suffused the darkness, like liquid gold. Ahkio shielded his eyes. A humming came from all around him.

"Kai Ahkio Javia Garika," a tremulous voice said, "welcome to the soul of Oma's seat. We've been waiting for you for some time."

53

Ghrasia arrived at the Liona Stronghold by Line. It had been a long time since she last saw its walls. The great living vines that bound the hold's walls were comforting. When she stepped out of the Line chamber, familiar faces greeted her, though far fewer than she would have liked.

She met the hold's temporary keeper, Arasia Marita Sorila, one floor up in Ghrasia's former office. Arasia had stacks of correspondence on the table and books scattered across the floor.

"Have you given up defense for strategy?" Ghrasia asked.

Arasia was a very round woman, at least three times Ghrasia's size. She held a magnifying lens in one hand and a Tordinian cigarette in the other.

"Thank Tira you've arrived," Arasia said. "Don't worry about this. We're working with the parajistas to shore up the west end. Lots of history reading. I didn't get into this for the reading, you know."

"What's happening on the wall?" Ghrasia asked. "Your note was brief."

"Best you see it for yourself," Arasia said. She took Ghrasia up the winding stairs to the ramparts. It was nearly dark. Ghrasia went to the edge of the rail and gazed across what must have been almost six hundred dajians camped at the bottom of the wall. She had seen groups of refugees camped before, but none like this. It was even bigger than the group she turned away during the Pass War.

Ghrasia stepped away from the rail. "They're just refugees," she said. "You know the policy."

"Yes, but see that?" Arasia pointed. In the far distance, Ghrasia could see smoke. "They have a tail behind them. You know what a tail with cook fires that size looks like."

"Hold the wall," Ghrasia said. "You know the policy."

Arasia seemed pleased. "I told the others that's what you'd say. They didn't believe it, but I knew the history."

"Only a miracle would have us open these gates," Ghrasia said. She tried not to think of how many people they just lost in Raona. She remembered Ahkio's speech. And his mother's. The same tired story. "Let's have dinner. I'll walk the ranks."

Lilia tried the obvious thing first, just to get it out of the way. She pounded on the little sally port at the gates of Liona and demanded entrance. She called up her name and her place at the Temple of Oma. No one answered.

There was no welcome for her at Liona. There certainly wouldn't be any welcome for the rest of them. She would have to make one. In a way that was more politic than burning the whole stronghold down.

When the moons set and the sky began to gray, Taigan said, "It's time for you to dress."

"Yes," she said. She took Taigan's water bag.

She woke Gian. Gian opened her pack. Lilia washed her own face. Gian helped her take off her clothes. Lilia knelt on her dirty clothes to keep her knees out of the mud. Gian unpacked Lilia's white dress. It wasn't as white as it should be, and it would look terrible up close, but from a distance, it would do. Lilia pulled the dress over her head. Gian tied the white ribbons she had gifted her at Lilia's wrists and on her fingers. They had already re-bound her hands in white bandages.

Gian moved her hands through Lilia's long hair and oiled and combed it. Lilia could not remember the last time she had long hair. The Woodlands, maybe. A long time ago. Her hair was ragged at the ends and needed a cut, but like the dress, it would do.

Gian braided back Lilia's hair into an intricate swirl of knots and bound them in white ribbon. She used a fine stick of charred wood to outline Lilia's eyes in black.

Gian helped Lilia to her feet and regarded her in the graying light.

"Are you afraid?" Gian asked.

Lilia looked over her shoulder at the height of the wall. "No," she said.

They walked to the gate where Taigan and the Seekers waited.

"You have sworn to her," he told them, "and to disobey that word forfeits your life. Remember that."

"She's gifted," Tulana said. "I still don't see why she can't do this herself."

"Faith Ahya wasn't gifted," Lilia said.

Taigan shrugged. "There it is."

"Superstitious Dhai nonsense," Tulana said.

Distant cries sounded behind them.

Taigan nodded to Lilia.

Lilia moved to the front of their half circle. Some of the Dhais and dajians camped around them had woken. They sat up and stared.

"All right," Lilia said.

Taigan held out his palm toward her. She felt a prickling across her shoulders. The air in front of her shimmered bloody red. She took a deep breath and shouted up at the wall, "I am a Dhai, and I demand entrance through Liona!"

The funnel of air Taigan shaped carried her words to the top of the wall. Her voiced boomed through the pass. She clapped her hands over her ears. The shout was deafening.

Cries came from the top of the wall, shouts, sounding small and plaintive after Lilia's cry.

"Who's there? What's happened?" someone called from the wall.

"Open the gate! I ask passage!"

"What right do you have for passage?"

"We are Dhai! That is enough!" An echoing call, the voice of a god.

Something in her hesitated before she said the rest – and committed herself to blasphemy.

Lilia closed her eyes and shouted, "I am the rightful Kai, and by the laws of our country, you are bound to open these gates for me and all those I harbor!"

Banging on the door.

Ghrasia started awake. Grabbed her sword. Shoved it forward just as the door opened.

The small woman in the doorway jumped back. "Ghrasia Madah!"

Ghrasia shook herself awake. She had been dreaming of blinding-trees. "I'm sorry. What is it?"

"One of the refugees is shouting. Arasia said to bring you upstairs."

"Of course they're shouting; they're–"

"The legionnaires are going to press them against the gates, just like in the Pass War. Please!"

Ghrasia swore. "I'm coming; all right." She knew why Arasia wanted her on the gate. She didn't want the blood on her hands. No one wanted the blood. Gods. She thought of Ahkio. And Nasaka, and what Nasaka could do to her daughter.

Ghrasia dressed quickly and walked up to the ramparts. It wasn't even dawn yet. On the ground below, she saw a girl dressed all in white, standing among a half circle of figures.

There were already two dozen militia on the walls. Arasia strode toward her. "She says she's the Kai," Arasia said.

"Well, that's obviously untrue," Ghrasia said. "I was just with the Kai in Raona, and I can assure you this person is of the wrong type."

"Well," Arasia said, low, "some people do say *he's* the wrong type, really. The Kai has always been able to bear–"

"Hold your ground. They are just refugees."

Lilia glanced over at Taigan. She was watching the sun rise along the horizon directly behind them.

Taigan held up a hand, telling her to wait.

Then Taigan nodded.

Lilia held out her arms. She felt the Seekers behind her tense. She took a deep breath. She heard more shouting behind them.

Someone screamed, "Dorinahs!"

Lilia focused on her breathing. She felt the heat of Oma just beneath her skin. She held it but did not draw it. Just in case. She had fallen too many times already.

"I'm ready," she murmured.

Her skin began to itch. She felt the suns at her back, cresting the edge of the world. She turned her head up, toward the top of the wall.

Something cold crawled up her spine. She resisted the urge to grab at it. The air around her became heavy, murky. She took deeper breaths.

Her skin began to glow, a soft amber light.

Her view of the wall altered. It looked like the wall was getting shorter, but she was actually moving upward. She kept her arms out, trailing white ribbons. She did not look down but concentrated on the top of the wall. A false wind caught at her bound hair, the streamers in her hands, and blew them back behind her. The wall was rushing past her.

Lilia flew.

Her skin felt hot. She did not look at her arms to see if the divine glow had become a blistering flame. She could not look at anything but the top of the wall and the figures rushing back and forth as her glowing body shot up through the air.

Lilia crested the top of the wall with the blinding glare of the suns-rise. She alighted on one of the big parapet stones.

She looked down at the walkway atop the wall and the dozens of skirted militia staring up at her in fear and awe.

Only one woman had not shielded her eyes. She was small and slight. She was familiar, though Lilia could not place her.

"You will open these gates," Lilia said softly, but Taigan's amplification of her voice set the militia to covering their ears. All but the little woman.

"I have come to free these people," Lilia said. "You will open these gates for them."

Lilia's skin burned. The heat of the suns throbbed at her back. Her fingers were numb from holding the ribbons. Her shadow swallowed the form of the woman in front of her. Her shadow was a great thing, a massive specter burning along the battlements.

Lilia dropped her arms. She had run out of words.

The little woman stared up at Lilia. Her jaw hardened. Her eyes were black under the length of Lilia's shadow.

Ghrasia watched Faith Ahya land lightly atop the parapet. The breath left Ghrasia's body. She had the absurd urge to kneel. Streamers of white cascaded from Faith's fingertips, like wings. How many times had Ghrasia wished for a world where she could take back everything she had done twenty years ago?

She remembered the little feral girl. Remembered the screams of the dying during the Pass War and the screams of her people slain by the shadow-men in Liona. Oma help her, she thought of the dead shadows, too.

"Am I any better than them," Ghrasia asked the girl, "if I slay you here?"

"Only you can answer that," the girl said.

Ghrasia thought of the woman in the tapestry. The woman her country thought she was. That woman would not open these gates.

But she was not that woman.

She turned to Arasia. "Open the gates," Ghrasia said.

"But you said–"

Ghrasia did not raise her voice. "Open the gates of Liona."

Arasia shouted at the militia on the parapet, relaying the order.

Ghrasia watched the girl. The suns' light was harsher now, and Ghrasia could see scars on her face. She saw how tattered her white garments were, some shoddy patchwork piece. The ribbons in her hair had obviously been salvaged from some other, finer garment. She leaned awkwardly to one side, and her left hand was a twisted little claw.

The girl was little more than a child – a child desperate enough to fly.

Lilia gazed over the wall at the crush of her people below. As the gates opened, her people began to sing. Lilia did not know the song. It was something in the patois of the camps. But it was very beautiful.

"You're very brave," the woman on the wall said.

Lilia had almost forgotten about her. "Yes," Lilia said. "I know."

EPILOGUE

Nasaka climbed into the mossy hills surrounding the Temple of Oma. She stood in a field of withered black poppies, their massive blooms frozen and crushed in the winter chill. She looked back at the amber haze of sunlight glinting from the massive dome of the temple. Out here, the temple seemed very small, nearly swallowed in the naked, grasping claws of the bonsa trees. It all looked very fragile. She gripped the hilt of her willowthorn sword, tensing her arthritic fingers. The pain was getting worse, and she would not be able to hide it much longer.

The air around her grew heavy. She turned to face the woods. As she waited, the air in front of her shimmered, as if tempered by a wave of heat. Black rents appeared in the air. She stepped back.

The seams between the worlds parted as if raked by the claws of some great beast. There were places where the fabric between the worlds was thin, and the cost to peer from one to the other was not quite so high, even with Oma's face still shrouded. This soft spot was closest to Oma's temple, and Nasaka thanked Oma each day that no adult could fit through the seams that opened here.

Through the tears between the worlds, Nasaka saw the other Kirana, dressed in shiny red armor. She stood in the sweltering ruin of some dead city. Nasaka saw the tail end of the black, dying satellite in the sky behind her. Scorched bodies hung from parched trees and lay mangled on broken plates of pink glass and blood-smeared marble. From what Nasaka could make out of the bodies' remaining clothes and features, the dead were of no people she recognized.

Three of Kirana's generals conferred nearby. Nasaka had seen them a few times before. One of them looked a lot like Gaiso, perhaps a bit plumper, but she had never asked the woman's name. She didn't like seeing the others. Knowing they existed was one thing. Seeing them was quite another.

"Is it done?" Kirana asked. She pulled off her left gauntlet and wiped the sweat from her face. She was a lean but powerful woman, far more physically fit than the Kirana that Nasaka had once known.

"He's left the temple for Liona," Nasaka said. "By the time I got back, he was already gone."

"Don't tell me your prized boy has become headstrong," she said, but she was not looking at Nasaka. She was looking off to the left at some commotion.

"I didn't know about Kirana's quarters in Garika," Nasaka said. "By the time I arrived to clear them out, he'd already done it. I had no idea she was meeting with the Garikas behind my back. But our deal still holds."

"What?" Kirana glanced back at her. "Yes, of course. So long as you control him, he's no threat to me. You can have the boy. To be honest, I was always surprised you asked for nothing else."

Nasaka sometimes wondered how different things would be now if her Kirana had been the sort of leader this one was. But their worlds were different. Her Kirana had not been raised in a world that would produce such a person. But it produced me, Nasaka thought. It was I who failed. I should have raised her to be a soldier. A fighter. If I had raised her to such a vocation, we wouldn't be in this place.

"I've seen how you deliver on your promises," Nasaka said.

Kirana raised her brows. "You got your boy on the seat. That's what you wanted, wasn't it?"

"You asked me to kill a good many people and lie and betray far more to get there."

"It's not as if lying is a new exercise for a woman in your position."

"Kirana's death nearly split the country apart," Nasaka said.

"That was her fault," Kirana said. "She should have parlayed. Instead, she chose the coward's way." The air between them wavered. "I don't have much time. Will the harbor gates be open or not?"

"I need time."

"I thought you controlled Ahkio," Kirana said coolly. "If you can't control him, he's not necessary. I can have him easily replaced with any number of my own people."

"Like Yisaoh?"

"Yisaoh?" Kirana seemed genuinely surprised, then laughed. "I am often heartened by the amount of ignorance you display in these conversations, Nasaka."

Nasaka gripped her sword hilt hard. The willowthorn branch snaked out, wrapping around her wrist. She bared her teeth. "He'll do as I ask." And if he wouldn't, his wife would.

"Good." Kirana pulled her gauntlet back on and barked something at her generals in the Dhai dialect they used. Nasaka had picked it up over the decade of their discussions, but the gate between them was becoming unstable, and the words were garbled.

"My son," Nasaka said, loudly. "He'll do as you ask." Just in case she had not heard.

Kirana glanced back at her and flashed a grin. It was a confident, reassuring grin that Nasaka had seen her own Kirana employ while charming clan leaders and Oras alike. It squeezed at Nasaka's heart.

"I know he will," Kirana said.

The air pressure suddenly decreased. The air shivered. The rents between the worlds snapped shut.

Nasaka let out her breath. She stood alone in the field. Her grip on her sword eased. She let herself fall to one knee in the poppies. Her heart was pounding fast. The surge of adrenaline was nearly overwhelming. She had wanted to cut across the gate and sever

Kirana in two. But the war was coming. Oma was rising. And the Dhai in this world were not prepared for it.

The outcome was clear to her from the first moment the other Kirana dragged her through to witness a death that even now, Nasaka could not bear to think about. This Kirana would win. It would be a rout. The army that flooded Saiduan now was just a taste of what they were about to experience. Kirana had already destroyed her own world. Now she was coming for theirs.

Nasaka waited until her pulse slowed, and then rose. The hourglass of the suns had tipped behind the mountains. The world went turquoise, then violet. Nasaka followed the hunting trail back through the field of poppies, down into the snowy foothills, back to the Temple of Oma and the son who despised her, though she was the only thing standing between him and death.

She was no fool, of course. She knew Kirana would come for them soon enough. But Nasaka had other plans. Plans she needed far more time to put into motion.

When Nasaka reached the temple, it was full dark, her way lit only by the moons. She pushed open the sally port and mounted the long tongue of the grand staircase.

Una, the gatekeeper, met her on the stair.

"He was in the basements a long time before they called him to Liona," Una said. "He wouldn't tell me what he was up to, but he had some kind of maps."

"Did he find Meyna? She's still secure in the gaol?"

"She is," Una said. "Don't worry about that. What was he looking for down there, Ora Nasaka?"

"I don't know," Nasaka said. "But I intend to find out."

GLOSSARY

AALDIA

Country on the southwestern shore of Grania, led by a conclave of three queens and two kings.

ABAS MORASORN

A Saiduan dancer at Kuonrada.

ABUYTU

The name of a month of the year, in early (low) spring.

AHKIO JAVIA GARIKA

Teacher in Clan Osono. Son of Javia Mia Sorai and Rishin Garin Badu. Brother to Kirana Javia Garika, the leader of the Dhai people.

AHMUR

The largest of Raisa's three moons.

ALAAR MASOTH TAAR

The Patron of Saiduan. A tirajista.

ALAIS SOHRA GARIKA

Birth mother to Yisaoh Alais Garika. Married to Garika clan master Tir, Moarsa, and Gaila.

ALASU CARAHIN SORILA
A member of the Kuallina militia.

ALBAARIC
A city on the Saiduan coast. Former home of Maralah Daonia's family.

ALMEYSIA MAISIA SORILA
An Ora and the Mistress of Novices at the Temple of Oma. A very sensitive tirajista.

ALORJAN
A Saiduan-controlled island north of Dorinah, currently under siege by Dorinah.

AMELIA NOVAO
A Seeker from Dorinah. Tirajista.

ANAVHA HASARIA
Zezili Hasaria's husband. Son of Gilyna Lasinya, a tax clerk in Dorinah's eastern province. The Empress awarded Anavha to Zezili as a token for her service.

ARAMEY DAHINA DASINA
A Dhai scholar, specializing in Saiduanese history. Married to Lanilu Asaila Sorila.

ARASIA MARITA SORILA
Temporary keeper of the Liona Stronghold in Ghrasia Madah's absence.

ARISAA SAARA
Politically formidable wife of Patron Alaar Masoth Taar.

ASHAAR TOAAN
A Saiduan scholar.

ASONA MOSANA BADU
Clan leader of Clan Badu.

BAEL ASARAAN
Record keeper for the archives at Kuonrada. Native of Caisau.

BLINDING TREE
Tree that emits a deadly acid that can eat through skin and armor, and melt bone.

BONE TREE
Tree with spiny branches made of the bones of its prey. Secretes a poisonous sap.

BOOK OF OMA
Denotes the collected writings of Faith Ahya and her early followers, which have become the basis for historical understanding and religious practices in Dhai.

BOOK OF RHEA
A collection of anecdotal stories and observations which form the basis of religious practices and laws in Dorinah.

BROODGUARD
The Patron of Saiduan's personal guards, a position which is often hereditary.

CAISA ARIANAO OSONO
Novice at the Temple of Oma. A parajista.

CAISAU
A city in Saiduan just south of Isjahilde.

Casa Maigan

An old acquaintance of Ura Dasai's living in Isjahilde before it was overrun by the Tai Mora.

Casalyn Aurnaisa

Empress of Dorinah.

Catori

Title used for the spouse of the Kai.

Chali Finahin Badu

Ambitious Ora living in Oma's temple. Brother to Roh. They share two mothers and three fathers but are not related by blood. A tirajista.

Clan Adama

Named for one of Hahko and Faith Ahya's children, Clan Adama's primary exports come from its orchards.

Clan Alia

Central clan in Dhai, just north of Clan Garika. Primarily known for its textiles.

Clan Badu

Clan bordering Clans Garika and Sorila, in Dhai. Politically close to Clan Garika.

Clan Daora

Coastal clan in Dhai.

Clan Dasina

Clan Dasina often allies with Clan Daora in political matters. The two are named after the twin daughters of the fourth Dhai Kao. Clan Dasina's exports include rice, sugar cane, and hemp.

CLAN GARIKA

Known as the most powerful single clan in Dhai.

CLAN MUTAO

Smallest and least economically powerful of the Dhai clans.

CLAN NAKO

Neighboring Clan Mutao, Clan Nako holds much of the country's wealth in copper and other metals.

CLAN OSONO

Central clan in Dhai. Chief commodity is sheep.

CLAN RAONA

Originally comprised of two different clans – Riana and Orsaila – Clan Roana is just a century old, and was created in an effort to tamp down the fierce feuding between the Riana and Orsaila clans, which resulted in nearly a dozen deaths.

CLAN SAIZ

Clan located in southern Dhai, politically aligned with Clan Sorai.

CLAN SAOBINA

Clan Saobina exports timber, herbal aids and medications— which it grows and mixes in its own fields and workshops.

CLAN SORAI

Named after a powerful daughter of the third Kai, Clan Sorai is often allied with clans Adama and Saobina in political affairs. They are also the clan responsible for the safety and security of Asona harbor, the country's single largest trading link to the outside world.

CLAN SORILA

Clan nearest the Temple of Oma, in Dhai. Primary export is timber.

CLAN TAOSINA

Named for Faith Ahya's second daughter, clan Taosina – like clans Saobina and Sorila – borders the woodlands. Pottery and complex, plant-derived technologies such as bioluminescent floor or ceiling lighting solutions, self-cleaning fungus floors and the like are generally created and installed by Taosina crafters.

CORA

A dajian who lives with Emlee in the Dorinah slave camps.

DAJIAN

In Dorinah, enslaved Dhai people are called dajians. They are often branded with the mark of the family that owns them.

DAOLYN

Dajian owned by Zezili Hasaria. Works as Zezili's housekeeper.

DAORIAN

The seat of the Empress of Dorinah. A broad, rambling city built on the ruins of the former Saiduan city of Diamia.

DASAI ELASORA DAORA

An elder Ora, over a century old, who teaches Saiduan language, culture and history at the Temple of Oma.

DHAI

Small country located on the northwest corner of the island of Grania, an island at the far tip of the Saiduanese continent. Also the name of the people inhabiting this country. Dhai was established 500 years ago by former slaves fleeing their masters in the neighboring country of Dorinah. It's said the satellite called Sina was especially powerful during that time, allowing Dhai sinajistas, who outnumbered sinajistas among the Dorinah, to escape their servitude.

DOKAI
Guards of the holds in Saiduan, bound to live or die as the hold itself does.

DORINAH
Country on the northeast shore of Grania, ruled by a long line of Empresses for the last 1800 years. Relies on the enslaved labor of Dhai people – known locally as dajians – to sustain its infrastructure and economy.

DRIAA SAARIK, SHAO
A Saiduan sanisi. Parajista.

ELAIKO SIRANA NAKO
An Ora at the Temple of Oma and assistant to Nasaka Lokana Saiz. Comes from a family specializing in tea blends. A tirajista.

EMLEE
Local healer/midwife/sorceress residing in a dajian camp in Dorinah.

ESAO JOSA
Granddaughter of Nirata Josa, a woodland Dhai.

ETENA MIA SORAI
Aunt to the Kai of the Dhai. Etena was driven mad by her own power and supplanted as Kai by her sister, Javia Mia Sorai. She was exiled from Dhai, and her current whereabouts are unknown.

EVERPINE

Massive conifer, the sap of which dissuades bugs and many species of sentient plants.

FAITH AHYA

Faith Ahya is regarded as the mother of the newest incarnation of the Dhai nation, founded five hundred years before when she led an uprising of Dhai slaves in Dorinah. With her lover, Hahko, she established the Dhai nation in one of the most contaminated areas on the planet, one few other nations would touch.

FAROSI SANA NAKO

A member of the Liona militia.

FINAHIN HUMEY GARIKA

One of Roh's mothers.

FLAME FLIES

Thumbnail-sized insects which create light when they fly. On settling, the light dims and eventually fades after a few minutes. To rouse a light, one must only shake the lantern.

FLOXFLASS

A yellow, thorny plant that creeps over and consumes its victims. It's leaves are slightly sticky, and taste sweet.

FOURIA ORANA SAIZ

A member of the Kuallina milita.

GAILA KARINSA PANA

Near-mother to Yisaoh Alais Garika. Married to Alais, Tir and Moarsa.

GAISO LONAI GARIKA

Elder Ora of the Temple of Oma in Dhai. She is responsible for the overall functioning of the temple and care of the people therein. Cousin to Tir Salarihi Garika. A tirajista.

GHAKAR KORSAA

Dance teacher at Kuonrada, in Saiduan.

GHRASIA MADAH TAOSINA

Leader of the Dhai militia in both Liona and Kuallina. Best known as the woman who pushed back the Dorinah invasion during the Pass War.

GIAN MURSIA BADU

A parajista trained outside of Dhai temples, niece to Kalinda Lasa.

GRANIA

The island continent that is home to the countries of Dhai, Dorinah, Aaldia and Tordin, located at the far tip of the Saiduan continent.

HADAOH ALAIS GARIKA

Husband to Meyna Salisia Mutao and brother to Rhin Gaila Garika, Lohin Alais Garika and Yisaoh Alais Garika.

HAHKO

Hahko was a former slave in Dorinah, and aided his lover Faith Ahya in leading the uprising of the Dhai slaves from the scullery of Daorian. The two became the first rulers of the independent Dhai state, the first in over eighteen hundred years, after the defeat of the Dhai by the Saiduan roughly the same time ago.

HALIMEY FARAI SORILA

A young parajista from the temple of Oma.

HIGH SEASON

There are eight seasons in a year on Raisa: low spring, high spring, low summer, high summer, low fall, high fall, low winter, high winter. In general "high" seasons tend to bring with them more extreme weather than low seasons.

HOFSHA SOREK

A mysterious interloper.

HONA FASA SORAI

Leader of Clan Sorai.

HROLLIEF

Southern continent on the western half of Raisa.

ISAILA LARANO RAONA

Tir Salarihi Garika's apprentice clan leader at Clan Garika.

ISJAHILDE

A city in northern Saiduan, Isjahilde has been the country's political center for thousands of years.

ISOAIL ROSALINA

A powerful parajista/tirajista living near Lake Morta in Dorinah. One of the Empress of Dorinah's seekers.

JAKOBI TORISA GARIKA

Ahkio's third cousin, a parajista.

JASOI (JANUVAR) OF LIND

Native to Tordin, Jasoi's title among the Dorinahs is Syre. She is Zezili Hasaria's secondary commander.

JAVIA MIA SORAI

Former Kai of the Dhai. Ahkio and Kirana's mother. Deceased.

JOVOVYN
A coastal city in Dorinah.

KADAAN SOAGAN, REN
A sanisi, and one of Maralah Daonia's first students. Left hand of the Patron of Saiduan. Called the Shadow of Caisau. A parajista.

KAI
Honorific used for the leader of the Dhai people.

KAKOLYN KOTARIA
Commander of the northern legion in Dorinah.

KALINDA LASA
A wayhouse keeper and parajista.

KAROSIA SOAFIN
Local priest and moderately gifted tirajista living near Zezili Hasaria's estate in Dorinah.

KEEPER TAKANAA
Keeper of the Patron of Saiduan's household.

KIHIN MOARSA GARIKA
A novice at the Temple of Oma. Tir Salarihi Garika's youngest son.

KINDAR
A strategy game played in Dhai which involves the manipulation, swapping, and managing of copious "family" pieces to achieve a numerical win and box in one's opponent.

KIRANA JAVIA GARIKA
Former Kai of the Dhai. Sister to Akhio Javia Garika. Daughter of Javia Mia Sorai. A tirajista.

KOSOMEY ORISA MUTAO
An Ora in residence at the Temple of Oma. Parajista.

KUALLINA STRONGHOLD
Central hold in Dhai where militia are stationed, led by Ghrasia Madah. Also serves as the hub for the Line system, which connects holds and temples throughout the country.

LAKE MORTA
Lake in northwestern Dorinah which is the subject of many stories, and thought to be a holy place, blessed of Rhea. Attracts many pilgrims and vacationers in the summer months.

LAKE ORASTINA
A lake north of Lake Morta in Dorinah.

LANILU ASAILA SORILA
A Dhai scholar who travels to Saiduan with Dasai. Married to Aramey Dahina Dasina.

LARALYN MAISLYN
A Dorinah Seeker. Tirajista.

LARN
A dajian who lives with Emlee in the dajian camp near Liona.

LI KAI
Title used for the successor to the Kai.

LIARO TARISA BADU
Ahkio Javia Garika's cousin.

LILIA SONA
Scullery maid in the Temple of Oma.

LINE

A living transportation system connecting major strongholds in Dhai. People travel inside chrysalises built expressly for the purpose, which crawl along a giant living cable. Chrysalises dissolve on arrival.

LIONA STRONGHOLD

Hold that occupies the pass next to the valley that cuts through the mountain range separating Dhai and Dorinah. The forces stationed here are captained by Ghrasia Madah Taosina.

LIVIA HASARIA

Zezili Hasaria's mother. A weakly gifted tirajista who specializes in the creation of mirrors infused with the power of Tira. Resides in the city of Saolina.

LOHIN ALAIS GARIKA

Husband to Kirana Javia Garika, making him the titled Catori. Brother to Yisaoh, Rhin and Hadaoh.

LORD'S BOOK OF UNMAKING

A Saiduan book with extensive appendices that include love poetry written to Oma by a sixth century Saiduan scholar.

LOW SEASON

There are eight seasons in a year on Raisa: low spring, high spring, low summer, high summer, low fall, high fall, low winter, high winter. In general, the weather in "low" season is less extreme than that of high season.

LUNA

A Dhai slave living in Dorinah, and a scholar of Dhai matters. Won by Shao Maralah Daonia in a card game.

MAHUAN

Type of river plant with bold blue flowers whose roots are ground up into a powder and mixed with water, then drunk as a philter to soothe symptoms of asthma.

MARDANAS

Quarter in the religious sector of Dorinah cities where men serve Rhea by bringing both pleasure and children to women. Also called "cat-houses."

MARHIN RASANU BADU

A Kuallina militia member.

MASURA GAILIA SAOBINA

Elder Ora of the Temple of Tira, Masura oversees everyday management of that temple. A tirajista.

MARALAH DAONIA, SHAO

A powerful sinajista, and acting War Minister for Saiduan. Also known as the Sword of Albaaric. Sister of General Rajavaa Daonia.

MASOTH CHAIGAAN TAAR, SHAS

A sanisi and the Patron of Saiduan's eldest son. A tirajista.

MATIAS HINSA RAONA

Ora and doctor at the Temple of Oma. A tirajista.

MEYNA SALISIA MUTAO

Ahkio Javia Garika's housemate and lover. Married to Hadaoh Alais Garika and Rhin Gaila Garika.

MISHAEL MIRO OSONO

Saurika Osono's apprentice clan leader.

MOARA FAHINAMA BADU
Near-mother to Yisaoh Alais Garika. Married to Tir, Moarsa, and Alais.

MOHRAI HONA SORAI
Customs master at Asona Harbor in Dhai. Daughter of the leader of Clan Sorai, Hona Fasa Sorai.

MORA SOAN
A mysterious interloper.

MORSAAR KORYN
Rajavaa Daonia's best friend, lover, and second in command.

MUR
Name of Raisa's irregularly shaped moon.

NAORI GASILA ALIA
A powerful parajista. Ahkio's third cousin once removed.

NASAKA LOKANA SAIZ
An Ora at the Temple of Oma. Religious and political advisor to the Kai. Ahkio Javia Garika's aunt. A sinajista.

NATANIAL THORNE OF YEMSHIRE
A Tordinian man.

NAVA SONA
Lilia Sona's mother.

NIRATA JOSA
A woodland Dhai and omajista. Kin to Gian Mursia Badu.

OHANNI RORHINA OSONO
An Ora and dance teacher at the Temple of Oma. Parajista.

OMA

A heavenly body which appears in the sky above Raisa every 2,000 years (or so). The light it shines is red. Those with the ability to channel Oma can wield the abilities of all satellites, and also gain additional powers, which may include opening gateways between spaces, healing grievous injuries, raising the dead, and/or enhancing the abilities of others.

Oma may also be called Lord of Heaven, Lord of the Dawn, Lord of Awakening, or Lord of Change and is referred to in Dorinah scripture as the Eye of Rhea.

OMAJISTA

Sorcerers with the ability to channel Oma. They can wield the abilities of all satellites, and also gain additional powers, which may include opening gateways between spaces, healing grievous injuries, raising the dead, and/or enhancing the abilities of others.

Additional names for omajistas: omajika, makers, breakers, worldbreakers, disrupters.

ORA

Title/honorific for a Dhai magician-priest, one who is able to channel the power of Oma, Sina, Tira, or Para. Oras often act as teachers and religious keepers/advisors in the temples of Dhai.

OSORAAN MHOHARAN, PATRON

Patron of Saiduan before Alaar Masoth Taar.

PANA WOODLANDS

Also simply referred to as "the woodlands" this area stretches from the base of Mount Ahya in Dhai all the way to the sea, blanketing the western half of the country. Dangerous, contaminated, and very wild, exiled Dhai or "woodland Dhai" have lived here for centuries.

PARA

A heavenly body which appears above Raisa for roughly four years, with a ten-year absence between appearances (approximate). Para's light is blue, and those who can call on it may be able to manipulate air to affect weather, use as shields, call tornadoes, etc. Many are also immune to wards, and cannot be bound by them.

Para has also been called the Lord of the Air, or "Rhea's blue daughter," in Dorinah.

PARAJISTA

Refers to those who can call on Para when it is ascendant. Abilities include the manipulation of air to affect weather, use as shields, call tornadoes, etc. Many parajistas are also immune to wards, and cannot be bound by them.

Parajistas are also known as parajinas and wind wizards.

PASS WAR

War between Dhai and Dorinah twenty years ago. Began when 800 dajians escaped Dorinah and demanded entrance to Liona, only to be crushed and killed by Dorinah legions when the Dhai would not open the gates. When the Dhai opened fire on the Dorinah, the war began. Its end is largely credited to Ghrasia Madah and Kai Javia Mia Sorai, who used both strategy and political savvy to placate the Dorinahs.

PATRON OF SAIDUAN

Leader of the Saiduanese people. Powerful Saiduanese families have traditionally gone to war for the title. Since it was established, eighteen different families have ruled Saiduan. When a new family rises to power, the prior family's adults are killed and the children raised as slaves.

RAINAA

A slave of the Patron of Saiduan.

RAISA

Name by which the world is commonly known in Dhai.

RAJAVAA DAONIA

Captain-General in charge of a Saiduan military regiment. Maralah Daonia's brother.

RANANA TALISINA SAIZ

An Ora, and the defense forms teacher at the Temple of Oma. A sinajista.

RASANDAN PARADA

A dancer at Kuonrada, in Saiduan.

RHEA

The goddess of Dorinah's primary religion, whose symbol is a great cat's eye on a field of purple. Para, Sina and Tira are said to be her daughters. The Empress of Dorinah is also known as Rhea's divine, as Rhea is her mother.

RHIN GAILA GARIKA

Shepard. Husband to Meyna Salisia Mutao and brother to Hadaoh Alais Garika, Lohin Alais Garika and Yisaoh Alais Garika.

RISHIN GARIN BADU

Father of Kirana Javia Garika and Ahkio Javia Garika. Deceased.

ROHINMEY TADISA GARIKA

Novice parajista at the Temple of Oma, with the ability to see through wards. Son of Finahin Humey Garika, Tadisa Sinhasa Garika, and Madinoh Ladisi Badu. Brother of Chali Finahin Badu.

ROASANDARA

Name of a Dhai city when those people were once an empire stretching from Saiduan to Hrollief. Best known as the city where the decisive battle between the Dhai and Saiduan was fought.

ROMEY SAHINA OSONO

A student of Ahkio Javia Garika's in Clan Osono.

RYYI

Title used to denote the leader of the Dorinah Seekers.

SAGASARIAN SEA

A sea on the eastern coast of Dorinah.

SAI MONSHARA

A top general among the Tai Mora.

SAIDUAN

Large empire which rules the northwestern continent of Raisa. The continent itself is also called Saiduan. The empire is led by an individual called the Patron, the eighth in the country's latest line of rulers. Powerful Saiduanese families have traditionally gone to war for the title of the Patron of Saiduan. Since it was established, eighteen different families have ruled Saiduan.

SANISI

The conjurer-assassins of Saiduan. Sanisi carry weapons blooded and infused with the power of Para, Sina and Tira.

SAOLINA

A small town in Dorinah where Zezili Hasaria's mother lives.

SAURIKA HALANIA OSONO

Clan leader of Clan Osono.

SEA OF HARAEO

The sea that separates Dhai and Saiduan.

SEEKER

Term used to refer to the gifted in Dorinah.

SEEKERS

Designation for those in Dorinah who can call on the satellites. Trained and employed for both military and public infrastructure projects.

SEEKER SANCTUARY

Coastal home of the majority of Dorinah's Seekers. Seekers must train and have their licenses renewed here.

SHANIGAN SAROMEI DASINA

An Ora and mathematics teacher at the Temple of Oma.

SHAO

Title among Saiduanese sanisi, indicating relative talent. Most powerful are Shao, then Ren, Tal and Shas.

SHIA AROSAI SAIZ

Clan leader of Clan Saiz.

SHODAV

A dancer and old friend of Dasai and Luna. A former slave.

SHORATAU

A prison in Saiduan, located northeast of Kuonrada.

SIIRA

Dhai name for one of the low winter months.

SINA

A heavenly body which appears above Raisa every 15-18 years, and is ascendant for five to seven years. Sina's light is violet. Those who channel Sina may be able to rend/unmake flesh, transform or transmute organic substances, remove wards and call flame. Sina is also known as the Lord of Unmaking.

SINAJISTA

Sorcerers who can channel the power of Sina when it is ascendant. Those who channel Sina may be able to rend/ unmake flesh, transform or transmute organic substances, remove wards and call flame. Other names for sinajistas include transmuters, unmakers, destroyers.

SOKAI VASIYA

A Dorinah seeker. Parajista.

STORM (LASLI) HISARO

Captain General of the southern legion in Dorinah.

TADISA SINHASA GARIKA

One of Roh's mothers. Also mother of Chali Tadisa Badu.

TAIGAN MASANO, SHAO

An outcast sanisi bound and warded to Maralah. Known among the Saiduan as an omajista.

TAI MORA

Mysterious interlopers.

TALAMYNII

Former enemies of the Dhai four thousand years ago, when the Dhai were a powerful nation. They were wiped out by the Dhai, who in turn were decimated by the Saiduan.

TALISA GAIKO RAONA

Leader of Clan Raona.

TANASAI LAOSINA

Captain General of Dorinah's western legion. Near-cousin to Zezili Hasaria.

TAODALAIN HASARIA

One of Zezili Hasaria's four sisters. Daughter to Livia Hasaria.

TIR SALARIHI GARIKA

Clan leader of Clan Garika. Married to Alais, Gaila, and Moarsa. Father of Yisaoh Alais Garika, Hadaoh Alais Garika, Rhin Gaila Garika, Lohin Alais Garika and Kihin Moarsa Garika.

TIRA

A heavenly body which appears above Raisa every ten to twelve years, which enjoys six to eight years of ascendance. Those who can call on Tira may be able to restore and heal flesh, grow/train/control plants and plant-based lifeforms, create wards.

Tira is also known as the Lord of Life.

TIRAJISTA

Term for those who can channel the power of Tira when it is ascendant. Those who can call on Tira may be able to restore and heal flesh, grow/train/control plants and plant-based life-forms, create wards.

Tirajistas are also known as tirajika, restorers, gardeners, spinners.

TORDIN

Country on the southeastern shore of Grania, led currently by a King named Nhatyn of Lind. Prior to his rule, the country was a morass of warring city-states controlled by Penelodyn, cousin to the Empress of Dorinah, and the Thief Queen, a former commoner turned warmonger.

TULANA NIKOEL, RYYI
Leader of the Seekers in Dorinah.

UNA MORINIS RAONA
Gatekeeper of the Temple of Oma. A tirajista.

VORALYN JOVYN
A Dorinah seeker. Sinajista.

WORLDBREAKER
Mythic term for omajista.

WRAISAU KILIA, REN
A sanisi in Saiduan. Tirajista.

YISAOH ALAIS GARIKA
Daughter of Alais and Tir Salarihi Garika. Sister of Rhin Gaila Garika, Hadaoh Alais Garika, Lohin Alais Garika and Kihin Moarsa Garika. Yisaoh once contested Javia Mia Sorai for the title of Kai.

ZEZILI HASARIA
Captain general of Dorinah's eastern legion. Zezili's mother, Livia Hasaria, is Dorinah and her father a dajian, but her mother claimed her and ensured her status as a free Dorinah as opposed to a dajian slave. Her title is Syre.

ZINI
The smallest of Raisa's three moons.

ACKNOWLEDGMENTS

This book would not have come to be without the help of my agent, Hannah Bowman, who shepherded this novel through endless rounds of revisions – a couple of which turned out to be a burning down and rebuilding from the ground up (seventeen page edit letter!). It's been great to have an agent involved in this process from pitch to proposal to publication day. Thanks, Hannah.

I'd also like to thank the folks at the Wellspring Writers' Workshop, in particular Bradley Beaulieu and Gregory Wilson, for their detailed feedback on what I though was a polished manuscript, but turned out to be a very rough, very early draft. Thanks for wading through endless disconnected travelogues and peeling out all the good stuff. For feedback on later versions of the book, thanks go to Dave Zelasco.

There's a lot of other invisible work that goes into bookmaking, and for that I have to thank my amazingly dedicated assistant, Danielle Horn Beal, who not only organized the entire wiki for this series but became the point-person for entering line edits on those numerous drafts and helping me collect, format and research work for ongoing projects while I kept my head down working on this. I would not have been able to manage such an extraordinary year of apparent productivity without her.

Copyeditors are another unsung hero of the business. Thanks to mine for this project, Richard Shealy, who was really the person we made that wiki for... I cherish all of my copyeditors, as it is a skill I sorely lack. Thanks for patience with the made-up plants and endless Robert-Howard-like word rep.

It also makes a huge difference at the publisher level when you have a true team at hand who's both passionate about your work and great at what they do. Thanks to everyone on the Angry Robot team for giving this book a shot. Thanks to Amanda Rutter for a rather sobering edit that helped me enter the panicked state necessary to take the book to the next level. Thanks to Marc Gascoigne for the easiest cover development process ever ("Looks great, Marc! Carry on!"), and thanks to Caroline Lambe and Michael Underwood for tireless marketing and publicity support. I do not envy them their jobs, and wholly appreciate and understand the pressures they're under to position and publicize so many books. Thanks, finally, to Lee Harris for taking the ultimate chance on this series. We'll see how things wash out.

Living with a writer who is always talking about other worlds and fake people can be a chore, so thanks to Jayson Utz for endless plot and creepy worldbuilding conversations. "How about the swords sprout out of their wrists!?" is just one example of the kind stuff that pops up in these conversations and eventually makes it into the books. Thanks for all the fish.

I would also be remiss if I didn't thank the science fiction and fantasy writing and reading community as a whole – agents, editors, fans, casual readers, and all – for supporting both me and my work through oftentimes grueling business entanglements and gut punches. It's a tough business, and you all make it worth getting up again.

Thank you.

The Big Red House
Ohio
Spring, 2014